Diamonds or Dust

Luann Reynolds

The Series:

Let The Wildflowers Bloom

This is a work of fiction. Names, characters, places and incidents either are the product of the author's imagination or are used fictitiously, and any resemblance to actual persons, living or dead, business establishments, events, or locales is entirely coincidental.

DIAMONDS OR DUST
THE SERIES: LET THE WILDFLOWERS BLOOM, BOOK IV
Luann Reynolds

A Skinny Leopard Media book/ published in arrangement with the author, Sarasota, FL

Copyright© 2013 by Luann Reynolds
Artwork and illustrations, Copyright© 2013 by Patrick Reynolds

All rights reserved.

This book, or parts thereof, may not be reproduced in any form without permission, except in the case of brief quotations embodied in critical articles or reviews. The scanning, uploading, and distribution of this book via the Internet or any other means without permission of the publisher is illegal, and punishable by law. Please purchase only authorized electronic editions, and do not participate in or encourage piracy of copyrighted materials. Your support of the author's rights is appreciated.

ISBN: 978-0-9858961-8-8
Library of Congress Control Number: 2013958386

Books By Luann Reynolds

From the Series: Let The Wildflowers Bloom

Soul Pebbles, Book I

Between Two Hearts, Book II

Highland's Secrets, Book III

Diamonds Or Dust, Book IV

Ride Like the Wind, Book V (Coming Soon)

DEDICATION

To my sister Pam:
To my loving sister who sees to everyone's needs and puts those she loves before herself. She looks after and loves my children as her own. She has always been there. Love you.

To my dear friend Kathy:
To an extraordinary friend, we laughed, we cried, we sang and we danced. No distance can divide us. I'm your Indian sister from 1823. Love you.

Thank You, Peter O'Rourke

Peter O'Rourke's knowledge and research of herbal and essential recipes are greatly appreciated. I met Peter in Sarasota, Florida in the year 2000. At that time, he supplied my holistic and wellness center, Arts Within, with his premium essential oils from around the world. Peter's six-generation lineage, makes him a living legend of knowledge. He's taught valuable information on aromatherapy and herbs for many modalities.

I thank you, Peter, for your expertise, knowledge and generous giving. You have helped people all over the world. Thank you, dear friend.

You may reach Peter by email: openskyaromatherapy@hotmail.com
"Open Sky" Aromatherapy
Professional Consultations
Therapeutic Aromatherapy Workshops & Training
Private Instruction
Professional Grade Essential Oils
Customized Perfumes
Crystals, Geodes

Also, Thanks To:

I would like to thank the museum staff at the La Plata Historical Society's Animas Museum for all the help I received in researching my book series. The museum staff shares the gift of history with all of us and if you are planning a trip to Durango, CO be sure to visit the:

Animas Museum, 3065 W. 2nd Ave., Durango, CO 81302

The museum graciously accepts donations. Planned giving supports their future. Send checks to: LPCHS, P.O. Box 3384, Durango, CO 81302. Visit the museum online at www.animasmuseum.org.

Map Credits: Copyright 1995, Russell A. Morse, Jr. Printed in the USA by Rusty's Maps, P.O. Box 5, Arvada, CO 80001-0005. A list of other, original and reprinted maps are available for a stamped, self-addressed legal sized envelope.

PROLOGUE

Have you ever fallen in love? I have, and he is a ghost in my life. He's real, but so far away, I live on. I still have hopes and dreams of my love and lover, and feel he is my soul connection in this life and those after. I ask the heavens to let another door open, for without him, something is amiss and I am not whole. Why? Because I know what love is. I had it, it was in my grasp, and I let it slip away. I will never give up, not until it is mine. I'm claiming it and I will live my dream.

I was born in Creede, Colorado in 1876. I'm eighteen and live alone in Durango, Colorado, a small smelter town for gold and silver. I have twin siblings, John and Rebecca, living on the east coast. I came upon hard times, and in order to meet my responsibilities I took a position at the Good Hour brothel. I live a somewhat normal existence and work as a seamstress during the day and become a lady of the tenderloin, entertaining men at night. My name is Victoria Alexandra Highland. Friends know me as Alex. At the bordello, I'm Vicky.

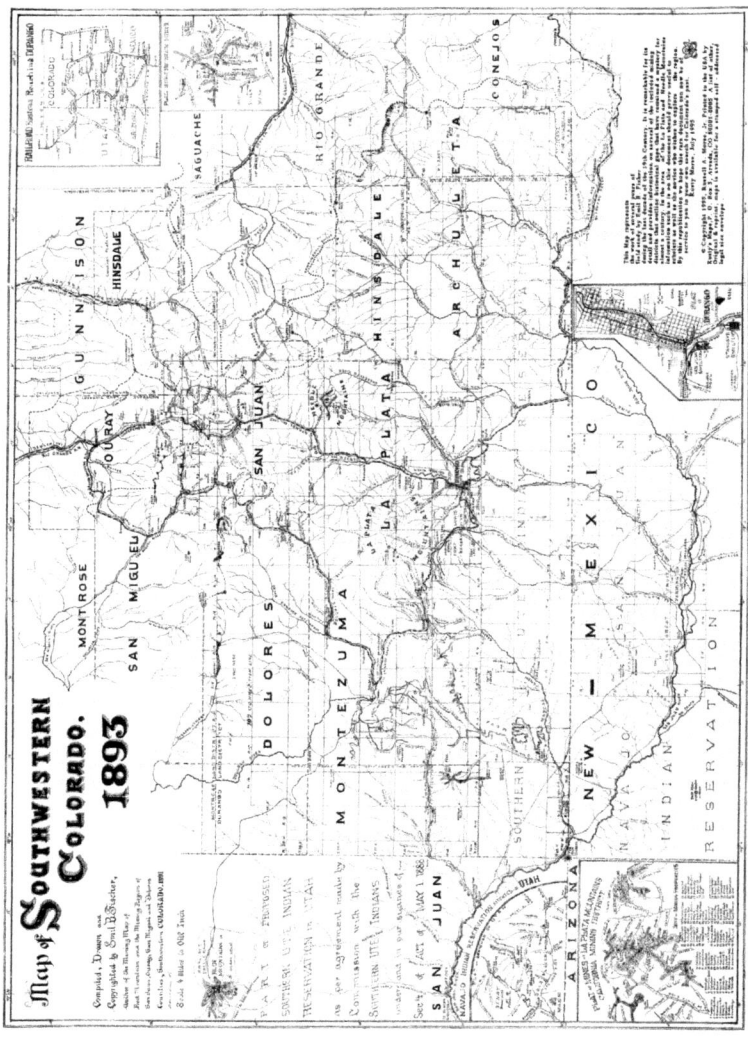

DURANGO, COLORADO 1894

Chapter One: BACK IN TOWN

The cold wind hollows through the valley of the small town of Durango. I live alone in a cozy flat above Brody's Mercantile. It is November in the Rockies, and it's always snowing. At five in the afternoon, it's already dark, making the days seem short and the nights long. For a prostitute, nights seem to go on forever.

Tonight, I won't be working at the Good Hour. No one is expecting me. No one but Mrs. Brody knows I'm back in town.

I pour the last bucket of hot water into the old copper tub for a soak. For a moment, I'm mesmerized by the steaming vapors induced by the room's cold temperature. I've been gone so long the cold has saturated everything, and even the potbelly stove could not take off the chill.

Testing the water, I let my robe slip from my shoulders and step into the steamy bathwater. Old Sam, my big orange cat, sits in the chair next to me. He leans over and touches the water with his paw. He's been on my heels since my return … unusual, as he loves staying with Mrs. Brody at the mercantile when I'm gone. She spoils him. "I think you missed me this time old Sam." Sam was my brother John's cat until he went away to school. I brought him from Creede in a carpetbag. He's my loyal companion. "Aren't you, Sam?"

It feels so good to relax in the old copper tub. Every time I do I think of Mother. She brought this tub west from Chicago, first on a train to Kansas City and then by wagon over the Santa Fe Trail to Colorado. Reading her journals tells me they faced Indians, raiders, Comancheros and terrible weather. How did people do it?

After my parents died, Becky and I had to leave Creede. We went through our belongings to decide on what few items we could bring to Durango. Mother's and Great Grandfather's journals and the copper tub were at the top of the list; awkward or not, the tub came with us.

I haven't fully recovered from the long train ride from back east, and I'm sure this is luxury compared to being in a rough old wagon, lumbering over some rutty, bumpy, dusty trail as Mother had endured. I sprinkle one of my muscle-relaxing potions into the bath water. After a short soak, I'll feel as good as new. I wish there were a potion to solve all my problems. I need to check Great Grandmother's recipe book. Maybe I have overlooked a concoction to make one invisible. I giggle. "Do you think that's possible, Sam?" He meows and hops out of the chair as I raise my wet hand to pet him. Then, I could be right under Mr. Brody's nose watching him like a hawk. Just think; I could go anywhere.

Tonight, I refuse to dwell on problems at hand, not the inspector, not James Brody, not Father, not J.W. nor Mac McClellan. Not tonight, tonight I claim as mine. I'm pretending this space is my haven and my sanctuary and that everything is good. I'm safe. I'm queen of my own castle. I hold the cobalt blue bottle up to the light. The blue wavy glass puts an interesting perspective on the room. I say aloud, "I, Queen Victoria of Blue Magic Island, dub this place peace and harmony." I giggle. How silly of me. I slide completely under the water for as long as I can hold my breath. After a time, I climb out. Wrapping in a thinly worn cotton towel, I stand close to the rosy potbelly stove to keep warm. Unpinning my long blonde tresses, my hair falls to my waist. I smile as I look at my sun-kissed skin that I acquired on a recent visit to Bimini Island. Dearest Uncle Scotty is a captain for the English Trading Company. He sails back and forth from Savannah, Georgia to the Spice Islands in the Caribbean. It was one of my childhood dreams to be able to sail with him.

I've been back just a few days in Colorado, and I already long for the hot Tropics. I loved sitting on the beach, digging my toes into the white crystal sand that seemed endless, breathing the oceans salty air as I dreamily looked through the tall, swaying, coconut palms along the ocean's edge. I can feel and hear the warm tropical breezes that make the palm fronds flutter against the brilliant azure sky. And, every sundown, the air reverberates with a deep mellow tone from an islander blowing into a conk shell, paying homage to nature's masterpiece of luminous colors. Shades of yellow, orange and pink stretch across the sky like taffy as the huge ball of fire meets the horizon, casting its reflection across the spectacular sea. The tranquil ambiance warms my very soul. I've lived in the Rockies all my life, but Bimini ... Bimini made me feel as if I were home. Maybe this is why it feels colder than it actually is. It's such a contrast from where I've been. The mountains are beautiful, but rough and raw; and the Caribbean is warm, serene and inviting, everything the Rockies are not.

When I'm standing in front of the dressing mirror, my hair looks lighter, maybe from the sun or just the contrast against my skin. It's so long that the soft wavy curls reach my hips. My hands roam over my breasts. I'm surprised to see how I've filled out. My body is taut, but my hips and breasts have rounded; and although it's not fashionable for a white woman to have color, it makes me feel healthy, as if I've been touched by nature. I like the way I feel and look. I don't consider myself beautiful. However, I have my own guise. Mother always said I was as pretty as a summer rose.

Chapter Two: A LADY OF THE EVENING

It was July when I went to work for Madam Grace Talbot. She owns the Good Hour brothel on Ninth Street. I guess you could say she was my saving grace. When my sister Becky was ill, I had to send her back east for surgery that took most of our savings. I was alone and desperate, and I still had responsibilities to meet. The value of silver plummeted, and since Durango is a smelter town, mines closed and hundreds were out of work statewide. The few jobs available were given to men, which brought me to this. I'm not complaining. I'm alive and well. Mother taught us to look on the bright side of things, and that's where I keep my focus. It's just that sometimes, like tonight, that things can get a little heavy. By morning, I'll have a fresh outlook on the day.

I've listened to many girls' stories. If you're a prostitute, something, or maybe everything, has gone awry. It may be the oldest profession but not an easy one. I came from a loving family of professional parents who wore fine dresses, had good shoes, never went cold nor went to bed with an empty stomach; but still, I ended up here. I have an above average education, speak two languages, and consider myself to have good common sense. My late mother was a teacher, and she taught me everything she knew. The other girls I work with aren't so lucky. They have neither an education nor a family who gives two hoots about them. Nevertheless, God blessed them with some pretty amazing qualities, at least for this line of work. Madam Grace runs a good business. She took a chance on me, as I didn't know anything about pleasing men. I told her of my situation, and she gave me an opportunity. I'm not one to forget when someone offers me a lifeline.

I consider the Good Hour my school. It's the best parlor house in town. It's certainly not the Ivy League curriculum Father had imagined, but it does require a specific set of skills. The girls at the

Good Hour are contributing to my honing talents. The place is known for the prettiest girls and cosmopolitan entertainment. Grace knows how to take care of her clients by serving delicious foods and the highest quality booze available. Her place is bejeweled with the finest furnishings. All a man need is money, and his wish is our command. Madam has what some would call a unique view on philosophy. She says a man's brains and emotions are strapped to his balls, which is not far from his wallet. We have what men want, and we have no problem taking their money for giving them pleasure. Grace has strict rules. She runs a clean house; she doesn't allow drugs. That means no Opium, Laudanum or excessive alcohol. It's not an easy life, and one can seek refuge from this line of work and become addicted to many different substances. Many prostitutes use it as a crutch, believing it will give them strength to make it through the night, but it brings only the banshees to rape their souls.

There are a dozen brothels in Durango along with twenty saloons, dance halls and other shady forms of entertainment. The high-class madams such as Grace Talbot, Martha Bruce and Bessie Meir are making a pretty penny. The word is that Bessie is the most worthy of trust. She has gained much of her fortune by miners asking to keep their valuables in her safe … some never returned because of sickness or the hard winters. She gives a lot back to the community and has the respect from high officials, even if she is a madam. Now, Grace Talbot is the queen of madams. She likes *rich*, and the gowns she purchases from me are as nice as any made in Paris. Grace says, "You've got to look successful to be successful." She sees that her girls are dressed nicely. You will find no tattered stockings or worn out clothes at the Good Hour. Her girls are clean and so are the beds. I've given Grace ideas about how to increase income, and now I'm the top earner. I have rules; no man comes to me ungroomed. I charge for everything, and nothing is free. I offer them a bath and a shave and massage (something I learned in the Islands, and I'm not talking of a man's genitals). I knead their back, neck and shoulders. My services make me a handsome ransom. Some men have teased me; saying I make my services so good that they use up their money before they can get into my bed.

There are many levels of prostitution, and that goes for the pay scale too. Girls on the outside work on renting their own cribs, an 8x8 room with a bed, with no one to protect them from rendering services for merely a dollar and sometimes less. The dance hall girls live under the protection of the establishment and reside in rooms above. Others, like me, live in brothels run by madams. Some are cheap, and others are expensive. It's common knowledge that you get what you pay for. Most of the girls earn less than twenty dollars a month before licensing fees and the cost of health certificates. It's just another way for the town officials to pad their pockets. Father was a doctor in Creede, and he said health certificates for working girls are a joke. There are no cures for what ails most in houses of ill repute. Prostitution is risky, for you never know whom you've sold yourself to, and every time you close your door you subject yourself to a world of disease and violence.

Chapter Three: THE PROPOSAL

I awaken this morning just as I hoped, rested. Things always look better in the morning. My first thought is of J.W. Reynolds. I met him last July. He was my first John, and I was extremely fortunate. J.W. is not only clean; he is intelligent, interesting, rich and knows how to please a woman. And, what's better than that is he made sex enjoyable and left me breathless. I had no idea a woman could climax more than once making love. Believe me, it was not my intent to enjoy my work, and at first I was perturbed he had invaded my senses.

Although I was in love with Mac McClellan, the Colorado Marshal at the time, I had to go to work at the brothel. I thought no one could possibly take Mac's place. However, J.W. Reynolds acquired my attention, and after spending time with him as a companion, I ended up enjoying his company immensely. J.W., with the madam's approval, asked me to escort him to Denver on business with no strings attached. Grace was happy, and we negotiated a percentage. I needed the money. What could be better than getting paid without getting laid? It was a gift from the Gods of sexual service. Everybody was happy.

Denver was a revelation. I had never been to a city, and I found myself enjoying J.W. Reynolds more than I should have. That's when things got complicated. In Denver, I found out that J.W. and Mac are related, and they found out that Vicky and Alexandra are one in the same.

The next time I saw Mac, I had to explain the circumstances and admit I had feelings for J.W. Mac said he wasn't going to interfere, and we made no commitments to each other. Mac, unfortunately, bowed out of my life.

Heartsick, I returned to Durango and received a letter from my sister, Becky; she was planning to marry. I asked J.W. to be my escort, and he accepted. We went by train to Baltimore. After the wedding, we traveled down the coast to visit his family in South Carolina and then to Savannah to visit my family as well. We became friends and lovers, but I never could get my mind fully off Mac.

After weeks of traveling, we came back to Durango. J.W. asked for my hand in marriage. I was very surprised. Thinking of him now makes butterflies in my stomach. I can't imagine how I looked when he asked me. I'm so glad he had to return to Denver. He is kind and considerate; he said I could take my time and give him my answer in Denver at Christmas. He stated that he didn't want to put more pressure on me than I was already facing with the issues of Father and Mr. Brody. I must say that J.W. puts me first every time. He is truly a gentleman. I needed time, and he graciously gave it to me. I recognize I'm fortunate to have his love. There must be a hundred women who would have eagerly accepted his proposal.

So then, why am I hesitating? I have a chance to step out of this bubble simply by saying yes. I'd never have to go to the Good Hour again. But, I cannot. I cannot deny I have profound feelings for Mac McClellan.

J.W. and I spent the last three months together, and it's been wonderful; we didn't disagree once. Things couldn't have been any more perfect between us. In the short time Mac and I have spent together, we've had our share of disagreements, and we are truly not the best at sorting things out without saying hurtful things. Denver was proof of that. Nevertheless, there are still strong ties for me, and the underlying hope of something more.

I wonder if things would have been different between Mac and me if we had spent as much time together as J.W. and I have. Would Mac have proposed? I guess I will never know.

J.W. Reynolds is a polished diamond, and Mac McClellan is one in the rough. The polished diamond has presented itself, and the industrial diamond has not. Answering yes to J.W.'s proposal makes Mac a foregone conclusion, which is frustrating, because Mac McClellan has my heart. He is my dream.

Chapter Four: THE INSPECTOR, BRODY AND FATHER

After my parents' accident on Aspen Ridge, Mr. Brody, a friend of Father's, offered his flat here in Durango. We accepted and moved from Creede. While my sister, Becky, was back east, I had a visitor, Inspector Hugo Southerland from Philadelphia. He was looking for my father, Dr. Frances Highland. He said they had unfinished business and then poured out his shocking news.

I learned that father was previously married to Inspector Southerland's sister, Harriett, and they had a son named Christopher. Frances had told the family they had died aboard a ship while trying to leave Savannah at the time of the Civil War. Later, Harriett's journal was found. She had written that she was concerned for her safety.

Years later, the inspector found his sister and nephew dead, buried behind a wall in the basement of the house in which they lived in Savannah, Georgia. A year ago, Father and Mother were supposed to have died in the accident on Aspen Ridge, in Creede, Colorado. However, the inspector believes that Father walked away and might have caused the accident that took Mother's life, and he is looking further into it.

The inspector said his investigation started when Harriett's first husband died an unexpected death. Father was his physician, but the inspector couldn't prove wrongdoing. The inspector believes that my father has killed many times. He also believes that my landlord, Mr. James Brody, is involved and aids my father in his hideous crimes.

His words rang true when I saw a brass box that looked identical to one my father had, in James Brody's office, which Father had forbidden us to touch. It went missing right after the accident on Aspen Ridge. I questioned Mr. Brody, but he said the box was his, and that it was just a coincidence. It also explains why

Mr. Brody offered his flat to Becky and me; maybe it was to keep an eye on us? For, we had never met the man or heard Father speak of him, for him to make such a generous gesture.

Becky and I found it very odd when we were writing friends and family about the accident that James Brody and our uncle's address, both of whom we have never met, were the only two addresses in Father's address book. Father was sixty-some years old, and one would think you would have many addresses in a book, since Father was from Philadelphia, lived in Savannah, and was Chief of Staff at Cook Memorial Hospital in Chicago before he moved us west.

I can't describe the horror and burden this has put upon the family. Unfortunately, and with deep heartache, I have done a little digging myself and found that the inspector's allegations are correct.

When J.W. and I came back from Bimini, J.W. went to see him. Inspector Southerland wanted me to let him know when I was back in town. He was waiting for something to break. He needed more evidence to put his case together. One thing that was interesting is that after the inspector had questioned Mr. Brody; and after that, Mr. Brody mysteriously left town. When I asked Mrs. Brody, she said he had gone away for a few days to see a friend. Of course, the first question that came to mind was, *Is Father really alive, and did Brody go to warn him?* It's all very suspicious.

Inspector Southerland had warned me it would not be safe for me to come to see him and that is why J.W. went in my place. If Mr. Brody is involved, then I could be in danger. The inspector told J.W. to tell me to be cautious, not to trust Mr. Brody, and never get myself into a situation where he could get me alone. The whole idea of Father being a murderer is unthinkable.

My body starts to shake. I throw a chunk of coal on the fire. It's early, but I need a drink to steady my nerves. I open a bottle of red wine and pour a glass. I felt safe when J.W. was in town, but now that he's gone, and although the inspector is still in town, I feel alone. I'm uneasy with all this thought of Father and Mr. Brody. I check the nightstand drawer for my pistol. I'd be a fool to turn my back and think I'm safe from either of them. My eyes well with tears, and I wish this would all go away.

Aunt Jenny, my late mother's only sister, and Uncle Scotty Michaels didn't want me to return to Durango. They know about the allegations against Father. We're all unsteady, not knowing what is true, or what may happen next. They invited me to come live with them, or move into the Mathieson house, my grandparent's house. It's empty, but I have hopes of building a life here and a relationship with Mac McClellan.

In front of the fire, bundled in my robe, I sit with pencil and paper and write a list of things I must do. First, I must stop by the post to get my mail. Second, I must gather Becky's things and ship them to Baltimore. Now that she is married, she will not be returning to Durango. How I miss her even if we did have angry words. I wonder how she's doing.

I wrap a blanket around me. I can't seem to get warm. I'm the last person she wants to hear from, since I conveyed the inspector's theory of Father's wrongdoing, she wants nothing to do with me. I will still compose a letter to tell her I'm home and safe; it's the responsible thing to do. Maybe by now, she's had time to forgive me. I didn't want to hear the news about Father any more than she, but she blames me, the messenger. Anyway, I will make sure her things get to her in Baltimore. I'm not going to be the one to break up what small family we have. I must write John too. I promised to let him know when I got home.

Chapter Five: GRACIE'S DILEMMA

I unpack the trunks filled with material and patterns, along with other things from my trip. The material and sewing notions will help me make money through the winter. I want to stay active, working as a tailor; it needs to be my first priority. I don't want to let myself get sucked into working at Gracie's more and more. It would be easy because the money is good, but I must stay focused. It's well known that in that occupation, women can be damaged … or worse … and survival is paramount.

Working in the sewing room, I finally have things put away and organized. I can't wait to get started cutting out one of my new patterns. For every piece of yardage I purchased from Aunt Jenny, she would find me a remnant for lining, or a half spool of thread, horsehair to reinforce collars or plackets to complete an outfit. I thanked her repeatedly, but I want to think of something special I can send her, and Uncle too, to show them how very grateful I am for all they have done.

I hate to break from putting things away, but I need to check the mail. I'm so hoping there may be a letter from Mac. With that very thought, I hurry and brush my hair to look somewhat presentable.

The boardwalk is wet from the melting snow. The air is fresh and crisp with a lingering smell of pine. My nose feels frozen as I take a deep breath. The town is busy, and as I pass the Strater House Hotel, I wave to Smokey Bearup posting the Thanksgiving menu in the window. It's a lovely bill of fare, with a nice piece of artwork in the corner. He pokes his head out the door. It is quickly covered with large moist snowflakes.

"Good to see you, Miss Highland."

"How are you, Smokey?"

"Real good. You've been gone a while."

"Yes, when I left I was trying to escape the heat, and now I'm trying to escape the cold." I hold out my hand and snowflakes land in my palm.

"It is beautiful though, isn't it?"

"Yes, it is."

"So, you went back east I heard."

"I did, for my sister's wedding, but it's good to be home."

"Maybe you'd like to have Thanksgiving at the Strater." He hands me a menu. I take a quick glance.

"It all looks delicious, thank you."

"I won't keep you. I just thought I'd say 'hello' and welcome you back."

"Thank you, Smokey, it's good to see you. If I don't see you prior, have a happy Thanksgiving."

Outside, two men begin to decorate the hotel windows and doors with pine boughs for the holiday. Smokey goes back inside, and I wave to him through the window and take a moment to read the holiday greeting and dinner menu. I do love the holidays, and I'm hoping to have company for Thanksgiving, a certain marshal friend of mine.

Celebrate with us at the Strater Hotel
Thanksgiving Dinner Menu

Raw Oysters
Mock Turtle Consommé Macédoine
Celery, Salted Almonds, Pickles
Fillet of Lake Trout, Maître de Hotel Parisienne Potatoes
Boiled Rex Ham, Champagne Sauce
Prime Rib of Beef Demi-Glace
Roast Young Turkey, Sage Dressing & Cranberry Jelly
Roman Punch
Spring Duck a la Marengo
Suckling Pig, Brown Sweet Potatoes, Apple Fitters, Fruit Sauce
Mashed Potatoes, Boiled Potatoes, French Peas in Cream, Escalloped Tomatoes
Fresh Shrimp Salad with Mayonnaise Dressing

Pumpkin Pie, Hot Mince Pie, Rhubarb Pie, New England Plum
Pudding with Hard Brandy Sauce
Assorted Cakes, Layered Raisins, Mixed Nuts
American Cheese, Roquefort Cheese, Bent's Water Crackers
Café Noir

It's a large menu. They must be expecting a crowd. I step aside to make way for two men taking up the boardwalk carrying in a big, full spruce tree into the Strater. The Strater House does everything magnificently!

At the post, I can hardly control my emotions. I'm elated to find I have a letter from Mac and decide to wait to open it at home. Trying not to slip and slide, I step in melting spots on the boardwalk. Reaching the mercantile, I stick my head in and say, "hello" to Mrs. Brody. I need to pick up a few things, such as fresh cream for Sam. She says she has heard from Mr. Brody, and he is on his way home. Chills run up my spine. I want to ask where he has been but dare not.

Taking my things, I return to my flat above the store. The sun is just now lowering over the La Plata Mountains, a beautiful sight. Shaking the snow from my cape and stomping my boots at the door on the stoop, I rush in, trying not to bring the cold air with me. The sun quickly sets, and I light the lamp on the kitchen table. I still am not accustomed to the alternating current Mr. Brody has installed. It's very convenient, but the light is harsh. Setting my things on the table, Sam comes to greet me, purring. I pour a little cream into his saucer. Before I do anything else, I want to read Mac's letter. With trembling hands from the cold and nerves, I tear open the letter. Just then, a knock at the door interrupts me. *Damn.*

"It's me, Gracie." I open the door.

"Grace, come in, you look like an icicle. Is something wrong?"

"Nah. Can't a friend just stop in?"

"Yes. Of course, but I'm surprised to see you here when you know I'll be coming to work in a few hours."

"I know, but I have somethin' I need to talk to you about. I didn't want the girls to hear."

I direct her to stand by the fire. She warms her backside. Her cheeks are rosy, and she looks young for being in her thirties. I've never seen her without a hat, no matter what the time has been. She's always dressed in her best. I've seen her be charming and intelligent, but what I know best about Grace is that she is a shrewd, calculating businesswoman. She runs a prosperous house, and sees no moral downside to what she does; she says there's a need for what she provides, and that this business was around before Jesus. She's an ace when it comes to training young women in the artful techniques of carnal knowledge. She told me that the better one performs, the higher the earnings. If you're not earning, you're out of Grace's house. The girls told me firsthand that there have been several of them that have breached Gracie's good graces and were sent on their way.

"I see. You've come to worry me instead," I say, closing the door, waiting for Grace to unbutton her wrap. "So, you're fine?"

"No ... I'm not fine. I have a dilemma."

"Here, give me your wrap and warm yourself. I'll put another piece of coal on."

"Thank you. It's colder than a well digger's ass out there. I want to thank you for comin' back to work so quickly. I've been a little under the weather, but I didn't want to say anythin'." She looks out the window. "Damn, if the snow doesn't stop, we'll all be six feet under."

"What a terrible thing to say."

"Relax, I'm joking."

"I would hope so. What's the problem?"

"I'm beginnin' to hate the cold. The Rockies are gettin' to me."

"Besides that, sit down. Let me pour you a cup of Chamomile tea."

"Your place looks good."

"Did you come here to tell me that? Don't make me guess, Gracie. Why are you out?" I serve tea for the two of us. I look at the letter from Mac on the table. I so want to read it, but listening to Grace is important. Grace takes a sip of her tea and sets the cup in the saucer on her lap.

"I'm startin' to warm up. You always have it cozy in here."

"I can't help it; I'm freezing after being in the warm climate. I don't think I'll ever be the same. If you like heat, you'd love it there."

"I want to hear more of Bimini. It does sound wonderful. Maybe I'll go someday."

"Really, just like that?"

"Why not, everyone needs a change. Change is good when things aren't going so well."

"Are you having a business problem?"

"No, not money problems, thank God."

"Then tell me."

"I will, I will. How's Mr. J.W. Handsome Tycoon. Is he still in town? He hasn't been in."

"He left to go back to Denver. I have so much to tell you I don't know where to begin."

"And I can't wait to hear. Can you stay late tonight?"

"Sure."

"Good, I'll eagerly await hearin' all about your trip."

Grace looks peaked. I know she's been working extra hours since I was gone, but there is something else in play.

"I saw all the fabric on the table in the sewing room when I came in."

"I have so much; you won't believe it. Do you want to be the first or take a look?"

"Absolutely, I always want to be first."

We go into the sewing room.

"Take a look at this. If I had more money, we would be opening a shop. Did you bring back the whole city?" I have fabric stacked on the table up to my chin.

"Look at this, I love this; I want it all." Grace circles the table thumbing through the different cuttings of material.

"I do have a great selection."

"Like I said, I love it and want everythin'. Did ya have any time to work somethin' up for me?"

"I brought six new patterns home, and I guarantee nobody here has these styles, at least not until the next season. My Aunt Jenny, she's sensational. You should see her shop. I'll have to show you the clothes she made for me. She has ideas you wouldn't believe, and she can sew anything. Look at the styles on the front of the envelopes. See? They have colored pictures; no more wasting time drawing them up. Someone has created it for you."

"I like your creations."

"I know, and I can use this for a base and then make adjustments. Each dress will have something different. No two dresses need to be alike."

"Is all this for sale?"

"It is."

"You're not keeping anythin' for yourself?"

"Don't worry, there's plenty to choose from."

"Okay girl, grab a tablet, I'll show you what I want." She flips through the bolts and cuttings, making her choices. I put them aside.

"I don't need to pick the patterns out. You know what I like." While she is choosing, I start matching lace and accessories letting her pick what she fancies. She's like a child in a toy store. I understand. That's exactly how I felt in Auntie's shop. I couldn't get enough. When she finishes, I complete my notes. Grace makes a few jokes ... and then becomes very quiet.

She opens her money belt and takes out a stack of bills and two gold nuggets.

"Here, I know these two gold pieces are worth two hundred and fifty dollars. I went to the bank on the way here. I realize that this isn't your final bill. However, I'd like to pay in advance ... just in case."

"In case? What do you mean?"

"You know me. I don't like debts hangin' over my head."

"Are you sure, Grace? This may take me some time to complete."

"Well, put me first on your list, girl. Ain't I worth it?"

"Yes, sure you're worth it. Now, why don't you tell me what's on your mind. Come, sit down."

We walk back into the other room and sit by the fire.

"I just can't seem to get warm. I don't mean to be pushy. I know you have other orders from more than just me, for Pete's sake. I seem to be in a hurry for everythin' anymore. Money seems to come and go lately. I had a great night last night, made a bundle. Therefore, I'm treating myself. Ya never know what tomorrow may bring. Besides, it's good to spread the wealth. Everyone needs work. We all need to make money. Now, about why I'm here."

"If it's about me just working three nights a week, Grace, I don't think I can give you more right now. I'm trying to make both jobs work."

"I see." She looks down for just a moment.

"What's going on?"

"I have to see a doctor in Denver. I need a little surgery."

"Grace, it must be serious, if you have to go to Denver."

"The doc didn't seem too worried, but then why would he be, he's not goin' under the knife." She chuckles. "I need to make the trip; they can't take care of me here."

"Then, you must go."

"I feel better already, just tellin' you."

"Well, I'm glad you did. That's what friends are for."

"I don't want to close the business. People will talk, and that's not the kind of talk a business needs, not in this rumor town. Men might think I'm closing up and go on down to the Pineapple Delight. That Madam Bruce, she's a smart gal, ya know? If anybody gets word I'm ill, they'll have themselves a fine day for sure. It could be the end of me, the end of the Good Hour."

"How can I help?"

"I don't know. I need to find someone responsible to watch over the girls and take care of things. They don't know anything about running the business. I hire them to fuck, and thank God they're good at it. But, the money end, ordering liquor and food, scheduling; they don't have a clue. I'd be broke in a week."

"Let me help, Grace. I can watch over things."

"Why honey, I appreciate it, but what do you know about my business?"

"Well, I know how to keep a ledger. I can do sums in my head. For my own business, I have to figure profit and loss. I know to have to provide a good service, buy what you need, but never run out and by the end of the day, I know you want to take more money in than you've spent."

"Damn, where'd you learn this?"

"From books, basic economics works for any business. I can make a menu, place food and liquor orders, and help Sadie in the kitchen. I can give orders, organize, and see the girls are ready for the evening … if they'll listen to me."

"They'll do as I say."

"You know my father was a doctor."

"No, I didn't."

"I grew up around helping those in need. I can clean and send out the laundry. I'm good at entertaining."

"You sure are girl, the best."

"And I know how to serve drinks, and I have a gun."

"Sweet Jesus, a gun? But, do you know how to use it?"

"I'm not a sharp shooter, but I know what end is the dangerous one."

"Wow, that's quite a résumé girl, but can I afford ya?" Grace rubs her chin and I pour us another cup of tea. "I will need to be gone at least two weeks."

"I can handle it. Besides, do you have another choice?"

"No, I don't. It's a lot for me to ask."

"Don't worry. If I need a strong hand, I'll send for Smokey Bearup."

"I've got Smokey's help. I guess he hired someone to help him at the Diamond Bell, so I can count on him to be there after eleven, and his brother William said he could fill in after dinner, from eight to eleven. So, I've got that covered. They are good men. I do believe, Vicky, you can handle it, and it sounds to me like you've got it all worked out already. Okay, you're hired. We'll talk money later, if that's alright. I have to get back. How soon can you cover?"

"Go ahead and make your plans. I'll be ready."

"Good, and thank you. I'll get my things together. I really can't thank you enough."

"You can thank me by getting well. The girls and I will do just fine." Grace gives me a hug, I help her with her cape, and she is off.

I look at the messy table in the sewing room, thinking I had just gotten things organized. However, I'm ecstatic to have Grace's large order and with payment. It gives me cash to purchase my train ticket and money to take care of my expenses going to Denver for the holidays. John's wedding is just weeks away. I'm excited and looking forward to it. Christmas in Denver with my family will be wonderful. Maybe we will go ice-skating and take sleigh rides. The extra I will make managing the Good Hour will help put some back into my savings, since I used it to buy materials in Savannah.

Rushing to Mac's letter, I sit down by the fire to read. I'm excited, but scared at the same time. I don't know what to expect. What if he said he never wants to see me again? The last time we saw each other was in July, in Denver, it was disastrous. I did a poor job explaining how I came to be with J.W. To make matters worse, I had to tell him I was working for Gracie Talbot at the Good Hour, in which he is well acquainted. His rude comments made my blood boil, and before I knew it, I had ordered him out of my room, like some mad woman. We were both hurt, but that was no excuse. My hands shake, as I unfold the thick, vanilla stationery that smells a hint of his spicy Bay Rum aftershave. I start to read …

October 9, 1894
Dear Alex,
I was a surprised to receive your letter, but glad to hear from you. You have been in my thoughts. I'm sorry for the things I said in Denver. I was totally befuddled and my choice of words was not the best by far. I hope you can forgive me. It just so happens that I will be in the area and I would love to have Thanksgiving dinner with you. I'm not sure what day I will arrive, so I'll stop by when I get into town. Thank you for the invitation. I would be happy to take you out to the Strater if you choose. However, if you choose to go out, will you be kind enough to make the reservations? For, I feel I may not arrive ahead of time. I'm looking forward to our visit.
Kind regards,
Mac
P.S. I bet you liked South Carolina. We will talk soon.

My heart is pounding. I want to scream. He's answered my letter! I'm so excited. The letter is vague, but he's coming. He's coming to be with me. It sounds as if he made special plans to be here. Oh my, my heart is aflutter. I dance around the room thrilled, I couldn't be happier. He's coming to Durango.

I have so much to accomplish and in so little time. I must get my things ready to take to the Good Hour. I need to be ready when Grace calls. I'll put a few outfits in my suitcase to take tonight. I need daytime and night clothes as well. In addition, what am I to do with Sam? I don't want Mrs. Brody to know I'm working or staying at the Good Hour. I'll need to keep the fire going and visit the mercantile once a day. I don't need her raising questions. I don't know how long I can keep my employment a secret. If word gets out, my sewing orders will stop completely. That means no money and no regular life to come home to. Even Mrs. Brody could put me out.

Exhausted, I pour water for a sponge bath and after I make a quick bowl of oatmeal and toast for dinner (I had forgotten to eat all day), Sam and I curl up in bed. We're warm in no time with the extra blankets and the thick, heavy sheepskin under the sheets. I feel good to have had such a productive day. Moreover, I give thanks to God that I received a positive response from Mac.

Chapter Six: COLONEL LEEDS

Back to work at the Good Hour, entertaining Colonel Leeds, I look at my reflection in the mirror. The haze of cigar smoke mingles with the fading light. I fantasize about my dreams and desires outside these walls, eagerly waiting for the day when I'm no longer under this roof as a working girl. I have an opportunity to leave it all behind if I could forget Mac and accept J.W.'s marriage proposal. J.W. has an outstanding résumé, and he's a great lover. He not only knows how to make love to a woman; he cares about her pleasure as well. That is a very rare and says plenty about his character. By marrying J.W., I would have property, jewels, money, the ability to travel and have practically anything under the sun, including my freedom. I know any girl I work with, including Grace Talbot, would take him up on his offer. I try to restrain any thoughts that connect me to my real world … or should I say, Alex's life, but it's not working.

In the interim, huge Colonel Leeds, in all his glory, is enjoying himself at his own expense, standing with his pants loose around his ankles, his long white legs bent at the knees with his hands grasping my hips. He lunges, making my breasts peak over my well-tied camisole, and the bed squeaks. I swear, every screw seizing this fancy ironwork will be loose if he does not surrender quickly!

"Please," I pray. "Let this man finish in a timely fashion." Mentally, I left this place an hour ago. Thank God, it's over. Upon his completion, the colonel walks over to the dresser while snapping his suspenders on his shoulders. He takes his time buttoning his coat over his massive chest.

"Vicky, I'll ask you once more, won't you come with me? I'll set ya up fine. You'll want for nothing, I promise you," the colonel says. I smile adjusting my bosom in my camisole.

"Thank you, Colonel, but I'm not going to be here much longer. I appreciate your invitation, but I can't accept."

He lays a brown envelope on the dresser and says, "The envelope is for you, a little something for the holiday, and the cash on the dresser is for the madam." Leeds is a generous man. He asks only for me since I came to the Good Hour. Many a time, he has offered to take me from Durango, just like today.

"Well, I'm jealous, Vicky that it's not me in your dreams, but just the same, I've left you something."

"I appreciate your generosity."

He is an older man with sparse hair, maybe fifty-two, and I know he has seen more than one war. I smile and thank him, placing my robe around my shoulders as I walk to the dresser. Opening the brown wrinkled envelope, I spy a mass of fresh new bills; it is not polite to count. However, I can tell it is a large sum of money. Occasionally, someone surprises me, and today it's the colonel. There are good people in the world. Tears well, and as I try to speak, my words do not come.

"It's okay, Vicky. You're a good girl, and I want to see you happy. You don't have to say a word, and the next time I'm in town, I'd be happy if I find you gone. Good luck, I hope the man you're waiting for is worth it."

He takes his hat and gloves in hand, steps out, and closes the door.

From under the bed, I pull out a washbasin to freshen up, and then dress in regular clothes to head home. I run my fingers through my expensive wardrobe fit for a queen and designed to allure any man. Gowns, dresses, robes and costumes made from satin, crepe and silk; from bold to subdued styles and colors, along with lace camisoles and stockings, and a variety of specially made high-heeled shoes. I smile at the thought that men do not mind waging their fortunes for my services. I make it my goal to find enticing ways to keep them coming back.

I put the envelope into my bag along with my diary. The diary holds expeditious information, notes on my posh clients, what they like and don't like. Time is money. I review the records. The trick of the trade is to surrender as little as possible and acquire all the stakes. You'd be surprised how the little things make me profitable.

I have plans of making a line of herbal blends from Great Grandmother's book, to use at work. Additionally, I've started selling a women's cleansing solution. Word is getting around, and I have plenty of madams to contact.

I hear Madam Grace outside the door, giving instructions to the girls. "Look, if you're through with your Johns, get downstairs and get another. Don't forget, get it up, get it off, and get him out, unless he's gonna go another round. Got it? You're here to make money, ladies. That's your job. Don't get chummy, don't get personal and don't get pregnant. Now shoo, go bring in the gold girls, the night is young!" She says merrily.

Chapter Seven: MOVING INTO THE GOOD HOUR

Gracie is at my door before eight o'clock the next morning. I answer, and a gust of frigid air wraps my gown around my frame.

"Grace, come in."

"Looks as if I woke ya." Grace stomps her feet and rushes in as I struggle to close the door with both hands against the forceful wind. "I said I'd let you know as soon as I could. I just went to the train station and got my ticket."

"So when are you leaving?"

"On the morning train. I know its short notice."

"Don't worry; I've already started putting my things together last night."

"I've got bad news."

"Oh no, what?"

"Everyone's okay, but Sadie, my cook left."

"What?"

"Her husband, he's a miner up at Silver Pick, and there was an accident yesterday afternoon. He got hurt real bad. What could I say?"

"Don't worry, Grace, the girls and I will be fine."

"But, what will you do? I don't have time to find someone else."

"We'll manage. We can cook for ourselves. Don't worry, I'm good at planning meals and I know a few nice dishes for company. When we take our breakfast in the morning, I'll put on a roast and vegetables in the oven for the afternoon. It will all work out. Stop worrying, will you?"

"It's easier said than done. There's always so much to do."

"I'll manage. You just have to relax."

"I'll give you the key to my desk. My moneybox is in there. In it, you will find an envelope with two hundred dollars. You can use it for groceries, medical supplies, booze and anything else you need.

I order liquor, whiskey or beer, from Smokey Bearup at the Bell. I have an account at Brody's mercantile. You can use it. Send Frannie. She's smart and has a level head. As far as anything else, you'll have to figure it out."

"It's going to be okay. Look, you are going to get yourself better. You will be back before you know it, and the Good Hour will be no worse for wear, really. You've got to trust me."

"I've never had to ask for anything from anybody."

"Good for you, but it's not my first time. I'll take care of things. What about firewood and coal?"

"You're going to need some by the end of next week, if it stays like this. I use Burgess. I'll stop by his place on the way home and tell him to check on you the middle of next week. He'll take care of the delivery, and you have plenty of money to pay him. Now, is there anything else I can do for you?"

"Not that I can think of. I would like a few days off when you return. I've got company coming."

"No problem, I'll try to be home by the holiday. I mean Thanksgiving, not Christmas."

"If not, don't worry. We'll be fine."

"I better get going."

"I'm bringing my things this afternoon. I'll be there a little early to get settled."

"Oh, the girls have cleaned your room. They're excited to have you."

"Good, that makes it easier. I was hoping there wouldn't be any resistance."

"Hell no, they're excited to have me gone for a while. I'll see ya later. Thanks for your help."

"No problem. See you tonight then."

I dress warm and head for the livery, bracing myself against the wind. It makes me feel good to be able to help Grace. It's snowing so hard I can't see the mountains. My nose and fingers are frozen before I get there. William sees me coming from his office window and opens the door.

"William, how are you?" I say out of breath.

"How ya doing, Alex? I heard you were back, but what the hell are you doing out in this mess?"

"I'm good, thank you. I'm sorry I haven't been down. Indy has probably disowned me. I brought you money."

"You didn't need too; I still have some from the payment you made before."

"Well, I like to stay ahead of things."

"Thank you! Christ, I wish all my customers would."

"How's Indy?"

"He's good. I hope you don't mind; I've put my niece on him for a little more exercise."

"No, that's wonderful. I've been here to see him a couple of times, after you had left for the day …William, I wonder if you can help me."

"What's on your mind?"

"I have a few things to take over to the Good Hour this afternoon, and I wondered if you have someone that can help me?"

"Sure, do ya need a wagon?"

"Gosh, no, a trunk and a couple of cases are all."

"I'll have Stan come over around four o'clock, if that's alright. He'll load ya up."

"Can you make it a little later, say four-thirty? Then, it will be dark."

"No problem, four-thirty it is."

"If he can come around back for me, they'll be fewer questions for me to answer."

"I understand, I'll tell him."

"Thanks for giving me a hand, I appreciate it. I'll say 'hello' to Indy while I'm here."

"Yeah, the good old boy is havin' some oats."

"How's your special lady friend Michele?"

"She's good, thanks for asking. Would ya like a cup of hot coffee?"

"I would like some, thank you." William pours me a cup and hands it to me.

"Don't worry. My hands are dirty, but the cup is clean."

"Thanks, William, I'm giving Grace Talbot a hand the next few weeks. She said you help her out from time to time."

"I do, when she needs it. Some nights, Smokey gets tied up at the saloon, and I've been known to fill in."

"Good, will you do the same for me? Grace has to make a trip to Denver, and she needed someone to help with things. I volunteered to give her a hand. It's all new to me, but she doesn't have anyone."

"No problem, just let me know."

"Okay, great. The fewer people who know I'm there, the better."

"You got that right. I mean … true."

"Thanks, and thanks for the coffee. I'll let you get back to work."

"Hey, you may not have someone to come get me, so how about if Smokey can't make it, he sends someone?"

"Perfect."

I take off my wrap and brush Indy down while I'm here. I've missed him. I haven't ridden since before I left for Baltimore. I just haven't had the time. Kissing him on his warm nose, he nudges me. I throw a blanket on his back to keep the chill off.

Back at the house, I clean up and do the dishes. I'm going to leave the fire burning. I'll have to come back each day to put on some coal. Sam has to be fed and kept warm too. At the same time, I'll stop in to the store to see Mrs. Brody, as usual. I've packed all my things and have them ready by four-thirty. It's dark, and I'm hoping the Brodys won't see. That way there will be no questions.

Young Stan arrives on time and is in and out in a jiffy. I decide to ride with him to the Good Hour.

Grace and I have a pleasant evening. Business is slow, and we retreat to her room for hot cocoa. She goes over her list of everything I need to know, gives me her key, and goes over her list again. Early the next morning, before sunup, we go to the train depot and I see her off. The last thing she says to me is, "Lick 'um and stick 'um, girl!" We both chuckle, keeping things casual. I pray everything goes okay.

The girls are still sleeping, which is fine. It's too late for me to go back to bed. I'd never sleep. I set up Grace's bedroom as a sewing room. That way, I can leave things out, but have it out of the way and when I have spare time. I will work on her dresses.

I make a schedule for the girls. With Sadie gone, everyone has more chores. Every morning, we will start with fresh linens. Tilly will be in charge of the morning laundry. Mae will help in the kitchen preparing vegetables for dinner. Frannie will clean up the parlor and wash the glasses. Bevie will tidy the rooms. There's still the washroom to care for, liquor to stock and fires to keep.

I hope Sadie's husband is okay, but this is the worst time to not have a cook. I will simply make oatmeal each morning. We will have a sandwich at noon and one good meal before the crowd comes at four. I just have to believe it will all be done. And before bed, I will see to the bookwork. By five, we'll be ready to greet our anxious guests. I plan not to entertain unless it is necessary. We have so much to do and have to look our best, besides, I need to make sure things flow smoothly and nobody has trouble.

I have Smokey Bearup coming each night at eleven. When his shift is over at the saloon, and on the nights Smokey can't, William has agreed to fill in. That's one big thing I don't have to worry about. I feel better with a man in the house. So far, we have not had the need for one, and that's okay by me.

I record all expenses into the ledger. I want to account for every penny. The house needs to run efficiently. We're organized, and the girls don't mind helping. Besides, it's their house too. We have talks and laugh a lot. After closing, we take a bubble bath. I bring a lilac and sage solution made from Great Grandmother's recipe book. We have only two tubs, but they're big. The five of us heave in, two in one and three in another, sitting with our knees to our chin. The hot, steaming water feels good, and it overflows onto the floor. From the table next to the tub, I pour five mugs of warm, spiced mulled wine that I made from the few open bottles left as a treat from one of the guests. We did pretty well, in terms of money, but I decide to count it in the morning. In dim candlelight, we take turns sharing our hopes and dreams sitting in the tubs.

I tell them about the adventures I had in the islands and sailing with Uncle. None of them have ever seen the ocean. They are all in love with J.W. and Mac's name comes up a few times. I say I have feelings for Mac and ask them to please not bring up their personal sexual activities with him. The girls chuckle but agree, understanding my position. For as much as we play and laugh, we finish with a short prayer between us. "God bless the whores," we pray. We mean it seriously.

The girls at the Good Hour are better off than most, and their circumstances are the best they have known. They eat three meals a day, have a roof over their head, a mother figure, sisterhood, and sometimes access to medical care. They don't care that they have to comply with strict house rules. They're not always happy, but they make the most out of what they have, and I'm grateful a thousand times over that I have a loving family and enough good memories not to be clouded with the bad. Life is good.

The girls are interested in learning to sew. They love looking through the fabrics and notions I brought to the house. So we agree, from two to four, after our chores are done, we will have class on basic sewing techniques. At first, it is hard to get everyone's attention, they babble like a bunch of young schoolgirls, but it's fine. I think it's good for them to have fun. "The more you laugh," Mother would say, "the healthier you stay." Once we get started, the girls catch on fast.

We begin by learning sewing terms, how to thread a needle, how to measure and how to baste. I talk about different types of fabrics and how they're used. We practice on our own clothing that needs repairing, buttons, hems and seams. After the first week, I show them how to lay out material and how to find the bias. We cut out our first pattern together, a simple dwindle skirt. They start to have fun sewing and the two hours go by too quickly.

Believe me, they're not your average sewing group, and the conversation is quite colorful. Listening to them makes me laugh, and I think of Becky and the women she used to meet with for knitting. Becky's group and this group are like night and day. Probably most of the women in the knitting group needed a good lay for what ailed them.

The girls look forward to doing chores early, to get an additional half hour of sewing time in. We talk of sewing fancy dresses and costumes as well. At the brothel, work is never done, and we take Johns in all night long. I didn't really need to put a sign on the door. Most of the time it's quiet in the mid afternoon. As long as I'm in charge, I'm open for ways to keep the girls happy and the morale up, and they like the fact that they're learning something.

Sewing isn't for everyone, and I don't think I'll make seamstresses out of them; but it's a skill, and they will use it for themselves, maybe their families later or as a part time job. Education changes lives. Who am I to say it will not for these girls? I want them to feel good about themselves. Living as a whore, you give everything, and sometimes it's hard to feel good about anything.

Chapter Eight: IAN BRUCE

I have a gentleman at the door around four in the afternoon; his name is Ian Bruce. He says he's from Chicago. I introduce myself as Vicky, the madam of the house. He scrutinizes me with his piercing emerald eyes. He's well groomed, and looks to be in his early forties, dressed in expensive clothes, tall, with noticeably large hands. Mr. Bruce tells me he is interested in leasing the Good Hour for a private party. I had dressed in my best, and I'm glad I did. It helps me feel confident enough to play the part. I believe he is thinking I'm far too young for the position. The girls upstairs are straining to hear the conversation.

"Mr. Bruce, may I ask where you heard of our services. It may save us some time."

"I've come here on Smokey Bearup's recommendation. He said Grace Talbot has one of the finer parlors in Durango and I could find the best of everything under one roof … so, you are not Grace Talbot?"

I realize my hands are shaking and immediately clasp them together and proceed to explain that Madam Grace is busy for the next few days, and I'm taking her place.

"I'm looking for the best, Miss Vicky. If I wanted anything but the best, there are a lot of places down the street."

"Well, we have the best, Mr. Bruce; I assure you."

"My sister will debate that."

"And who is your sister?"

"Martha Bruce, madam of the Pineapple Delight. Before you ask, I don't feel comfortable doing business at my sister's house. You do get the picture?" He says with a sassy smile looking down.

"Of course, Mr. Bruce, and I'm very happy to have you here. Please, come in, so we may discuss business."

"Very good, that's why I'm here. I have six men traveling with me, plus myself of course, and I'd like to have the house for two nights. Do you have enough women to handle us?"

"There are five of us girls at the Good Hour, that's our specialty, pleasing more than one man at a time. You know the saying, 'the more the merrier'?"

"And, you're one of the five, Miss Vicky?"

"Yes. Now so you know, I'm prepared to serve two delicious meals a day, all the liquor and beer you can drink. We shave, bathe and give massages for an extra charge, not to mention our talents of pleasing our male guests. Just as Mr. Bearup suggested, everything under this roof is premium." I glance to my right and see the girls dressed and standing quietly at the banister on the second floor. I smile, they are right on cue. "Would you like to see the girls?"

"Absolutely."

"Girls, please come down and meet Mr. Bruce. He is considering our accommodations to entertain his friends."

The girls put on a sultry exhibition, strutting down the stairs, one by one, with alluring and sensual smiles.

"They are pretty, very pretty, Miss Vicky."

"And pleasing, Mr. Bruce. Would you like another drink?"

"Yes, thank you."

I motion to Tilly to bring the crystal decanter of our finest to fill his glass. She's a beautiful redhead, with soft curls, bright blue eyes and skin as pure and as white as snow, with shapely full lips and perfect breasts. She bends over and slowly pours him a drink and lightly wets her bottom lip, showing perfect cleavage. She says in a sultry whisper, "I'm so glad to meet you, Mr. Bruce. I hope you're enjoying Durango. The sun goes down early in the west, and we have long, cold, nights. But, with the best whiskey and warm thighs, I'm sure you'll find us pleasurable."

Frannie promenades over to Mr. Bruce with the humidor in hand, dressed in a seductive, short dress, showing off her long, shapely legs. Frannie smiles and bends over to give him full view of her ample breasts, which are exposed to the nipple. Mr. Bruce's neck turns red. She opens the box of fine quality cigars, and touches her bottom lip with her soft pink, tongue before offering him one.

"Aren't they lovely, Mr. Bruce?"

"You have me convinced already, Miss Vicky. Let's talk money."

I dismiss the girls. They gracefully make their exit. He watches them go. "Fine, what's your price?"

I have to think quickly, "Two nights with meals, drinks and the best ladies of the evening in town," I say with a smile, "Two thousand."

"That's considerably more, Miss Vicky, than I had in mind."

"We have a very good reputation for pleasing our customers, and we're healthy. As you know in any business, there are expenses, Mr. Bruce. I don't believe in compromising the quality we offer over a few extra dollars."

"You are a very wise business woman, and you make a good point. I'll pay it."

"I do ask one thing."

"And that is?"

"That your men do not raise a hand to my girls."

"There will be no problems. You have my word."

"And I retain the right to ask that the men be clean and shaved. My girls will love to assist them in that area if they choose. Of course, that would be extra."

"How much extra?"

"Two hundred."

"Fair enough, Miss Vicky. And now it's my turn. I reserve you." Mr. Bruce stands and reaches for his wallet. He counts out his money and puts it on the table.

"There's twenty-two hundred."

"I'm pleased, thank you." Inside I'm screaming. I know Grace will be pleased. I extend my hand in a very delicate fashion, and he gently kisses it.

"We will be ready at five o'clock tomorrow evening." My heart is pounding, and I feel my cheeks flush. I show Mr. Bruce to the door. He leaves and I close the door. Now, my knees start shaking and the girls squeal with glee. I never thought I would have to make a deal such as this. Frantic, I call them to get their behinds down here. "We have work to do."

Every spare minute I have tonight, I'll write a list of things that need to be done. I have a limited number of hours to get the house ready for their arrival. Luckily, it's not a very busy evening and the others take care of the guests, leaving me to serve drinks and mingle.

Chapter Nine: SINK OR SWIM

I'm up before dawn and wake the girls. I give Frannie a long list to take to the mercantile; she has the best head on her shoulders. I remind her to ask for the groceries to be delivered by eleven a.m., if possible. She looks over the list and makes a few suggestions, surprising me. I think I can count on her to help, and she seems to keep the others in line, not in a bad way, but the girls have a tendency to lollygag. I post a note on the front door, *The Good Hour is closed Friday, Saturday and Sunday for a private party,* and advise patrons to please visit us another time. I added an extra day just in case Mr. Bruce's party stays longer than planned. Mr. Bruce is a man with money, and I want to make sure he gets exactly what he pays for. I can't believe he's Madam Martha's brother. How lucky for us he is not using the Pineapple Delight. I wonder how she feels about that. I need everything to go perfectly. If he says anything, I want it to be something good. Martha is Gracie's top competition.

I check the house and make sure we have enough bedding and towels. The closet is full, and there's enough to change the bedding twice a day if necessary and towels to dry a small army. I take a quart of boiled water from the stove and place it in a jar, adding a few sprigs of lavender to the water. I'll let it set, strain it and sprinkle it on the clean sheets when we make up the beds. There's nothing like the smell of fresh linens. I check the washroom. The razor is sharp, and there's a new bar of shaving soap in the cup, close to a full bottle of Crown's Hair Tonic for men, and six bars of Ivory soap on the shelf.

I've read about Ivory, a product from Proctor & Gamble. It smells nice. I'll have to try it. I know it will not be anything like Mother's soap. Tomorrow, we will strip the sheets and send them to the Chinese laundry if there is not time to wash them ourselves. Mae walks through the back door with an arm full of snowy, green pine boughs, and sets them by the fireplace in the kitchen to dry. She plans to decorate the mantel and make an arrangement for the table of fresh boughs and red holly berries. I check the kitchen linens for tablecloths and napkins and find both. The glasses shine, and the silver serving trays are polished.

Mae and I put on white, cotton gloves, to prepare vegetables for soup. The last thing we need is to smell like onions, or have orange stains from carrots on our hands. I look around the kitchen; the coziness brings a smile to my face. Grace has made this place very nice for a woman on her own. I remember times in our kitchen at home in Creede, helping Mother chop vegetables, and watching her pick leaves of dried sage hanging from the rafters. Like my mother before me, she liked having a warm broth on hand daily in the winter months. I can smell the soup simmering now. "Love you, Mother," I whisper quietly. I scrape the vegetables from the cutting board into the black iron kettle hanging over the fire. I can hardly believe it has been over a year that she has been gone. At times, like now, it seems like a lifetime ago. I snap out of it, realizing there's no time to lose being melancholy right now.

After food the food is prepped, I dash over to the Diamond Bell Saloon. Going in the side door, I discover Smokey on the sly. Grace says she orders everything from him. He has his own small business selling booze on the side, and if he doesn't have what I need, he'll buy it from the Strater. The two Bearup brothers have their hands in everything. They are ambitious, and make things happen.

The Strater has the largest stockpile of booze, besides the General Palmer Hotel in town. I give Smokey my order, and pay him up front for three cases of fine whiskey. None of that burnt sugar and chewing tobacco stuff. I get a barrel of beer and two bottles of imported Scotch, which is gold in these territories, practically going on a hundred dollars a bottle. He says I'll have the order by three this afternoon.

I tell him about Sadie's husband and being in a pickle with company coming. He tells me of a woman who can give me a hand by the name of Mrs. Kane. She lives two streets over and is in need of work desperately. He's sure she can come over right away. I'm delighted. Smokey sends someone to fetch her. He says she's a good cook; she bakes, cleans and has a son who can give us a hand and run errands. I thank him by slipping him a twenty-dollar gold piece for his trouble. On my way out, I stop and turn around, "Smokey, one more thing, are there any entertainers in town?"

Smokey squints and chuckles without a sound. "Other than you girls?" he jokes. "How about a piano player, do ya need one? Lorenzo Parrish is in town."

Lorenzo Parrish is a good friend of Mac's and J.W.'s. He was an attorney originally from Savannah and practiced law in New Orleans until he encountered some trouble. I met him at the Diamond Bell when Mac took me to dinner last June and introduced me as his girlfriend. The second time, he was playing the piano at the Good Hour, while I was working as a whore. The first and second meetings were weeks apart. You can imagine Lorenzo's confusion; it was the most awkward situation. First, I'm a respectable woman out with the marshal, and then I'm J.W.'s whore at the Good Hour. Anyway, he was polite enough not to say a word to J.W. about seeing me with Mac.

Well, I have to put clients first, I need a piano player, and they don't come better than Lorenzo Parrish does. I need him.

"If he's free, please send him over; but if not, send somebody that can fit the part. Smokey Bearup, you're much more than a barman. You're like the town crier." He laughs and pushes up his green, satin garters that are holding his shirtsleeves in place. "You know everybody and everything that's going on."

"I do it all for money, Miss Vicky, all for the money."

"I know what that is like." We both laugh, and he says, "See ya tonight."

Smokey is a bouncer for the Good Hour on nights he's off work at the Diamond Bell. Talk about having irons in the fire; I don't know when the man sleeps.

I'm elated to find Mrs. Kane at the house by the time I get back. She's ready to work, with her hair pinned on top of her head, hands and nails clean, wearing a white starched apron, and waiting for instructions. She seems pleasant, willing and able, and doesn't mind that her dollars are coming from a house of ill repute which suits me fine.

She introduces her son, Jessie; he seems to be a pleasant young man. I tell him to help his mother. His chores are to tend to the fires, keep the water heating on the second stove, empty and clean the chamber pots, all to be done without being seen. And, after this is over, I'll make it worth his while. He's happy and eager, and dashes off to get started. There's no doubt Jessie doesn't mind he's in a house of ill repute either.

Mrs. Kane and I sit at the table to go over the menus for all meals. She says her sister is willing to do the baking, while she takes care of everything else, if I'm interested. Gratefully, I accept, and she sends Jessie to fetch her at once. We'll discuss what baked goods I will require, and she can bake at home and Jessie can do the running back and forth. The oven here will strictly be used for roasting meats and such.

The deliverymen show up with the groceries and liquor early. Not another person can fit into this kitchen. Bottles are clinking, stoves are being fired, a man is tapping the keg of beer and Mrs. Kane is cooking. She says she can stay through to Sunday; just in case we need help cleaning up. Smokey has saved the day. He's in love with Mae, and she likes him.

Now with manual chores taken care of, we girls will concentrate on what we do best, taking care of the men. Everyone knows his or her responsibilities. I put Frannie in charge of the costumes and a pageant. They're working to create a little act to entertain the men this evening. Frannie says that "girls doing girls" always get things rolling. From there on out, the Johns will be primed and easy. She knows men and has the most amazing résumé, if you can call it that, I have ever seen. Frannie leaves nothing to the imagination. She's my greatest teacher when it comes to sex.

We spend the last hour before their planned arrival doing our hair and makeup. The girls are wearing their best gowns and ready for company. We need to show them this is no cow-town whorehouse; the girls and the house are laid out in Chicago fashion.

I break out new playing cards for the tables. The house smells delightful with the scent of rosemary and sage. Mrs. Kane is roasting a small rib roast with all the sides for dinner. I have her make enough meat, potatoes and vegetables to feed an army. I have no way of knowing how much six men eat. However, I remember when Mac came for dinner he would eat four to my one of everything.

Jessie comes through the back door with two warm apple pies, sets them on the mantel to keep warm above the fireplace, and runs back to his aunt's to get more. Mrs. Kane prepares a tray of cheese, crackers and hard sausage, and sets it on the cocktail table in the parlor, along with a tray of fresh oysters. I hope they like them as they cost us a dollar apiece, but it's a luxury not most can serve. I carry in a tray of clean glasses to the bar. Everything seems to be in its place, and we're stocked and ready. The men arrive at a quarter to six, and I greet them at the door.

"Good evening, Mr. Bruce." The men parade inside. "It's a pleasure having you with us tonight."

"Thank you, Miss Vicky. The men are glad to join me."

The girls merrily introduce themselves. They've dressed in fashionable, reserved attire. My philosophy is, if you dress like a whore you're treated like a whore. This is the Good Hour, and we have a reputation to uphold and have taken a large bankroll as well. I will treat and serve them like royalty, and the girls will give them an erotica experience they will not forget. If he breathes a word to Madam Martha, I want it to be good!

The men are dressed nicely in business suits, and they are clean and shaved. I think to myself, "We're starting out right." The girls pour the men drinks, and they start to get to know each other.

At seven o'clock, Mrs. Kane, dressed in one of Sadie's uniforms, sets the buffet. Everything looks delicious. I announce that dinner is served. The girls escort the men to the table, and fill their plates for them at the buffet. I excuse myself when I see Lorenzo come through the door. I go to meet him. Our eyes make contact, and he gives me a big smile.

"Mr. Parrish, thank you for coming," I say softly.

He leans forward and says, in a quiet voice, "It's Lorenzo, and I'll call you Miss Vicky if that's what you're going by," he smiles.

"Vicky, it is," I say with raised eyebrows. "And thanks for not giving me away the last time you were here. I'd like a chance to explain."

"No need. Women have secrets."

"Have you had your dinner?"

"I have, thank you, but I'd like a drink."

"Whiskey, beer or bourbon?"

"Bourbon sounds good." I take Mr. Parrish's coat and fix him a drink.

By the time I return, he is already playing the piano. He's debonair as well as talented.

For a short time, all you can hear is the sound of forks and knifes while the men are eating, and everyone seems to be enjoying dinner. After, Mr. Bruce approaches me and tells me that the meal was exceptional. *Good,* I think to myself. *It's one more thing I can check off the list and not have to worry about.*

The girls go upstairs to change into their costumes, while I pour the after drinks and hand out the cigars. The music creates a comfortable ambiance. The men unbutton their suits, loosen their ties and get relaxed. I offer Ian a glass of Scotch from a bottle of dense, hazel-red, single malt. The girls return and flirt with the men to build a little excitement for the show. Mrs. Kane clears the dining room table, and the girls use it as a stage.

They give the men what they want to see, plenty of skin, girls touching girls, girls kissing girls in every position imaginable. Frannie and Tilly team up with two of the men. Mr. Bruce asks for my company. They all go upstairs, laughing and fooling around. Bruce's deep green eyes seem to look right through me, making me a little uneasy. He reminds me of someone, but I can't put my finger on it. I check with Lorenzo, before me seeing to Mr. Bruce.

"You play beautifully. Thank you for coming on such short notice."

"Smokey said you were kind of in a tight spot, that you had big company come in from Chicago."

"I hate to ask, but are you free for a few hours tomorrow night. They've rented the house for Friday and Saturday."

"No problem, I can give you a few hours. How about seven to nine, will that do?"

"Sounds perfect, I appreciate it. I'll pay you whatever Grace pays. Drinks and the girls are at your command on your next visit."

"Command? Ooh ... I like that. I am good at commands," he says, laughing.

"It seems as if the girls can take it from here. Feel free to leave anytime. I'm sorry, I'm going to have to excuse myself." I say, turning my head slightly toward Mr. Bruce.

"Yeah, I see you've got a live one. Yes, ma'am, he's been watching your every move ... this may not be the time, but are you still seeing Mac McClellan?"

"I am, but it's complicated. He's supposed to be in town for Thanksgiving."

"Great, maybe I'll run into him."

"I'm making Thanksgiving dinner, why don't you join us."

"Let's talk tomorrow. I don't want the wolves to get restless."

"Thanks, Lorenzo, for the favor, I'll settle with you tomorrow night, if that's okay."

"Sure. I'll have another drink of the good stuff, if you don't mind, and then I'll hit the road. I've got a game at the Strater."

"Good luck, and help yourself to the booze. Mrs. Kane is in the kitchen if you want a sandwich before you go."

I take Ian Bruce by the arm, smiling. We make small talk and proceed up stairs. The bedroom door on my right is open. There's an orgy going on, and in the next room, Tilly has her own ménage à trois. It's a mild group, fairly quiet, and there's no fighting. The girls seem to be safe. Smokey will be here shortly, and then I can relax.

We enter my room. The lamp is down low, and I help Mr. Bruce with his jacket. He is a well-built and attractive man. He takes off his shirt and tie, throws it to the chair and his braces falls to his sides. His chest is broad and muscled, with sparse, jet black hair. I hang up his shirt and move the chair out in front of the mirror, and motion for him to take a seat. He does it with a smile, and I hand him a drink. I put on a show, slipping from my clothes. He doesn't take his eyes off me. I take my time, and make slow, smooth moves and strip down revealing a pink and white lace corset, trimmed in silk with black satin strings. Breasts full and firm, my rosy pink, taut nipples are barely concealed. I lift my foot and rest it between his legs, giving him a full view. He unsnaps the garters and peels the net stockings to my ankles and removes my shoes. Mr. Bruce likes a show. He's in no rush and good spirits. He pulls me onto his lap.

"That's nice, Vicky." He takes my hand and lays it between his legs. I feel his warm flesh. I can't believe his length. He's watching for a response.

"You like that?"

All I can think of is that this could hurt me. "I'll let you know," I whisper.

"Fair enough." He picks me up and carries me to the bed.

"You just lay there, beautiful." He removes the rest of his clothes.

My eyes travel to his erection. I take a deep breath. I think Mr. Bruce has fun shocking women by the look of his expression. I decide to give him no encouragement. He lies down beside me on the bed and brings his warm lips to my breasts and up to my lips. I turn my head and say, "I don't kiss."

He turns my head to his, "I paid you, remember? You gave me your terms, and that wasn't one of them," he whispers in a deep husky voice.

I smile and say, "You're right, Ian." He takes my chin and presses his lips to mine. Not wanting to, I kiss him in return. He's right. I set the terms. He makes the moves; he likes to be in charge.

"Your skin looks like a peach. Have you been in the sun, pretty lady?" he asks with a devilish smile. I say nothing and try to relax, knowing what's coming. His lips reclaim mine and his fingers probe. "You're tighter than I expected. I must do my best to entice you to be ready for me." Mounting me, he spreads my thighs and teases the oyster's pearl with the tip of his hard penis. I'm trying to relax, but the sight of him scares me. I close my eyes and concentrate on his touch. My tension starts to subside. He gently eases into me. I moan loudly and hold his hips to stop him from taking me too fast. I'm sure the look on my face is not one of pleasure. My body is quick to adjust, the pain eases. Mr. Bruce took his time getting there, but once the dance begins, it is over. I thank God and hold my breath as he withdraws. I've heard the girls talk of a man's size, but Ian Bruce is huge. He takes me by the hand bringing me to the side of the bed.

"I like you, Vicky. I knew you'd be good."

I smile and ask, "But will I ever be the same?"

He gives a little chuckle. I slip into my robe. "Ian, if you'll excuse me for a minute, I'd like to see to the girls."

"Of course, but don't be too long," he says grinning.

I freshen up his drink and step out into the hall, hearing sounds of pleasure. I pass the rooms slowly. Everyone is enjoying everyone from what I can see. Two men are downstairs having a drink, taking a time out. I check the kitchen. Jessie has six huge kettles steaming and cold-water buckets set next to the tubs, if needed. Mrs. Kane brings two pitchers of beer and two silver platters of sandwiches into the parlor. She has baked a chicken and added it to the broth and vegetables for the girls.

It's early yet, about two-thirty in the morning. Mr. Bruce lingers down the hall and takes an interest in Bevie. I hear her give a positive comment on his enormous member. I'm ecstatic, maybe he'll like her better and I won't have to service him again. After I do my rounds, I'm the first one in the tub. His first plunge stung. I want to stay out of his reach the rest of the night. I chat with Mrs. Kane; she is exhausted, too, and takes her leave until morning. She will be back in five hours and plans to serve brunch for the men at noon.

The men have enough by about four a.m. of eating, drinking and making merry. They leave to go back to the General Palmer Hotel. I help the girls bathe and wash their hair. We leave the beds until morning. The girls sleep in the dorm and I sleep in Grace's room. I'm thankful the first evening is a success.

The morning goes well. We change the linens and have the house straightened by ten o'clock. The girls and I have oatmeal and canned apricots before they arrive.

The men come in as fresh as daisies. They'd sought their own baths. That is a relief, but they're hungry and love Mrs. Kane's brunch. She has prepared two-and-a-half dozen eggs, three pounds of bacon, two pounds of link sausage, dozens of griddlecakes with warm syrup and butter and two-dozen biscuits with pan gravy.

The men play cards for several hours, drink beer and smoke cigars until we can hardly breathe. Once they're tired of their man play, they want the girls to play a different game. I'm fortunate, Mr.

Bruce has an unexpected business meeting and he has to take leave for a few hours. He says he will be back by eight-thirty in time for dinner.

At first, I'm relieved, but then he says he'd like to see me tonight. Mrs. Kane serves the men a snack of meat sandwiches, relishes, two dozen cherry tarts and three pots of coffee at four. Mrs. Paul, Mrs. Kane's sister, arrives with a three-layer chocolate cake for dessert. While she is there, she cleans the washroom and tubs. Mrs. Kane had already washed and seasoned two twelve-pound turkeys and had them in the oven an hour before she served the men lunch. Things are working like clockwork. Jessie checks the stoves and does his other chores while the men are eating.

The men take a break and go to the Strater for a drink around five. It gives us girls a chance to dress for the evening and relax. Later, Mr. Bruce enjoys Bevie and Tilly together; they love and praise his length and girth. I love the way they feed his ego and he, of course, has to take them both, twice. I'm so glad to see the morning come.

The men stay all night, Mrs. Kane too. The guests are starving at six a.m. She's a dear and puts on coffee, makes a big batch of biscuits, puts a half-dozen ham steaks into the oven, fries two-dozen eggs and makes a huge pan of gravy from the ham drippings. Again, I think of Smokey Bearup. He was right about Mrs. Kane. She surely can cook. How in the hell did I think I could do all this? I'm glad I didn't have to find out. I owe him. The men finish everything, along with a pan of warm coffee cake that Mrs. Paul baked.

We've barely slept in two days. I have a pleasant conversation with Mr. Bruce. He's a very interesting man. He tells me before he leaves that he saw my shaking hands the day we met, and he decided to give me a chance. Now, he's glad he did. The men enjoyed their stay and they went together and bought gifts for each of us girls, a bottle of Eau de Cologne, promoted by the Empress Josephine of France and the consort of Napoleon Bonaparte. The girls thank them for their gifts. It is very thoughtful of them.

"Did you enjoy your stay in Durango, Mr. Bruce?" I ask.

"I did. It's small, but the people are nice."

"Are you going back to Chicago?"

"No Ma'am. I owned a meat packing business and got into a little money trouble and decided I better take my money and run."

"I see." I chuckle. What else could I say?

"I bought a place south of Park City, Utah. My sister was supposed to supply me with girls, but we had a little squabble. You know how family can be."

"Yes, I do," I say and think of Becky.

"You wouldn't be able to help me out, would you?"

"No Ian, I don't have the connections."

"Well, you did real well here, Miss Vicky," he smiles. "I guess we'll be on our way, via San Francisco. But, I have to do a little whore buying first. If you ever want to bring your girls, I've got a big place, and I'd pay you well. I like your company. You're a real nice lady, and you know how to entertain."

"Well, Mr. Bruce, if you're ever in Durango again, please calls on us at the Good Hour."

"I will do that." He takes my hand and places a wad of bills in my palm.

"Thank you once again." Bruce tips his hat. "Vicky, you run a first-class brothel," he says as he goes out the door and the other men follow. After they are gone, I open my palm and throw the money into the air. The girls take hands and twirl with one another, giggling.

"Good job, girls, good job."

They count the money. "He gave us a three-hundred dollar tip, Vicky!" They scream happily.

I send Mrs. Kane and her son home for the rest of the day. We all need to rest. Tomorrow, we'll clean up the house. It's really not too bad. I flee upstairs to tally the books and say, "We did it, Gracie. We did it first-class. You'd be proud."

Chapter Ten: LIFE'S SIMPLE THINGS

We're moving slowly this morning. Thank goodness Mrs. Kane and Mrs. Paul come through the back door early, with smiles on their faces and ready to go to work. I don't need to say anything. The two clean the kitchen, washroom, parlor and dining room. The house is as good as new in no time and is back in shape. The girls see to the stripping of beds and bring the dirty laundry downstairs.

Mrs. Kane's son stuffs the bedding into a bag to take to Mr. Lu Chi at the Chinese laundry just a few blocks from the Good Hour. I've heard from Mrs. Brody that he's a fair man; how she knows him I'm not sure. I would love to see whether he has oils from the Orient. I'm excited just thinking about what he may have to sell. There was a man in Creede that Mother dealt with. That is where many of her oils came from, but now all I have left are her empty bottles. If I'm going to find another source, I must do the legwork myself.

"Hang on, Jessie. I'm going with you."

"Miss Vicky, I'm pretty young, but I don't think you want to go down there."

"I thank you for your concern, but what is there to be afraid of?"

"Just people, *them* kind of people, Miss Vicky."

"What do you mean by *them* kind?"

"All I know is what I hear. There's dealin's there … money for dope and stuff. I know Joe Black got the life kicked out of him one night; for what, I don't know."

"We'll be careful. We're only taking the laundry."

"Okay, but don't say I didn't warn you."

I heed Jessie's warning and keep my eyes open. It's wise for me not to go alone, but this is as good a time as any. I want to meet the headman in charge of the operation. I'm sure, as Jessie mentioned, there's a lot more than the laundry going on there. I've heard the girls talk of friends getting drugs and paraphernalia from the Chinamen.

I take a minute to get my pistol, placing it in my pocket. I don't expect any problems because I'm not looking for one. However, it's better to be safe. I take a gold piece that I know is worth twenty dollars and place it into my coat pocket, and put my six empty bottles into a small sugar sack. He may have herbs and spices as well. Just the thought of someone here having what I need makes me excited. I'm hoping to replenish what has been emptied in Mother's case.

Jessie and I walk on a snow-packed path the three blocks over to the west side of the river, to a place that some call the Orientals. The small poverty-stricken buildings are just shanties. They have their own little town. We draw much attention as we walk through, but nobody speaks with us. My eyes grow wide exploring the surroundings. There's a lot of chattering going on when Jessie and I pass by the rough, run-down buildings.

Passing two men in front of the icehouse, one looks up at me before striking the head from a chicken. The site sickens me, seeing the red blood run freely down the ice block he uses as a chopping block. It creates a large puddle of blood swirled in the packed snow. The other man hoists a gutted pig to hang on a large iron meat hook, placing it next to a dressed deer with its head still on. This is too much for me. I may not eat meat for weeks. The one man says something to me in Chinese. I give him a half smile, nod my head and continue walking. He might have just asked me if he could help. I don't know. It seems strange that they wear fine silk clothing but live in shanties.

"Miss Vicky, these heathens can't be trusted."

"Lower your voice please."

"That's what I hear. They're Godless heathens. That's why they can't look you in the face, they are Godless souls."

"Who told you that?"

"Everybody talks about them in town; they worship a naked fat man."

"They're a different culture, Jessie. That doesn't make them bad people, just different."

"Well, they live down here in these shacks."

"Maybe they don't require much. Don't be so quick to pass judgment."

Out in front of the laundry, several women are tending three big black caldrons, all boiling clothes. They do not make eye contact. Others are cooking something on an open fire across the way. Smoke and steam fill the air, and I catch a whiff of a familiar smell of clove, anise and cinnamon. One woman is serving petite bowls of rice from a small black caldron and a steamy hot broth from another.

At the laundry, Jessie hands the man our bag of sheets. I show him one of my bottles from the sugar sack in which I used to carry them. He pops the cork off and takes a whiff. He says, "Inside, Lu Chi." I thank him and continue through a leather-hinged door. The smell inside is something unfamiliar. An oriental man with a stern face greets me.

"Mr. Lu Chi?" I ask. He gives a quick nod. I show him my bottles. He nods again. We follow him through a maze of small rooms used for living quarters and enter a larger room filled with smoke from Opium pipes, the origin of the strong order I smelled at the door. A dozen people, men and women, lie on pallets in a comatose state. Two elderly Chinese women assist those smoking pipes. There's an uncomfortable feeling within these low energy chambers. I hate that I've brought a boy of maybe fourteen here.

The large, round Chinese man with a black braid, turns to me, and holds out his palm. I think he expects payment, but then he pretends to sniff. I understand. I place one of my bottles in his hand and the others on the table. Individually, he removes each cork, brings each to his nose, rummages through a long teak box with various pigeonholes and retrieves the oil required. I tell him I want his best.

He nods and says, "Good?"

I say, "Yes, good."

There are different grades of oils, and Mother always said to buy the best.

He says, "You try."

He gives me what I need. I reach into my pocket and produce a twenty-dollar gold piece. He quickly takes it from my hand and smiles. He bows and says, "Good." Placing it into his belted purse. I guess I'm not getting any change. It's a good thing I didn't bring more. He'd be taking it all.

He wraps the amber bottles in brown paper, bows and says, "You go now, miss."

I notice herbs hanging from the low rafters and recognize a few that I use. I point, and he takes them down and lays them of the counter. He says, "Two dolla'."

I tell him I don't have any more money with me. He picks up the herbs, holds them in a tight fist, and with a stern look on his face, says in rapid secession, "Two dolla', two dolla'."

I tell him, "Bring the herbs when you deliver the laundry, and I will have your two dollars." He nods yes and says, "Two dolla."

"Thank you, Mr. Chi."

He looks at me without facial expression and says, "Lu Chi, Lu Chi."

"Thank you, Mr. Lu Chi."

He smiles, and we find our way back through the maze of inadequate construction. I feel dizzy and light-headed from the Opium. I look at Jessie and say, "Lu Chi, Lu Chi! Two dolla', Two dolla'! I should call him Mister Two Time; he says everything twice." Jessie and I are now laughing, probably from the light buzz we encountered in the thick smoky den. The cold air does us good and clears are heads on the way home. Coming upon the Pineapple Delight, Madam Bruce comes down the steps dressed in a rich burgundy wool cape trimmed in fox fur, with her beautiful red curly hair feathering out at the sides. Martha Bruce is a beauty.

"Good morning, Madam Bruce," Jessie says with a big smile.

"Good morning, son, but you're too young to visit me," she says, raising her brows over her bright baby blues. "Good morning, Miss Vicky."

"Good morning, Miss Bruce. I'm surprised you know who I am."

"Why would that be? I make it my business to know all the girls in Durango. I like staying on top of things," she says with a giggle, "if you know what I mean. I know all my competition. Where's Grace? I haven't seen her around."

"She's in Denver or on her way home."

"Damn, is she up buying new girls again?"

"I don't really know the madam's business."

"Well, maybe I'll see her myself, if she's coming in on the morning train. I'm expecting a new girl from Chicago. I'm just going down to meet her. I expect her presence to rattle this town."

"I wish you the best, Miss Bruce."

"I don't want to speak out of line, but this being my business I must ask, is Grace paying you what you're worth? Because if she's not, I'd gladly raise the stakes. You're one of the prettiest girls this side of the Rockies, Vicky, and I don't give many compliments. Word gets around and from what I heard from my brother, Ian, you've got some kind of magic, girl. I'd be interested in knowing just what it is that you do for the men."

"I thank you, Madam, but I'm doing just fine at the Good Hour."

"We'll, you know, I hear that Grace has a little bit of a temper, and if she ever uses it on you or you change your mind for any reason whatsoever, come see me. I'll make it worth your while. Just so you know, I'm jealous Ian took his men to the Good Hour, but I do understand his reasoning. He said they got the royal treatment and that's a compliment coming from Ian. Ian and I have few things in common, but one of them is that we like everything first-class. Congratulations, you made him happy, and that is no easy task. Well, I better get going. I don't want to keep the new damsel waiting."

The madam steps into the fine carriage that is waiting, looks ahead and is gone. So that is the Martha Bruce I've heard so much about. She has an air of confidence that almost bowls me over. She has money, and money gives you power. When I was at the bank last, she was paying off her new place. Hell, she's only been in Durango for as long as I. There's something to say about good business. If she and Grace teamed together, they'd own all the pussy and all the money in this town.

I see her girls in the window; they give Jessie a little show.

"Come, Jessie." I take him by the coat sleeve. "We've got to get a move on."

"Do you know, Miss Vicky, how many brothels there are in town?"

"No, Jessie, I don't. Are you going to tell me?"

"There are twelve, plus the cribs."

"I'd ask you how you know this, but I'm not your mother so I'll pretend I didn't hear."

"Do you know how many saloons there are in town?"

"No, Jessie, I don't."

"I can name them, the Office, the Open Door, the Senate, Link, Hub, the Coliseum, the Keg, the Silver Brick, the Central and the Diamond Bell."

"How many books have you read? Can you tell me their titles?" He stammers. "You're a smart kid. Start using your head. If you're going to count something, do your arithmetic and count something more than the low-life establishments in Durango. I'm sure it will make your mother happy."

I've seen Durango change from the time I arrived. A new contrast is easily seen from one side of the tracks to the other. Durango's rough side is the west, with dance halls, cribs, brothels and saloons. The more refined people live on the east side of town. Grace knowingly made some changes in her business to lure a more genteel audience to her place, much like Madam Bruce.

Back at the Good Hour, the girls are having a bowl of hot vegetable soup when we return. I thank Jessie for helping and pay him what is owed. He's more than pleased. I pay Mrs. Paul and Mrs. Kane and thank them for all their help. I ask Mrs. Kane and Jessie if they would like to stay on. They say "yes," and we come to an agreement and explain she will have to talk to Grace when she comes home. I don't know whether Sadie is returning.

I tell the girls we shall celebrate! I have Tilly get paper and pencil and while we have lunch, I make notes at the kitchen table.

"How are we going to celebrate?" The girls shout in excitement.

"Okay, we're going to buy treats. Everyone gets to name one thing we can buy at the mercantile."

"Great! I want to make ice cream," Tilly says excitedly.

"Alright, what do we need, Mrs. Kane, to make ice cream?" She names the ingredients, and I make the list. "Next."

"Swiss chocolate, creamy milk chocolate bars. I can taste it now," Mae says dreamily.

"Okay. Next."

"I want a roast like Mrs. Kane fixed the men the other night. My mouth was watering," Bevie says.

"A prime rib roast." I write it on the list. "Frannie, you're next."

"Another bottle of French perfume for all of us."

"And me, what do I want? Let's see, I want one of Mrs. Brody's three-tiered chocolate cakes with ice-cold milk."

"Oh, that sounds good," the girls say. "Can we get one more thing?"

"One more."

"Let's get a huge jar of hard candy."

"Okay, but that's it. That's enough treats for today." I add in hard candy and say, "Frannie and Mae, you may take the list to Mrs. Brody's. Remember, don't mention my name. I don't want anyone, especially the Brodys, to know I'm here. Here's ten dollars. It should be enough. You can spend it all. Now, tell Mr. Brody the roast needs to be ten pounds and that you want the bone cut off and tied on. Got it? After you're done, come right back. Don't let anyone touch you. Grace would have a fit, especially if it were Mr. Brody, you hear?"

"We don't want Mr. Brody's pudgy fingers touching us anyway. Now, if we run across a tall handsome cowboy …"

"I don't want you touching any of that unless it's here. Just get the items and come home."

I tally the books and figure Grace's profit for the twelve days she's been gone. We've done extremely well I see as I compare it to other weeks. I take five envelopes, one for each of the girls, Frannie, Mae, Tilly, and Bevie and put fifty dollars in each. The tip money from Mr. Bruce belongs to the girls; the rest is Gracie's. I wait until the girls are back and hand them out. They open them, scream and do a little dance. It's more money than they've seen at once in a long time, maybe ever, I don't know.

"Now pay attention," I say, "we will not be young forever, that means you can't turn tricks for the rest of your lives. Right?"

"Yes." They answer in unison, still bubbling.

"Okay, now we have a responsibility to ourselves to save a little of our earnings. Who's with me?"

Everyone raises their hands, holding a fistful of dollars.

"From now on, you need to put a little away, either in the bank or in a secret place. Christmas is right around the corner and some of you have family and friends you would like to buy presents for, but don't spend it all. The most important thing to remember is things happen; you might need money for an emergency, you could get sick or something unexpected may come up. Do you think you can save some money?"

"Yes," they shout. There's an undercurrent of conversation as I talk to them about setting goals.

"Tomorrow, those of you who want to open a savings account; I will take you to the bank."

I leave the closed sign on the door for today. We aren't taking customers. I don't know whether Grace would agree, but today I'm in charge, and I'll take the brunt of any repercussions. After chores are done and the house is back in order, we play games. The girls and I do a little sewing. I've made new friends, and it's a good feeling to have them as my family.

The girls seem happier. Tilly starts her list of goals right away. Her son Jimmy lives with her parents in Philadelphia. His name is at the top of her list. She shared her dreams the other night of having enough money to get home so they can be a family again. I hope she gets her dream. People love Tilly. She is kind.

The last two weeks we've learned a lot about one another. Tilly and I are the only ones that have family. We all depend on each other; this is family, and we are sisters. They've made me a part of their group and have allowed me to take what knowledge I have and share with them. It makes me feel good to contribute.

Mrs. Kane calls us to dinner. We fly down the stairs to the dining room. The table is set as if we are guests. Standing behind a chair, we marvel at the food she has prepared. The rib roast looks delicious, carved to perfection. Our mouths water at the sight.

"Wow," Tilly says, "Look at this."

"We're like regular people," Bevie says.

"We are regular people, worthy of all things," I say smiling at each of them.

Tilly asks to say grace. We bow our heads, return thanks, and bless Mrs. Kane for this spectacular dinner and from which it came, and I remember to include our dear Gracie.

We sit down and pass the food. Mrs. Kane asks to be excused and says we will see her tomorrow. The conversation is plentiful. The girls plan to decorate for Thanksgiving. There's lot of chatter at the table. I hope Gracie is home by Thursday. Thanksgiving is just three days away.

Later, around the fire, the girls talk of using their talents. After we put their sex talents to rest with laughs and giggles we get to their real talents, like singing, playing the piano and cooking. Mae loves to cook and hopes to marry or get a job on a ranch somewhere. Tilly wants to go back home to her son. Frannie loves the theater and dreams of being an actress someday. She hopes by next November, she'll be in San Francisco on stage playing in Moulin Rouge. I've encouraged them to look at other avenues; but for now we are whores going to work and saving our money. The girls go to bed early. It is rare they get to go to bed when they wish, and actually sleep through the night. I'm going to take a long hot bath, soak and think about where my life is going.

Chapter Eleven: TWO DICK HENDERSON

While half-asleep, I hear Mother's voice call out my name, "Alex." Startled, I rise up in bed. I had left the window cracked for fresh air. The moon is almost full and lights the room dimly. I'm chilled. I'll close the window. A wary feeling penetrates my soul. The curtains sway with the light breeze. I see a shadow to the left of the window. Alarmed, I search for my pistol in the nightstand. The pistol isn't there. Out of the shadows, a man comes forth, grabs my wrist, sinking his nails into my flesh with his one hand and holds my pistol with the other.

"Is this what you're looking for?" He flings it into the corner of the room. "Goin' for your gun are ya, you girlie bitch?" he says in a low growl.

I try to jerk from his grasp, but his hands make three of mine. I'm shocked. He stands naked with his stinking thing in my face. I push away as hard as I can.

"Let go of me, you filthy animal."

"Lower your voice, pretty girl. You utter one word or squeal; I'll cut your tongue out and then your throat. Ya got it?" He smells terrible. "Ah, you were just a little young thing when we first met."

He moves my hair from my shoulder with his stinking fingers and his foul breath. He reeks strongly of drink. Pinching my cheek, he lodges his thumb under my chin, hurting me as he lifts my face toward him.

"You were attached to your mother's apron strings the first time I saw you. Your sweet mother dug a couple of bullets out of me, and left my brother to die, the bitch. You made a mighty fine impression with your long blonde curls. I should have taken you all, but all these years, I've had ya in my bed. Do you remember me now, you little wench?"

I'm trembling. I remember him like it was yesterday. He's the bastard that broke into our home, demanding our father help him, but he wasn't there, so Mother had to do the dirty work. He held a gun on us. Yet, despite that, somehow, Mother got the upper hand. She took care of him alright and dug deeply into his torn flesh to retrieve the bullets someone gave him.

"Mother was a better person than I. I would have left you rot, you filthy beast."

"Shut up, you whore. Your mother let my brother die!"

"I remember, he was too far gone and bled out on the table, you asshole. She didn't kill him. It was you that got him killed. You must be a bad shot!"

"Shut the fuck up, bitch."

"The day you tried to attack me in town, I'm glad I kicked you in the face."

"Something had you in a hurry. You were wide-eyed and hateful," he says, spitting bubbles on his chin from between missing teeth. "You needlessly kicked me in the face." He turns his head showing me the left side of his ugly mug. "Now, I got this to remind me of your sweetness." A long scar runs from his chin to ear. He gyrates his hips flinging his male part in my face. He sees my disbelief and throws his head back and laughs. Let me introduce myself," he takes his penis and shakes it. "I'm Two Dick Henderson. I got one so big; they call me Two Dick. I can make ya scream, and I'm planning to do just that."

In the dull first light I see his crazed grin with tobacco-stained teeth. "I stripped for ya, right over there. You got me all excited just watchin' you sleep. I guess you didn't know; I spent the night in your fancy little chair doin' myself." He laughs.

Struggling to flee, I try to slip from his grasp.

"Oh yes, good ol' Two Dick has enjoyed watchin' ya toss and turn. You're a whore now. You're not so high and mighty." He pushes me back on the bed, pulls up my gown, and tries to open my legs. I let out a half scream before he covers my mouth with his stinking hand; he strikes a hard blow to my chin. "Your sweet blonde pussy must be stretched out with all your whorin'. Let's see if you're big enough to take me." He leans over me with his left forearm weighing heavily across my throat; he searches for what he craves. "I hear you're an expensive little banger and Two Dick gets ta rip your seams, lady." He's so angry; he drools on my face. "I'm gonna make ya feel me."

I want to scream, but I don't. I need to stay calm; he has the advantage all the way around. He's a dangerous maniac, and he has me right where he wants me. He has trouble directing his penis where it needs to go and repositions himself, swearing and spiting in my face. I can't stand it, even with pressure on my throat I tussle and say, "No wonder you do yourself, you pig."

"Shut up. You think you're too good for me. I saw you in the saloon with that marshal. I'm gonna kill that bastard too. I like to kill, and if you don't shut up and let me do this, I'll crush ya."

"He'd kill you for touching me." He rises up and releases another powerful blow. I'm in a fog and seeing stars. Realizing I'm not being held, with all my might, I sit up in hope of escape. My mind is racing, and there is a flash of steel. He lunges at me with his knife. I roll, and the steel blade plunges into the pillow. A poof of feathers fly into the air, some are sticking to his bare, sweaty skin. His anger heightens, and his face twists, his eyes bulge and he drools down his chin. His contempt is real, and his arm comes forth with another jab, this time making contact. He cuts my arm from shoulder to elbow. I lunge from the bed, fall to my knees and scamper to my feet, trying to get away before he strikes again. I'm back against the dresser. In two steps, he is there. I reach for the heavy silver hand mirror, my only weapon. Swinging hard, to my surprise it lands, hitting him across the face. The mirror shatters. It stops him for only a second. He touches his face and finds a triangle piece of glass is sticking out the side of his temple. Blood is squirting everywhere.

He yells, "I'll get you, bitch!" He's off balance from the blow. I strike again, this time his hand grabs the broken mirror and his knife flings across the room, but he keeps coming. I duck as he lunges for me. I scramble to get the knife sticking out of the baseboard. I pull hard, for its freedom and for mine. His vision is blurry from the blood-dripping cuts. He uses his arm to wipe his eyes, pushing the fragments of the mirror deeper into his flesh.

"Fuck," he says violently. Blood gushes and he spits froth from his lips. Our eyes meet. He stumbles around the end of the bed to the chair where his clothes and holster are lying on the floor. He's mumbling something I can't understand.

"You're mine. You can..."

This is it, his life or mine; I struggle and pull with all my might. The knife springs loose, and in one swift move, I spring like a cat onto his back, jumping as though I am mounting a horse. Screaming, I take the knife with both hands and plunge it into his neck. I hear a gunshot as he crumples to the floor. My heart pounds out of my chest. There, I sit on the back of the beast, breathless and traumatized. I hear someone shout, "Stand back, girls!" There's a loud crashing noise, the door is kicked in and slams against the wall. Smokey Bearup blasts into the room with his Schofield Colt in hand. He takes aim at the naked man lying in a puddle of blood.

"Jesus Christ, are you alright, Vicky?" He walks closer, and kicks the gun away from the man's hand. Miss Vicky, you're bleeding." Smokey tucks his gun into his belt and helps me to my feet. "Get the doc!" He yells. Blood has saturated my gown making it cling to me like an extra skin. The girls rush into the room and start to panic.

"Quiet down! Miss Vicky, you're going to be alright," Smokey says.

My eyes dart around the room, but my body doesn't want to move.

"Smokey?" I whisper.

"Yes, it's me, Vicky. You're hurt, let me help." He takes me into his arms and sits me in a pile of feathers on the bed. One of the girls wraps a robe around my shoulders. I sit limp. He tears my sleeve open and rips the sheet for a bandage, wrapping my arm tightly. "Who is he, Miss Vicky? Nobody came through the door."

I look at the man with the knife sticking out of the side of his neck. "Two Dick, he calls himself, Two Dick Henderson." My body shakes uncontrollably. Eyes start watering.

"It's okay, Miss Vicky; you're not hurt bad."

"There's a dead man in my room, and I had to put a knife in him."

Chapter Twelve: THE UNFORSEEN

"I swear, Miss Vicky, nobody came in from downstairs."

"Don't worry about it, Smokey, look." I point to the window where a rope hangs from overhead.

"The bastard came from the roof."

"What's going to happen? I just killed a man."

"Yes, but in self-defense." Smokey rubs his brow. He opens the dresser drawers, paws through my clothes and pulls out a nightgown. "Here, go behind the screen and put this on, hurry. The doc will be here any minute." I do what he says and let out a sigh in pain as I struggle to put on the clean gown.

"Hurry, Vicky." I step out from behind and over the dead body.

"What are you thinking?"

"Come, let's go to Gracie's room." He tells the girls to close the door and takes me to her room, pulls back the covers and puts me to bed. My clean gown is already bloody. He tells Mae to pour some water on and get a cool cloth. I use it to wash my face. Tilly applies pressure to the wound. Bevie puts out a sign that the Good Hour is closed for the afternoon. The doc appears.

"What happened, miss?" He takes my chin in hand. "You've got some bad bruises here."

"He got a little rough with me."

"Yes, I see that. Let us see that arm. Are you hurt anywhere else?"

"Just my arm, Doc."

"Well, you're lucky. It's not deep, but you may need a few stitches. Guess you can't do what it is you do and not get hurt." The Doc asks with attitude, "Where is the prick now?"

"He's dead in the other room," Smokey says.

"It all happened so fast. He had a mean streak in him, Doc."

"Who's the bastard?"

"I don't know, someone from out of town. I think he said Creede."

"Hell, that could be anybody. No one's really from Creede."

"Have ya seen him before?"

"We don't have that kind of dirt here. He's filthy and smells. He belongs at the Frontier House."

"Damned if I don't get tired of fixing you girls up or seeing you buried."

The doctor cleans the wound, bandages me up and gives me instructions to lay low the rest of the day, and to get a new profession if I want to live to be an old woman. I try to smile, but it hurts and I thanks the doc for coming. He said he would put it on Gracie's bill.

Smokey sees the doctor out and tries to give him a few extra bucks. The doctor turns it down, speaking in a low voice, "I don't want your money. Just do your job, will you? I'm tired of patching up the whores. I liked this place better when it was a sleepy town."

As Doc is heading out the door, Smokey says, "Ya know, Doc, it may be time for you to retire too." He rolls his eyes and closes the door.

Chapter Thirteen: REMEDIES

Frannie brings me a cup of chamomile tea and straightens the bed.

"Are you alright, Vicky? I know you're battered, but we girls are concerned about what that bastard put you through."

"I'll be okay; I just need a little rest."

"Do you want me to brush your hair? I know it always makes me feel better."

"That would be nice."

"I'm going to go down to get some lavender water; it will help take out the snarls. I'll be right back."

Sitting with my knees to my chin, I gaze through the sheer lace curtains to the street below and recall what Mother said in one of her journals after an attack by Comancheros, "Bastards never die." I throw back the covers and get out of bed and walk down the hall. The door to the guest room is closed. Resting my head on the door jam, I take a minute before opening it. It looks like a war zone with blood splatters on the walls, feathers are all over, and Henderson, with his flesh turning blue, lies in a pool of blood on the wood plank floor with the knife that I stabbed him with still sticking out of him. Smokey and Mrs. Kane appear.

"Miss Vicky, you should be resting," Smokey says. "We got this."

I stare at the unsightly scene and say softly, "I just need to be sure he's dead."

"Oh he's dead alright, I'm sure of it." Smokey walks into the room, careful not to step in the blood. He rolls the body onto its side. The dead man's eyes are rolled into the back of his head. Smokey lets the body flop face first with a thud.

"The sheriff will be here any minute. Why don't you go back to the other room? He'll want to talk to you."

I'm dazed, but I do what he says and crawl back into Gracie's bed, rolling up into a ball.

Frannie comes in, "There you are." She brings a brush and lavender water, sits on the edge of the bed and gently brushes my hair.

"His horrid face is still in my head."

"Well, you took care of him; you've got nothing to worry about now."

I hold my wrist; it pains me when I move. I'm not complaining. I could have been the one dead on the floor. Thinking back, something had wakened me. It was Mother, I heard Mother's voice, and she was warning me. The bastard she nursed some years ago had come back to hurt me.

There's a knock on the door and the door opens.

"Excuse me, miss, I was told you killed the man in the other room. Is that right?"

I sit up. "Who's asking?"

"I'm Sheriff Brookstone and you are…"

"Vicky … Highmount," I lie.

"Is that supposed to be funny?"

"No sir."

"Good, are you registered as a working girl at the Good Hour?"

"I am."

"Are your fees paid up to date with the commission?"

"Yes, sir. Are you clean?"

"What does that have to do with anything? Look, I'm the one asking the questions. So what happened? I can see you stabbed a man in the back. Are you in the habit of killing? Have you been in jail before?"

"No, to both your questions. He beat and threatened me. He was going to kill me. He came after me with a knife, cutting me all down my arm. I hit him with the hand mirror, and the knife stuck in the baseboard. He went for his gun, and I pulled the knife free. When I heard the hammer go back, I jumped onto his back."

"So, it wasn't your knife you drove between his shoulder blades?"

"No, I didn't have a weapon."

The sheriff holds up my small pistol with one finger. "So, this isn't yours?"

"Well yes, I mean, I had a weapon in my nightstand but he took it. I'd never seen him before. He kept calling me Gracie." I was lying, but why open another assortment of problems? It wouldn't do me a bit of good; it could only hurt me if I tell him the whole story. It would show I had a motive.

The sheriff tells me not to get any ideas about leaving town. I ask Smokey want he means by it. Smokey says to forget it. It was just his way of dealing with the situation, or not dealing with it; and the sheriff did not intend to investigate the knifing of this deadbeat any further. He said he's the kind of sheriff who doesn't want to make more work for himself. In other words, he doesn't really care. The man wasn't of any importance, and if he was traveling alone and nobody comes forth asking questions, his marker will read John Doe, and that will be the end of the story. He isn't going to spend the law's money on a nobody. "Besides," Smokey tells me. "When I went for him, he was sleeping one off or he might have locked you up. Today, you are lucky all he wanted to do was get out of here."

I ask Tilly to have Mrs. Kane pour me a bath. I feel dirty from him touching me. Mrs. Kane comes up to tell me it's ready and takes me by my good arm, and we walk down to the washroom, passing two strange men coming in the back door with a sled to carry Henderson's body off.

I ask Mrs. Kane if she would help me prepare an energizing bath, opening Great Grandmother's book, I flip to the page reading:

INVIGORATING BATH RECIPE

Take one handful of fresh Rosemary leaves and a small handful of Juniper leaves. Bruise or chop the leaves to release the healing oils and combine them with a generous handful of salt or bicarbonate of soda. Wrap the mixture in cheesecloth and tie the ends to form a ball. Put the ball in the bath when you start to draw the water (the hot water will cause the herbal oils to be released into your bath, and the salt will ensure dispersal in the water) and leave it there until you have finished bathing. This will relax and soothe your tired, aching muscles leaving you refreshed, and if used upon rising, sufficiently invigorated to face the day.

INVIGORATING REMEDY RECIPE TO BOTTLE

Take one generous handful of fresh Rosemary leaves and place them in a glass bottle. Add one pint of olive or sweet almond oil and cork the bottle. Shake the mixture, and then place the bottle in the sunlight to warm. Shake the bottle each day for 14-21 days, after which time the oil will be ready to use. Strain the oil through a fine cotton cloth (to remove the solid matter). One tablespoon of the infused oil serves to invigorate the user at any time. If Rosemary is not available to you, substitute a similar amount of chopped Peppermint leaves.

I take a long hot soak, but keep my damaged arm high and dry. I relax with thoughts of my stay on Bimini. What wouldn't I give to have a massage from Chilie. I can hear the ocean rushing onto the white, sugar-sand beach and feel the hot sun's rays on my back. Lost in thought, I am brought back when Mrs. Kane knocks softly on the door.

"Yes?"

"I brought you some warm whiskey and honey."

"I thought that was for a cold, Mrs. Kane."

She smiles, "Maybe, but I think it will do you good." I take the cup form her hand and sip the hot amber drink.

"It does feel good all the way to my toes."

"Then it's doing the trick."

"What trick is that?"

"Helping you relax, so you can heal."

"Thank you, Mrs. Kane, I'm grateful for all the work you've done here."

"You're welcome, Vicky. I just want you to know, they've taken the body out of the house, the floors are scrubbed, and I'm going up right now to make the bed. I don't mind staying with you tonight, if you don't want to be alone."

"Thank you, but I'll be fine."

I dress for work. There is no way I can keep the Good Hour closed. We already had Friday and Saturday listed as a private party; Sunday was closed for cleaning and recovery. We have to be open for Monday night's business. I can only hope Grace is on the afternoon train.

The girls and I are ready at four in the afternoon; we have some early patrons and perform business as usual.

Chapter Fourteen: GRACIE COMES HOME

It hasn't been easy filling in for Grace. I don't want to do this every day. I take the sewing I have completed back to Mrs. Brody. I need to be seen at home and check on Sam. Old Sam greets me at the door, but snubs me for leaving him. I see where he has pawed his way down into the covers of my bed. The fire is nearly out in the stove. I pick him up anyway and tuck him under my coat. It's no time until I have a crackling fire built in the potbelly, as well as the cook stove, warming the house up. I'm so anxious thinking of Mac coming to town. I hope everything goes smoothly. I tidy up the house before going back to Gracie's, this way I can use my time to make Mac a tasty Thanksgiving dinner. This reminds me that I need to settle with Lorenzo. I have his money in my bag. I pour a bowl of cream for Sam and write a list of groceries that I will need from the mercantile and run downstairs to get them. It's as good as time as any. Mr. Brody is behind the counter.

"Good morning, Mr. Brody," I say, pleasantly, although I think he is slime. If he does have dealings with Father (if he is alive as the inspector says), or wants to bed me at the Good Hour, either way he makes me sick.

"Good morning to you, Alex. It's been awhile."

Not long enough, I say to myself. To him I lie, "It's good to see you home. Did you have a nice trip?"

"I don't know if I'd call having to do business a nice trip, but I accomplished what was necessary."

I wonder what he means by that. I try not to make eye contact with him. He makes me feel uneasy, and the last thing I need to do is let him know he has a hold on me. I don't know what business he is talking about, and I don't want him to think I'm curious. As the inspector said, "Stay collected, you do not want him to expect that you surmise anything." He comes around the counter and puts his hand on my back.

"Are you still working at the Good Hour?"

"Mr. Brody, I wish to keep our relationship as family and friends. I can hardly do that if you want to fondle or bed me. So please keep your hands to yourself."

"You're such a pretty thing."

"Pretty or not, I hope you'll respect my wishes. Oh…" I quickly change the subject. "Maybe you can tell me whether you've seen the marshal? I'm expecting him."

Brody quickly removes his hand. "The marshal, huh?"

"Yes, he's supposed to be in town."

"Really? No, I've not seen him." He walks away and begins to restock the cracker box. "Have ya had anybody else visit ya?"

"Visit? No, why do you ask?"

"I was just wondering. There was a man who came around asking questions."

"About me?" My feet want to freeze to the floor. He's talking about Inspector Southerland.

"Yep, your family anyway," Mr. Brody says.

"I can't imagine who that would be, someone from Creede perhaps? I can't say I've had a visitor. Traveling to Baltimore for Becky's wedding and visiting friends in South Carolina, I've been gone for a month. When I got back, I stayed with a friend to help her out … I wonder if it was Pastor Roy, but he would have left word, I'm sure." I go to the pie rack, hoping to change the subject. "I'll buy two of Mrs. Brody's custard pies, a venison tenderloin, two butternut squash and a quart of Mrs. Brody's canned green beans."

"I guess you're not spoofing about the marshal coming'."

"No, why would I do that?" I can't wait to get out of here. Mr. Brody gets a basket and loads me up. "How much do I owe you?"

"Aren't ya going to put it on the books?"

"Not today, I want to pay for this, if I may."

"I'll take your money. I got no problem there."

"Thank you, Mr. Brody, tell the missus I was in, will you?" I walk out as fast as I walked in, and I don't wait for him to say goodbye. I need to see Inspector Southerland; I wonder if he's back from Creede. J.W. mentioned before he left that the inspector said he might return once again.

I hurry back. I told Mrs. Kane she may have the night off, and I plan to cook the dinner meal. The girls have been busy cleaning. The house looks nice. Jessie brought a half dozen pumpkins and gourdes from his mother's garden. Everyone is getting in the mood to celebrate Thanksgiving.

I have a few hours before I'll start dinner. We put our idle time to good use and sew. Earlier, we cut out five dresses, and now we will baste them. The dresses are taking shape, and the girls are excited. Today, I'll teach them how to fit a dress. Frannie is the least bit interested in the actual sewing. However, she likes the idea of new clothes.

We sit down to dinner when Gracie comes through the door. We all rush to greet her. She looks white as a ghost, holding her stomach. We help her into the house.

"Gracie, are you alright?" We all talk at once, including Grace. She tries to catch her breath and says, "I just need minute, girls." We help her with her coat and boots. "I'm hungry. I haven't had a lick of good food since I left."

"Good, you're just in time. We were just sitting down to dine."

We make our way to the kitchen. The girls help Grace and pour her a glass of beer.

"This will help you, Gracie. I know you love your beer," Mae says.

I hand her a wet cloth to wipe her face and hands and proceed to make her a plate of food. We let her rest and settle in before asking questions.

"What's going on here? You never let me eat in peace." The girls break the silence with a laugh.

"We're glad you're home, Grace," Frannie says.

Grace takes a bit of venison. When she finishes she announces, "I had all my women parts taken out." Everyone is silent for a minute.

"Does that mean ya can't fuck anymore?" Bevie asks, inquisitively.

"No, it doesn't mean that. I just can't have kids."

"I'm sorry, Grace," I say softly.

"Me too, I know you wanted a family someday," Mae says.

"Well, there's no way that's gonna happen now." Tears start to roll down her cheeks, and she wipes them away quickly. "I'm just feeling a little sorry for myself."

"That's okay, Grace, you have every right to," Tilly says.

"Are ya goin' to be alright now? I mean, did they fix ya so you're all better?" Frannie asks.

"Yes, the doc said I'd be fine in a few weeks, although it's been over a week and I'm still not too perky."

"I can stay tonight if you'd like, and I can go home tomorrow. You'll feel better getting a good night's rest in your own bed."

"Vicky's right you know; you'll feel more like yourself again," Frannie says.

"That would be real nice, Vicky, if you could work for me one more night. I just need a little more time is all."

"Of course, it's no problem. The girls and I have worked out a routine, and things are going very well."

"I'm glad to hear it."

I cut the pie and pass it around and then pour us coffee.

Tilly asks, "Did you make the coffee, Vicky?"

"Yes, why do you ask?"

"Because no one will tell you."

"Tell me what?"

"You make the worst coffee ever." The girls laugh.

"It took you two weeks to tell me?" I taste it and make a face. The coffee is weak and bitter. "You're right. I can't make a good pot of coffee. Maybe that's why I hardly ever drink it. Who can make coffee?"

There's a show of hands.

"It looks like everyone but you, Vicky," Gracie laughs. "Maybe we should stick with drinking beer!"

We sit and listen to Grace's stories about her travels and hospital stay before telling her about what happened here while she was gone. She is surprised to find out that we leased the brothel for two nights, and even more surprised to hear how we handled it. We all take part in telling her the details about Ian Bruce's guests, and the terrible night Two Dick Henderson came in through my window.

Grace comments that she can't believe all we had to contend with; she hasn't seen that kind of activity ever.

We have to stop and get to work when four Johns come through the door. I help Grace upstairs. I think she should go right to bed, but she insists on going over the books. I sit down with her. If it were my business, I'd probably do the same. I see by her face she is amazed by the entries.

"It looks to me, darlin', you did real well."

"Thanks, Grace." She scans the books further.

"Damn, you made a lot of money. This Ian Bruce, do you think he'll be back?"

"I don't know. He was going on to Salt Lake City. You'll never guess who his sister is."

"Who?"

"Martha Bruce."

"You've got to be kidding!"

"No, I'm not. He said she was upset about him bringing the men here, but he can't do the thing with his sister underfoot." Grace laughs.

"Well, that's good for us."

"I'll say. He gave us a huge tip; I shared it with the girls. I hope it was okay."

"It looks like you collected on him dearly, and the girls deserve it. So, I need to settle up with you."

"Why don't we wait until morning?"

"No, I want to do it now."

"You'll find all the receipts in cash box. I was able to keep on budget." Grace opens the cash box, counts out some bills, folds it and gives me the money.

"I gave you full percentage, just like a partner, if I had one. You're a natural for this business; you got all the female attractions and brains too."

I put the money away, tuck Grace in and close the door behind me when I leave.

I wake in the morning feeling incredible. It's a nice day, the sun is out and the weather is mild. I let Grace sleep in, and I tell Mrs. Kane I'm walking down to the livery to get a carriage. She says

Jessie will be by later if I want to wait, but I'm excited to get a start on the day. I just have today to get ready for the holiday, and maybe, just maybe, Mac will arrive early.

"Bearup's Sign" Rharmoos

75

Chapter Fifteen: THE CIRCUS IS IN TOWN

It feels wonderful being out in the air; besides, I miss Indy. I walk faster the closer I get to the livery. I hope William has a carriage or wagon he can spare for an hour. I see William and Smokey standing in front of the livery discussing something of importance. I hear bits and pieces of their conversation as I approach and see a large, beautifully painted new sign hanging over the main doors. The sign is approximately a third of the building, and it will be easily read from halfway down Main Street. It reads, "William Bearup – Owner. Bearup Livery" in letters four feet high, painted bright yellow with a gloss black outline. On the bottom, he advertises, "Ferrier, Wheelwright, Shoes and Tools." It's the biggest sign in town; no one can miss it.

"William, Smokey," I say with a smile.

"Good afternoon, Miss…" William says, "You'll have to excuse me, I don't know which name to use," he says quietly.

"I'm sorry for putting you in an awkward position, half the time I don't know myself. When I'm not at the Good Hour, please call me Alex."

"You got it. Hey, what do you think about my new sign, Miss Alex?" William says proudly.

"Wow, you spared no expense."

"No, no I didn't. It's one of a kind," William says.

"It's a really big sign," I say, smiling, "a real attention getter."

"Yeah, it looks like the circus is in town," Smokey says cynically. "Where's my name? How come my name's not on that, I'm an owner."

"Why would I put your name on when you're never here?" William asks.

"But I own half this place."

"I don't give a shit. Excuse me, Miss Alex," William says.

"It doesn't matter. I don't want people to know I have to shovel horse manure to put food on the table," he says, puffing out his chest and snapping his britches. I'm a diversified business man."

"You're a what?" William asks, with a strange look on his face.

"I've got my fingers in many different pies."

"It's more like you got your head up your ass," William says with a jutting chin.

"Hey, watch yourself. There's a lady present," Smokey cautions.

"Sorry, he really gets my goat," William says.

"Don't worry, I've heard all these words before. But, tell me, why so fancy, William?"

"I always wanted to own a hotel, something grand like the Strater or General Palmer. I don't see that happening, so I decided to have a fancy sign made for the livery. I know one thing."

"And what's that, brother?"

"There isn't any livery within a thousand miles showing this much class," William says proudly.

"Well, I'll say this, if you were in charge of a lighthouse, brother, you could see it from China," Smokey laughs and slaps his brother on the back.

"Kiss my you know what! You know it's a classy sign, and you're just jealous I didn't have your name put on it."

"Yeah, William, the Bearup brothers are nothing but class, and our business deserves a first-class sign." Smokey slaps him again and has a change of heart. "Ya know what I like about it? The spelling is correct," Smokey says with a certain pride.

"How the hell would you know if it's spelled correctly? Are you telling people you are educated now?"

"I can read and do sums, the same as you."

"I'll give you some. Get over there and start mucking the stalls, Mr. Owner, unless you're afraid of getting your green garters dirty."

"You better see to Alex."

"Are there anymore Bearup brothers?" I ask.

"No ma'am. It's just us two, thank God," William says.

"I got all the brains and the looks. That's why I don't spend my days mucking stalls," Smokey says snidely.

"Haven't you got some place to be, or some spittoons to empty, big boy?"

"Anyway," I interrupt. "I want to thank you, Smokey, for helping me out this week."

"How did things go?"

"Very well, thanks to you."

"Look, I've gotta get going, I'm glad I could be of help. See ya later brother."

"Yeah, I'll meet you for a beer after work," William says.

"You're buying."

"What's new?" he asks with a chuckle, shaking his head. "He's a cheap so-and-so."

I see Indy and feed him some oats. I promise to take him for a ride this week. I need to get him out as much as possible before the heavy snow falls. William's hired hand loads my things and takes me home to the mercantile.

I cannot wait until Mac arrives. I'm so excited. This is my big chance to have him in my life again. I want everything to be perfect. I want us to have good conversation, a nice meal and whatever else transpires. I don't want to set myself up for a fall. Down at Brody's, I buy the smallest small turkey they have. Mrs. Brody keeps insisting I need to come there for dinner. I thank her and whisper I have company coming. She takes the hint and says, "I'm still hoping for you, pumpkin." I buy potatoes, bread, winter squash, onions, fresh sage and a pound of apples to make pie. They are like gold right now. However, there's nothing like hot apple pie with whipped cream.

Chapter Sixteen: THANKSGIVING

I'm up at six o'clock, and I still haven't heard a word from Mac. I'll just die if he doesn't make it. The damn snow is really coming down hard. We got another four inches last night. Sam comes through the open window in the sewing room. I close it tight, now that he's inside, and take a towel to dry his fur.

I'm going ahead with dinner as planned. I just pray he will be able to make it through. I put wood in all three stoves and prepare pastry for the pies. I love to cook for the holidays and especially for Mac. The turkey looks like a perfect one. When the skin is a rich yellow, it's always a sign it will make good gravy. I rub the turkey with butter and sprinkle it with salt and pepper, and toast my bread on the cook stove for a sage stuffing. I was fortunate enough to get cranberries and an orange to cook down with a touch of cinnamon for a delicious sauce just like Mother used to make. I stop for a moment, feeling melancholy. Mother's been gone a year, John and Becky are having their own Thanksgiving, and Aunt Jenny and Uncle Scotty are probably enjoying a country boil and eating outside. I miss them.

I'm going to stop what I'm doing and prepare a bath. I'll be clean before I do anything else. I'm nervous as a new colt away from its mother. After my bath, I sit with Sam by the stove to get warm and towel-dry my hair. I think I'll wear my deep green, velvet skirt and waist jacket. I look at the clock. I have plenty of time; it's only nine.

The room takes on the heavenly smell of apples and cinnamon from the pies baking in the oven. I keep watch out the balcony doors for Mac to come riding into town. Soon, I see someone wearing a snow-covered cowboy hat, and what looks like a long, wool duster with the collar turned up at the neck. I can hardly make him out, but as the rider gets closer, my hearts starts to pound. I think it's him, and he's coming here. Sure enough, the man out front ties his horse at the hitching post and comes up to the store. I quickly pin my hair up and run to the door, opening it, just as Mac is ready to knock.

"Mac!"

"Hello, Alex, it's been awhile."

"Too long, I'm afraid." He's snow covered, and his hair and eyebrows are iced. He brushes the snow from his shoulders and stomps his boots on the deck.

"Come in, you look frozen."

"It certainly is cold. The train stopped in Rockwood, and everybody had to get off. The snow came down as high as the engine and covered the tracks. It will take a good long while before they can dig out. Arapaho and I knew we would miss Thanksgiving if we didn't get started, so I saddled up and made our way down the mountain from there."

"Here, let me help you."

"Before I take my coat off, I need to see to Arapaho. He needs a double order of oats and a good bed of straw in the shelter of the livery."

I hurry to get Mac a towel to use to dry off. He takes a moment to wipe the snow and ice from his face. "Thank you." He looks me over, and pauses before saying, "You look good, Alex. How are you?"

"Good now that you're here safe and sound." I reach up to touch his face. He takes my hand and kisses my palm.

"I've missed you, Mac."

"I was hoping you would," he says with a warm smile.

"You're always so sure of yourself, aren't you?"

"A man's got to be in today's world."

He steps closer, lifts my chin and gives me a kiss. As our lips meet, it sends a rush of hot, molten lava pulsing in my veins. The thrill is still there. I feel it down to my toes.

"It was still dark when we left Rockwood. Luckily, there were others riding with me. We took our time until daylight, hugging the mountain as we came down."

"It sounds dangerous."

"Oh it was. We moved as quietly as possible. We didn't need an avalanche to let loose. I didn't know whether we'd make it. I couldn't see twenty feet in front of my face. We'd been pushing snow all the way from Silverton, but when we reached Rockwood, it was too deep to continue. Everyone had to get off." There's a silent moment, and then Mac says, "It's good seeing you, Alex."

"Do you have a place to stay?"

"Not yet. I thought I would try the Strater or the General Palmer Hotel."

"You're welcome to stay here with Sam and me."

"I don't want to be any trouble, and let's see how things go."

"Sure, I understand."

"How's old Sam?" Hearing his name he slides off the chair and starts his slow approach to Mac like a gun fighter. Sam rubs up against him like a long lost friend. Mac reaches down to scratch him behind his ears which is appreciated. "Smells good in here."

"I just took apple pie out of the oven. Have you had breakfast?"

"No, but like I said, I need to get Arapaho settled."

"I'll walk down to the livery with you."

"Are you sure? It's brutal out there."

"You've come all this way, the least I can do is walk with you. I've waited a long time for your company, Mac McClellan."

"Bundle up; it's really coming down."

I grab my coat, boots and gloves and quickly dress. Out the door we go and ease down the slippery steps. Arapaho is covered with huge snowflakes. The visibility is getting worse. There's no one around. You can't see the mountains or even the other end of town. We're walking down Main Street; everything is snow plastered. It's pretty, like something out of a Charles Dickens novel. Everyone has taken refuge inside. We run into Mark Rich who runs the ladder brigade; he's shoveling snow off the boardwalk.

"Hey, the last time I saw you it was July. You had just won the horse race on Fiesta Day. Good to see ya, Marshal, Alex," Rich says.

"Yes. That day was a little warmer, and if I remember right, we were sipping cold beer."

"I haven't heard the train. Did you ride into town?"

"The train is stuck up in Rockwood. It will be there awhile. Yes, I rode in."

"Damn, you chose a bad day for that."

"I had a pretty lady and a turkey on my mind," Mac says with a chuckle.

"That will do it every time. Well, I got to keep shoveling." Rich looks back to where he has just been. "I don't know why, it's coming down faster than I can move it. I think this calls for a beer. You guys have a happy Thanksgiving."

"You too, Mark. Take it easy."

The snow is deep, making it difficult for me to walk. Mac stops, picks me up and sits me in the saddle, takes the reins, and then we continue.

"I'm glad you made it, Mac."

He turns around and says, "Me too, I didn't want to miss your turkey dinner."

"Is that all you can think of?" He looks up at me in the saddle, smiles, showing his pearly white teeth.

"I'm just teasing you."

We come to Gracie's street.

"Do you mind if I stop in, so I can check on Grace? She just got back from Denver. She had a little surgery."

"We're here. It's okay with me."

He lifts me down. I bound up the icy steps and stick my head in the door. Gracie is in the parlor, playing the piano.

"Happy Thanksgiving, Gracie. How are you feeling?"

"Good. Come on in."

We step inside.

"We girls are having a party today." The girls swarm to say hello, and they aren't dressed for winter, I can tell you that. "Girls get from the door before you take a chill."

"Is that you, Mac McClellan, under all that snow?" The girls giggle.

"Yes, ladies, it's me. Happy Thanksgiving."

"Oh Mackey, we wish you a happy holiday. Won't you two come in? We can have some fun," Bevie says. "Tilly's been here waiting for you, Mac, but she won't say it in front of Vicky. She wants to curl your toes, and we all know how you love Tilly." Mac's face turns a deeper shade of red.

"No, thanks girls, I'm here with Miss Alex." The girls giggle.

"He's here with Alex," they say in unison.

"Why Mac, Alex or Miss Vicky won't care. She's one of us, you know."

"Thanks, ladies, but not today."

"I just thought we would say hello and wish everybody a 'Happy Thanksgiving'. Are you feeling better, Grace?" I ask.

"I'm doing fine. Don't you worry about me. The girls have been telling me all you did while I was away. Thank you."

"We made a real good team."

"Were having a fine turkey dinner and pie this afternoon. My door is always open. You look real good, Mac."

"You too, Gracie. Alex said you were little under the weather."

"The doc fixed me up and I'm alright now."

"I'm glad to hear it," Mac says.

"I'm glad you're doing well, Grace, and thank you for the invitation, but I'm keeping Mac to myself today."

She laughs. "Honey, I would too. The girls are like vultures. The last time he was here for two days. They've been practicing their roping, ya know," Grace says to Mac.

"We have to run," I say.

"Take care, Grace," Mac says.

"You too. Thanks for stopping by." We close the door and hear Grace playing the piano and singing.

"Did you really stay for two days?"

"I don't know, it seemed like a week," he says jovially. "I could hardly wait to get back on the trail to get some rest." Mac tries to muffle a chuckle. I scrape enough snow off the rump of Arapaho to make a snowball and let him have it.

"Damn you, McClellan!"

"Well, don't ask. If you've been around Gracie's girls, you probably know more about me than I know about myself."

When we arrive at the livery, we learn that William is not in, but the hired man says he'll give Mac a hand. Mac politely declines and explains that he will take care of Arapaho himself. He removes Arapaho's tack and rubs him down with straw. He gives him a double serving of oats before we start back home. Mac picks up some snow and we have a little snow toss, laughing. I fall on my butt, trying to be quicker than he.

"Oh, I forgot to tell you, Lorenzo Parrish is in town. I saw him the other night and asked if he would like to have Thanksgiving dinner with us."

"You were sure I was coming?"

"Well, that's what you said, cowboy." I look up and watch the huge flakes drifting to the ground. Scooping up snow, I pack a tight snowball and quickly fire it at Mac's head, and with a loud *whap*, his hat is gone.

"So, this is how it's going to be? Prepare for a salvo, Miss Highland." As quickly as I turn my back to him, a snowball whizzes past me. Then, it begins, each of us dancing around in a circle dodging and weaving, laughing and giggling, like children playing in the snow. I brush the snow from my clothes and shout out, "That's enough, I give up! You remind me of Becky. She was a crack shot with a snowball. I could be hiding around a corner, and she could hook it right around and get me."

"How is your sister? Have you heard from her?"

"That's another story, and it has to go with a drink."

"I like stories with drinks."

"Well, I know I'm going to need one."

He picks up his hat and brushes it against his thigh.

I run to him, throw my arms around his neck like an ornament on a tree, and give him a kiss. Gazing into his eyes, he makes me want him here on the spot, snow and all. Mac McClellan stirs my blood.

Chapter Seventeen: LORENZO DOW PARRISH

"Is Lorenzo staying at the Strater?"

"Yes," I answer as I tuck my arm under his.

"Let's stop and see if he's coming. Does he know where you live?"

"No, I hadn't thought to tell him."

"That's a good hostess," he replies teasingly.

"If I didn't know you were playing with me, I'd give you a little piece of my mind."

"I'm not going to comment on that statement because I'd be in serious trouble," he laughs.

"That's fine by me," I giggle.

We stop at the Strater. Mac says, "If he's still in town, he's probably banging keys in Bell or flipping cards." We enter the Diamond Bell. Lorenzo immediately sees us and waves. "He saw us coming. That's a sign of a wanted man," Mac says, smiling.

"Hey, cowboy, what brings you to the Bell," Lorenzo asks.

"Looking for you, Parrish."

"Well, I don't see a warrant."

"I didn't know I needed one to invite you to Thanksgiving dinner."

"Hello, Alex," he says with a warm smile. "So it's true, you are inviting me for a home-cooked meal?"

"We'd love to have you, Lorenzo."

"I thought you'd be at the piano tonight."

Lorenzo displays a bandaged hand by laying it on the bar.

"Shit, what happened? It looks serious," Mac is concerned.

"It could have been worse. I got this and my pride hurt. I think I'm losing my touch."

"Don't tell me, someone did this to you with a knife?"

"In one of the tunnels, of all places. Some rude bastard pushed me up against the wall just to get past me. I called him on it and told him I didn't tolerate rudeness. Before I knew it, I was in a knife fight. He was good, real good; but I know he tasted my steel. I had blood on my blade, but I never even felt this." Lorenzo holds his hand. "The blade he used was as sharp as a razor."

"When was this?"

"Last night. I was coming back from the Pleasure Place."

"Would you recognize him?"

"Maybe. It was dark. You know there's just a torch at the end of the tunnel, but there would have to be a serious cut in his mackinaw."

"You should check in with the sheriff so he can put the word out."

"Good enough. I'll do just that, even though I don't really want to grace the jail doors." The two men chuckle.

"So, can we count on you for dinner?" Mac asks.

"Are you a good cook Alex?" Lorenzo asks with a cute smile. "Don't answer that. Now I'm the one being rude. I thank you for the invite, and I would love to come to dinner."

"Good, dinner is at seven," I say.

"I'll be there. Thanks for thinking of me."

"You're very welcome," I answer.

"I'd shake your hand, but…"

"I guess this will interfere in your piano playing," Mac says.

"I'll just wait until the crowd has a few more drinks, and nobody will know the difference." He laughs.

Mac tells Lorenzo where I live and to come over anytime.

Smokey's behind the bar serving the patrons. "Hey, good to see ya, Marshal."

"How are you doing, Bearup?"

"Business is good, and that's money in my pocket."

"What more can you ask for? Happy Thanksgiving."

"You too, partner."

Back in the apartment, there is a delicious aroma of roast turkey and apple pie.

"I don't know if I can wait for Lorenzo, that turkey smells so good."

"Will a biscuit and honey hold you over?"

"I haven't eaten all day."

"And that's my fault? You're a grown man, Mac."

"I thought you'd feel sorry for me."

"You just have to hold out a little longer. I've got mashed potatoes, sage dressing, winter squash, corn, biscuits and apple pie." He spins and reaches for his coat.

"Where are you going?"

"I'm getting Lorenzo."

"Alright, I'll give you a couple of biscuits."

"Deal."

"As long as you still have your coat in hand, do you mind bringing in some firewood?"

"I can do that. Maybe I'll get some of that plump breast in return for doing the chores," he says with a wink and chuckle.

"Get the wood."

Mac heads back out into the snow.

I take the turkey from the oven. The skin is golden brown, and the drippings look rich. I know it will make a tasty gravy. From outside, Mac brings in several armloads of wood and a bucket of coal. After he sets them down, he hangs up his coat and rubs his hands together to get them warm.

"This is one hell of a storm. If I would have been just one hour further north, you wouldn't have seen me today."

I pour him a cup of strong black coffee and set a plate of warm biscuits and ham on the table just to hold him over. He reaches and pulls me to him, kissing me. I feel his hard muscular arms under my palms and melt. We stand in silence, just looking at each other.

"I missed you, love. I'm always missing you."

"Nobody's ever called me 'love' before."

"Do you mind?"

"No, I don't mind. It's kind of nice." We kiss again. "No matter where I'm at, or whom I'm with, I'm always thinking of you. Whether you know it or not, you made the trip to Bimini with me." His hold tightens.

"I thought of you too. The last time in Denver, I didn't want to leave. Oh hell, I didn't want things to end that way."

"Me neither. I was confused. I had mixed feelings, and your sister didn't make it any easier. I want you to know, I love J.W. He is the nicest and kindest man I know, but I'm not in love with him. It's you whom I'm in love with."

I put my lips to his. My knees go weak as he kisses me passionately. There is a rough side to Mac. When he holds me, there's an assuredness.

"I'm glad I accepted your invitation. After Denver, I couldn't get you off my mind. I kept thinking that I wished I had said things differently. For as much as I didn't want to hurt you, I did. I'd give anything to take it back, but what was said, was said. I just hope we don't quarrel again."

"Do you still have feelings for me?" I ask.

"I've always had feelings for you. When you said J.W. was in the picture, I didn't want to stand in the way. He's like a brother; we've been together through thick and thin. You made it clear there was another man in your life, and it seemed serious. Is that still the situation?"

I start to panic. Now I'm going to have to tell him about J.W.'s proposal. "J.W. is in love with and he has asked for my hand."

"When did you plan on telling me, or didn't you?"

"I wrote you when I was in South Carolina. It was weeks before his proposal." I take a deep breath.

"Go on."

"J.W. surprised me. I had no idea that he was going to propose. We had just gotten back to Durango. He asked me to have dinner with him. It was the night before he left for Denver, just a few weeks ago. I was stunned. I couldn't give him my answer."

"How did you leave it?"

"I didn't. J.W. was the one that gave me an out, and said that if I couldn't give him an answer, I can when I head to Denver for John's wedding at Christmas."

"I see. So it sounds like I'm here to help you sort your feelings out?"

"No, that's not the way it is at all. I'm hoping we can have something together, you and I."

"Have you told him 'no'?"

"No, I haven't said anything yet."

"You're confusing me, Alex."

"I don't mean to. I'm turning down his proposal."

"When did you decide that?"

"It doesn't matter when I decided it. I'm not marrying him."

"Are you sure? Because I'm not getting into a fight with J.W. over this." A knock on the door interrupts our conversation. "We'll talk about it later," Mac says. I nod my head in agreement. "Let's just be thankful for today, Alex."

"I agree, it means a lot to me that you're here. Can you get the door? I'll check on the turkey."

"Fair enough." Mac opens the door. It's Lorenzo, covered with snow.

"Come on in, Parrish. We've got turkey to eat."

"Hey! Happy Thanksgiving! Let me brush myself off. It's snowing balls out there."

Mac laughs. "You've sure got a way with words."

"I've been dreaming about this dinner since the night you asked me. I've brought my big appetite."

"Good, because Alex made a lot of food. Here, let me take your coat. Sweet Jesus, you're right it's snowing like crazy."

"Thanks, I brought us a couple of bottles of wine and a bottle of the good stuff."

"Are they full or empty?"

"When have I ever brought an empty bottle?"

"Well, let me see. I do remember one time."

"What? When?" He asks as he hangs his hat on a hook by the door.

"You really don't remember?"

"Hell no."

"Galveston."

"Holy sh… you remember that?"

"I sure do. I left you for three hours, and when I came back you had finished our stash. You didn't want me to know, so you foolishly filled the bottles with some poor soul's warm milk."

Lorenzo starts laughing, "Damn, that's right."

"I took a big gulp and almost choked on it. You were passed out on the veranda with your face in some pretty gal's lap."

"You're telling stories, partner."

"No, I'm telling truths." They laugh and pat each other on the back.

"Come on, you're lucky we're with Alex, so I don't remind you of the whole story."

Lorenzo laughs and says, "Well tonight, I got this from your cousin's stash, straight from the Strater's cellar."

"He'll never miss it," Mac says.

"Hell no! You'll have to excuse me, Alex, I don't often bring stolen goods to the hostess," he says with a smile, "but good wine is hard to come by in these parts. If you don't bring it with ya, you're not going to find it in Durango".

"I don't mind. I like a good glass of wine."

"As high and mighty as the townfolks think they are, they don't have a clue about most of the finery in life. Wouldn't you agree, Mac?"

"They're missing a few things, no doubt."

"I'm glad you're hungry and that you could come to dinner," I say warmly.

"It surely smells delicious," Lorenzo says.

"Well, everything is ready. How about carving the turkey, Mac, while I make the gravy?"

"I can do that."

"Is there anything I may help with?" Lorenzo asks.

"You sir, can open the wine."

"Very good."

"I'm starved," Mac says.

"You're always starved, Mac," I say happily.

"It's your good cooking that I look forward to."

I lift the food from the stove and place it in serving bowls to bring to the table. Lorenzo pours the wine. I ask Mac to say grace. I'm melancholy, remembering all the things I have to be thankful for, and especially the company that is with me today. My eyes begin to water. I dab them with my napkin.

Lorenzo notices and says, "Holidays can be tough, with or without family. I've had it go both ways. I, for one, have plenty to be thankful for and being invited here today is one of them," Lorenzo says as he pats my arm.

"Thank you, Lorenzo. We're family today."

"Here, here," Mac says as we raise our wine glasses together.

The food and wine are spectacular. I enjoy watching the men eat several servings. It is a holiday feast, and we have our fill. I cut the warm apple pie and place a slice of strong cheddar cheese on the plate.

There's a knock at the door. I excuse myself to answer. Mac and Lorenzo stand up from the table. Mac follows me to the door. It's Mr. Brody with a bowl of vanilla ice cream. Mr. Brody is surprised to see the marshal here.

"Mr. Brody, happy Thanksgiving. Do you remember Marshal McClellan?"

"Yes, yes. How ya doing, Marshal?" The two men shake hands. "I brought you some ice cream the missus made. She thought you might enjoy some."

"That's very nice. Please tell Mrs. Brody 'Happy Thanksgiving'. We were just getting ready to have pie. What a nice surprise."

"We'll enjoy it," Mac says.

"Good seeing ya Marshal," Mr. Brody says as he takes the steps down." I giggle.

"What?"

"He is surprised to see you here although I told him you were coming. Mr. Brody can't seem to keep his hands to himself."

"Really?"

"Yes."

"I'll take care of that while I'm here."

"Come, lets have pie and ice cream before it melts," I say.

After dessert, we sit around the cozy fire in my modest little quarters. Lorenzo and Mac chat while I sit quietly thinking of my aunt and uncle, Becky and William. I hope they too are enjoying this very special holiday.

"Hey, I almost forgot to tell you, after you left the Strater, I got to thinking about what you said and went down to talk to the sheriff. He said that a lady of the evening was murdered down by the river last night, only twenty feet from the opening of the tunnel. That was just about the time I had that run in, and he thought there might be a connection. The killer used a sharp blade and slit her from stem to stern. It was done with one pull, the poor girl."

I drop my coffee cup onto the saucer. Lorenzo's comment strikes home. There are several underground tunnels in Durango running from major business establishment to the river and beyond, and all are in close proximity to most of the brothels. Men discreetly trying to seek company frequently use them.

"I'm sorry," I say as I mop up the spill with my napkin. A woman was killed. Some nights, I walk home from the Good Hour. It could have been me.

"Did you burn yourself?" Mac asks.

"No, I'm alright," I answer while thinking to myself that the killer was someone who is excellent with a knife, a razor or maybe a scalpel, like my father. My God! I swallow hard and take deep breath.

"I'm sorry, Alex, I didn't mean to upset you. I should have told Mac later. It's definitely not table talk. Forgive me."

I'm in my own world during the next few minutes of conversation. Thoughts of Father flood my mind. Could he be here, or is this just some other sick bastard?

"Are you sure you're alright, Alex?" Mac asks, "You seem distant."

"Yes, yes, I'm fine. Would you like more coffee? Or, I can open Lorenzo's bottle of bourbon."

"That sounds good to me," Lorenzo says. "That is, if I'm not wearing out my welcome."

"Not at all," I say with a smile and wonder, *what if it's Father?*

Mac brings up that I have just gotten back from a trip to Bimini. I hand Mac the bottle to pour. I welcome the change in conversation. Trying to control my nerves, I stumble over the first words, and then go on to talk about the island.

It's just after ten o'clock when Lorenzo says he'd better head back. He jokingly says he may be lost along the way in the blizzard. I thank him for the wine and remember I still have his envelope in my handbag.

"Just a minute, Lorenzo. I forgot to give you this from the other night." I hand him the envelope. He tucks it into his coat pocket. Mac has a puzzled look on his face.

"Thanks, I appreciate it, he says.

"You did me a great favor."

"Well, you're welcome. Thanks for dinner and the company." Mac sees him to the door. I hear them chuckle while Lorenzo puts on his coat. They say goodbye and Mac comes back into the room. He puts a chunk of coal on the fire.

"I should get going too."

"I thought we would continue our talk?"

"I think it's going to have to wait. I need to call it a day, love. I hope you don't mind. I'm exhausted."

"I thought perhaps you might stay tonight."

"It's been a long day, and I don't want to put you to any trouble."

"It's no trouble, really."

"I need a bath and a shave, and I won't have you waiting on me. You've worked all day, putting a real fine meal together. We have tomorrow."

"I'd like to make you breakfast."

"Instead, how about lunch? I want to check in with the sheriff and see if they have any information on the man Lorenzo ran into."

"Of course, and lunch is fine. We'll have turkey."

"I don't mind. It's even better the second day. If you don't mind my asking, are you still working for Gracie?"

"Yes, a few nights a week."

"I see, and do you stay overnight there on the nights you're working?"

"No, I usually don't. I like to come home."

"I don't need to tell you how dangerous it can be after dark. That's a real concern, Alex. I'm going to find out the particulars. I remember having many incidents like this in Creede. In fact, I remember talking to your father about them."

"Father," I say in a whisper and my mouth goes dry.

"Lorenzo's real good with a knife. I've never seen anyone better; so for this man to cut him, he's more than dangerous." I want to tell him about Father, but I can't get the words out. "You get some rest. I'm going to do the same. We'll talk tomorrow."

"Mac…"

"Yes?"

"I'm glad you came, really glad."

"Me too." We kiss goodnight. He thanks me for the wonderful meal.

"I'll see you around noon, and don't forget to lock your door."

"I won't."

I see him out, lock the door and go to the balcony. I can't see a thing; it's snowing so hard.

Slipping from my clothes, it feels good to get undressed. I'm tired and it's been a long day. I'm glad they enjoyed my dinner. I love preparing big meals, but I hate the cleanup. I give Sam a little turkey and gravy. He purrs and digs into his saucer as if he hasn't eaten in a week. I go about cleaning up the kitchen, but can't help thinking about the poor girl who met her ill fate. Mac is right; I shouldn't be walking home. I wonder who the poor girl was. I feel so bad for her. I hope it's not Father. When I think back to when we lived in Creede, Mac was right, there were murders there, girls in the red light district. I hope Father didn't have anything to do with them. It gives me the chills, and something is telling me he did.

I wanted Mac to stay, I do love him, and tonight I needed to feel safe within his arms. With all that's been happening with Father, I must tell Mac. It's frightening. We have many issues to discuss. I can see that he is being very careful not to jump in too quickly, or he would have stayed here overnight. It's okay; I know he wants to know exactly where he stands and what my feelings are. I can't blame him. After all, I was the one to put the strain on our relationship, even if we had not made a verbal commitment. We made love and shared feelings that shouldn't have been ignored.

And I went to J.W.'s bed willingly. Plus, I accepted gifts from him, gifts meant only for a wife or mistress. I wasn't prepared to tell Mac about J.W.'s proposal, and that I was still at Gracie's. Damn, I knew I would have to address these things, but when I looked at him, I got flustered and nervous. I probably sounded like a child trying to explain a wrongdoing. Why can't I talk with him as I talk to J.W.? Maybe it's because I don't feel as if I have to defend myself with J.W. I open the sewing room window to let Sam outside. He jumps on the sill, gets snow on his paws, shakes them and jumps back inside. I guess he's not going out tonight. I close it and start to walk away, stop and turn around and remember to lock it.

Tomorrow, I'm telling Mac about Inspector Southerland and Father. How can I expect this conversation to go well when the subject is about murder, mayhem and deceit? It's easier to put on a simple face and just say; 'I love you'."

Chapter Eighteen: COLD DAYS

Waking to a clear, bright day, I'm feeling invigorated, even if I do have to tell Mac about my troubles. I've wondered for more than three months if I'd ever see him again. I'm damn fortunate he made the trip after our dispute in Denver. He must still have some feelings toward me. I really didn't believe he would come, and now I have more drama to share, and none of it is pretty.

Outside, the town's people are up early and eager to get out after the storm. Mr. Thorpe unlocks the bank and goes inside, and I see the postmaster do the same. Mr. Brody is shoveling the boardwalk. It's early in the year to have so much snow. I wonder … does that mean it will be another hard winter like the last? Heaven forbid. I remember last year. I was practically crawling the walls. We had days where the snow was piled up so high that it covered the windows in Creede, making it dark and dreary and confining us indoors.

Pouring a hot cup of tea, I sit down on the edge of the bed, looking at the bookshelf that holds Mother's journals. It's November; the year went by so quickly, and some days it seems that the accident was a lifetime ago. Other times, it's as if it just happened yesterday. I miss her. Some days, I go through her things just to feel close to her. You can have friends, but you only get one mother, and nobody, but nobody loves you as she does. Losing my mother has left a huge void in my life, and it has been a while since I felt her presence. Thanksgiving is here, and Christmas is around the corner. It's the worst time on the heartstrings. Here I am feeling sorry for myself when Mother met her death on Aspen Ridge. In addition, Father's own hands had something to do with this ugly twist of fate.

I run my fingers over the soft leather-bound journals, thinking that maybe someday a son or daughter may care enough to read my own writings. I can only hope that I live my life as well as she lived hers. I'm angry. There, I finally said it! I'm angry that her life was brought to an abrupt end. *Hear my words, Father, Frances Harrod Highland.* I think to myself. *If you took her life, watch out for me. I'm alive and well, young and strong, and if it takes me all my days to rectify this wrong, I will kill you.*

Standing at the window, I look out aimlessly at the street below. Mr. Brody spies me from the window and waves. I do nothing. All I can think of is that he might have assisted Father in some dreadful way. He pays a couple of coins to a young boy and hands him the shovel. I put a log on the fire, wrap up in my robe and make up the bed. Mac said he would be here around noon. I'm nervous, thinking how I will make my confessions, but I plan to get everything off my chest.

I think of J.W., my good, loyal friend and lover who wants much more than I have to give. He deserves more, and I feel badly that I have been so intimate. I may have encouraged him to fall in love. I want to give him my answer. I would write, but he deserves for me to tell him face-to-face. The last thing I want to do is hurt him. He has been there for me when I needed someone, every step of the way. Most would have said goodbye, but not J.W.

Slipping into my clothes, I fix my hair and take myself to the kitchen. Baking is always good therapy. I get out a bowl and ingredients to make an apricot and banana loaf to have with coffee later. I don't want a sink full of dishes, so I butter a Dutch oven to heat the leftovers. First, I put in the sage dressing, then gravy, slices of turkey, a little more dressing and even more gravy to keep it moist. I save the mashed potatoes for the top and dab it with butter, cover, and put it into the oven to heat through.

By the time it's ready, Mac is at the door.

"Mac, come in."

"Hey, how are you this morning?"

"Wonderful, it's such a pretty day."

"Calm and mild, actually, after the storm." Mac crosses the threshold and steps into the room. "Something smells good. Are you always cooking?"

"No, not always, but I promised lunch, didn't I?"

"After everything I ate yesterday, I shouldn't have to eat for a week."

"Oh, you're not hungry?"

"I wouldn't go that far. I can always eat, and it surely smells good."

"We're having leftovers."

"Sounds great to me. I won't argue with that." I help him with his coat. He hangs his hat and holster, picks up Sam and gives him a rub. "Did Sam have turkey too?"

"Of course. He's a turkey boy."

"I stopped at the livery to see William. I got us a sleigh for this afternoon."

"That sounds wonderful."

"I'll take you out toward Vallicito if the snow's not too deep."

"It's so beautiful out there. Indy and I have gone out there a few times. My favorite place is Transfer Park."

"That's a long way, lady; I hope you don't go alone."

"No, I ride with Henry. It takes us all day. I've gone with Rob Baker too."

"It's beautiful country. Someday, I want to take you to Cascade Canyon, or have you been there?"

"No, I haven't. Isn't that up by Lime Creek, where the road goes up to Silverton?"

"That's it, another beautiful place for a picnic."

"Will you take me next summer?"

"I will. There are some good trails. Or, we can follow the railroad tracks north."

"Have you been west of here, to the cliff dwelling?"

"No, but I would like to. Rob showed me photos of his last visit. It's just incredible. While I was staying at the Strater, I heard about the man from Sweden that was under house arrest. He took artifacts from the dwellings and shipped them to Sweden. What was his odd name?"

"Gustaf Nordenskiold."

"That's right; he was under lock and key at the Strater Hotel a few years ago."

"Anyway, the train runs west and makes a stop there now. We can take the horses and stay a few days to explore if you like."

"I would love to. I wish you were in Durango more often. There are so many things I'd like to do. By the way, did you see the sheriff this morning?"

"Yes, apparently the woman who was murdered was one of the girls from the cribs; she solicited near the tunnels regularly."

"Do you know her name?"

"Rita Bell."

"I'm sorry for her."

"Did you know her?"

"No, I can't say I did. It's a shame so many of these girls spend one day after another struggling for their existence. I've given food to some of them before, on my way to Gracie's."

"Well, that is very nice, but I wish you wouldn't linger on the streets."

"You're right. I will be more careful."

"Supposedly, she had a fight with a John earlier last week and he came back for revenge."

Thank God, it is not Father; I think to myself. "Lunch is ready if you are."

"It smells good. Let's eat. What can I do to help?"

"You can set the table." I hand him the plates and silver.

I pick at my food and Mac asks whether something is wrong. I figure that is my cue. I have to tell him sooner than later. I dive right in and tell him about the inspector coming to the house late August, right before I left for Baltimore. When I pour our second cup of coffee, after talking for an hour, I offer him a little bourbon. He declines, but I pour myself a shot. I'm just getting started. Through tears, anger and grief, I press on. Later, Mac takes the bottle and pours himself a touch. I give him every detail about Father, the inspector, Becky's wedding and her reaction. He lets me talk, and after two hours, the facts are on the table.

"I'm sorry, Alex. I know this is hard."

"It's one of those things you wouldn't wish on anybody. It's so hard for me to believe we lived with this man and didn't know anything about him. As I said, I didn't want to believe any of it, however, reading some of Mother's journaling is pretty much proof there was so much more to him."

"It concerns me. I'll be gone and J.W.'s in Denver. You're alone, going back and forth from the brothel at night. Can't you stay there and come home in the morning?"

"I'll consider it."

"I'd like to at least talk to Southerland before I leave, if that's alright with you. I want to hear what he has to say about Brody, if he thinks he's involved."

"Yes, it's fine with me. Last night, when Lorenzo told us about the girl, my first thought was that Father is here."

"Where is Southerland staying?"

"Last I heard he was at the Rochester House. Do you want me to come with you?"

"No, it isn't wise for you to go near the inspector. You never know who may be watching. As long as Mr. Brody and your father think you know nothing, you're safe."

"I'm sorry you have to spend your time this way," I tell him.

Mac gets up from the chair. "Don't worry about me. Why don't you get ready for the sleigh ride, and I'll pick you up in less than an hour?" He gives me a quick kiss.

"Perfect, thank you, Mac."

"How good are you with that pistol?"

"Don't know, I've never shot it."

"Bring it with you."

Chapter Nineteen: SLEIGH BELLS & PISTOLS

We could not take the sleigh as far as we would have liked. However, from one to three o'clock it was lovely. Yesterday's snow was heavy, wet and stuck to everything, but with today's hot sun, the large limbs covered with snow let loose their bounty from the tall pines and rooftops. In the valley, we see herds of elk, snowshoe rabbits and red tail fox along the Animas River. The river is iced over in many places. The snow easily packs and makes it a little harder for the horses to pull the sleigh. The sun on the snow makes it glisten, and it's so bright we can hardly see. Wrapped in warm furs, William has made us comfortable; he even tucked in a bottle of something to keep us warm. The mountain air is fresh and crisp, and having Mac by my side couldn't be nicer.

We stop into a little saloon for coffee and are lucky to get a bowl of tasty venison stew. Mac tells me about the conversation he had with the inspector and shares his concerns. The inspector told Mac that he had hoped to uncover something by now that would tell him he is on the right path. He said that Mr. Brody's smart; and if he is connected in any way, he's playing it by the book and staying level headed. He said that even Mr. Brody's little excursion didn't lead him to my father. Discouraged, he's out of leads. Unfortunately, he has to wait for the next encounter, and that means another person's life is in danger.

Outside the little saloon, Mac looks over the countryside for a good place to shoot.

"This will do. Get your pistol, Alex. There are many trees that back right up against the mountain. We'll just pick one."

I get the pistol from the sleigh and bring it back to where he stands. Looking at it, I smile, admiring the artisanship.

"Tell me, love, what's the smile all about?"

"This pistol was a gift to my mother. She got it from John Henry Holliday."

"Holliday?"

"Yep, he taught her how to shoot."

The look on his face is one of surprise and moderate disbelief.

"Are you serious? Doc Holliday taught your mother how to shoot?"

"He did. He had a crush on Mother."

"Damn, how'd that work?"

"Well, it was the year before I was born. They met in Dodge City." I relate the story that Becky had told me. "Apparently, my mother was a good student of Holliday's because one terrible night on the Santa Fe Trail, their wagon train was attacked by Comanchero's. Her sharp shooting saved my father and many others. Becky told me Mother shot ten men that night."

"I hope I'm as good an instructor as Doc Holliday, and I'd like to hear the whole story sometime."

"I'll be glad to tell you. I don't mind telling you I really don't like guns, and I hope I don't ever have to use one."

"Well, in your line of work, knowing how to use a weapon should be a prerequisite. Let me show you how to handle this so you don't shoot yourself."

Mac goes through the safety aspects and the instructions begin.

"I want you to know that if you carry a weapon you must be willing to use it because having one means that it can always be turned on you. If you're threatened, you must use it."

After my lesson, we head back to the house for a game of gin rummy. The wind comes up fiercely.

I tell Mac how I sailed with Uncle Scotty on board the Spice Queen to the Spice Islands in the Caribbean. It makes for an interesting conversation when I share that Uncle's friend, Gillson Estavan, gave him half of a treasure map for safekeeping before he was found murdered under the docks in St. Lucia. The map references a fleet of eighteen treasure ships that sank during a hurricane in the year 1733 along the Florida coast. We speculate for an hour on whether the treasure is still there. Later, I show him the sketches I drew during the trip. My best drawing is one of Tall Trees Plantation, the other is of the Spice Queen and Royal Duchess, anchored in port.

"They are all very good. I had no idea that you liked to draw."

"My mother and John are the real artists but I do want to paint one day. I need to get some new brushes," I say, putting them aside.

"You should, you're very good. Not to change the subject, but there is one more thing I want to talk to you about."

"Okay."

"Down at the jail, the sheriff was hashing over the last month's events. He said there was a murder at Good Hour, and that a Vicky Highmount was involved. He said there was a squabble, and a man tried to take her life. He said the man was some low-life from out of town that nobody claimed to know. He claims the man was stabbed in the back, and that Miss Highmount claimed self-defense. What I couldn't believe is that he didn't arrest her for trial. Do you know anything about that?" I look down at the table and pull the ribbon holding my hair. It falls to my waist.

"Yes, yes I do. Damn, it seems as if I can't get in out of the rain, can I? So, that's what he calls a squabble."

"Is that the name you go by at the Good Hour?"

"Usually I go by Vicky Highland, but I was afraid when the sheriff asked me. 'Highmount' was the first name that came to mind on short notice. And, I was pretty shaken up when he paid me a visit. I think I was in shock. Smokey said the sheriff was sleeping off an inebriated state when he went to get him. Lucky for me he was sick, and all he wanted to do was get out of there or I know I would have been put in jail."

"That's true. Well, I guess that explains a few things."

"I'm careful about what I call myself there. I don't want people to know I work at the Good Hour. It will hinder what few sewing clients I have if they know about my part-time prostitution!"

"Don't get upset. I agree."

"So, why are we talking about this?"

"Please, I mean no harm or disrespect. I'm just concerned for your safety."

I take a deep breath. "I'm sorry if I worry you," I say and change the subject. "Would you like something to eat? The time just got away from me."

"Is there any of that pie left from last night?"

"You're making it easy on me."

"The stew is still with me, and a piece of pie is all I need."

I get two plates, cut the apple pie that is left into two slices and set it on the table.

"Do you want to talk about it, Alex?"

"You mean about Two Dick?" My hands shake as I warm our coffee. "I said that when I started at Gracie's I didn't intend to die by some demented beast. That is what he was, a beast. He cut me from my shoulder to my wrist, but I was lucky, really lucky; the man wanted to kill me."

"Damn, Alex, I wish you would let me help you."

"Smokey was on watch that night, but Henderson came through the window, sat in a chair, and was there for hours watching me sleep, the creep. I heard a voice, in my head; it was Mother trying to warn me. He threatened me, tried to rape me, and we fought," I pause… "He cut me. He wanted to do worse, but the tables happened to turn in my favor. An opportunity arose, and I took it. I killed him," I say holding one hand over my mouth. Mac gets up and wraps his arms around me.

"Did you know the man?"

"You mean, did I know the beast?"

"Yes, did you know the beast?"

"I did, he had been to our house in Creede, he and his brother, over a year ago. They were pretty shot up and came to the house looking for a doctor. Father was gone, and so it was Mother who took care of them. I remember, it was the first time I heard bad words come from her lips; but the way she said them, I knew she had had a lot of practice. I heard a strange tone in her voice, a voice a mother must use to protect her young. She surprised me that day; she took control. The second time I saw him, I was in town riding to Aspen Ridge. It was the day of my parents' accident. He was crawling drunk in the middle of the street and took me by the leg and was yelling obscenities. I kicked him in the face. He fell in the mud, bleeding. I held my shotgun on him, and Becky and I rode away. He said he'd find me someday and he kept his word. I was scared out of my wits but I wanted to survive. It was him or me. I hardly remember what happened, but I still see him lying there with that knife stuck deep in his back … the bastard."

"How's your arm now?"

"Healing," I say with glassy eyes staring as if I'm staring at the dead man again. "It's good. It's fine, thank you."

"You've had a rough go of things this past year."

"I'm okay now that you're here."

"But that's just it, Alex, I'm only here a few days. I can't protect you from a distance."

"I know. I'll watch myself."

"I don't want anything to happen to you."

"I'm not going to let anything happen."

He holds me. I'm strong and hold back my tears, but I want him in my bed, at least for tonight.

"Will you stay with me, Mac?"

"Yes," he says softly. He lifts my chin to take my lips, and my body is pliable to his touch; I open up to his mouth just like a bloom opens to the warm sunlight.

Chapter Twenty: WARM HEARTS, HOT NIGHTS

It has been a long, emotional day, and I want to take a hot bath to make myself pretty. Though I'm a lady of the evening and have slept with many men, I'm nervous. Nevertheless, I still have that incredible feeling when Mac kisses me, the same sensation I had when we first met. I'm in love.

I had put water on to heat for a bath earlier and Mac kindly fills the tub. He tells me to take my time and relax. He will fill the wood box and coal bucket. I excuse myself to undress behind the transparent fabric screen. I vaguely see him standing in the middle of the room, so I know he can see me. I wonder whether he is looking. I hope he is. Don't all women want to look sexy for their lovers? Lavishly, I pour two tablespoons of warm coconut oil in my bath. I brought a large bottle home from Bimini that Chilie's sister gave me. Chilie is one of the housekeepers at Tall Trees. She introduced me to her sister who has a knowledge of the healing nutrients on the island, such as coconut and different roots than we have here at home. Nothing makes your skin smoother and gives you a healthier glow. Mac dozes off in the chair before I'm finished. I let him sleep as I clean the kitchen before waking him.

I take a moment to watch him sleep. His hair is darker than before. Usually, it's bleached out from the hot summer sun. He opens one eye, as he instinctively knows someone is watching him.

"Sorry, Alex, I dozed off. I didn't hear you get out of the tub."

"I was just getting ready to wake you. The water is still hot, and I laid a towel and washcloth out if you'd like a bath."

"You don't mind?"

"I prefer it," I answer with a big smile. He stands and stretches, and begins to unbutton his shirt as he walks behind the screen.

"It's always nice to smell clean. Do you happen to have a razor?"

"I do."

I go behind the dressing screen. The quarters are small, and my bosom brushes up against his tight bare chest. I look up as he looks down. He gives me a devilish grin.

"If those get any bigger," he says, "we'll have to draw straws to see who goes first,"

"Mac, you're embarrassing me." I blush. I carefully hand him the razor. Can I get you anything else?"

"Now that you ask, you could…"

"Never mind," I interrupt. "I'll let you have your space."

I hear him splashing and humming as he washes in the tub. Afterward, clean, shaved and in his trousers, he stands next to the blazing fire. The light flickers and inundates him in a warm, amber glow, making his skin look bronze. His chest is still moist with water that looks like golden honey. Warmth rises in my cheeks and spreads through my loins. His broad, strong shoulders make a large silhouette on the wall. His trousers sit very low on his narrow hips, and I can't help but focus on the fine line of hair running from his muscular chest down his torso to the glorified masculine form. I'm awakened from my private thoughts when he asks,

"We haven't really talked about sleeping arrangements. Where would you like me to sleep?"

Without hesitation, I say with a smile, "In my bed." He looks me over from head to toe, with a hungry gaze. *God, he is handsome.* He tends the stove, as I turn down the bed and get in.

He drops his trousers and stands naked at bedside. My eyes canvas his body and there's nothing I do not like or do not crave. I want him, all of him, and I want him to want me. My nipples tell the story; there is no hiding as I feel the tingling sensation of excitement. He crawls into the bed beside me, putting his arm under my head and reaches to turn down the lamp on the bedside table. He smells of soap, clean and fresh. I lay in his arms in the dark room. I've dreamt of this moment, a hundred times. I know I'm right where I should be. I love him, I have from the first night we met.

"The sleigh ride was a wonderful idea, it was so beautiful out today, and thank you for the shooting lesson," I say softly.

"You're welcome, and the ride with you by my side was perfect." I move closer. Sam jumps up on the end of the bed and makes himself comfortable in the fold of the blankets.

Mac leans up on one elbow, and moves a strand of hair behind my ear. "Why don't you show me your arm?"

I hesitate at first. He helps pull my arms free of my sleeves and then pulls my night dress over my head. You can still see with just the light of the fire.

"I'm sorry you had to encounter this. No woman should have to deal with violence," he says sincerely. "This scar will never take away from your beauty." He kisses my damaged shoulder softly. "I feel bad I wasn't there to protect you."

I lay back on the bed, tears run down my cheeks. His hands glide over my flesh, and his kiss is as soft as a feather. I've never seen this side of him. "Tonight, I'm going to call you "dove", because it doesn't matter whom you've lain with, you're as white and pure as snow to me," he whispers. "Let me love you tonight." He softly kisses me from head to toe, missing nothing in between. I close my eyes and feel his touch.

"You're a delectable sweetness." His hand sweeps across my taut belly and opens my thighs. I love the feeling of his warm, strong hands caressing me. His tongue takes possession of mine as he explores me with tenderness, kissing me.

"You're a delicious assault on my senses, Marshal," I whisper as I lovingly stoke his muscular arms and shoulders. His thighs push between my thighs, but instead of taking me with his hard manhood, instead, he lifts my hips and lowers his lips to my warm valley, using soft swirls of his tongue, the French way, taunting my pink flesh. The tantalizing sensation is more than I can endure. I ask him to stop, but he tells me to savor the pleasure. It sends me yearning, and I feel as if I'm spinning out of control. His talent intensifies, and my hips slowly dance with the burning desire for more. I open my thighs further as a moaning escapes my lips.

He whispers in a husky voice, "Come, dove, give yourself to me. I want to feel you quiver on my warm, moist tongue." I can't take any more. It's beyond anything I have experienced. It's an inescapable and indescribable pleasure. I grab a fistful of sheet, biting my bottom lip, trying not to make a sound. I can't hold back. I don't want to hold back. A blissful sound escapes as my body shudders with an immense release. Tearing the sheets with tight fists, I softly cry out his name, "Mac." After laying as limp as a willow, he cradles me very carefully in his arms, while kissing my tears away.

In the rosy aftermath, we're silent. He strokes my forehead and cheeks with his fingertips.

I squeeze my eyes shut, as if I can stop the emotional tears, while my lips take his with urgency.

"I love you, Mac McClellan."

"And I love you, my dove."

Chapter Twenty-One: THE SURPRISE

Sitting up in bed, I smile because my first thought is that Mac's here. I stretch, moving my arms overhead. My hair is a mess. I see he is partially dressed and tending the fire.

"I smell coffee," I say.

"Good morning, dove. I think you slept like a baby," he says grinning.

"I did sleep well, thanks to you."

"I'll take credit for where credit's due."

"Don't you be too pleased with yourself, lawman."

"Oh come on, sometimes it's good to stroke a man's ego."

"Okay, I'll allow you this one," I say, jumping out of bed. "It's cold! That's why I loved Bimini. You wake up, and the temperature is already perfect. I could have stayed."

"Why didn't you?"

"Because of you, silly! You're here, and I want to be with you," I say, throwing my arms around his neck giving him a good morning kiss.

"That's music to my ears, thank you," he says, kissing me hard on the lips.

"Would you ever want to go there?"

"I don't know, dove, its three thousand miles away, and I can't see the state letting me take off work for several months."

"Work, work, work. I hate it when it's so demanding."

"Would you like a cup of coffee?"

"Yes, please." Mac pours a cup and hands it to me. "You do make better coffee than I do."

"Really, you're surprised? I hate to tell you, but I think everybody makes better coffee than you," he chuckles. I try giving him a disappointed look, but I burst out laughing. "My sister says I can't bake either."

"Well, you've made some pretty good cakes and cornbread."

"Yes, but I buy Mrs. Brody's pies and bread sometimes."

"Oh, you don't play fair."

"That's not true, I do buy them, but I've never taken credit for baking them."

He stands in the kitchen and watches my every move. The sun is coming through the balcony doors, and it dawns on me; he can probably see right through my nightgown.

"Mac!"

"What? Oh, now you've spoiled it."

"You can see right through this gown."

"Yes, and what a pleasant silhouette you make, Miss Highland. You're a picture; I haven't seen such a fine piece of art in a very long time."

"Really, Marshal," I say with a smile. He, too, is a vision in the morning sun, standing tall with his white shirt unbuttoned, exposing just a sampling of his muscular torso. His trousers are unbuttoned, and a dark hairline travels down his belly. He rakes his hair back with his fingers with a predatory look on his face, as if he is hungry for something and that something is me.

I say, "I'd like a minute to freshen."

He kindly moves aside to let me through to the modest bathing area. I quickly take a sponge bath and brush my teeth, making myself presentable, dabbing a little of my favorite oil in the hollow of my neck and between my inner thighs. I smell like bergamot, orange and nutmeg and come out wearing a silk shawl, just barely covering my peachy golden flesh.

"Mac, are you hungry? Would you like breakfast?"

"What did you have in mind?" He turns around to look at me. "Wow, I like what I see," he says with a sexy grin.

"Call me "dove". I'm your French tart."

He says nothing, advancing toward me like a panther, while discarding his shirt. He lifts me off my feet and lays me across the bed with my arms stretched out over my head. He's out of his pants in a flash and lowers over me. He opens the silk wrap with one tug of his teeth. He gingerly bites my rosy pink nipples.

"Ouch, easy cowboy."

"The tantalizing curves under your gown got my full attention." His white teeth flash a wicked grin that sends a ripple of excitement through my veins. So many nights have I closed my eyes and made believe he was in my bed, making me ache for his touch. His hot lips part mine and demand a response. I have no need to hold back, I desire to have him inside me as much as he wants me. I take control. He smiles as I guide him into my warm, moist valley. Lifting my hips, I take him deeply, hoping to fill my scorching desire by feeling every inch of Mac McClellan. Devouring me with his mouth and tongue, I open further for his delicious assault. Our lovemaking grows wilder, and more frenzied. Waves of heightening bliss immerse me. I'm aflame, riding him on top at first and then I roll beneath him. Moisture of our heat drips from our bodies, hearts hammering. His voice is intoxicating as he says my name. I'm lost in his liquid green eyes and he in mine. Together, breathless, we take our pleasure.

"You were a panther, Marshal."

"And you are insatiable, dove." We burst into a hearty laughter as he rolls off and pulls me on top of him. I'm so happy when I'm in his arms. I'm so in love with this man; I let him take me repeatedly until we collapse on the bed. I lay against his hard chest; his heart is beating wildly.

"I've had you many times in my dreams, but there's nothing like having you beside me."

"Are you sure they were dreams or was I haunting you, love?"

"If it was, I enjoyed it immensely."

He chuckles.

Chapter Twenty-Two: DANCING IN HIS ARMS

Mac splits wood and carries it upstairs, piling it high right outside the door. I hear him stomp his boots as he comes in.

"Damn that wind. You should have enough wood for a while. Do you know anyone who can give you a hand?"

"Yes, Jessie. He runs errands for me at the Good Hour."

"Great, I'm going to lay a few dollars here on the shelf. I want you to get Jessie to split wood and stack it for you this winter."

"That's very nice of you, thank you."

"I don't think Mr. Brody will be around much. We had a talk. I don't think he'll give you any more trouble, but watch yourself. Try to stay out of his way. Get your groceries when the missus is around; she seems to be a sweet woman."

Mac leaves for a few hours to take care of some things in town, and I go down to the mercantile to get what I need to prepare us a hearty dinner. I buy a pound of ground venison and a half-pound of ground pork for a meat loaf. I peel potatoes, carrots and onions to roast along with the meat in the oven. I also want to make Mac his favorite desert, chocolate cake. I have everything I need: flour, eggs, sugar, baking soda, baking powder, cocoa and so forth. While baking, I whip butter and sugar to make a creamy frosting.

I hear him coming up the stairs. He knocks and opens the door. "I'm back," he says in a lively manner. He hangs his holster, hat and heavy sheepskin coat out to dry. "Something smells good."

"I baked your favorite. I'm just finishing the frosting now."

"Can I lick the bowl? I'm just kidding, but I'd love to have a piece."

I cut a big slice. "Would you like a glass of milk?"

"I'd love one. You can't have chocolate cake without a cold glass of milk." Mac takes a bite. "It tastes like Matilda's, and that's a compliment. You must have tasted her baking when you visited the Reynolds plantation. She's the best cook in the South. She would bake all kinds of goodies for J.W. and me. She sure can cook, but then you probably already know that."

"You're right. Her cooking is that of the Gods. Everything she made was delicious."

"My mother can't cook, besides Matilda wouldn't let anyone in her kitchen."

"I you know just what you mean," I laugh. "She doesn't like to share."

"Mother never had a chance, and Matilda is not one to share secrets. She would come right out and say, 'I'm not teaching ya a thing, child. This is my kitchen.' She is a good woman ... when I talked with the sheriff; he said that things have been a little rough in Durango. With the economy down and men out of work, tempers flare, and there are just some bad people out there. Be careful. Always scout the streets and don't go out at night unless you absolutely have to. If you stay aware of your surroundings, you can stay clear of danger the majority of the time. Is the pistol the only gun you have?"

"No, I have a shotgun under the bed."

"When you ride, I'd take it with me if I were you. It probably needs cleaning. I'll see to that for you, if you like."

He cleans the shotgun. I don't remember if it's ever been cleaned. He also puts up two shelves for Sam, one in the sewing room and another on the back window, facing east, so he can lie in the morning sun.

"Now that I'm done with that, I have a surprise for you," he says.

"What, what kind of surprise?"

"Close your eyes. Let me lead you. It's in the sewing room."

"The sewing room? Did you finish all my sewing orders for me?"

"Are you kidding? I can sew a patch and a button, but that's as far as my skill goes." We head to the sewing room.

"Okay, you can open your eyes now." There, on the table, is my surprise.

"A phonograph," Mac announces.

"Oh, my stars! Wow, is that for me?"

"I saw it today and thought you would like it."

"Like it? I love it! I've always dreamed of having one!"

"Well, wait until you hear it."

"We can thank Edison and Bell for their wonderful contributions."

"Do you know how it works?" he asks.

"'Yes, my Aunt Jenny and Uncle Scotty have one. Actually, it's a gramophone."

"Now you're being smart. Greek, right?"

"*Gramo*, meaning word, and *phone* for phonetics or voice … something like that."

"You're right." He bends over and picks up a small box from under the table.

"And in here are a half a dozen records."

"Mac, this is such a surprise. I don't know what to say."

"Say you'll dance with me, dove. Let's play some music. When we're in Denver I'm sure we will find some other selections as well." He moves the furniture from the center of the room, takes me in his arms, and we waltz away.

Throwing my arms around his neck, I give him a big hug. "Thank you, Mac McClellan. It's a wonderful gift."

"I'm glad you like it."

Chapter Twenty-Three: A WONDERFUL EVENING

Dancing leads to an intimate evening and Mac offers to bathe me. We play music with candles burning, creating a cozy ambiance. I bathe first, and he washes my hair by sitting on a stool at the end of the tub. He gathers my hair over the side and pours a pitcher of warm water over my forehead, allowing it to run into a large pan below. He delicately massages my scalp, my temples, my forehead and the base of my neck. It feels heavenly. He hums as the music plays.

"It feels so good, Marshal. It always feels better than doing it yourself." I tilt my head back, looking at his face. He is so handsome. He leans over and kisses the tip of my nose.

"I'm so happy you're here," I say warmly.

"I'm glad I am." He sponges my arm carefully and then the rest of my body.

"I like your honey-gold skin. You must have bathed nude in the Islands."

Afraid of where that conversation might lead, especially since it was times I shared with J.W., I smile and say nothing.

Finishing my bath, he pats me dry. Now, it's Mac's turn. He slips into the tub. He seems to enjoy my touch and I gently stroke his body. He's aroused and sits up abruptly; the water spills over the side. He jumps out and says, "That's it. That's all I can take. I want you, woman." He doesn't even stop to dry off. He lifts me to his hips, and our bodies mesh. With hands under my bottom, he buries himself deep into me. His voracious appetite clearly astonishes me, but I'm touched that his need is so ravenous. My body heats with passion, and I wrap my legs around his narrow waist, pressing harder against him. He backs my body up against the wardrobe. His mouth covers mine, and his velvet tongue invades my searing lips.

"You're a voluptuous temptress, dove," he whispers breathlessly, before he surrenders. Wrapping my arms tighter around his neck, I feel him explode, bringing me to ecstasy. With strong arms, he lays me onto the bed, towering over me. He's my dream. He's my lover. Tears stream down my face.

"I'm so happy, Mac," I whisper.

"You're a pleasurable woman, Alex."

Just hearing him say my name, I would let this man do anything he desired.

We lay together, sleeping through the night.

Chapter Twenty-Four: THE LOST PENDANT

I tell Mac about losing my wildflower pendant in Bimini. He is very understanding. However, it doesn't make me feel any better.

"Don't feel bad. I'll have another one made."

"Oh no, it wouldn't be the same. I met a woman on the islands. Her name is Kena. She does juju."

"Does what?"

"You know … juju … like in magic."

"Magic, like the Gullah in Georgia and South Carolina?"

"I believe so."

"They believe in witchcraft and call it wanga or voodoo … something like that. So, what did she say?"

"She said the necklace will come back to me, and I should never take it off again or bad things will happen."

"Well, don't believe everything you hear."

"I know, but I'm glad to know I will find it. You know they say witches can cast a spell by putting powerful herbs or roots under a person's pillow or at a place where he usually walks. They call these special individuals, Root Doctors or Doctor Buzzards. They are known to provide protection against witchcraft or withdraw the effect of a curse. Do you believe any of that?"

"I don't know too much about it, but I have heard things. I do know the Gullah believe in dangerous spirits capable of enslaving a person by controlling his will. How did you meet this Kena?"

"Uncle Scotty introduced me to her while in Bimini. Where did you learn about magic?"

"I grew up in South Carolina, with blacks and their religions."

"Uncle has known Kena's family for years. When I went to her house, I saw newsprint on her walls. Later, I asked Uncle about it. I thought maybe since they didn't have much, they used what they had, but he said 'no'; it is used because of their superstition. They believe the newsprint will keep bad spirits away because the bad spirits must first read each and every word before taking action."

"I have heard some of this; Matilda told me once that the custom is derived from West Africa, and they practice wearing a protective amulet called a sebeh or gri-gri, containing written passages from the Koran."

I tell him it was Kena that drew something in the palm of my hand and said that my necklace would come back to me.

"Alex, you're over three thousand miles from Bimini."

"I know, but I believe her."

"You have every right to your beliefs."

"Thank you, and I want my pendant back desperately. So, I'll just have to wait until I find it again."

Mac chuckles and gives me a kiss on my forehead. After dinner, we clear the table and refresh my memory on how to play cribbage.

"Mac, do you remember you said you would take me to your cabin in Ouray?"

"I do, but it's winter. There's no way I can take you now."

"Will you take me in the spring?"

"I don't see why not."

"Good, let's plan when we can go." I get up from the table to get a calendar. I flip the pages back until I come to the month of June. "How about June?"

"June should be alright if the weather is decent. Most of the snowpack should be melted off by then. And you want to do this on horseback?"

"Yes. I'm an experienced rider."

"It's not an easy ride."

"I know, but I'd like the challenge," I smile.

"Okay, we have plenty of time to figure out the details."

"How's the fourth of June?"

"Actually, I'm thinking more like the fourteenth of June. If we have a late spring, it will give us a few more weeks to warm up."

"Okay, June fourteenth. It's a date."

"You'll have to take the train to Silverton. I can meet you there."

"Perfect, I can't wait. Hmmm … I've never packed for any significant length of time before."

"You may never want to go again. The Rockies are rugged. It's pure wilderness."

"You could be right; but how will I know if I don't try it once?"

"I'll have everything we need; you just need to show up."

"Great, it will give us something to look forward to."

"We'll ride out from Silverton; I've got a couple of friends that live in between who would be glad to put us up for the night if we need to. We'll ride the mountain trails. Depending on the weather, it could take us a couple of days. Are you sure you can ride that far?"

"I'll practice."

"Don't go alone. Ask William to recommend someone he trusts, and take your shotgun."

"I understand."

"I know you'll like Ouray. It's beautiful, and you'll love the hot springs."

"I'll just love being with you." I write the date on my calendar. "It's official, June fourteenth. Now for the question I don't want to ask. How long are you staying in Durango?"

"I have to leave tomorrow. I need to make my rounds if I'm going to make it to Denver for Christmas. I've heard from my sister Peggy."

Peggy is Mac's only sister, a beautiful fiery redhead who likes to stick her nose into Mac and J.W.'s business. She's married to Phillip Bouvier and lives on Capitol Hill in Denver's most prestigious area. "Mother is coming from Ireland for the holidays. In fact, she may be in South Carolina already. I'm excited to see her; it's been two years. I guess my father is busy with work as usual, and is not making the trip. I don't like her traveling alone although she has a woman companion, but traveling with a man is safer. I would like for you to meet her while you're in Denver."

"J.W. was asked to John's wedding. It seemed right at the time."

"That's fine. Will you be staying at the Brown Palace?"

"Yes." There's a strange awkward moment between us. "It will be nice to see Peggy again, I hope?"

Mac laughs, "Peggy has good intentions."

"Really? I'm not sure about that."

Mac stays overnight. My first thought when I awake is: *This is his last day*. I lay on my pillow watching him sleep. The sun's rays stream through the back room's window onto the bed. Mac throws the comforter off since I stoked the fire when I got out of bed. He lies naked on the white sheets. I'm already sad thinking of him leaving, but it will only be weeks before I will see him again in Denver. I'm quick to get my sketchbook and quietly move the rocking chair to a better position to sketch his form. I want to capture the light shining across his body. At this moment, it is perfect. He sleeps for the next hour which gives me time to get what's important on paper. He squints, opens his eyes and stretches.

"You look as if you swallowed a canary," he jokes as I quickly close my sketchbook. Without saying a word I set it back on the bookshelf. I go to the bedside and sit down next to him.

"What I'm I doing is waiting for you to wake up, sleepy head." I move his hair from his brow.

"I need one of these sheepskins you have on your bed for a bed roll."

"It keeps you warm in the winter and cool in the summer. I'll see if I can find you one."

"What would you like to do on our last day? I'd like to at least take you out to dinner tonight."

"I'd love that."

"Your wish, dove, is my command."

Chapter Twenty-Five: DINNER AT THE STRATER

I take the afternoon to get a few things accomplished while Mac is busy and pamper myself for an evening out. I lay out my burgundy, velvet bolero jacket and press my white, high-necked ruffled blouse and black silk skirt to wear. After a long soak, I primp my hair, put on a little perfume and dress.

I'm surprised; but it's a nice surprise that Mac shows up early, bathed, shaved and wearing a new suit and hat.

"I hope I'm not intruding on your time. My, you look lovely tonight. I like that color on you. Burgundy makes your cheeks rosy."

"I dressed early. You look mighty fine yourself."

"Topped off with a new chapeau."

"You look handsome, Mac McClellan, with or without your clothes."

"Why Alex, I didn't think you were looking."

"Well I did. Does that surprise you? You're blushing, Mac."

"Only a little ... allow me," he says and helps me with my wrap. "You smell like mandarin and spice. Very nice, it makes me hungry for you."

"We had better go then, or I'll miss out on dinner."

"You could be right. So let's shuffle on out of here."

We take a carriage to the Strater for dinner. It's cold, but I don't mind, as long as I'm out with Mac. The stars are bright against the dark blue sky and the road is icy. Steam rolls from the horse's nose. When we stop in front of the hotel, he helps me down, and we enter the Strater. The dining room is in the back. Passing the inside entrance to the Diamond Bell Saloon, we see Smokey tending bar; he waves and holds up a finger. We stop and wait.

"Will you excuse us for just a minute, Miss Highland?"

"Of course."

Smokey knows who I am; but outside the walls of the bordello, he is nothing but a gentleman to me and only calls me Alex or Miss

Highland. While the men are talking, I watch a dozen men at the bar discussing the day's events, eating pickled eggs and hocks and smoking cigars. A table of five is playing poker. It seems to be a quiet evening at the Diamond Bell Saloon. I look at the piano. No one is playing tonight, and I can't help but wonder where Lorenzo is. Maybe he's left town or sitting at one of the high stakes tables in the private room.

When the men finish their conversation, Mac holds his arm out for me to take and we walk into the dining room. Someone is playing the harp this evening, how romantic.

We are shown to our table. Mac pulls out my chair and I take a seat. He lights the candle on the table.

"Would you like a glass of wine?"

"That would be wonderful."

The waiter comes, "Good evening, Marshal, what can I bring you?"

"Would you bring us a bottle of J.W.'s best wine?"

"Yes, sir."

We both smile. "He doesn't mind. He has a case sent in every other month ... I plan on being in Denver for the holidays. Do you think we can spend some time together?"

"I don't see why not."

"When do you know what day you'll be leaving for Denver?"

The server brings the wine.

"How is this, sir?" He shows Mac the bottle.

"That will do, thank you."

"I would like to leave on the twenty-first."

"Maybe we could have dinner one night."

"I would like that."

He pours a glass of wine to taste. "J.W. sure knows his wine. I was thinking about continuing our talk about us after dinner. I hope you're over him. That's the only way it will work for us."

"As I have said before, I love J.W. He is a dear friend; I need you to understand."

"What I understand is that you two are lovers and friends. And to J.W., it's more than that. For him to propose, he's madly in love.

He's never proposed to any woman. You surprised the hell out of me. I've never known him to be serious. It is out of character."

"Maybe after dinner would be a better time."

"Why don't you tell me about your trip back east?"

"You won't mind?"

"No. I mean, why I should? Maybe we will be family one day, and we will have to sit across the dinner table from each other and have civil conversations," he chuckles.

"Okay, where do I start? In mid-August, we left for Becky's wedding. She had fully recovered from her illness and fell in love with her doctor, William Stanton. My brother, John, came home from Paris with a fiancé; her name is Teresa. She is actually from Denver. My Aunt Jenny and Uncle Scotty came with their three sons, Terrance, George, and Christopher from Savannah. My cousins are all older than I, and it was the first time I had met them face-to-face. Becky's wedding was beautiful, however, we didn't part on good terms after I told her the news about Father. Anyway, we left Baltimore and went on to the Reynolds plantation."

"Peggy said J.W. took you home to meet the family."

"Yes. It's a beautiful place."

"I'm sure you were treated well."

"Oh yes, they couldn't have been nicer. After a week, we sailed to Savannah to my aunt and uncle's. That was a new experience for me, sailing. I had never even seen the ocean, let alone sailed on one. Uncle Scotty invited us to sail to Bimini with him. I had always wanted to see the Caribbean, ever since I was a little girl. The trip was eventful. We got in a storm, and I hurt my knee before we ever got to the island. Bimini is so beautiful; I love it there. In some ways I feel as if I had been there before."

Reaching for my hand, he says, "I'm glad you had a good time. I guess we should order." He motions for the waiter and asks, "Is there a special tonight?"

"Steak and mushrooms or pork chops with cornbread dressing."

"Alex, what would you like?"

"I'll have the steak, please."

"And I'll have the same, rare."

"You look beautiful tonight, as always," Mac says to me after the waiter leaves with our order.

"Thank you."

They bring out fresh baked rolls. Mac butters my roll and sets it on my bread plate. I like the little things he does for me. He pours us another glass of wine. "I have excellent taste in wine and women." He smiles and lifts his glass. "To you, Alex, the woman who stirs my heart." Soft music is playing in the room. "Would you like to dance?"

"Yes, that would be lovely."

He helps me from my chair and leads me to the dance floor. "Your blue eyes remind me of the crown jewels," he whispers to me. I smile, thinking he is so incredibly handsome. I want to savor being in his arms.

Chapter Twenty-Six: FEEL ME DEEPLY

Back at the apartment, Mac stokes the fire, and I light the candles next to the bed. I start to close the draperies at the balcony door windows. He stands behind me and rubs my shoulders, and nuzzles his nose in my hair.

"You smell of Mandarin," he says softly, "Fresh and sweet."

"The sky seems really bright tonight with all the stars. Look there." I point up at the night sky. "What's that?"

"That would be Venus."

"Venus? Do you know about the stars and planets?"

"A little, I studied astronomy in college."

"Tell me about Venus." I lean back into his arms. He moves my long tresses from the back of my neck, and presses his warm lips to my ear, kissing me softly.

"Let's see what I remember about Venus. She's the brightest star in the sky, kind of like you, dove."

"Why thank you, Mr. McClellan, go on."

"Apart from the sun and moon, she's bright enough to cast shadows."

"I often stare at the stars and wonder about what's out there. Tell me more."

"The reason it's bright is due to its size. It's just a little smaller than Earth, its distance comes closer than any other planet, and it is completely covered with clouds that are highly reflective to sunlight. You can see Venus either in the west after sunset, or the east before dawn.

"It is so bright and beautiful." He slowly unbuttons my dress.

"Like you, dove… An interesting footnote is that Venus can't be seen fully and is closer to the sun than the Earth, so we can only see it in phases, never full."

"You're very smart, McClellan."

"I'm trying to show off for you. Is it working?"

"I'll answer that when we get into bed, lover."

"Who's feisty now?"

In bed, lying in each other's arms we tastefully play. I dread the fact that he is soon leaving. I close my eyes to focus on his warm touch and the way his lips feel as they brush against my skin. The candle flickers, but in the amber light I see his deep green eyes with thick lashes and I feel as if our souls connect. He tenderly tucks a curl behind my ear. I turn and put my back to him, snuggling up as close as possible. He nibbles on my ear, kissing the back of my neck and presses his hardness against me. With my arm overhead, I run my fingers through his hair. He rises on one elbow, kissing my full ivory breast from the side as he stimulates my secret, coral flesh and slips his fingers inside whispering, "I love it when you're so tight and warm." Placing my hand over his while he is touching me feels erotic, and he teases with his fingers and thumb until I'm scorching with desire. Inhaling short shallow breaths, he sweeps me onto my back and enters me in one swift move. Devouring me with his mouth and tongue, hands slipping under my buttocks, he lifts me to meet him. I feel him deeply, and I take his lips and mouth savagely. Harder and harder we meet, he rises up onto his knees, my legs bent. He grasps my thighs, lifts his chin, burrowing his manhood excitingly into me. Seeing him in the shadowy light, he's gorgeous and I release in a frantic, fluttering, heightened state of bliss as he meets his. Folding onto the bed, he holds me close, our bodies moist from the fervent lovemaking, but just minutes later, he brings me to my knees, swells inside me and takes me again. We make love continuously, until it's painful and our greedy, insatiable bodies can take no more.

In the morning, I can hardly speak. Mac is leaving today. I make breakfast, and we sit quietly at the table.

"I don't want to leave today without saying that I hope we can work this out between us."

"I think we have," I say smiling.

Mac puts on his sheepskin coat, pulling the curly buffalo collar up around his neck. I hand him his gloves, watching as he stretches them over his hands.

"I will see you in Denver, dove." He kisses me one more time. "Oh no, I never made it over to the train depot to get your ticket to Silverton."

"Never mind, I can get my own ticket. I'll do it tomorrow," I reassure him.

"Don't forget, June fourteenth."

"Don't *you* forget."

"I've got to ride, dove. I'll be thinking about you."

"Stay safe. I'll see you at Christmas."

I rush out to the balcony to watch him ride to the train depot. It takes only a minute to put on his saddlebags and tie his guns on. Arapaho is dancing. I suppose he is eager to go. Mac mounts up and adjusts his coat. I feel my face turn red, and the tears flow down my cheeks. Mac looks up and I smile. He tips his hat and touches his spurs to Arapaho. They go prancing off. I watch until he has ridden out of sight. I stand there for the longest time. I'm frozen in one position. The cold wind whips around me. It isn't until then that I move.

It's the end of November. I have to concentrate on completing my sewing orders, and I need to go to Gracie's tonight. I am sure she can use the help. I heat water for my bath. It feels good to soak. It's so quiet; I miss Mac already, and it's only been a few hours.

Chapter Twenty-Seven: TICKET OF DREAMS

I am glad the sun came out, especially for Mac's sake. He took the train north, heading for Denver, planning to make several stops along the way.

I need to get a few things done. When he's here, we spend all the time we can together. I stop at the post office to check for mail, and I'm surprised to find I have a letter from John. I don't have time to open it now if I'm going to make it to the depot before closing. It's not that I have to buy my train ticket today; I just want to. It's a representation of the time we plan to spend time together next spring. The wind picks up, and I tighten the ribbon of my hat under my chin and turn up my collar. As I come to the Strater, Smokey is in the window of the Diamond Bell Saloon. He acknowledges me and I wave. This time last year, Becky and I were in Creede waiting for winter to pass. So much has happened this year.

Opening the door to the depot, I step inside, stomping the snow from my shoes and walking up to the cage window. A man with a visor, dressed in a pristine, pinstriped shirt sits at his desk in the middle of the room. I look at the clock; it's five minutes to four. I wait at the window to be recognized. Finally, I say, "Excuse me; I'd like to purchase a ticket please."

He remains at his desk and says, "Sorry, miss. I'm getting ready to close."

"It's two minutes to four, sir."

He looks up, stands and comes to the window. "Look miss, I'm closing."

"I'd like to buy a ticket. I promise to be quick."

"We're sold out for tomorrow."

"That's okay. I want to buy a ticket for next spring, June fourteenth, to be exact."

"June fourteenth of 1895? That's six months from now, lady. I think you have plenty of time."

"Please, I'm already here and it will be another sale for the day," I say, upbeat with a smile.

"Whatever you say, miss." He starts the process of writing the ticket and says, "This is a bet on the future you know."

"How?" I ask.

"Not only does this ticket say you're going to be here; but so is this place and the people you're going to see." He hands me a bright yellow ticket with black markings with the date of June 14, 1895, passage for one from Durango, Colorado to Silverton, Colorado. The departing time is ten a.m. with an arrival time of three p.m. "Planner or not, lady, I think you're way ahead of yourself."

"I am a planner, sir. Thank you for your service. It is important to me."

"You're welcome. Now is there anything else I can do for you? My old bones are tired, and my missus promised me a big bowl of venison stew when I get home."

"No, you've been very kind. I hope you enjoy your dinner."

Looking at the ticket, I smile and place it carefully into my handbag.

The wind has come up out of the north. I put my head down. My shoes slip and slide as I try to get a better grip walking in the snow. It will be dark soon and time to go to Gracie's.

Back home, I dress for an evening at the Good Hour, wearing my forest green, sleeveless dress that has a tight-fitting bodice and a low, square neck. I slip on black elbow-length gloves. I made a wide fabric belt to wear with an old Rhinestone buckle that Mother salvaged from a dress I don't ever remember her getting to wear. Most of her city clothes were kept in a trunk in the hallway closet upstairs in Creede. Heaven knows there was nowhere to wear fancy things. The soft flowing fabric of the skirt puddles onto the floor. The dress has a wristband on the hem to pick the skirt up by. I can draw it up to show my knees and kick up my heels.

Tonight, Grace has a favorite client here, so we change positions and I'm working the floor. I pour drinks and have long conversations with boring men, showing a little breast and leg. It earns me tips. It's after two when the last John leaves. Grace's bedroom door is still closed. I think her fellow is staying the night.

I'm ready to close up and say goodnight to Smokey. "I'll go out the back and you can lock up," I tell him.

One step out the door he sticks his head back inside, "Miss Vicky, it's like a blizzard out here. Do ya want help gettin' home?"

"Really, Smokey? Is it that bad?"

"It surely is. I'm takin' the lantern sitting by the door to see my way. If you don't mind me sayin' so, I think you should stay put tonight."

"Thanks, Smokey. That's a good idea. I'll do that. Be careful out there."

"Thanks. I don't have far to go."

That's just it. You don't always have far to travel; but when the weather becomes extreme, things happen. I remember two men in Creede lost their way one night and froze to death. In the morning, they found them just a few feet from their home. I try to look out the kitchen window, but the cold wind and snow have frosted it over. I put a large chunk of coal in the stove before I came, so I know that Sam will be fine. Smokey is right. It's best for me to stay put. I pour myself a hot cup of tea. I guess I'm the only one up. I take a seat at the long table closest to the fire. Warming my hands on my cup, I hear the gusts of wind as the icy snow pelts the house.

Chapter Twenty-Eight: WINTER IN DURANGO

The winter days are short, and the nights are long. I'm spending more time with the girls, and today, Gracie's friend, Annie Rapp, is taking us for an afternoon sleigh ride. There's nothing like being in the crisp, clean air and the sweet smell of pine as you glide over a sparkling new snowfall with sleigh bells ringing. The Rockies put you in the holiday spirit. We huddle together under wool blankets to keep warm. The cold makes our eyes water and our noses bright red. A picture of us would make a jolly painting. We head north along the Animas River where the elk herds are plentiful in the valley, and you know the snow is deep when the elks are standing and it reaches their middle. We veer east toward Vallecito Lake where it's thick with snow-covered pines in order to pick out a prize Christmas tree. Annie comes prepared, bringing with her a saw, hatchet and rope. It's something she and Grace do every year. We all take turns cutting the tree. Annie takes over, and we stand back out of the way and watch the tree fall. We tie it to the back of the sleigh, and the horses pull us home. I breathe in the smell of pine and look at the mountains above. It reminds me of Father and me cutting our trees in Creede.

"It's beautiful, isn't it," I observe.

"What is?" Frannie asks.

"Everything, the mountains, the trees and you, Frannie."

"I am pretty cute," she says with a smirk. She gives me a push, and I fall backwards into the snow. She flops down beside me. We make snow angels and everyone follows our lead. Grace and Annie plan a day to take us ice skating between Christmas and New Year's. We laugh, sing and have a snowball fight. Today, we play. We're just girls.

Mrs. Kane put on a ham and sweet potatoes to bake before we left. Jessie brings the frosty tree through the front door and stands it in a corner window. He secures it in a bucket with heavy rocks and wood wedges to hold it straight. We invite him to stay for dinner, and there's no twisting his arm. The girls promised Mrs. Kane they wouldn't bed him before his sixteenth birthday.

In the afternoon, Frannie and Mae are busy in the kitchen making dozens of sugar cookies and tins of chocolate fudge. The rest of us gladly sample their efforts. Tilly pops corn, and Grace and I sit at the kitchen table in front of the fire stringing garland for the tree. Bevie comes in from the cold with her arms full. She has cut holly berry branches to fill in the tree's bare spots, making it even prettier with the contrasting colors of red and green. Later, we gather everything we can think of to make decorations. The tree is shaping up beautifully. Everyone has made something special to hang on the tree. Gracie plays the piano, and we have a sampling of her secret Christmas punch recipe before bed. We gather around the tree holding hands and making vows to one another to fulfill our dreams. I remember Mother saying how important it is to have them.

In the morning, home with Sam, I go over my sewing orders. It's a relief to have them finished, and now all I need to do is to make the deliveries. There's a knock on the door. On the stoop, a man has delivered a trunk from Savannah, Georgia. I can't wait to open it and quickly cut the ropes securing in. Upon opening it, I find a letter on top from Aunt Jenny.

Dear Alex,

Surprise, and Merry Christmas early! I hope everything fits like a glove. By the time you receive this, we will be on our way across country to Denver. The boys are coming, and we are looking forward to seeing you. Your room will be ready and waiting at the Brown Palace. All you need to do is check in.

We enjoyed your stay with us and can't wait to see you again! We hope there's a chance you will visit us in the spring. Don't forget the Mathieson house is open and yours if you ever change your mind. We would love to have you. Have a safe trip north, and we will see you soon.

Love,
Aunt Jenny

I have chills; I'm so excited. Our family will be together for Christmas and I hope Becky and I can mend our relationship.

I pull out one surprise after another, stripping on the spot and trying on all my new outfits. I dash to the mirror. They're lovely, truly beautiful, and they fit perfectly. I'm so excited. *Just think, Alex, you're going to Denver*, I say to myself. I love the city, and most importantly, I will see Mac. This is a good time to select what I'm taking and start packing. I lay everything out on the bed, matching shoes, gloves and such. The wonderful outfits Auntie made will go back in except for a lovely, blue wool suit. I plan to wear it now. I'm so fortunate and I know I have so much to be thankful for. I think of the girls at the Good Hour and count my blessings. I have family, and I'm going to be with them. I pray for Tilly. I hope she gets her wish to go home to her son soon.

I play the gramophone and think of Mac as I sing and dance around the room. I love being in his arms. While singing, I pick Sam up to dance with me. He resents being my partner, but he's tolerant.

I look at the time and see it's after two. I'm starving and run downstairs to Mrs. Brody's to get something I can cook for supper, when I spy a new stack of horse blankets in the window. My first thought is getting one for Arapaho and Indy. It has been years since Indy had a new blanket, and he deserves one. I go through them and pick out two, an oatmeal-colored one with black and red zigzags that's perfect for Arapaho and a bright blue with red stripes for Indy. I place them on the counter with the rest of my things.

"Are you Christmas shopping, Alex?"

"I am, Mrs. Brody, I love the holidays."

"Is this for Indy?"

"One for Indy and one for a friend."

"How nice. Will you join us for Christmas dinner? We would love to have you. We're having a big turkey and all the fixings."

"I would love to, but my brother John is to be married in Denver on Christmas day."

"What a special time to be married! Would you like me to watch Sammy boy? It's no bother. I think he likes it here."

"Why wouldn't he? He gets fresh cream, table scraps and the run of this place."

"Yes, he does, and I like his company."

"I think you should get a cat."

"Oh, I had one once, but Mr. Brody … well, he didn't take a liking to him."

I purchase a pork chop, a lone potato and a can of green beans. Mrs. Brody sticks a chocolate bar in my basket.

"Mrs. Brody, you're too sweet."

"I don't have anyone else, Alex and I like you; you're a good girl. Consider it an early Christmas gift."

"I like you too, Mrs. Brody, thank you."

"Before I forget, I just wanted you to know I'm enjoying my pretty wildflower teapot you brought me from Savannah."

"I'm so glad. If I ever get back, maybe I'll find the teacups to match."

"Oh, glory me! Why, I'd love to have the set. Maybe we can have tea sometime after the holiday rush."

"I'd love that. Well, I better get upstairs. It's getting late."

I spend the evening packing and embroidering Mac McClellan's name in small letters on Arapaho's new blanket. I plan to do the rest of my Christmas shopping in Denver. I wrap gifts in brown paper to take with me including the silver tray I bought from the silversmith for John and Teresa's wedding gift. I can't wait for Becky to see the colorful yarns and spices I purchased for her in the islands. Oh, and I don't want to forget to put in the men's leather gloves I bought in Savannah.

It is around midnight when I bathe and finally get into bed. Snuggled down into the covers, I think about having to tell J.W. my answer. I don't want to hurt him or ruin our friendship. It makes me almost sick to my stomach just thinking about. I do have feelings for the man. He's been so good to me, and I've enjoyed his company immensely. I remember what Aunt Jenny said, "You will make better decisions when not intimately involved with the two men at the same time." She was right, and I knew it. And, if I hope to have a relationship with Mac, I can't be in J.W.'s bed.

Chapter Twenty-Nine: FAT SAM

The girls and I get ready for clients at the Good Hour. I'm helping Tilly with a letter to her son when the first John comes. Soon, everyone is busy except me, when Sam Bowdean comes through the door. He's the big man I've heard the girls talk about from Yellow Jacket, Colorado. I remember Grace saying he is running for some public office. Anyway, he's a long way from home tonight. I can't help but say that Mr. Bowdean is not on my list of wishful clients. I introduce myself and stall as long as possible, serving him whiskey in hopes one of the other girls will finish up and come downstairs. Then, maybe Sam would choose one of them instead of me. After three drinks he asks, "Are you busy tonight, Miss Vicky? I don't recall seeing you before."

"I'm new, Mr. Bowdean. I haven't been here too long. Would you care for something to eat?"

"No, no. I had my dinner, and I thought I'd have my desert here," he says with a chuckle. I feel sick. I take a deep breath and look at the ceiling before taking Sam's hand to take him upstairs. *God, help me,* I think. Inside the room, he undresses. I can't help him. I know my duties, but I'm dreading what is coming next. When I finally look at the man who has discarded his clothes, I can't hide my revolt. I grab my robe and tell Mr. Bowdean to excuse me for a minutes. I'm out the door, marching down the hall. I knock loudly upon Gracie's door. I hear her ask, "Now what?"

"Are you alone, Gracie?"

"I'm alone, but can't it wait?"

"No," I say, opening the door and progress into her room. "I need to see you, Grace. This is important. It can't wait."

"Shut the door. You're the second one in here tonight with a problem. What the hell's going on?" She sits in her chair behind the desk, with pen in hand waiting to hear. The words fly out of my mouth.

"Look Grace, my job is degrading enough without having to entertain a fat man. I'm disgusted, and don't tell me how important he is, or give me that bullshit story that he is a pillar of the community. I don't care how much money he has; a girl has to draw a line somewhere. This man has enough skin hanging from his balls to make kneecaps. I'm not doing him, I just can't. This is one memory I don't need. I am telling you, Grace, the sight of this man is damaging," I squeal in a high-pitched voice.

Grace rolls, laughing and trying to catch her breath. "Oh my God, Fat Sam is here." Grace pushes away from her desk, slaps her knee as the tears roll down her cheeks. "Honey, I'm sorry. I would have given him to Bevie; she takes care of Sam. It's okay now. Calm down, and go get Bevie." Grace stands from behind her desk and starts to walk me out. "You sure have a way with words, girlie." She slaps my bottom. "Fat Sam is a good soul and enjoys a bath, too!"

"And where does she do that for him, at the livery?"

"Just get Bevie," she says as she escorts me from the office. "And get back to work."

I whisper, "This could be more like a circus act, and we could probably charge to watch." Gracie hears and says, "You ain't tellin' me nothin' I haven't thought of, girlie."

Chapter Thirty: INSPECTOR SOUTHERLAND

I leave town in a few days for John and Teresa's wedding. I know I should be here in case the inspector needs me to assist him in watching Mr. Brody. The inspector thinks Mr. Brody is the link to Father's conviction. I hate calling him Father for he doesn't deserve it.

I ask Smokey after work to take a letter to the inspector. The letter asks him to meet me on Second Avenue at the church on the corner. It's the best place I could think of to meet for I know Mr. Brody wouldn't be caught dead there. Every Sunday, if I'm in the mercantile, he is spouting off to Mrs. Brody about how going to Sunday service is a waste of her time. I wear my red wig, and zip down the back stairs taking the alley up to Second Avenue. I wait around the corner to make sure I don't see anyone before I go ahead and check my watch. It's ten fifty-five. I asked the inspector to meet me at eleven. I want an update on what he's found out and if he saw the brass box that I think is Father's, while I was gone. I open the large, arched doors to the church and see a man sitting down toward the front. Clicking my heels, I shed the snow and walk down the aisle and take a seat behind him. Upon clearing my throat, he glances back in my direction. I see his face; it's the inspector.

"Miss Highland."

"Inspector, thank you for coming."

"Let's keep this short."

"Yes, I wonder if you've found out anything new?"

"I went to the mercantile and I was able to glance into Mr. Brody's office, but I didn't see the box where you said it would be. Then, I had a few minutes alone so I actually stepped into the office; but there was no brass box."

"What? The box isn't there?"

"Shhh … calm down. I didn't say it wasn't there. I said I didn't see it. Don't jump to conclusions."

"I think we should break in. It's got to be there."

"He must feel that something is going on if he moved the box after you saw it. He's put it somewhere for safekeeping."

"You're right. If the box were truly his, it would still be there."

"Correct. So it's good news in a way."

"I'm impatient and tired of watching my back every time I go out."

"You must continue to be cautious."

"Inspector, you've been on this case for a long time. You know the box is a vital part of what's going on."

"It is an important clue, yes; but you will not catch your father by taking the box. Mr. Brody is a pawn, and he may be a killer. However, more than likely, he's your father's boot licking lap dog, if you know what I mean. If we take that box, we may never see Dr. Frances Highland again. We'll find out where the box is; but we're not going to take it, understand? We need Mr. Brody and Dr. Highland to come together with that box. Besides, we don't know whether there's anyone else involved in this. I've spent twenty years on this investigation, and I'm not going to ruin this now. Therefore, I believe it's best you do go to Denver, just as planned, and leave the investigating to me. I know what I'm doing."

I look in his eyes and know instantly he is right. He is the inspector, and he should be the one. I want this over. I want to know the truth; but I'm not an investigator, and I'm too close to the subject not to get emotions rolled into my good judgment.

"Very well. I will go to Denver; but as soon as I return, I'm coming to you."

"Agreed."

Inspector Southerland nods his head and tips his hat. "Good day, Miss Highland."

I watch the broad shouldered man walk away. I can't imagine what it might be like for him and I surely wouldn't want twenty years to pass with this weight on my shoulders. I don't know how he has done it. He does his job, but simultaneously, he must want revenge. How he does it without coming undone, is a puzzle to me. I've known about this situation with my father a few short months and I'm a mess. Dr. Frances Highland is the hunted, but he's not afraid. All this time, he has been ahead of his game. He is very smart and almost arrogant about it. I feel it in my bones.

Chapter Thirty-One: BIG MAN FROM TEXAS

At the Good Hour, we entertain some big-time rancher from Texas until three o'clock in the morning. He pays Gracie to close for the night to accommodate his request for an eight-handed massage. He is approached north, south, east and west, and when done with one side, we flip him over like a pancake and proceed to massage his front. This is a first at the brothel. He must have been over six-foot-five, with the artillery to go with it; at least that's how Grace describes him. He is a big man with big money. He eats and drinks until I think he will burst, dispensing fistfuls of dollars to watch us women having sex with each other. The girls don't usually make more than twenty-two dollars a month; but he hands out silver like a promotion man handing out circus fliers. Gracie has an extremely profitable night, and we don't do too badly ourselves.

I stay over, and in the morning I hear Mrs. Kane moving about in the kitchen when there's a knock on my bedroom door. It opens.

"Vicky, I didn't know you were staying last night."

"Good morning, Tilly. It was too late to go home."

"I just want to let you know Gracie promised us a surprise this morning, and it's to be delivered at ten o'clock, so come on down and have some breakfast."

"A surprise? What kind of surprise?"

"I don't know. I have no idea, not a one. Hey, did ya count your silver from big James? I did, I got six. Can you believe it? I hope he comes to see us again."

"I doubt that he will."

"And why is that? He said he loved us girls."

"He said he was heading back east of the Rockies to ride the Goodnight-Loving Trail this spring before he's too old to do so. I can't imagine how hard that would be."

"Well, how far is it?"

"A couple thousand miles ride from San Antonio to Cheyenne."

"Who would want to do that?"

"Men, men who can afford to live out their dreams."

"How do you know these things?"

"I read, Tilly. My mother made me read. I read just a few years back about the longest cattle drive ever. Drovers took their cattle to the junction of the Margaret and Fitzroy Rivers, in 1886, and right there a station was established, and they called it Fossil Downs. It was the longest cattle drive in history."

"I've never heard of Fossil Downs. Is that in Texas, too?"

"No, silly. It's in Australia."

"And what's a drover?"

"A cowboy, a rancher. It's a long way from here, but I hope to go there one day."

"You have so many plans, Vicky."

"You can too." I grab my robe and Tilly takes my arm. Being arm-in-arm reminds me of Becky when we were young girls growing up. It gives me a warm and happy feeling.

"Vicky, since you're here and it's Wednesday, does this mean you're coming to the hot springs with us? Don't say 'no'. You're already here, and you said yourself that you've completed all your sewing orders, so you've gotta come. It will be fun." I smile at Tilly; she is such a beauty with a head of flame red curls. Out of all the girls, Tilly always walks on the sunny side of the street.

"Well, since I'm here and I don't have plans for the evening, I'd love to come."

Tilly breaks into a wide smile and squeals, "Vicky is coming to the springs with us!"

Gracie says, "One more pussy in the pool. It will be good for you, and you deserve a night off."

There's a knock at the back door. Mae runs to open it. It's Mr. Winter from Winter's Hardware.

"Good morning, ladies. I have a delivery for Grace Talbot."

Grace comes to the door. "Good morning; I'll show you the way." Grace invites Mr. Winter and another man inside. They follow her to the bathroom. We wait and wonder what is happening. The two men bring out one of the old tubs.

"Grace, what's going on? Where's our tub going?" Mae whines.

"Stand back, girls. History is being made at the Good Hour! We have ourselves two big new copper tubs!"

The girls let out a scream followed by a joyous hoot and holler.

The men set the old tubs outside and bring in the new. They're beautiful. The tubs are shiny and sit in heavy wood cradles that have four, fancy-carved wooden feet. The new tubs are two feet longer than the old ones. The girls "ooh" and "ahh" and say they won't have to draw straws to see who will bathe first anymore. Two can easily fit without touching in these beauties.

On Wednesdays, Mrs. Kane makes her fabulous scrambled eggs, and we all eagerly await them. She also makes crispy fried bacon and hot griddlecakes with honey butter. I pour the first round of coffee.

Everyone is in good spirits. Mae looks out the window, "Damn, it's snowing again. We may not be able to get the carriages or wagons through if the snow gets too deep."

"Don't worry, I saw William yesterday at the livery and reserved one of the big sleighs if we can't take the road. We'll go down the river. He said it's frozen solid."

"I love you, Grace. You think of everything," Frannie says. "I don't want to miss soaking in that hot pool."

"Me neither," Tilly agrees. "It feels so good."

"You got that right. I like to feel the bubbles between my legs," Frannie says.

"Girl, you're so bad," Mae laughs.

"At least, I'm honest and say what I mean."

"As soon as we're through with breakfast, Mae and Frannie, you help Mrs. Kane clean up the kitchen and the rest see to straightening the house and makin' beds. Mrs. Kane, why don't you let the girls do the dishes and you make up a basket of sandwiches, cake and such for us to take along? You're welcome to come along, too, if you like. Girls, we're going to make a day of it."

All the girls hug Gracie.

"Oh, Gracie, we're going to have so much fun. Can we be the first ones there?" Tilly asks.

THE TENDERLOIN TRAVEL TO TRIMBLE!

The girls go to Trimble Hot Spring, eight miles north of town, in the Animas Valley. The madams of Durango rent one of the swimming pools and take their girls for a soak and dinner. Trimble Hot Mineral Springs is "The Spa" of the Rockies, and is patronized by the rich and the poor. For centuries, the native Indians bathed in the bubbling warm water of Trimble Springs. The spring's temperature ranges from ninety to one hundred and thirty degrees, depending on the various pools. There are three large ones and some small ones. In the spring, there's a path where you can ride a horse or bike from Durango along the Animas River. It's a beautiful ride. Indy and I have taken it many times. The Trimble lodge was built to accommodate both the health and pleasure seekers. The madams usually rent a buggy when the weather is good and take the scenic trip at the foot of the mountains to the springs. Some of the more prosperous madams have their own buggies and carriages. There is talk that next spring the D&RG railroad will make a stop there on its run to Silverton.

Our work is done, and we dress in our warm clothes. Outside, I see William pull up in the sleigh. We're excited about the sleigh ride and the fact we have the day and night at our leisure. Out the door we go, like a flock of chattering magpies.

"Hello, ladies, it looks like you're dressed warm enough; but I put couple of coke-burning stoves on the floor board. So, keep your lap robes back and your feet where you can see them. Don't get too close. You can set yourselves on fire real quick."

The coke stoves give off a reddish glow with no smoke or fumes, and it's enough to keep our legs and feet warm. We are blessed with a beautiful day after all. The clouds have cleared, the snow stopped; but it's getting colder, and after the sun goes down so will the temperature in the Rockies. The snowfall this morning was like goose down feather floating softly from the sky, making it look like a painting from Currier and Ives.

I can't help thinking of Mac. Just a few weeks ago, we took a sleigh ride. My memories make my cheeks rosy. I hope he's somewhere safe and warm. I pull out my sketchbook and start to draw. Gracie opens the basket a few miles from the springs and we peal back the brown paper-wrapped sandwiches and eat. Afterward, she passes a bottle. There's nothing like spirits to keep you warm. Mae starts us out in song; Grace and William sing bass and the others fill in. It's really beginning to feel a lot like Christmas. William guides the sleigh up to the lodge. Smoke is rolling out of the chimneys, and there's a fire built in the pit outside near one of the pools. Without seeing any other sleighs in sight, we must be the first ones here.

The girls jump down into a foot of snow. We go into the lodge to undress and put on our heavy robes. What a picture we are in our fuzzy robes and winter boots; I follow the girls down the path. This is my first time here. There is so much steam rolling off the water I can hardly see the pools. We hang our robes and bloomers, and dash toward the pools in the buff. I can't believe how warm it is, almost too warm.

"Where does this water come from?" Tilly asks.

"Do you know what a volcano is?"

"I'm not sure."

"A volcano is molten rock. They call it lava. This lava flows through tubes to other openings under the earth, and as it passes underneath or close to the watershed, it heats the water in the springs. It's kind of like you putting a pot of water on the stove to heat; but you don't see the flame."

"If I did see the flame, I wouldn't be getting in."

"Right, me neither."

"Oh, but it sure feels good, especially on my bottom."

"Let's have a race to the other side," Fran says.

"I don't know how to swim," Tilly pipes up.

"I'll teach ya."

"I want to learn how to swim too," Mae cajoles.

"Okay, everybody who wants to swim, comes on over here," Fran spouts. "I'll show you, like I have to show you everything else."

"Kiss my you know what, Miss Fran."

"You do me first, Mae," Fran answers, giggling.

I go along with the rest of the girls although I know how to swim. A few hours pass, and other working girls arrive. Fran has to show off, making nude snow angels shouting, "Jack Frost, bite my ass!" We laugh until our sides hurt, and it turns into a huge snowball fight with more than fifty naked girls. The whole valley is echoing with laughter. It's strange; it's snowing but here we are standing in the nude, and we're not really cold. And, when we get cold, we get back into the hot springs. I haven't had this much fun in a long, long time.

"Do the madams ever come out?" I ask Frannie.

"Oh yeah, but they talk business first. I heard Grace mention something about an election of the new city officials and wondering if the taxes are going up. Those jerks already get more than their share. You don't see them offering up their butts, the bastards. Grace pays twenty a month in brothel taxes. And, of course, you know, we pay six dollars each, and we're lucky to make twenty. So, if Gracie's taxes go up, so will ours. We have it better than most of these girls because Grace pays two dollars for our medical certificates every month. The other houses don't."

I can't help but look at the Negro girls from The Hanging Gardens of Babylon. It's the first time I've seen a black girl nude. They are no different than we are, except their tight, black curls on their heads and private areas, and their skin tones range from cocoa brown to ebony. We're all about the same age. I talk to many of the girls today. Some come from as far away as Maine and San Francisco, and most have similar stories.

We have dinner in the lodge at six. Huge blazing fireplaces warm the room. There are sixteen tables to seat three hundred easily. The food is served buffet style. The menu is roast pork, venison, baked sweet potatoes, mashed potatoes with brown gravy, baked corn casserole, candied carrots, BBQ baked beans, yeast rolls, cornbread, applesauce, applesauce cakes, chocolate pudding and frosted sugar cookies with a spiked fruit punch. After dinner, there's music and dancing until the wee hours of the morning. We have a great time dancing with a bunch of cowboys from the James Ranch. Thank goodness, William is here to take us tipsy girls home.

Chapter Thirty-Two: GIFTS FOR THE GIRLS

Today, before I leave for Denver I want to finish the girl's Christmas gifts and run them over to them. From the remnants of some of my finest materials, I've made five beautiful velvet drawstring handbags, gold for Grace, silver for Fran, blue for Mae, red for Bevie and green for Tilly, all with satin cord and decorated with pearls and glass beads, and inside, I stitch in their initials. I hope they like them.

At home, on the floor in front of the fire, I roll out yards of white butcher paper I got from Mrs. Brody's. It was Mother's tradition for birthdays and Christmas to paint her own wrapping paper. I get out my paint box and start painting; bells, wreaths, snowmen, trees and bows. After the paper dries, I wrap the handbags in paper. I can't wait for morning to come so I can give them to the girls!

Chapter Thirty-Three: MRS. BRODY'S CHRISTMAS HAT

I spend the rest of the evening completing Mrs. Brody's Christmas gift. She's a wonderful person and deserves something special. I hope she is surprised with her beautiful new Christmas hat. I bake pinecones at a very low heat for a few hours to kill any bugs and melt the sap from them. I gather a colorful variety of nuts, placing them in a cutting of silk from an old silk stocking and tie it with a very fine piece of wire. I use a cluster of dried red berries, waxed holly leaves and pheasant feathers, attaching it all to a green felt hat and add a band of red velvet, yards of green tulle and a bow made from white satin. It's so very festive.

In the morning, I deliver my sewing orders and come back to the flat to pick up the Christmas gifts to be delivered. The girls wanted to wait to open them on Christmas day. Mrs. Brody opens her box right away, and she loves her new hat. She has gifts for me. I unwrap them. She has made me three jars of homemade applesauce, a jar of raspberry jam, a jar of sliced pickled beets and, my favorite, baby gherkins. She is so good to me.

Before dark, I take a walk to the liquor store and buy a bottle of the best whiskey. By the time I reach the livery, William has gone home. I leave the bottle on his desk with a painted Christmas card that reads:

Dear William,
I wish you a very merry Christmas. Thank you for taking good care of Indy.
Enjoy a bottle of the good stuff!
Alexandra Highland

It has been a full day, but everything is done and I'm packed and ready to go. The train leaves at nine a.m. I want to be well rested and don't want to have to rush around in the morning. I tidy up the house, and after my bath, I pull one of Mother's journals from the shelves. I flip it open to December 22, 1884. I would have been eight years old, and John and Rebecca would have been almost seventeen. I believe this was John's last year home before he left for Chicago to go to college. It reads:

I hardly have time to read or write, between teaching school and taking care of the household. I love the season and look forward to Christmas every year. It's a warm and cozy time to spend evenings with the family.

John is getting restless, and Becky is in love with Gates Barlow. Alexandra, my, she has grown. She has a lovely disposition and is outside playing with the animals every chance she gets. It doesn't matter if the snow is over her head. There's not a boring moment in Alex's life, for she always has a project. Becky is progressing on the piano nicely and will be playing at Sunday service.

Frances seems unusually quiet. I'm not sure what's on his mind. Behind closed doors, I beg him to let me go home to Savannah to see Jenny and the boys. Whenever I bring it up, he doesn't talk to me for days. I don't understand. Our relationship is shallow. I stay involved with the children. They are a delight. The winter snow creates a warm ambiance as we cuddle inside baking and making special gifts to give to friends. Tonight, we painted our wrapping paper. Tomorrow, we will wrap our packages. It's a family tradition.

At this time of season, I get a little melancholy. I miss Mother and Father. Each Christmas, hanging ornaments on the tree brings back memories. One year, old Jeffrey made up little bags of something that we'd put in the fire to change the color of the flames. He'd spend afternoons pushing me on the swing or baiting my fishing hook. I still have the dress that Jenny made me the first Christmas without Mother and Father. She insisted I open it early. She had bought the fabric by selling our eggs.

There are times I think I can smell Father's pipe tobacco and Hattie's special pecan tarts. It's the small things in life I miss. It's been almost seven years since I have seen my dear sister. God bless her. I would give anything to be home to place a Christmas wreath on Mother and Father's graves. For now, I'll make the best of it, close my eyes, and take myself there.

Although I'm two thousand miles away, I have great gratitude for life and the journey.

I close the book, holding it to my chest in silence. My eyes fill with tears. I miss Mother, and her words I find moving. I set it back in its place and kneel down at the bedside to say my prayers.

Early the next morning, I take Sam down to Mrs. Brody's and wait for Earl, William's helper at the livery, to pick me up. I dress in my new navy, brushed wool suit from Savannah and my warmest boots. I can't wait to get on the train.

I wrote Becky in Baltimore weeks ago, but she did not respond. It's been over a month since I shipped her belongings. I would think she would have at least let me know that they had arrived. For John's sake, I pray we can resolve our differences and enjoy our time together, time we have so little of.

Looking out the balcony doors, I see William pull up. I wasn't expecting him. He dashes up the stairs and knocks on the door, breathless.

I answer, "William, this is a surprise. I didn't expect you."

"Good morning. I've got Earl on another run, so I thought I'd come get ya myself. Are ya ready?"

"Yes, how nice of you. My bags are over here."

"Before I forget, thank you for the whiskey. It's a mighty fine brand."

"I hope you will enjoy it."

"You bet I will. It's not like the stuff my brother gets." He laughs and rubs his hands together to warm them.

"Well, it's up to you if you want to share it with him."

"Yeah, I'll think about. He's a pretty good brother," he says, flashing a smile as the frost melts off his eyebrows.

He helps me to the wagon and puts my belongings in the back. We ride off to the depot. William is a good man. I try to pay him, but he won't hear of it. I wish him a very merry Christmas and tell him I would be happy to make him and Michele dinner when I return. Michele is his lady friend that I met last summer. He's pleased and says they'll take me up on the offer.

The train depot is busy, I'm sure it will be more so in the city. Finding my seat, I get situated. It's starting to snow and I hope we can get through the mountain passes. Stranded on the mountainside at ten thousand feet is not where I want to spend the holiday. I have my warmest clothes, just in case. People have been stuck on the tracks for days before anyone could get to them. The train whistle blows and the heavy iron wheels spin before catching the rails, and the train jerks forward. The train is chugging, and we head north through the Animas Valley and climb slowly up the mountains. A herd of elk has bedded down along the frozen river. They are close. I can see their heavy winter coats and steamy hot breath. We invade their resting space. A few remain, but the majority stand and bolt. I love nature.

I'm so excited to be going to Denver, and I'm happy that John has found someone special. He said a Christmas wedding is Teresa's dream. I know it will be beautiful. Staring out the window, I watch the winter-scape pass. I wish Mother were here. It was her dream to spend a holiday with all the family. I whisper, "Mother, I hope you're with me." I feel a sensation by my right temple, where Mother used to kiss me and I can barely keep my composure. I know it's her. I keep looking out the window.

I have my journal and plenty of time to write, but I just continue to watch the scenery. The snow is coming down harder and the windows have steam. I can't see much of anything now. I decide to stroll to the dinner car for a cup of hot tea, and to my surprise, I see Mr. and Mrs. Johnson from Creede. They owned the hardware store when we lived there. They ask me to join them, and we talk for hours. Mrs. Johnson says she had tea with the Widow McAfee just yesterday. The widow was one of Mother's best friends in Creede. I ask how the widow is doing. She fills me in on all the current events, and I share about Rebecca becoming ill, going to Baltimore and marrying her doctor. Before we know it, it is time to order dinner. We have an enjoyable meal and, before the evening is at an end, we make plans to have brunch before we reach Denver at noon. It is the first time I have seen anyone from Creede since we left home. In the morning, I give a letter to Mrs. Johnson and ask her if she will deliver it to the widow when she returns.

Chapter Thirty-Four: DENVER COLORADO

It's December 22 and I arrive in Denver. It's so cold the snow packs and squeaks under my feet. I'm surprised to see J.W. waiting for me on the platform holding a bouquet of flowers. I wait my turn to get off the train.

"Vicky!"

I wave my arm to acknowledge him. He weaves through the crowd, flashing his beautiful smile, picks me up, and twirls me around and says, "You look great."

"I didn't expect you to be here, J.W., but it's a nice surprise. How are you?"

"Good now that you are here, it's been six weeks, and it seems like a lifetime without you." He hands me a bouquet of flowers. "These are for you, love. Enjoy them, for I fear they may only last a short time in this cold." My heart immediately plummets, thinking about answering his proposal.

"Thank you. They're beautiful, it's been such a long time since I had flowers."

"A beautiful woman like you should be surrounded by them."

"Thank you. You always make me feel so good."

"My pleasure."

Since he left Durango, I've missed his company. No, I've missed much more than that, his handsome face, his tender touch, the romance and his smile that says, *I'll take care of you in every way possible* and he does happily. I'm convinced there isn't anything J.W. wouldn't do for me.

"How did you know when I would arrive?"

"I have my ways, love." He gives me a quick kiss. "Here, let me take your bag and I'll see to your luggage. Come, you must be freezing."

"I'm so glad you're here. There are so many people. It might have taken me hours to get my things and find my way to the hotel. I've missed you, J.W."

"I was hoping you couldn't get me off your mind," he says, flashing perfect white teeth in an electric grin.

"Oh, J.W., you are something."

"My dear, *something* these days can be a man's *everything*. Come, I've got a carriage waiting."

"I'm so spoiled."

"Yes, you are, and that's how I think it should be. I consider myself lucky to have such a delightful woman in my life. Like I've said before, you're a breath of fresh air, Vicky."

It's not hard to enjoy his company, he always has a smile even when I've known he's had no rest. J.W. greets each new day as if it is his last. How does he do it? Meeting him tonight is something I didn't plan. I have rehearsed my decision about his proposal, but it was on my terms. It all seemed so well defined before I arrived but now I've been in his company for less than half an hour and my thoughts are muddled. I've gone over and over this many times. I told Mac on his last visit I was prepared to tell J.W., but now I'm already questioning my decision. What is wrong with me? When J.W.'s around I find him irresistible. If the two were only one, I would be the happiest woman. I love J.W., I truly do, we have never had a bad day between us, but I must admit that when with him I have profound thoughts of Mac. When a woman is in love, that shouldn't be happening.

The station is crowded with holiday travelers. Many have Christmas packages stacked to their chins and need a few more hands to carry things.

Within minutes, J.W. has my luggage loaded, and we are on our way to the Brown Palace. The city looks different covered with snow. The horses lurch forward with their nostrils flaring, puffing steam in the cold night air. The carriage bells jingle and many have evergreen wreaths. The store windows are dressed in holiday colors with tinsel and trees. We pass the Capitol building, lights burn brightly in the elite neighborhood on Capitol Hill. The city feels alive, and I love it.

I count my blessings to be here. I look at J.W.; he is dashing wearing a long, black cashmere overcoat and a high crown, medium brimmed beaver Stetson with a red silk scarf circling his neck.

"Ooh, its cold," I say.

"Pretend it's Bimini and all this snow is sand."

I lift my shoulders and jokingly ask, "Where's the beach?"

"I'm sorry, dear one, we're hell and gone from there, I'm afraid," he says squeezing my hand. He looks into my eyes, tilting his head slightly and says seriously "But I'll take you back if you like."

"Oh, J.W., you really would?"

"We can leave right after Christmas dinner if you like, I'll do anything for my woman," he says with a wink and a grin.

My stomach turns when he says "his woman." He takes such good care of me. I know everything he does is from the heart. I must stay with my decision and tell him as soon as possible, the last thing I want to do is hurt him.

He covers me with a lap robe, and takes my hands between his black, kid gloves and rubs them briskly to warm them. He points out the Christmas tree in the square and says, "Ta da ... for you, my dear," making a gesture as if this is his accomplishment.

"Did you really," I ask, feigning gullibility.

"No, I had nothing to do with it, but it's nice." We chuckle, and he pulls me closer to him.

From a distance, I see the famous flat iron building, the luxurious Brown Palace. The carriage comes to a stop at Seventeenth and Broadway. The tall eight-story building of granite and sandstone looms above. The entrance looks like a Maharajah Turkish palace. I marvel at the powerful, exotic overhead stained glass of two colorful griffins. One would expect to see two ancient Moore warriors standing sentry, wearing white turbans and bejeweled wrist armor with turned up pointed slippers from out of the stories of Arabian Nights. The Palace's character has changed with the season. In the summer, she blends with warmth and richness of the surrounding mountains in colors of brown and green; but tonight, in the dead of winter, her vision is one of interior warmth. The hotel lights are casting elongated amber figures onto the wet sidewalk.

J.W. helps me down and says, "The Palace is for you." He takes my hand and raises it to his lips. The magnificent lobby is decorated for Christmas. A thirty-foot tree stands in the middle under the atrium. A harpist is playing William Dix's sixteenth century English melody, *What Child Is This*. It sets the mood.

"Oh, J.W., everything is so beautiful."

"Isn't it? Now, you wait here, love. I'll check you in."

"Aunt Jenny said she has a room reserved for me."

I walk to the tree and stare up to the mezzanine. It is beautifully decorated with pine boughs and bright red bows. The staff is hustling and bustling, seeing to their guests' needs. People are in the holiday spirit, especially me. A hotel server comes with a tray of hot cocoa and asks if I would like a cup. I'm pleased, and say "yes." He shows me to a seat and pours for me. I sit and sip the warm, creamy chocolate which instantly warms me. I can't wait to see my brother John and the others. This is going to be a wonderful holiday.

I see J.W. taking out his wallet and making payment. I do not expect him to take care of my expenses. I overhear him say to the desk clerk, "Whatever Miss Highland desires."

"Yes, sir. We'll take good care of her, Mr. Reynolds."

"Please run a tab and I'll settle with you upon her departure."

"Very good,"

J.W. signs the register and walks over to me, smiling. I start to say something about payment, and he put his finger to his lips, but I don't feel right and I must.

"J.W., please, I don't expect you to pay for my stay, I've come prepared."

"Merry Christmas, Vicky."

"I…"

He cuts me short by saying, "I see you have a cup of cocoa, good."

"Thank you," I say faintly. This is why this can't go on. I will not take advantage of his good will. "Would you care for a cup?"

"No," he says with a chuckle, "I have something a little stronger in mind."

Upstairs, the elegant suite has two bedrooms and a fireplace. The furnishings are lavish and the room is impeccable, just as I remember it. Greenery, pinecones and red satin ribbons adorn the mantel and a festive arrangement of red poinsettias and white fluffy mums are on the dining table with a cornucopia of fruit and nuts.

The bellman helps us off with our coats and hangs them in the closet.

"Is there anything else, sir?"

"For the present, we have everything we need, thank you," J.W. says and gives the man a tip as he leaves.

"Earlier, I took the liberty and asked the maid to run a bath. She will be up within the hour."

"That sounds heavenly, after being on the train twenty-four hours it's just what I need, thank you."

"I hope you had a good trip."

"It was fine."

I think any minute the question may come up.

"I ran into neighbors from Creede. We had dinner together and a fine time reminiscing."

J.W. takes an envelope from his suit coat pocket and hands it to me. "This is for you from Peggy." I open the envelope, admiring the expensive stationary; it is an invitation to Peggy's Christmas Eve dinner, for my whole family.

"I know she sent invitations to their house,; but you know Peggy, formality."

"I'm sure everyone is looking forward to it."

"Good, I've checked the train schedule, and the rest of your family should arrive late this evening. I ordered an assortment of fruit, breads, meats and cheese, with a pot of hot coffee to be waiting for them."

"You think of everything."

"I try, everything will be closed by the time they get in, and they made need a little something to carry them over till morning. Would you like to have dinner this evening?"

"That would be nice. I need a chance to talk with you…"

House service interrupts by knocking on the door. J.W. answers the door and says, "She's here to run your bath. You go ahead, angel. I'll wait in the parlor. We have all night to talk."

I melt into the warm bathwater. My muscles are sore from twenty-four hours of jiggling on the train. It feels so good to soak and to be in such luxury. I can't complain about the train. Just think, before, people rode in wagons and stagecoaches, for goodness sake. The train is a dream compared to other choices of transportation.

Patting dry, I put on a robe and sit at the vanity to brush out my hair. The maid is very helpful, and she hangs my clothes and puts the rest of my things away. I feel like royalty with all the attention. I dress quickly. I don't want to waste a minute. Besides, J.W. is waiting and I'm starved, when I'm not thinking about giving him my answer.

Hurriedly, I choose a skirt and waistcoat of burgundy taffeta. The waistcoat has three silver buttons and a square neck and is trimmed with a two-inch, stand-up ruffled, black velvet collar to match the inlay panels of the skirt which opens gracefully when walking. I wear pearl earrings and Mother's simple strand of pearls. In the parlor, J.W. is waiting patiently, sipping bourbon from a crystal glass by the fireplace. I walk into the room. He smiles and raises his glass, "To you, beautiful."

"Thank you, J.W. You look very handsome."

"Would you care to join me for drink before dinner?"

"I think not. I'm already tired and one drink of that may put me to sleep."

"Are you ready for dinner then? I made a reservation for the dining room at seven o'clock; it's just about that now."

In the elegant dining room, our table is by the fireplace. We order drinks and the server brings us a menu. The restaurant is nice and festive. However, all I can think about is the issue at hand. There's a part of me that would be happy in J.W.'s arms as well as being in Mac's. Is love supposed to be so incredibly complicated? The server lays a napkin across my lap and pours water. I nervously glance around the room. This is it. I have to tell him. There is no way to deter this conversation and there shouldn't be. He has given me plenty of time to answer. Why should I keep him waiting? The server recites the specials. They are serving a prime beef rib roast au jus with mashed potatoes and buttered lima beans or a thick, smoked hickory ham steak with a baked apricot sauce, cornbread dressing and glazed carrots. We choose the prime rib roast and J.W. orders a bottle of Merlot. The server allows J.W. to taste the wine. Upon his approval, the wine is poured. I try and relax to the tasteful music, but instead of giving my answer, a question pops out of my mouth.

"Is your family in town?"

"They got in yesterday. They are staying at Peggy's, of course. The girls are asking about you."

"How are they?"

"Good. This is their first trip west of the Mississippi. They loved the train and were able to take in a few sights along the way. You know, they're young girls excited to be in the city."

I sip my wine. He doesn't take his eyes from me, and there is a moment of passionate silence. He takes my hand. "I couldn't wait to see you, Vicky."

"I'm glad to be here. It's good to see you, too."

"I was just thinking today about being together in Bimini."

"I love Bimini."

He looks at me happily.

"What are you thinking, Mr. Reynolds?"

"One of my favorite days comes to mind."

"And what day is that?"

"The day we rode horseback on the beach and back into the rainforest to the falls, do you remember?"

"I'll never forget. That day is embedded in my mind forever. It was perfect, wasn't it?" I say with a heartfelt smile.

"You were perfect then and still are, love." There is a moment of silence. "Oh, I checked the train schedule and arranged for someone to pick up your aunt and uncle, also Becky and William. They should arrive at the hotel around eleven o'clock tonight."

"That's very nice of you. I know they will appreciate not having to find their own way after their long journey. I was glad you were waiting for me."

Everything is delightful, and the Brown Palace has first-class service.

"The beef is very tender," I say.

"Yes," he says taking a bite. "Are you tired, dear? I notice you're hardly eating. Would you like me to have them bring something lighter?"

"No, thank you. I'm hungry, but exhausted. I just need a good night's rest. The last few days I worked hard to get everything done. I guess I've pushed myself a little too much."

"We'll call it an early night." He hasn't come close to finishing his meal, but he calls the for the check.

"J.W., I'm fine, please finish your meal."

"I've had all I want, don't worry about me. Do we have something to toast to, dear?"

My face flushes and my heart starts to race. "J.W., we must talk."

"Go ahead. I see your hands are shaking."

I straighten in my chair and lean forward, "You know I love you, J.W., and I consider you my very best friend."

J.W. looks down at his plate and then looks up and says, "This isn't what I hoped to hear."

"I'm sorry, I have deep feelings for you, and this is difficult for me as well." Wiping my tears, I continue, "I've enjoyed every minute we've had together. You treat me as if I were a queen…my family too…without ever expecting anything in return." My chin quivers and I struggle to hold it together.

"You can talk to me about anything, you know that."

"I know, but it's difficult, because I think so much of you."

"Vicky, your honesty is a virtue. Go ahead and say what you need to say. I hate to see you like this."

"Damn, J.W., there you go again, putting me first."

"You'll always be first in my life. When I told you I loved you, I meant it. I don't use words lightly. I fell in love with you because you're kind, caring…let me just say, you're the most beautiful person I've ever known." He hands me his hankie. I dab the hot tears streaming down my face.

"I love you in my own way but it wouldn't be fair for me to accept your invitation having someone…"

"Having someone what… someone else in your dreams?" There's a pause. "I see, even though I don't want to hear. I love you, Vicky. I can't help but say I'm terribly disappointed, but I want you to be happy."

"I don't know what to say… I love everything about you and I love how you love me."

There is silence. J.W. squeezes my hand. I look into his eyes. "I'm so sorry. Please, I pray can we still be the best of friends?"

"Always, love. May there not be a woman, or man, that comes between our friendship. I love you and that will never change, but I'll love you from a distance. I'll not make things difficult for you. God knows, I want to see you happy."

I squeeze his hand, and wipe my tears.

"You'll always be in my heart, J.W., always."

Quietly sitting in the flickering candlelight, it has been a painful discussion. I should feel better having explained, but I don't. I believe silence is best for right now, so I say nothing more.

J.W. takes a deep breath, and gives me a half smile and helps me from my chair. I take his arm as we walk back to the room. Standing outside the door, our eyes connect. I lower my head. I can't bear the pain. If I've made the right decision, why does this hurt so badly?

"I will admit I'm sad that we are parting ways," J.W. says.

I look up, choked with tears and reply, "Me too."

He kisses the palm of my hand, pulls me close and takes my lips, slowly, tenderly and passionately. "Thank you for being honest." He opens the door to my room.

"It's a long way out to Capitol Hill. Won't you please stay here tonight?"

"Thank you. I'll sleep in the other room of course."

Inside I say, "I can explain to the family if you are uncomfortable about escorting me to the wedding."

"I gave you my word as a gentleman and a friend."

His answer is no surprise. "I'm glad, John and Teresa asked you and I want you to come." He kisses me on the cheek, "I'll say goodnight, Vicky." He leaves me standing in the parlor and goes to his room. The covers are turned down in my room, and a red rose is lying on the pillow. I bite my knuckle, trying not to cry and think *what more could a woman want?* My heart is heavy. I get out of my clothes as fast as I can, do my toiletries and crawl between the lavender-scented sheets. My mind reels with thoughts of both J.W. and Mac. Exhausted, I fall into a deep sleep before I can say my prayers.

I'm startled by a knock on the door. For a moment, I don't know where I am. I throw back the covers; J.W. opens my bedroom door.

"Vicky, is that you knocking?"

I rub my eyes. "No, it's not me." There's another knock.

"May I answer the door?" J.W. asks.

"Yes, please," I answer as my hand pats the bed, searching for my robe. J.W. opens the door. It is Becky and William. I let out a squeal, running to her and we embrace.

"I'm sorry, Alex; I'm so sorry, please forgive me. I didn't mean any of what I said. You have to believe me." We both start crying. I take her by the hand, pulling her inside.

"William, how are you?" J.W. says as the men shake hands.

"Better now that we're here, and Rebecca has a chance of mending their relationship."

"I'm glad. Would you care for a drink?"

"No, we're not staying; Becky just couldn't wait till morning to apologize. Sorry to wake you," William says.

"No problem," J.W. says.

"I've missed you, Alex," Becky says with tears. "I feel so bad about things. I was going to write, but I needed to apologize to you in person. I've been such a fool to let things come between us. It was such a shock, and with the wedding ... Anyway, there's no excuse for how I've acted."

"It's okay, I forgive you. I've missed you too."

"I couldn't wait until morning; it's been too long already." She looks at J.W. and then me. "I'm sorry if I interrupted..."

"You didn't interrupt anything. J.W. is staying in the other room. It was too late for him to go back to his sister's."

"It's none of my business," she says. We both smile, and our eyes fill with tears. "Let me look at you. You look great, Alex. How have you been?"

"I'm good." We embrace again.

"I've come to realize what a sacrifice you made for me. I'm sorry. I'm sorry that I got sick and even more sorry that you had to take care of me. Thank you, Alex," Becky says.

"Our train was an hour late," William says to J.W. "I want to thank you for having a carriage waiting. I was surprised when a driver asked if we were the Stantons. It was thoughtful of you."

"You're welcome. I hope it made your trip easier."

"It definitely made things easier. I hate coming into a strange city tired, cold and in the dark. There were two carriages, ours and another waiting on the Michaels family. Their train is due anytime, but Becky was so tired we decided we needed to come on ahead."

William comes over to warm by the fire. Becky and I have a seat on the sofa. J.W. pours himself a brandy and asks if we'd like to join him.

"Tell me, what you have been up to?" I ask.

"I don't know where to start. I'm working two days a week at the Baltimore school, helping with the children's music program. I'm volunteering two days a week at the hospital. I don't know how good I am. You know it was always your area, nursing … you were the one always mending someone. I'm deliriously, happily married. He's so thoughtful. Every day it gets better and better."

"I'm so happy for you."

"What about you?"

"Life has been interesting. I must say, not quite like yours."

There is knock on the door. J.W. goes to answer.

"Surprise!"

It's Aunt Jenny and Uncle Scotty, Terrance, George and Christopher. We are all talking at the same time. J.W. excuses himself, goes to his room and comes out dressed. And, in twenty minutes, he disappears briefly and returns with servers who are wheeling in carts of hot coffee and tea, biscuits with honey, slices of smoked ham, scrambled eggs, mushrooms, and an assortment of fruit and almond cakes. He bows and whispers, "J.W. Reynolds, at your service, Miss Highland."

"Oh, J.W., how kind of you, I thought you said the kitchen would be closed."

"It was. However, with a little coaxing and with the order I placed earlier, I just intercepted the delivery to each of the rooms, and convinced them to cook a couple dozen eggs and mushrooms."

Everyone is starved and happy to be together. We fill our plates and sit in the parlor and at the table. No one cares that it half past midnight. We talk for a several hours and decide there is no way in the world we can cover all of our topics tonight … this morning … whatever the time. We need rest and say our goodbyes for the night … or rather, day.

J.W. walks me to my bed and kisses me goodnight.

"You are the perfect man, J.W., and I do mean perfect," I say in a half whisper as I turn onto my side.

"You think? If I were perfect, love, you would be going to bed with me," he says solemnly.

He turns out the light and softly closes the door. I lay in the dark, thinking.

In a few hours, the sun is up, and we have plans to meet John and Teresa for brunch at noon here in the hotel. Having the morning together will give us time to catch up with ourselves. I'm taking a soak in the tub when J.W. calls to me from outside the door. "Are you decent?" he asks and peeks around the corner.

"You can come in. I'm up to my neck in bubbles."

"I see, love. Do you need any assistance?" he asks with a devilish grin, pushing up his sleeves as to render his services.

"No, J.W., I'm doing just fine," I say joyfully.

"I just want to tell you that your brother and future sister-in-law are downstairs."

"Great! How long have you been up?"

"Well, I never went to bed. You left me wanting, and I couldn't sleep." He chuckles.

"Stop teasing me."

"I found a poker game in the Grand Salon after you fell asleep. I just excused myself to meet you for brunch. I want you to know it cost me a bundle to leave the table."

"I'm sorry."

He chuckles, "Oh, don't be." He fans a stack of high dollar bills.

"J.W.!"

"I did lose a bundle, but you're worth every penny. Now get dressed, love, before I ravish you and keep your family waiting. Oh, by the way, I'm nominated to take the women holiday shopping."

"That must be Becky's idea since we had so much fun when you took us out in Baltimore."

"Ah, that's why I'm elected."

"I'm so excited. I can't wait to see John. Can you hand me a towel?"

"I was hoping you would ask."

I stand covered with bubbles, and J.W. holds out a towel, pretending not to look.

"Are you peeking?"

"No, Ma'am. I wouldn't be a gentleman if I did, would I?"

"I don't believe you," I say laughing. "I'll be out in a minute. I have my clothes laid out. I dress in record time, and hurriedly we go downstairs. Frantically, searching for my brother, I see him and Teresa standing by the Christmas tree. "Fabulous," I say, "The entire family is here."

"John! Teresa!" I call from a distance and dash to them. I can't get over how much John looks like Mother and Teresa, the bride to be, is beaming.

"Hello, John, I'm so glad to see you. You know I'd be here, even if I had to walk the mountain passes."

"I'm so glad. How are ya? Is everything okay?"

"I'm fine, not to worry. You both look healthy and happy. Hello, Teresa, it's good to see you. It's just a few days away."

"Yes, and I too, am extremely glad you're here. John has been worried ever since you left Baltimore." John and Teresa are holding hands and smiling. "Yes, just two days," Teresa says happily.

"Well, I think we're ready. We can't wait for Christmas morning," John says happily.

"I bet you can't. I'm sure the wedding will be beautiful," J.W. answers.

"I hope so. The wedding at eight o'clock on Christmas morning before the Christmas morning service, and brunch will be here in the dining room right after the ceremony," Teresa says excitedly.

"We are looking forward to it," I say.

We have a delicious breakfast together and catch up on family business. No one mentions Father, and I'm sure not bringing the subject up. After we bundle up to go Christmas shopping, J.W. hires four carriages to take us. The weather is windy and cold; but it doesn't stop the crowds from doing their last minute shopping, and it doesn't dampen our spirits. I'm glad I'm wearing my winter wool plaid suit and double-lined ivory wrap trimmed in fur; everyone is dressed in holiday colors. We take our places in the carriages and off we go to Larimer Square where there are dozens of shops to choose from. Surprisingly, the men have one request, and we stop in front of the new Goorin Brother's hat store. It's the first time I've seen men excited and having a good time shopping. There are so many styles to choose from. All the men make at least one purchase.

Our second stop is to an incredible bookstore. We file into the store, ringing the bell. The smell of leather, glue and ink mingle in the air. Thousands of books are stacked and shelved to mull through. It's shoulder to shoulder with people, but everyone is in the spirit and does not mind. In the back, on a large wooden table, there is a pile of old maps for sale.

Terrance says to Uncle, "There are a lot of maps here, but I bet you won't find one like your treasure map, Father." He is referring to the treasure map of Estefan's.

I like one map in particular. It's of the Caribbean Islands, and it even shows the island of Bimini. It will make a perfect gift for J.W. Without J.W.'s knowledge, I make the purchase and arrange to have it framed. I pick out a card and write, *Merry Christmas, J.W., a time I will never forget. Love, Vicky.* I'll have them attach it to the back of the frame. The salesclerk will make the delivery Christmas Eve morning. They also have a collection of ships in glass bottles, and I find one very similar to the Spice Queen. I ask to have it wrapped so Uncle Scotty doesn't see. It even comes with a brass plaque that he might have engraved. It's perfect for his desk in his study. I buy a small book of quotes, entitled *Friends* as a hostess gift for Peggy from all of us for tomorrow evening. Before leaving the store, J.W. points out Arthur Conan Doyle's new collection, the *Adventures of Sherlock Holmes*. I decide to buy three copies, one for each of the cousins. I've spent more on Christmas this year than all my years put together, but this one is special, and who knows when we will all be together again?

Our agenda for Christmas day shall be the wedding at eight o'clock, brunch, gifts and cake. Later, we'll have our Christmas dinner and share gifts in one of the private sitting rooms at the Brown Palace. It will be a full day.

J.W. has the drivers stop in front of a French bakery in the square.

"Time for coffee and pastries, everyone." We all "ooh" and "aah" over the aromas of sugar and spice as we come through the door. John says it reminds him of two of his favorite bakeries in Paris, La Bonbonnier La Farm, and La Chatelaine Patissarie. The case is full of all kinds of delectable goodies. John points to the Napoleons. He says they're delicious. "They are made with layers of puff pastry, interspersed with whipped cream and iced with fondant or topped with chocolate and confectioner's sugar," he says. Another is a tart, filled with a lemon curd or coffee cream. He explains that the pate sucre is a sweet pastry that resembles cookie dough. "You have to make it in advance and allow it to mellow. The tart and tartlets are filled with a cream base and topped with fresh fruit covered by a sugar glace, making this an exquisite dessert."

"John, how do you know all this?"

"I worked. For not all my hours in Paris, did I have the luxury of painting," he says with a smile.

"You worked at a bakery?"

"Yes, and not just any bakery, one of the finest in Paris, the *Bonbonnier la Farm*."

"Tell me, what are these?" I ask, as I point to a shell-like, shaped cookie.

"Madeleines, they're small sponge-like cookies often served with afternoon tea. They do look like elongated shells from being baked in special tins. There, now that you've had a lesson in French pastry, let's eat."

"Now I want one of everything," I say excitedly, but I choose the éclair with chocolate frosting with a white creamy filling. The waiter pours us hot steaming coffee and brings us samples of their freshly baked meat pies, which smell heavenly. They're so good that Uncle says to bring us each one and we'll have lunch. We eat the hot meat tarts with a salad.

Aunt Jenny points to a fine jewelry store across the street. She says she would like to explore. The store is full of people and it's standing room only. I'm trapped in the corner where there is a showcase of silver and gold pocket watches. I see one that strikes my fancy and ask if I may see it. It's a fine silver piece with horses engraved on the front. It would make a wonderful gift for Mac. The watch is silver with hands of gold. Inside, there is a place to hold a photo. I decide I'm going to take it and ask them to engrave it with his name and date. The salesman reminds me that the owner of the watch will need a fob. I say, "It will need to be substantial."

The man asks, "What line of work is he in?"

"He's a marshal."

"Ah," he says. "This watch is a good choice. It's one of the new ones. You don't need a key too wind it. You use this knob."

"Wonderful. What about a fob?"

"I have just the one for him." He takes the heaviest silver chain from the case. "Do you like the look of this?"

"Yes, it's perfect."

"It is our most substantial chain, and it has a clip on the end so he can attach it to his vest. He won't lose this watch."

"Very nice. I'll take it."

"If you have a few minutes I will do the engraving myself."

"Thank you." He hands me paper and pen to write exactly what I'd like to have engraved. While waiting, I see an exquisite 10K yellow gold, hand-etched pencil. When the salesman comes back, I ask if he can tell me about it. He takes it from the case and shows me. The pencil is actually a telescope that opens and closes with a flush-set finial citrine-colored stone on the end. I ask what the price is. It's expensive, but it's so beautiful and with such a feminine line. I just have to have it for Aunt Jenny. I look into my handbag and count my money. *Do I dare spend so much? Will I have enough if I have an emergency? Can I get home on what I have left?* The man waits patiently, which I commend him for. There are so many people needing to be waited upon. If I dismiss him, he may be caught up with others and I won't have another opportunity to buy.

"I'll take it," I say, releasing a deep breath. I love it and I know she will too. I feel good that I've purchased such wonderful gifts. I watch the man place them both in small velvet pouches and put them into boxes.

We sing carols on our way back to the Brown Palace. J.W. drops us off, and he goes on to Peggy's for the night. As a family, we sit around the Christmas tree, listening to the harpist and drinking mulled hot cider.

Morning comes early, and my first thoughts are of Mac. I'm hoping to see him today. A knock comes at the door. A bellman is holding a silver tray with an envelope upon it. He extends his arms. I ask him to wait, and I give him a tip. I sit down on the settee. It's from Mac.

Dear Alex,
I heard you arrived safely in Denver. I'm looking forward to seeing you at Peggy's Christmas Eve. I know J.W. is your date for the wedding. However, I thought we could spend the 26th together. I have a special place I want to take you for dinner, and your family is welcome to come. I'm staying at my sister's while I'm in Denver. If you like, you may contact me there.
Sincerely,
Mac

My hands are shaking, and my heart takes a leap. I'm anxious to see him.

Becky and Aunt Jenny come to my room at ten o'clock. We are wrapping our gifts together. The bookstore had a marvelous selection of ribbons and paper. This is the first time I've ever bought papers for wrapping packages. They're gorgeous, and we all bought dozens of colorful twines and ribbons. Nothing is too good for this celebration.

We order a tray of fancy sandwiches, hot tea and red ribbon cakes for our lunch. Sitting on the floor next to the fire, we wrap our packages while the snow is falling outside.

We all have new dresses for this evening and are looking forward to meeting J.W.'s and Mac's family. I give them a detailed description of the elaborate Bouvier mansion.

Later in the afternoon, Becky and I meet with the chef in the kitchen to plan our Christmas dinner menu. He suggests roast turkey, turnip mashed potatoes, cranberry relish, sage and celery stuffing, gravy, glazed carrots, scalloped oysters, buttered corn, green beans and a fruit salad. For a dessert, we choose a variety; a warm fig pudding with a heavy brandy sauce, apple pie and pecan tarts.

I'm so excited for so many reasons I can hardly stand it. Aunt Jenny has gone back to her room to take a leisurely nap. Becky and I come back to my room and lay by the fire. It's our first moment alone together.

"I have something I want to share with you."

"What? Tell me?"

"William and I have talked about moving to Durango!"

"What? You're joking."

"No, I'm serious. He's the one who brought it up."

"I can't believe it."

"It's true. He's so good to me, Alex. He said he knows how much I miss you."

"Oh, you're going to make me cry."

"Don't cry, please, and I can't say for sure yet."

"But don't you like living in Baltimore?"

"Yes, but without you or John, I feel so alone."

"I know that feeling. Oh, I would love to have you near."

"I want to thank you for sending my things. The day they arrived I was alone and when I opened the trunks, one by one, I sobbed." Becky starts to cry. I embrace her.

"Now who's crying, silly?"

"It was like everything I touched came alive, Mother's quilt, Father's pipes; everything spoke to me. It was then I realized how foolish I am. I don't want to bring up the horrible stuff about Father, but I find it hard to keep it from my thoughts."

"I understand. It's the same for me. I don't like it either."

"I've been writing John practically every day discussing my thoughts, both good and bad. It's helped me to get to where I am now. At least I'm coping with it. I mean that the possibility horrifies me."

"You're not alone. No one would ever dream of such a terrible thing."

We talk and dry each other's tears, bathing our faces with cold compresses so we don't look as if we have been crying. We worry that the Bouviers might think we were drinking all day.

"We need to change the subject," I admonish.

"Good. Tell me something wonderful. Tell me about you."

"J.W. Reynolds has proposed to me, but I have turned him down."

"You're just now telling me? When did this take place?"

"He proposed after we got back from Savannah."

"Oh my gosh, Alex; I thought you were in love with him."

"I do love him, but not like I love Mac."

"But last I knew, Mac was out of the picture. Are you sure that's wise?"

"Now don't start; we've had a really good day."

"I'm not; but you can't blame me for being concerned about you."

"Thank you, but I'll figure it out."

Chapter Thirty-Five: CHRISTMAS EVE

We decide it's time to freshen up and dress for dinner. The men had lunch together and played cards and billiards until five. That gave us time to bathe and dress for an evening out.

I take a long soak and reminisce about Mac's visit at Thanksgiving. I dream, but I wonder what kind of relationship we may have together. I'm certain I want Mac McClellan in my life; but in his line of work, I can expect him to be away most of the time. I think I'm putting the cart before the horse, as he hasn't asked me to marry him.

I want to look my very best. I will be meeting Shannon McClellan, Mac's mother, J.W.'s aunt who raised him. I splurge and have a beauty worker from the hotel come up to do my hair. I've spent a lot of my savings so far, but this is a special time. I'll just have to work harder when I get home to put some money aside for a rainy day. Mother always said, "Women need to be able to take care of themselves." I believe she was way ahead of her time. From what I have read in one of Mother's first journals, my grandmother was too. Mother talked about her mother taking on a whole group of women in Savannah as she defended her views against the war. Women in those days did not voice their opinions, and if they did so, there could be consequences.

Finishing with my toiletries, I use a hint of color on my face and dab a little of my best perfume behind my ears. I'm wearing a dress Aunt Jenny has designed; she reminds me so much of Mother. The dress is made of black cherry colored crepe, with a square-neck cut just above my bosom, sleeveless and with a full skirt. The bodice is dotted with black seed pearls backed by sequins. I look into the mirror and pull a few soft curls down around my face. I brought Mother's single black pearl necklace. It goes perfectly with the dress. It's simple, yet elegant. I read it was a gift to Mother from Doc Henry Holliday. I can't wait to read her entire journal on the trip home. I look at it closely in the mirror, "Mother, I'm wearing this for you tonight." Instantly, I smell a whiff of gardenias, one of my mother's favorite flowers. I think she approves.

One last look, I'm ready. In the lobby, I wait for the others. My stomach is full of butterflies, thinking about being with Mac and J.W. in the same room.

It's not long till the family gathers, and we take the carriages to the Bouvier mansion on Capitol Hill. The sky is cloudy, and huge snowflakes are floating in the air. We are covered with heavy wool blankets trying to keep warm. The carriage takes us across town to the Hill. We pass Margaret Brown's mansion. She is one very humble woman, and as sharp as a pin. She comes from regular folk and entered into the high society of the rich after her husband struck gold. I enjoyed speaking with her at Peggy's party last July. Too bad Peggy's guests aren't all like Margaret Brown.

The carriage circles the drive, and the driver stops in front of the house by the nine-foot double doors. They are dressed with huge evergreen wreaths and ribbons. I look at Aunt Jenny and Becky's face.

"I see what you mean, Alex," Aunt Jenny says.

"Yes, you were not exaggerating when you said their home was like a castle," Becky agrees.

Streaks of light emanate from every window of the mansion, making the snow look as if it is scattered diamonds. For as much as Peggy likes everything perfect, I bet she shoos the deer off her property so there are no hoof prints.

"It is a grand place. Let me help you down, ladies," William states.

Peggy and Philip are there to greet us at the door, wearing their holiday attire.

"Come on in, folks. It's so nice of you to join us on Christmas Eve," Philip says.

"Peggy, Philip. It's so nice of you to have us," I say happily.

The foyer is breathtaking. A five-foot centerpiece sits on the large marble and gold gilded table, and the grand staircase is swathed with evergreens and red and white silk ribbons. The house smells of bayberry, pine and citrus, and the marble floors reflect the light and colors and shine as if they're ice. A doorman takes our wraps. I introduce my family to the Reynolds and the Bouviers. We're shown to the parlor and served drinks and hor d'oeuvres. Philip puts everyone at ease, for the surroundings are more than a little pretentious. It is nice to see J.P. Reynolds, Maggie and the girls. The girls are all talking at once, and they're so proud to show me their new gowns. And, they have to tell me all about the shops they have already visited here in Denver. It's fun to hear them bubbling with excitement.

I'm introduced to Shannon Connor McClellan. She's very beautiful, tall and slender, small boned with an ivory complexion, stunning red hair and deep green eyes that match the color of her gown. J.W. says he loves her like his mother, and it is not a secret that his father J.P. thinks much of her too. She looks like royalty, and her actions suggest the same. We are told that Mac and Peggy's father, Shawn McClellan, will not be joining us. He is home in Ireland and could not make the trip. They say he hardly travels across the water, although he has business in Boston. I notice as Shannon holds out her hand, on her index finger she wears an emerald cut diamond, larger than any I've ever seen, and a ruby pendant hangs from her neck the size of a cherry.

"Alexandra, I've heard a lot about you. That is what you liked to be called?"

"Alexandra is fine. It's a pleasure to be here tonight, Mrs. McClellan."

"Please call me Shannon. So tell me, I understand you are in town for your brother's wedding?"

"Yes, they couldn't join us this evening and send their regrets. They are having a special dinner with the bride's family this evening."

"We understand. How very nice for them."

"Thank you. The wedding is tomorrow morning before Christmas mass."

"Maggie tells me you visited the Reynolds plantation with my nephew J.W., in September."

"I did, and it is lovely. I had a wonderful time."

"How nice. It's my favorite place in the world. My nephew and my son have talked a lot about you."

"J.W. tells me that you practically raised him."

"Yes. My sister died right after his birth. Maggie, J.W.'s grandmother, and I are his mothers."

"Well, it's fortunate for him to have you both in his life."

"Why thank you. By the way it sounds, both J.W. and Mac have an interest in you. How charming."

"They're delightful men."

"I feel the same. I pray there's a reasonable outcome to this infatuation, and no one gets wounded. I love them both. I hear J.W. coming in now."

He looks dashing in his tails. We make eye contact, and I smile warmly as he makes his approach.

"Aunt Shannon, don't you look lovely this evening."

"You look debonair. You make me very proud. J.W. Just who are you going to slay this evening?" Shannon asks. "You see, Alexandra, my son and nephew are among the most handsome, eligible men in the state."

"Aunt Shannon, you're biased."

"That may be true, but Alexandra feels the same way. Don't you?"

I smile, thinking that it probably is true. J.W. looks me up and down.

"Victoria, you look lovely this evening. I see my Aunt Shannon is filling you with nonsense."

"Hello, J.W."

He kisses her and gives me a peck on the cheek.

"Where is Mac?" J.W. asks.

"I believe he's doing Peggy a favor."

"So, he's in town? Good, I have some business to discuss."

My heart drops.

"Yes, he got in early this morning, from Leadville, I believe he said. We're expecting him any time. I hope nothing is wrong. You sound so serious," Shannon says in a concerned voice.

"Nothing for you to worry about, Auntie. It's just business."

"I've learned from your uncle when a man says, 'it's just business', something is happening."

"Philip and I are taking care of things."

"Good. Alexandra and I are talking about South Carolina and the plantation."

We hear Mac's voice echoing in the hall. My heart skips a beat, and I feel my throat close. The anticipation of being at his side this evening is of the upmost significance. I'm so eager to have this time with him. I've been dreaming about this for a month. I'm stressing, thinking about being at Peggy's with J.W. and Mac here together. I need to relax. I'm among family and friends. Even Peggy doesn't seem as if she wants to throw me to the wolves tonight. On my last visit, I was here with J.W., and that's when Peggy found out it was I whom Mac wrote home about. Mac knew me as Alex and J.W. knew me as Vicky. I do not care to relive that night again.

"I do believe that there's the man now," J.W. says.

"Good, I think everyone is here," Shannon says.

I smile as he steps around the corner, and my heart leaps. A second later, my eyes go wide, seeing a stunning woman on his arm. My heart drops to my feet, my knees grow weak, and I'm dazed.

J.W. says in a monotone, "Now there's a surprise, Elizabeth Van Buren. I thought she married."

"One could only hope," Shannon says softly.

J.W. looks at me. I try to hide my astonishment, but I'm not very good at it. I already feel the heat rising to my cheeks as my eyes meet Mac's across the room. I feel as if I've been caught between a clap of thunder. What in the world is he doing here with another woman? Shannon sees my distress and takes my hand.

"J.W., why don't Alexandra and I have a drink. Will you be so kind?"

"I'm sorry. I'll get the two prettiest women in the room champagne," he says with a hospitable smile.

"Oh, child, I see by your expression you have a sincere interest in my son, and just maybe it goes deeper than that. You never know who he's going to have by his side."

"Do you know her?" I ask.

"She's Elizabeth Van Buren from Louisiana, daughter of big money, whose fortune lies in oil. She's a friend of Peggy's. The two girls went to school together. She's a Southern beauty; but there's something about her that cries out, 'beware'. I have no idea what Mac is doing with her. He mentioned that you would be here this evening, and he said he was looking forward to our little gathering."

"I admit my bubble has burst. Forgive me, but I must take a seat," I say fighting back the tears. "She's very beautiful," I whisper.

"Oh yes, and she knows it. I don't imagine she knows about you."

"I could have sworn Mac intended for me to be his date this evening. He invited me to dinner the day after Christmas. If he wants my company, you would think he would not flaunt another in my face."

"True, so what's this about bringing another woman into the lion's den? I think this may be Peggy's idea. She likes to plan interesting evenings."

Mac takes Elizabeth around the room to introduce her to everyone.

J.W. comes back with the champagne.

"Ladies."

"Thank you," I say.

"Vicky, if you're okay with Aunt Shannon, I thought I'd make sure the captain is being tended to."

A familiar gentleman's voice speaks from behind. "How about taking care of me too? I can use a drink."

Without turning, J.W. replies, "That voice can always use a drink." He turns around, "Merry Christmas, Lorenzo. Glad to see you could make it."

"Thank you for the invitation. This is one of the few houses in which I'm still welcome."

"This is my sister's house, but you can always call wherever I am, your home."

"Mrs. McClellan, Alexandra, you look lovely tonight."

"We're glad you're here, Lorenzo. I'm sure your mother misses you," Shannon says.

"I'd like to think so."

"Hello, Lorenzo, it's good to see you again," I say warmly.

"Good to see you too. We do make the circuit, don't we? Alex was kind enough to invite me for Thanksgiving dinner. She's a marvelous cook."

"I'm sorry it was so meager compared to this."

"No need to apologize. Your place is very comfortable. It's all about friendship."

"Let me get you a drink," J.W. says.

"I think Philip is already getting me one, but thank you."

"What are you doing this far north, Lorenzo?" Shannon asks.

"I've come to participate in the Dead Man's Hand, a poker competition at the Palace on New Year's Eve. I'll never be Doc Holliday, but that's my goal. He was the best western gambler, with just the right mixture of authority and manners."

Lorenzo is dressed flamboyantly, a gentleman pirate in a cut-away coat with black satin lapels. He sports a ruffled white shirt beneath a gold brocade waist coat, tailored trousers of a matador with a crimson sash, and leather knee-high boots with a high buff shine.

"That's a dashing outfit you have, I think you've outdone me. Are you carrying?" J.W. asks lightheartedly.

"Of course not. This is party," he says with good-humor. "It would be in poor taste for me to carry a pistol."

"But I do see you have a cane, which matches your attire."

"Now, this here is a weapon. It is supposed to have belonged to Doc Holliday. It has his initials engraved here."

"It's a pretty intricate handle," J.W. comments.

"Isn't she lovely? A nude carved from ivory," Lorenzo points out.

"John Henry Holliday ... isn't it ironic that both of us have on something of his tonight?" I say.

"Really?" Lorenzo asks and J.W. is all ears. Between finger and thumb, I take the black pearl I'm wearing around my neck to show them.

"This was my mother's, a single black pearl," I say, as I fondle it. "John Henry gave it to her. They were good friends before I was born. They met in Dodge City."

"You don't say," Lorenzo replies. "Tell me more."

"I also have a pistol that he won at the tables playing poker. He gave that to Mother too.

He taught her to shoot before she went west on the Santa Fe Trail. I never knew him myself, but I would have liked to."

"Your mother and he were friends? I'd like to hear more about it sometime," Lorenzo says as he looks at his cane.

"I'd be glad to tell you what I know."

"I'd like to hear too," J.W. says inquisitively.

Philip heads in this direction with drinks in hand, and the three men start to talk of a Daniel Caruthers. Apparently, he is a partner of J.W.'s and Philip's. However, by the sound of the conversation, he's not well liked. The three men ease away, talking business.

"I see Elizabeth is meeting your family," Shannon says.

"Yes, my sister is looking my way. I should make my way over to them."

"Of course. I know Elizabeth. She thinks the world of Mac. However, she thinks more of herself and Mac knows this. He's not one to be fooled. They used to court one another in college. I thought, at one time, she'd be my daughter-in-law. J.W. dated her for a short time too. He said she was definitely not his type. Neither of them cares for showy women. I guess that is why they like you." My eyes go wide. What does she mean? "What I mean to say is, that you are warm, considerate and genuine."

"I will take that as a compliment."

"You may my dear. It is meant to be."

Mac and Elizabeth come our way, meeting the three men first. J.W. says hello to Mac and Elizabeth. I know he's said something because they causally look in my direction. This is the first time I've seen the men side by side. They are different, yet alike in so many ways. My hands tremble. Shannon places hers on mine.

"You like both J.W. and my Mac, and I hear both men are infatuated with you. You're a prime candidate to be in our family, one way or another. If you don't mind my saying, don't be intimidated by Elizabeth. She and half the women in Denver are after these two men. You're a beautiful young woman, and you must be very special to get my boys' attention."

"I'm not like the other women. I've never been after either of the men. I'm not a chaser, Mrs. McClellan."

"Of course not. Come, let us mingle, shall we?"

Chapter Thirty-Six: VAN BEAUTIFUL

Peggy and Philip joyfully lead us into the great dining room. She has set the table for royalty, with candelabras and flowers. The back of each dining chair is decorated with swags of evergreen and large satin bows. The room looks like something out of a fairy tale. The amber light reflects the lit candles in the room, making everything shine of crystal, china and silver. Peggy shows the men to their seats, and Philip shows the women. At each place setting, there is a place card with each guest's name. My heart is racing while waiting to see who will be sitting on the other side of the table. Mac and Elizabeth enter the room. *Oh no, please don't let them be seated by me.* Too late, they are standing right in front of me talking to J.W.'s grandmother, Maggie. Becky comes to my side.

"Are you alright? What is going on," she whispers in my ear. "I thought…"

"Me too, but I guess I thought wrong. I can't believe he would do this."

"There must be an explanation," Becky says.

"Just wait. We are going to be sitting together; I know it."

The host and hostess invite us to take our seats. J.P. Reynolds pulls out my chair and takes the seat next to me, and Becky takes her seat next to J.P. Reynolds. J.W. comes over, kisses me on my cheek, whispering, "You're the most beautiful woman here."

"Thank you, J.W., how thoughtful." Even now, he is supportive.

Glancing at the end of the table, Peggy sits like a queen. She is glowing and gives me a flippant smile. I thought we were friends. After all, she invited my family as her guests. What have I ever done to her? The last time we spoke, she had kind words.

A waiter places a napkin in my lap. I look across the table. Mac smiles, I want to die. I can't sit here with this torture. My breath catches in my throat as I watch him circle the table. He comes to my side.

"Alex, you look beautiful this evening," he takes my hand, and, before I realize what's happening, kisses me hard on the lips.

"You look ravishing this evening, dove," he says loudly, so everyone may hear. He flashes a devilish grin, and my fears begin melting away. "I'm sorry I arrived late, and we didn't get a chance to talk." I'm silent. "I had to see to a friend. I don't think you have met Elizabeth Van Buren?"

She is flawless, tall and slender with raven hair, porcelain skin and delicate features. I notice her jewelry. She wears diamonds and sapphires that are as big as my eyes. Her gown is midnight blue velvet with a white satin sash. It's fabulous and very expensive. She is beautiful. I can't image any man not wanting her in his bed. She must have many suitors, but she makes it no secret that she has eyes for Mac. I'm sure that isn't all she has for Mac.

Poised, I reply, "No, I have not," forcing a smile.

"Elizabeth, this is Victoria Highland. She goes by Alex."

"It's nice to meet you, Alex. Your gown is lovely. Peggy told me you are a seamstress and have a small shop in a frontier town … what is it called … Durango?"

"Yes, I do have my own place."

"Maybe I will engage you to make my next party dress," she says with a smirk. How dare she degrade me?

"I'm sorry, I only design for the upper echelon."

"I didn't know there were any upper echelon in Durango."

"Actually, we have indoor plumbing, telephones and alternating current, just like the other frontier town … San Francisco, for example. But Durango had it first. You know, they are so behind."

Mac bends down and whispers, "Ouch. There's a little jealously. That's my girl."

I turn from my chair, toward him, whispering, "Are you senseless? Of course there is. Look at her. She's perfect."

"She is no match for you. Play nice," he says with a sassy grin and goes back to take his seat. While circling, he asks the waiter to bring him a double and stops to shake Uncle's hand.

"What is it that you do, Elizabeth?" I ask with a cold smile.

"Anything I want to," she answers for only me to hear.

She changes her attitude like a chameleon changes color. Peggy is doing her best to put Elizabeth between us. She must be jealous of my relationship with her brother and cousin. She's evidently been the center of attention for too long. Why else would she go to such lengths to put pins in me?

Feeling heat in my face, I take a sip of wine from my glass. I look at his mother seated next to Peggy; she smiles and takes a drink. Mrs. McClellan is right. Peggy is a game player. I wonder where she has learned her moves. I don't feel as if Shannon approves of Peggy's games, but I'm not sure she approves of me either. Appraising the situation, being the outsider, I believe Mac's mother would choose Elizabeth over me. She's schooled and rich. Money attracts money, is what I've heard. However, it's neither Shannon's nor Peggy's decision; it's Mac's. My question is, why didn't Mac refuse to be her escort? Did he really think it wouldn't be a problem? That's it. He didn't think.

I smile and make conversation with Aunt Jenny. I look at Mac. He takes a gulp of whiskey from his glass before sitting. Elizabeth can't do enough to get his attention. She wants him all to herself. I see her hand leave the table ever so delicately, and by the look on Mac's face, she is doing what she can to get his full, undivided attention. I'd like to slap her. He stretches his leg out to touch mine, and I pull back. I'm sore at him for not taking my feelings into account, but I'm surprised he displays such affection for me in front of the others. His cheeks are rosy. I wonder how many drinks he's had. Philip asks us to bow our heads; he gives thanks, and dinner is served. It takes all my will to keep my emotions intact. I take a deep breath and sip my wine and sip some more. I like its warming effects. It's relieving my tension. I'm running through frontier terms that are not suitable for the table. I must not let any improper remarks come out. I had better watch my drink.

"So Alex, I hope you had an uneventful trip," Mac says as he sees the server pour me another glass of wine.

"Yes, the tracks were clear. However, heavy snow started to fall after leaving Silverton. When did you get into town?"

"Early this morning. I came in from Leadville."

At least he has the same story as his mother told us. He tries to make conversation, and I try to talk to anyone but him.

"You still have a little color on your face," Mac comments.

"You know what they say," Elizabeth chimes in. "You should protect your face and stay out of the sun."

"I just spent time in the tropics, and I'd much rather have a rosy glow than look like paste."

She gives me a slight leer.

"I like that you have a little color. You look healthy," Mac says warmly.

"Thank you."

A trio of musicians begins playing dinner music. I hear partial conversations at the dinner table that are very interesting.

J.P. says he would have loved to have been in England to see the opening of the Tower of London Bridge this year, and makes a point of how important it is, at his age, to do the things one has always wanted to do. Aunt Jenny and Uncle agree.

Abigail, J.W.'s half-sister, is intrigued with John talking of Paris and shares her desire to see the Eiffel Tower. It was built in 1889 as the entrance to the World's Fair. She says Paris sounds like the most romantic city in the world and she wants to visit desperately. Teresa shares the exciting features about living in Paris, telling the girls how magnificent it was seeing the ballet premier, "L'aprés-midi d'un faune" of Debussy, and visiting the Louvre Museum where they saw the *Venus de Milo*, the *Victory of Samothrace* and Leonardo da Vinci's, 16th century *Mona Lisa*. It sounds fascinating to me. Mother always wanted to go. Her mother came from France. Mother died too young, before she could fulfill her dreams.

At the other end of the table, Christopher and Pamela are exchanging their views on the new comic section published in the New York City *Times* Sunday edition. Pamela shares her desire to become a journalist for an important city newspaper, such as San Francisco or Boston. All these wonderful conversations are taking place, and I sit like a bump on a log. I can't seem to think while I'm stuck with Elizabeth Van Beautiful. I debate on whether to try to have another conversation with her, but decide to let sleeping dogs lie.

The wine flows freely around the table. The servers file in with a bounty of holiday side dishes; stuffing, cranberry sauce, carrots, with a variety of potato dishes ... roasted, mashed, baked and boiled, and a special spicy pressed beef loaf (one hot and one cold). And lastly, four perfectly roasted fowls on huge silver trays surrounded by grapes, oranges and herbs and a Christmas goose. It all looks wonderful, but I find it is an unusual combination. I must have had a peculiar look on my face as the dishes of food are being set because Mac says, "It's a typical Irish Christmas dinner. I hope you enjoy it."

"Everything looks delicious," I answer.

I make my choices. There is so much food to choose from. Elizabeth is watching my every move, as if she is grading me on my table etiquette. How much longer do I have to look at her? She's flawless, making me completely lose my appetite.

For dessert, we have Christmas cake, decorated with marzipan and icing and made with delicious vine fruits, cherries and French brandy.

Philip says, "It is our holiday tradition, after our Christmas Eve meal, to set the table again with bread filled with raisins and caraway seeds and a pitcher of milk. This year, we need to do more. We were going to take Christmas dinner to the shelter by the riverfront; but another family made plans first, so we decided we'd take our dinner to the shelter on the twenty-sixth. Anyway, it will take us day and night to prepare what is needed. We plan to take six whole hams and all the fixings. I feel that it's our duty to take care of those less fortunate."

"Here, here!" J.P. cheers.

"There are many out in the cold tonight," Mac adds.

"We would also like to contribute to the cause, if it's not too late," J.P. chimes in.

Everyone applauds.

"It's never too late," Philip says.

"I would like to volunteer my services, and make a donation, if you need help taking the food to the shelter," Lorenzo offers.

"Thank you, Lorenzo," Philip answers.

Uncle Scotty says he would like to make a donation as well.

Denver, along with other cities, is severely hurting financially after the government's devaluation of silver. Thousands of men and women are out of work and are homeless. I overheard on the way here that some train companies are giving away tickets to help take people to other states to find work; but for many, there's nowhere to go, so they search for the next opportunity. Many a business has closed, banks too, and with no insurance, people have lost their savings.

We take hands after dinner. Mac rises to make a toast.

"Bless everyone Father, Lord of all. We ask for peace and goodwill for all men."

"Amen," we say in unison.

"Shall we move into the parlor?" Philip asks.

We stand and move into the parlor, chatting as we go. Shannon shares an old family recipe as she pours us Irish coffee.

SHANNON'S IRISH COFFEE
Warm a stemmed whiskey goblet.
Pour in one shot of Irish whiskey.
Drop in three white sugar cubes.
Fill the goblet with strong black coffee, leaving an inch from the rim.
Stir very gently.
Slowly pour heavy cream over the back of a spoon, filling the goblet.
The cream should float on top of the coffee.
Do not stir. Sip this drink through the cream for full flavor
(For today's drink, buy cream without any additives or it will mix with your coffee.)

Elizabeth makes it obvious she doesn't want to share Mac. She clings to him, using all of her Southern charms and trying her very best to hold his attention. Abigail and the girls play the piano and sing carols. I sit with the women but I overhear J.W. and Philip talking about business with the man named Caruthers.

Afterward, we move into the ballroom where Philip lights a decorated twelve-foot tree. It's beautiful. The musicians play music to dance too. Mac comes to me.

"Will you dance with me," he asks.

"I thought you were engaged with Elizabeth's company?"

"It's not what you think. She's a wart on my behind tonight. I don't know what her issue is … wait a minute, I do know. She's jealous of you," he says loudly.

"Hush… it's your whiskey talking. I wouldn't normally say anything, but I don't want to see you embarrass yourself."

"Embarrassed? We're Irish. We *are* an embarrassment. No one on the hill wants us here except the Browns. Have you ever met Margaret Brown, now *she's* a woman."

"Actually, I have."

"You have? You do get around."

"Yes. I like her, and I like her attitude."

He takes my hand, and we waltz away from the rest, sweeping around the dance floor. He pulls me close and whispers with heavy whiskey breath. "Why don't you meet me in the hall? We'll get away from here," he says with a heated stare. When the music stops, he kisses my hand. I excuse myself to go to the powder room. When I come out, he is waiting. We hear the doorbell ring. Peggy and Philip have more company, and a dozen or so couples join us. There's much noise between the introductions and the music. Philip is passing out cigars, and some of the men gather and go into the billiard room, while the women insist Peggy show them the west wing she's decorated for Christmas. Mac quickly takes me by the arm, and we duck into a dark corner. The girls enter the hall chatting, but do not see.

Chapter Thirty-Seven: THE LIBRARY

We kiss with my back against the wall.

"This is the perfect time for me to steal you away. Come." He takes me by the hand, and we flee up the main staircase. My eyes dart right and left to make sure we have not been seen.

Whispering, "Mac someone might miss us."

"Not for a while. Peggy has the brood."

The musicians strike a tune, and the music echoes to the hall above. The only other sound is the clicking of our heels. We enter the library through large mahogany doors. I know because Philip had previously taken me on tour on my first visit to the mansion. Inside, it is quiet. The moonlight streams in from the twelve-foot leaded glass windows. The cool white light bleaches all colors, making the room surreal. Affectionately, he pulls me to him. His breath rises and falls. He's hungry, and it excites me. Our lips meet feverishly. His tongue invades, but it's soft as velvet. He smothers me with ardent kisses that grow stronger.

"God, you look gorgeous. I couldn't wait to taste your sweet lips." He dances me across the room in the milky cascading light, backing me up to the desk.

"Mac I can't..." I whisper, "Someone may come in."

"No one will come." He takes me in his arms. "Tell me you want me, love, for I need you badly."

I feel his hardness against me and start to whisper my response as he practically bruises my lips with his. His hands are all over me.

"I couldn't get to you fast enough. You lit my fire as soon as I stepped into the room."

A flashback of Elizabeth on his arm is disturbing, and I push him away. "What about her?"

"What about whom?"

"Elizabeth."

"Elizabeth? What about her? She's nothing to me."

"Friend of the family? It didn't look that way to me."

He gives me a devilish grin and says, "She with me? Did it anger you, dove? I see fire in your eyes."

"Damn you! Don't be too sure of yourself, Mac McClellan."

"Look, dove, if I wanted her, I wouldn't be here with you right now. Would I?"

He clears the end of the massive desk in one sweep. He lays me back onto the cold leather top. Breasts spilling from my dress, my nipples are taut. He quickly pulls off his tie, discards his coat, and has his vest half-unbuttoned before my next breath. He steals a kiss in between his movements, and his clothes are dropping to the floor. Unbuttoning his shirt, I swear I can almost hear the pounding of his heart, but I can't, for mine is beating wildly. The sight of his bare chest feeds my frenzy and my desires. I shouldn't let him take me here, but why not? I want him now more than ever.

"You should know better than to show me so much flesh, dove."

His hot lips devour mine. Eagerly, he nibbles my neck down to the hard peaks of my bosom. His touch is intoxicating. He pushes my dress up to my hips. A chill runs through me as my bottom touches the cold leather top of the desk. He stands and relishes the view of my long, legs with fancy garters and stockings. I see his face light in total surprise when he sees I have no panties on. He rubs his chin and brazenly grins, shaking his head side to side as if to say he doesn't believe it. He opens his trousers and lets them fall, and with hands behind my knees, he pulls me to him. I experience a rush of sexual energy as his curly hair brushes against my valley, heightening my senses. With his tongue, he tastes me, holding me in the palm of his hands. The feeling is so intense I can't move, and I search for something to grab onto.

"Take me, I beg you."

Diving into the warm ocean that makes a man weak in his knees, he takes me fully. The sight of him in motion is erotic, and leaves me burning to open and take him deeper. I try to contain my desire, but a moan escapes my throat as I wrap my legs around his neck.

"Ooh, you're a greedy little thing; I love it when you're wanting," he says in a sultry voice.

He is a god, having his way with me in the moonlight. I stifle my cries of passion; he takes another deep thrust, and I am reeling with him from the scorching pleasure. He lifts me to him to muffle my cry. The pleasure is beyond what I've ever experienced. We hear voices.

"Mac…oh God. I look as if I've been tossed."

"You have, love, and I'll gladly take the credit," Mac says grinning.

"That's not funny. Don't embarrass me. Help me. I need to find a place to fix my hair and cool down."

He takes me by the hand, leading me to a small water closet.

"You will find what you need in here."

I freshen as quickly as I can. Mac opens the door to the balcony; the cold night air instantly helps revive us.

"You are beautiful," he says, as his thumb caresses my face, looking into my eyes. "I love you, Alexandra. I always have and always will." I want to savor the moment. This is what I've been waiting to hear. I take his lips, kissing him tenderly, "I love you too. I fell in love with you on the dance floor. The first night we met, you stole my heart."

We have finally spoken those tender and intimate words, and I long to stay in his arms forever.

IN THE DARK

Mac says softly, "I'll make my way back to the party, and you come down when you're ready." He goes to the door, and I follow. We kiss, and he leaves me. I walk back to the balcony for one more breath of cold air, hoping it will take the excess heat from my body and my color will return to normal. I look up at the stars before closing the balcony doors. I want to rejoice and shout to the world, telling them Mac is in love with me, but for now, I must be content. My eyes well with warm tears, and I wipe them away, "I wish you were here, Mother. Merry Christmas."

Exiting into the dark hallway, I pray for an opportunity to ease back into the party without anyone knowing I left. I close the massive doors. The heavy latch is noisy and echoes. I see someone in the dark shadows of the hall smoking. The amber glow tells me someone is there. J.W. steps out into the dim light.

Startled, I hold my chest. "Oh, it's you J.W."

"I didn't mean to startle you. Are you alright? You sound winded."

"Yes, I am fine. I just needed to get away from the crowd for a bit."

"Me too. I was just going to venture into the library, but it sounded occupied." I feel guilty, and my heart is pounding as if I am hiding a deep, dark, secret. "I guess everyone had the same idea. I saw Mac come out and decided to give you time to get yourself together."

"I'm sorry you had to see."

"I didn't see anything, and there is certainly nothing to say."

Damn, I hate that he knows we were together. I would never intentionally hurt him.

"Forgive me, J.W. This wasn't the time or the place…"

He interrupts, "No need to explain. I've been around long enough to know that some days are diamonds, and others are dust."

He leaves me standing there aloof. "Diamonds or dust," I repeat softly. I watch him saunter downstairs. My feet don't want to move. I pick up my dress and go swishing down the hall. Under my breath, I say to myself, *"You're a whore, Victoria. I know it, and J.W. knows it. He's just too much of a gentleman to say it. I think I would feel better if he would have blasted me with the truth."*

I make a quick stop at the bar for a glass of wine, as if I'd been there all along, and then leave by mingling with the other guests who are moving slowly back into the room. Aunt Jenny and Becky give me an inquisitive glance as they converse with the other women. Uncle Scotty enters the room and asks us women if we should call it an evening. I'm delighted as I'm so ready to leave. We start saying our goodbyes. I find Mac's mother.

"We must be going, Mrs. McClellan. The wedding is early tomorrow morning."

"Yes, I understand. We didn't get a chance to talk after dinner. I guess my son kept you to himself." My eyes go wide, and my face turns fifty shades of red. I open my mouth, but words don't come out. I swallow and force a smile. "It's true. He monopolized your time. Don't be embarrassed."

"I'm sure Peggy told you, I did not know they were related. They are both very special to me, and I know they mean everything to you. J.W. had asked me to marry him, but I have declined. I hope we remain friends."

"You don't feel that will be a problem? And is it fair to him?"

"We are adults, and I hope it's not a problem. He's the kindest man I've ever met, and I love him. However, I'm in love with Mac. Mac says he feels the same."

"I thank you for your honesty. They're gown men, and I know they'll work it out. It's not their first dance, and it doesn't surprise me in the least to know they've chosen the same woman. I will look forward to seeing you again. I hope you have a very merry Christmas."

"It's been a pleasure, Mrs. McClellan. Merry Christmas."

Turning away, I say my goodbyes to the rest of the family, including Mac, and thank Peggy and Philip for including us. Peggy says she will bring the girls to an afternoon tea at the Palace. They're staying another two weeks.

"It's a wonderful way to spend an afternoon. I love the Devonshire cream and the fancy cucumber sandwiches," I say.

"Maybe you would like to join us."

"I would love to, if I'm still in town."

J.W. rides back with my aunt and uncle. I ride with Becky and William. Becky whispers, "I noticed you went off with Mac."

"He was showing me the family library. Philip has a large collection of first editions."

"Really, I thought you might have slipped off for a minute alone with him."

I'm glad it is dark out. I know my face is red, and if she could see my eyes, she would know it was much more.

After we arrive back at the hotel, Uncle Scotty tells the family they've been invited to spend Easter at the Reynolds Plantation. Aunt Jenny comments that she will look forward to a spring visit to the Carolinas; it is a beautiful time of year. I believe Uncle has made a couple of new friends with Philip and J.P. Reynolds. George and

Christopher enjoyed meeting the young Reynolds women, Abigail, Pamela, Andrea and Cynthia. They both fancy J.W.'s half-sister, Abigail. I warn him that she has a strong personality and is very spoiled. Boldly, George says he and Abby exchanged addresses. Over all, everyone had a wonderful time.

 The Bouviers sent us off with three large gift baskets of wine, assorted chocolates and nuts and Irish Christmas cakes, along with copies of her grandmother's recipe. It's nice that she is so willing to share.

Irish Christmas Cake

3/4 lb. plus 3 tablespoons butter
1 1/4 cups plus 2 tablespoons flour
3/4 cup candied cherries, chopped coarsely
1 cup sundried raisins
1 cup white raisins
1 1/4 cups dried currants
1 cup of mixed candied dried fruit, minced
2 tablespoons candied angelica, finely chopped
1 1/4 cups sugar
7 eggs
1 teaspoon ground allspice
1 tablespoon salt
1 cup walnuts (chopped
Directions: preheat oven 300 degrees
Butter bottom and sides of 9 x 3 spring form pan- dust with flour.
Combine fruit in a bowl and add one ½-cup flour and toss, set aside
Cream butter and sugar by beating with a wooden spoon.
Beat in eggs one at a time, and then slowly beat in remaining flour, allspice and salt.
Combine nuts and fruit with batter slowly, beating well.
Pour batter into pan and spread evenly.
Bake for 1 1/2 hours or until golden. Use cake tester.
Cool completely before removing from pan.
Serves 8 to 10

J.W. walks me to our room. He is staying at the Palace overnight and is to be my guest for John's wedding. It feels complicated, but I don't want it to be. After our goodnights with the family, it's just the two of us. I say to J.W., "I must tell you, Mac visited over Thanksgiving."

"I know about him coming to Durango. I ran into him last week and he told me. I know it was more than dinner, Vicky. We have no secrets between us; we agreed last July that we would see where this would go. I told him I asked you to marry me, and you hadn't given me an answer. I was still hoping you would say yes. I respect Mac. We surely do have good taste in women," he says with a soft chuckle.

"I want us to be friends," I say softly.

"You're more than my friend, Vicky, but that's my quandry."

"You're making this hard."

"I don't want you to be uncomfortable. I don't have to go tomorrow."

"I want you to come, if you want to."

"I will attempt to come as your friend, nothing more."

We go inside. I retreat to a hot bath while J.W. leaves the room. I surmise he is going down to the Grand Salon for a game of poker. Relaxing in the tub, I think about Mac making love to me in the library. I immediately feel aroused. He has such an effect on me. I can't believe we did what we did. I let myself get out of control. I would be so ashamed if anyone found out. The company I keep has influenced me. When would I have never worn panties? I pick up my clothes, scolding myself. Vicky and Alexandra seem to be folding into one. That is not what I had planned. I pick up my clothes and go to bed.

I hear J.W come in after midnight. I slip on my robe and go out to the parlor. He is standing by the fireplace with his arms extended as if he is holding up the mantel. He turns when he hears me enter the room.

"Hey, I thought I heard you come in."

"I was trying to be quiet. I didn't want to wake you. I was just thinking about getting another room. This seems a little awkward."

"We're adults and friends, aren't we?"
"Yes, but what about Mac?"
"What about him?"
"I don't want to make things difficult."
"What, by us sharing a room? We have two bedrooms."
"As long as you're alright with it, I don't have a problem."
"So why don't we relax and get some rest. You must be tired, J.W."
"A little. You looked beautiful tonight."
"Thank you."
"Did you have a good time?"
"Yes. Everyone did. You heard them on the way home; the whole family enjoyed themselves."
"Good."

I sit down on the settee, patting the cushion with my hand. "Come sit with me." He takes a seat. He looks at me and smiles. I place my hand on his leg and put his hand over top of mine. He looks down at them and then brings my hand to his lips, kissing my palm. Without a word, we gaze at the fire. He places his arm around me and pulls me closer. I look up and kiss his cheek.

"You're a good man, J.W. Reynolds."
"You think so, Victoria?"
"Yes I do. I'm sorry if I've hurt you."
"Don't worry about me. I'll be just fine. You never made a commitment to me. I'm fortunate to have had your company for the last six months. I've enjoyed every minute of it."
"We'll always be friends, won't we?"
"Of course, and I will always cherish you. Maybe someday we'll be family."

He gives me a smile, patting me on the arm. Watching the fire is hypnotic, and I fall asleep. He gently wakes me with a kiss on my temple.

"It's time to go to bed, love," he whispers. We stand, and he takes me by the hand. I kiss him on the cheek.

"Will you wake me at five? I know you are always up."
"I will, love. Get some sleep."

I walk into my room, and close the door. On the table, I see a package. How could I have overlooked this before? The gift is wrapped in pretty shiny red paper tied with thin green satin ribbon and accompanied by a card. I sit down on the edge of the bed, holding the small package. My eyes fill with tears. This man is so sweet. I open the card, it reads:

May the blessing of Christmas be upon you. From your friend, J.W.

I unwrap the gift and open it. I can hardly believe my eyes. Inside are my initials made into a gold pin, V.H,. studded with small, brilliant round diamonds. It's stunning and fit for a queen. *Oh, J.W.,* I whisper to myself, *this is gorgeous.* He shouldn't have. It's so extravagant. I go to the parlor and see his bedroom door is closed. I stand for a moment in front of his door, deciding if I should wake him. I knock and wait. He comes to the door and opens it. I stand speechless, in tears, holding my pin. I throw my arms around his neck. We hold each other, and I sob. Through my tears I say, "It's beautiful, J.W., so beautiful. Thank you."

I run back to my room. "I have a gift for you too." I come back with it.

"You want me to open it now?"

"Yes, please. It's after midnight. Merry Christmas," I say warmly.

He walks out to the settee to sit down, slips the giftwrap off carefully, commenting on how nicely it is wrapped. My back is to him. He turns it around and smiles.

"Where in the world…"

"At the bookstore."

"Where was I?"

"You were outside when I found a table of maps piled high. I started looking. It was meant to be when I found this one in particular. I was so excited. I love old maps, and this one is so artistic. I could hardly keep it a secret."

"The Bahamas. It's beautifully done."

"Look, this is Bimini."

"It's great, Vicky, thank you. I'll be sure to hang it on the wall in the study at the plantation."

"There's a card on the back." He opens it.

Dearest J.W.,
I will never forget the wonderful times that we have shared. You have changed my life, and all for the better. I don't know how I will ever thank you. I hope you know I will always be there for you as you have been for me. No one has ever been so good. Thank you. You are truly my very dearest friend, and that will never change.
Merry Christmas,
Love, Vicky

J.W. leans over and kisses me.

"When I look at this, it will remind me of all the good times, and there's been nothing but good times. It's the perfect gift. Thank you again."

"I'm glad you like it. I love my pin. It's so extravagant and you really shouldn't have."

"I had it made as soon as I got to Denver. I'm glad you like it."

"I love it!"

"We better get to bed, love. Morning will come early. It is already after one o'clock. I will be waking you in just a few hours. Come, I'll tuck you in."

He pulls the sheet over me, tucks it in and kisses me on the forehead. I grab for his hand before he can leave the bedside.

"Merry Christmas, J.W."

"Merry Christmas, Vicky."

Chapter Thirty-Eight: CHRISTMAS MORNING WEDDING

Waking, I rush out to the parlor. J.W. is up, looking out the window.

"Is it snowing?"

"It's coming down, and it's pretty dark." He turns around and says, "Merry Christmas."

"Merry Christmas to you! I'm so excited. It's my first Christmas with family and friends."

"I'm happy for you."

"Is there any coffee?"

"I went down earlier and ordered us breakfast. They should be up in just a few minutes."

"Good, I'll go ahead and take my bath."

"I'll call you."

Completing my toiletries, I slip into my robe and join him. The warm amber glow of a fire makes a warm, cheery, comfortable ambiance.

"I'm excited for John and Teresa starting their union on Christ's birthday. What a perfect day this will be, and we will have a new addition to our family."

"She seems to be a very nice. John is fortunate."

The servers are at the door with our breakfast. J.W. greets them and they roll the breakfast cart inside.

"Please allow me," J.W. says.

"But sir ... we can get that for you."

"Not today, thank you. You are working today, away from your family to make this day special for those of us visiting." J.W. reaches into his pocket and pulls a number of crisp dollars from a roll of green bills and places them in one of the server's hands. The server looks at him in disbelief.

"Do you have a family, sir?" J.W. asks.

"Yes, sir. We all do." The other servers nod as well.

"Good. It's nice to have family, and now you each can add to their Christmas."

The servers thank him over and over. They see themselves out.

"Victoria, they have prepared us a beautiful meal. Come, I will serve you." He pulls out my chair, and I take a seat at the table. I unfold my napkin as he uncovers a platter of freshly baked warm cinnamon rolls, a platter of plump brown sausages and another of eggs cooked over easy, buttered toast, sharp cheese and two bowls of hot baked apples sprinkled with brown sugar and cinnamon, fresh juice and a steaming pot of coffee.

"Thank you, J.W. You made several people very happy this morning."

"Well, I'm happy."

"Tell me what makes you so happy."

"Being here, sharing Christmas morning with you."

"Oh, J.W. You are the sweetest man."

"Thank you for the compliment. I'll give thanks if it's alright with you."

"Yes, please do."

He sits down at the table, and places his hand over mine.

"Lord, I thank you for this day and we wish you a happy birthday. We fuss, prepare and try to make everything perfect, when it already is. Thank you for all your blessings big and small. Let us be your light today and forever more, sharing with friends, family and strangers that will be no more. Amen."

"J.W., that was beautiful. I want you to know I'm extremely thankful for you coming into my life. You have been wonderful. I feel as if we've known each other forever."

"I'm just as fortunate. You're a beautiful, fun-loving woman. I'm glad you're in my life in whatever capacity you choose it to be." I squeeze his hand and give him a warm, heartfelt smile. "Oh," he continued. "I took the liberty this morning to make sure everything is ready for your family dinner this evening. I figured that with everyone just getting into town, they have enough on their minds."

"Thank you. You're welcome to come."

"Thank you, but I think I'll just play Santa and ask to borrow a luggage cart."

"A luggage cart?" I asked.

"After the wedding, I'll load up the Christmas packages from your rooms and take them down to the private dining room and put them under the tree. You'll feel as if you're right at home."

"That is a wonderful idea," I agree.

"Everything should be in place for you and the family to relax and have a beautiful Christmas. I will then go on to Peggy's for our Christmas dinner."

"I wish you could be in both places, but I understand."

"It is exciting that they're all here for Christmas too. Peggy's dinner is at four o'clock. This is the first Christmas Mac and I have spent together in years."

"Oh, J.W., That's wonderful. What did you get him?"

"I had a new saddle made for him in Durango. The last time we went riding he complained his saddle never broke in the way he wanted it to. This one turned out very well. I hope it fits him and that Arapaho and he like it."

"I'm sure he will. What a great idea." I ask what gifts he has in store for his grandmother, Aunt Shannon and the girls. He tells me, and I can see he is excited. "It sounds to me if you've been working on your shopping list for quite some time."

"I have. It gives me great pleasure buying. I have never been much of a shopper except for my clothes. I've done more shopping with you than I ever have on my own."

"Me too, and you made it possible."

We have a very pleasant morning together. I finish dressing and come back into the parlor wearing a gold velvet dress, fitted bodice, full skirt and simple capped sleeves, complemented with white elbow-length gloves. Later, I plan for Christmas dinner, and will add a red sash and red shoes.

"You're a vision this morning, Vicky, but I thought you looked perfect in your robe."

"J.W., you always have the perfect compliment."

"It's not hard when your subject is as pretty as you," he says kissing me on the cheek. He walks over and sets his glass on the mantel. He looks dashing wearing a fine black wool, three-quarter length coat and charcoal grey slacks. His vest is gold and green brocade with an expensive crisp white cotton, embossed paisley print shirt underneath. He's smoothly shaven except for a thin mustache. With his arm outstretched on the mantel, I see his nails have been neatly manicured. Just being in his presence is making it hard for me to resist his charm. I find myself wanting him, and I'm lost in the thought of his bedding me right here in front of the fireplace. I hear him ask, "Are you alright, Victoria? Your face is flushed, and your neck is blotchy, love."

My hand flies to my throat, "Oh, yes. I was just lost in thought for a moment."

"Well, where ever you were, I'd have liked to have been there with you."

If you only knew, I think. He is genuinely handsome. His presence makes it difficult to entertain another thought. J.W. loves life, and I love that about him. I know before the day is over, my best gift of all is J.W's friendship. I will treasure this morning for the rest of my life. He's a special man, and whomever he may marry ... I hope she's good to him. He deserves the very best.

We meet with the family downstairs. We're all excited to have this special time together. We take a carriage to the church, arriving for the morning service at seven forty-five. The service will be in candlelight. The pews are decorated with winter flowers and greens and satin bows. It's the first time I've been to a church this early in the morning. The candles give off a warm, soothing glow, and the music is playing. We meet with Teresa's immediate family and are seated in the first row on the groom's side.

The bride is lovely and is dressed in a simple white velvet gown with a twelve-foot voile train held by flat velvet bows at her shoulders. The gown resembles a medieval style, with an empire waist, long, fitted open sleeves and laced gold cords from shoulders to wrists. The dress is elegant. She wears a diamond tiara with a veil of tulle that is as long as her train.

Teresa's sister Cynthia sings *Ave Maria* at the beginning of the ceremony. John looks handsome and nervous. There is a joyful noise as six trumpets play as she and her father walk down the aisle.

The wedding ceremony is beautiful. When the bride and groom are ready to leave, two white horses pulling a white carriage appear and take them back to the Brown Palace Hotel for the reception. The weather holds until we all arrive, and then it starts to snow heavily.

At the Palace, we greet the newly married couple. Becky, John and all of us have tears in our eyes. Our family is introduced to the rest of Teresa's family and friends. The gala room is decorated all in white with candles, bows, tablecloths, napkins and flowers. It looks like a winter wonderland, glittering. The music plays softly. The specially prepared brunch consists of baked salmon in a creamy white wine sauce, smoked honey-glazed ham; boiled potatoes with parsley; green beans; golden brown waffles with warm maple syrup; fresh whipped cream and peaches; bacon and egg quiche; quail on toast tips; and a vegetable, sausage and rice casserole. For dessert, there are baked apples in a caramel brandy sauce, almond cakes and vanilla egg custards. The bride's father gives a champagne toast.

John and Teresa make a handsome couple, and they seem extremely happy as they open their gifts. They're showered with linens, china, silver and more. They serve the wedding cake and coffee at noon. I go to dance with John and am so proud he is such a fine man. I'm hoping he and Teresa stay in the states; but if not, somehow, I will find a way to go visit them in Paris.

J.W. comes back after leaving to put our gifts under the tree in a private dining room.

"It is time for me to leave."

"I hate that you have to go, but I'm happy that all your family is here too. You have a wonderful time with them."

"I will," he says as we hug. "I need to say my goodbyes to John and Teresa."

"I'll go with you." We wait our turn as others are saying their goodbyes to the bride and groom.

"John and Teresa, the Reynolds' wishes you forever happiness." He hands them an envelope.

"Thank you J.W. We're so glad you could make it. It means a lot to us, especially on this Christmas day."

"Teresa, you are beautiful."

"Thank you J.W. I hope we meet again.

"I'm going to see J.W. to his carriage, John."

"Merry Christmas," Johns says.

"Happy New Year's to you both."

"Thank you," John answers.

"I'll walk to the door with you." Taking his hand, I feel the tears welling up inside me. I'm so emotional. "When will I see you again," I ask.

"Whenever you like. I'll be in town for the next few days, and then I will probably go back east and stay until spring. We'll see. I plan to stay at Peggy's tonight and maybe tomorrow. Aunt Shannon wants the family to stay together for a few nights, at least until New Year's."

"Please wish them a very merry Christmas for me?"

"I will. I enjoyed today Vicky."

"Me too. For some reason, I feel as if we're saying goodbye."

"We are saying goodbye, in a way, but not farewell by any means. I loved being with you, and the way I look at it, our time together was a good way to end the year. I feel fortunate to have met you darling."

I wrap my arms around him holding him tight. I don't want to let him go; but it is my doing. I've chosen Mac over him.

We look into each other's eyes and J.W. says, "You'll always be in my heart Vicky." Trying to make the moment lighter he ends on an upbeat note by taking my chin between his thumb and finger, "This is the first time I've ever been jealous of my cousin."

"I'm sorry," I say as I wipe my tears, and smile with a quivering chin.

"Don't cry and ruin that pretty face of yours. You have to do what your heart tells you. I'll be in town, but I don't think seeing each other too soon will help either of us."

I nod in agreement. His eyes are so blue. I'm so drawn to him. Without hesitation, I take his lips, kissing him long and tenderly. He returns the affection, holding me in his arms. Our eyes connect into a desperate sequester. There is a serious and heartfelt interlude between us. I'm so torn. Without a word, he lets go and walks away. I watch him go out of the door and into a carriage. I run out as the carriage rolls, but for what? I don't know. There's nothing left to say. I watch the carriage disappear into a vale of snow. The cold wind whips my hair into my face, blinding my sight. The doorman says, "Miss, you're going to catch your death without a coat. Please let me take you back inside." He takes me by the arm, and I follow. "Are you alright miss," he asks.

    I can't speak. My heart is in my throat. I nod yes. Inside the hotel, I take a seat next to the window, staring down the road to which he traveled, not that I can see a thing. I just stare. A large part of me feels broken. He's been gone minutes, and I already miss him. *Oh J.W., I'm sorry. I'm so, so, sorry.* I have someone, someone whom I know I love. So why in God's name do I feel this miserable? Shouldn't I only have feelings for one man? I wish someone could explain this to me. Mother, what do I do? I sop my tears with a handkerchief to dry my eyes. I look down the hall to where everyone is celebrating, thinking I must get back. I take a couple of deep breaths, stand and take one more glance outside. This doesn't feel right. I hope I did the right thing. Looking down at the floor, I think of Mac. I smile. I have so much to be happy for. I know I love him. I've told myself time and time again. Nevertheless, this beautiful man just walked out of my life and left a deep void inside me. What is that? How can it be? And yet, the other half of my heart, when I think of Mac, is full of joy. Victoria Alexandra Highland, you now know how it feels to be between two hearts. Uncommon as it may be, it's true.

Chapter Thirty-Nine: OUR FAMILY CHRISTMAS

The guests had left by one o'clock in the afternoon, and our family dinner is at five. We decide to take a respite before dinner. Teresa and John are planning to join us before going to her parents. I returned to my room alone and I'm surprised to find a gift with a card on the table in the parlor. I open it. It's from Mac. He must have stopped by or had it delivered. The card reads:

My Dear Alex,

Merry Christmas. I was thinking of you today and wishing we were together. Would you like to spend tomorrow with me? I can be there at noon. If you have other plans, I'll understand. Just leave a message at the hotel desk. I'll check there before I come to your room. Have a wonderful day with your family. I'm looking forward to our time together.

Love, Mac

I take the gift and sit down on the sofa, gazing into the fire. The last two days have been nonstop and very emotional. I look at the bow on the package. I know Mac had tied it himself because I smell just a hint of spicy Bay Rum aftershave on the ribbon. I hold it to my nose, breathing it in deeply. I pull the ribbon, and the paper unfolds. There are three boxes.

I open the first. Inside is a selection of squirrel tail hairbrushes for painting. In the second package is an assortment of minerals to mix with linseed for oil painting. In the third is a beautiful, leather-bound journal with an engraving of my initials, VAH. He remembered when I said someday I would buy a set of brushes. I smile. What a wonderful gift, and I love the fact that he remembered. I feel the soft brushes and admire the craftsmanship. Mother would have loved them. If only she were here she to paint with me.

Warm tears flow down my cheeks. I say aloud, "Merry Christmas Mother. I love you." All morning I had a feeling she was with us today. It pains me to my very core to think Father took her life. If he's still alive, I hope he gets what he has coming to him tenfold. I wipe my tears. Damn, this is quite a day. "Anyway Mother," I continue. "Teresa is a beautiful girl. I know you would like her." The flames shoot high in the fireplace, giving me a startle, making me clutch a hand over my chest. "You scared me." I remember it happening another time in Creede. "I should be used to your visits by now. Don't get me wrong, Mother. I like you here. Becky said you visit her all the time. I'm glad you're here Mother. I miss you so much."

I lie down on the sofa with my head on the pillow and put my feet up. Memories of past Christmases flood my mind. I think, I'll rest my eyes, but fall fast asleep. I wake when I hear a knock on the door; it is Becky and William coming to get me for dinner. I invite them in while I quickly wash my face and hands. I show them my gifts from Mac and J.W. I tell Becky on the way downstairs that Mother had visited as she did before. Her eyes get as big as saucers. She smiles and grabs my arm and says, "We have to talk." Downstairs, I stop at the front desk to leave Mac a message saying that I would love to spend the day with him.

We enter the private dining room. The room is lovely, and in it, there is a gramophone playing holiday songs. A large decorated tree stands in the corner, with snow scattered underneath, just as J.W. had promised. Our dinner is delicious. The cooks have outdone themselves, and the amount of food is endless.

We give thanks for being together, and we gather around the Christmas tree. Uncle Scotty plays Santa and passes out gifts. Becky adores her colorful yarns from Bimini along with her spices. Uncle Scotty loves his ship in a bottle and Aunt Jenny is enamored with her gold telescope pencil. Terrance, George, and Christopher can't wait to read the new Sherlock Holmes books. Everyone loves his or her gifts. Becky got me a small table easel for painting. I'm able to ask Aunt Jenny about the dress she made Mother for Christmas when they were just girls during the war. We share stories and drink mulled wine. We laugh, and we cry, talking about past times. She told us how her mother's friend came from Germany to visit one year and taught them to make ornaments for the Christmas tree; some we still have. I love hearing about old times.

Aunt Jenny says she would like to have a memorial for Mother in the spring, at the Mathieson House in Savannah. It feels right to do so. Even if it has been a year and a half, we all need closure. I don't bring Father into it, although it's hard to separate the two; but Aunt Jenny seems to do a very good job of keeping the subject on Mother. I'm grateful. This is a time of celebration.

It is well after midnight before we say goodnight and retire from truly a lovely, and eventful, day.

Chapter Forty: THE DAY AFTER

I sleep in and miss going out with the family for breakfast. I don't remember hearing anyone knocking on the door. Maybe everyone is still sleeping. After I finish with my bath, I hear the maid. She's at the door. She's comes in to make the bed and stoke the fire. I pin my hair into a twist and try to manage the little strands of wet hair sticking to my face, when there is another knock. This time, the maid answers. I hear Mac's voice. She comes to the bedroom to ask me whether I'm expecting someone. I say "yes" and to please tell the gentleman I will be right out. She leaves as I slip into my robe, and goes out to greet him.

"Mac, you're here," I say as I step out of the bedroom.

"Good morning, dove." He looks me up and down, rubs his chin and smiles. "Should I come back?"

"No, I'm so glad to see you. I was just getting dressed."

"Not for me I hope. You look beautiful the way you are," he says flashing a smile. "I got your message downstairs."

"Thank you. I'm glad you've come early. Did you have a nice Christmas?"

"Very nice. It was good to be with family, and now it's even better because I'm here with you." He raises a brow and says, "It's better than the last time we were here together."

"Oh Mac, did you have to bring that up?"

"Now wait. It was just a little joke, and I like that we've mended our relationship."

"Me too," I say putting my arms around his neck and give him a kiss.

"You look pretty this morning."

"Why don't you have a seat, and I'll get dressed."

"Why don't you stay as you are," he says with a chuckle.

"You're full of yourself today Mac."

"I had a good breakfast. Oh, when I was downstairs, I ordered some coffee to be sent up. I hope you don't mind." Just then, there's a knock on the door. "It must be the coffee. Let me answer, and you do what you need to do."

I'm thrilled he's here. I think he gets better looking every time I see him. Especially today, in his tight-fitting Levis, leather vest and jet-black shirt, open at the neck with cuffs rolled to his forearm. His leather holster rides low on his hip. He wears a weapon as comfortably as an old pair of boots. Seeing him stirs a fire within. I sit down next to him on the sofa, almost crushing his hat. He pulls it out just in time, and gives the hat a quick inspection before putting it out of harm's way.

"What's the matter? Don't you like my hat?" He asks with a half chuckle.

"I love your hat. Maybe you should wear it to bed sometime."

"What?"

"I like you in your hat."

"That's a first."

'No one has ever said that. Usually, the girls like me with nothin' at all."

"Well your hat looks pretty good on you."

"I'll wear it if it gets me what I want."

"What is it you want?"

"Good question. Let me think. I don't want to rush into answering and cut my requests short. Besides, what is it about the hat you like so much?"

"I don't know. I guess it gives you a ruggedly handsome look."

"I thought I was ruggedly handsome without a hat," he says with a smirk. "No really, that's a good thing. I'll be glad to accommodate you and wear the hat. Should I bring the rope? Do you want to ride bronco? I can make it hard to stay in the saddle." We start to laugh.

"Well, I'd just synch you up a little tighter Marshal and grab the horn."

"Wow, there really is another side of you I don't know." Looking seriously he asks, "Have you really done that before?"

I give him a wink and smile.

"Since we are putting in requests, maybe you'd consider wearing your chaps without your pants."

"Damn girl, what's making you so naughty? I think you've been with the girls too much," he says with a chuckle.

"I heard you liked naughty girls."

"You've heard too much."

"Are you blushing Mac McClellan?"

"If I'm red, I guess I am. Chaps with no pants ... you've got me on that one."

"Not yet I haven't," I whisper in his ear.

I take his lips, and he responds eagerly. Our heat builds. When I'm with Mac, I always feel as if I can't get enough. We've never had much time together, so I've learned to savor every minute. Mac unties my robe and places his hands around my hips. He pulls me onto his lap. I flinch as the cold steel of his weapon touches my skin.

"Are you taking that off? I think there need be only one gun at a time."

"Let me lose one."

"Make sure it's the right one."

"No need to fear that." He unbuckles his rig and sets it next to his hat.

I smell the spicy clean scent on his skin and the new leather vest. It's manly and seductive. I'm delighted to be in his arms.

"Make love to me Marshal."

He wastes no time picking me up and carrying me to the bed.

I unbutton his shirt and feel his smooth muscular chest under my palms. He is still dark from the summer sun. He sits on the edge of the bed and uses the hotel bootjack. From behind, I rub my hands over his chest. I feel a tingling sensation in my loins as my breasts ride on his back. My hands roam over his hard body and forearms. He stands and slips out of his jeans, half turns and says, "Wait, I'll be back." He disappears into the living room and comes back nude with his hat on.

"Oh my God, that's the funniest thing I've ever seen."

"No jokes or I'm getting rid of the hat. I'm complying with your request."

I slip out of my robe, and scoot under the sheet and say in a low giggle, "Yahoo, cowboy."

He comes to me with a heated gaze, and in a low voice he orders, "Come here you delectable sweetness."

Naked, I let down my hair and crawl to him like a cat. Taking his hat, I set it on the nightstand. "You can put that on later. Lie with me." He lays me back and takes my lips. I feel his strong hands as he caresses me. My nipples stand taut as he encircles them with his velvet tongue. Teasing him with my touch, he closes his eyes and moans. I know he's more than ready. Feeling his dewy silk, his eight or nine inches will soon to be mine.

He bites my lip gently. He wastes no time, seeking the moist valley between my thighs. He lies back and pulls me over the top of him, lifting me to his hot lips. My hands grip the headboard as he gives me the most delightful pleasure with his keenly edged tongue.

"Mac please take me," I whisper. He suckles, and I can't help but cry out and scoot down over his hardness, plunging down to meet his soft hair, resting my palms on his hard flat belly. He moves profanely under me and says, "I like a woman sweet, wild and sassy."

"You think that's me?"

"I know it's you. Every time I'm with you, it's like opening a bottle of wine. I never know what the bouquet will be, until I drink your sweet nectar."

"I love to hear your voice when you're making love to me."

Moisture covers our heated bodies. Wildly we roll from the bed to the floor. On top of him, he grasps my tight buttocks. His arms and chest ripple as he rakes me against him, and, once again, I take my pleasure.

"You are pleasurable, dove," he says breathlessly. Picking me up, he lays me on the sheets and pours us a glass of water from the pitcher on the side table. We lay together, staring at the ceiling while trying to catch our breath. We fall asleep, nuzzled together.

Waking at two in the afternoon, we're starving and the coffee is cold. Someone has slipped an envelope under the door. I take time to open it. It's from Becky. It seems as if everyone slept in, and they're meeting for dinner at five. We freshen up and dress to go get something to hold us until dinner.

"I need a little air. Do you mind if we go outside the hotel for lunch?" I ask.

"Whatever you choose is fine with me."

Downstairs, Mac recommends a little restaurant around the corner. We bundle up and carefully walk arm-in-arm down the icy sidewalk. The sky looks as if it is going to open up any minute.

"Come, let's get warm. The food is great here." Mac holds the door, and we're shown to a small table by the window. The place is the Cozy Hearth. I look around; the tables are small, with checkered cloths, and the windows have little café curtains. It is cozy and smells of fresh baked bread. He hangs my coat and helps me with my chair, and then sits with his back to the wall. I mention that there may be more room where I'm sitting, but he said he is fine.

"I like to sit with my back against the wall. It's a habit. That way, I can see what's going on."

"Now, what would you like to eat? They don't have a menu. Everything is written up there on the blackboard."

"Okay, I'll have a half of a cheese sandwich with a cup of tomato bisque."

The server comes to our table and takes our order. Mac orders scrambled eggs, ham and toast.

The waiter brings a pot of hot steaming coffee.

"I'm content when I'm with you."

"I'm so happy we have this time together," I say smiling.

"We must have got six inches of new snow so far today."

"I love to watch the horse and sleighs and the bustling people. Somehow, it makes it seem so romantic in the city."

"Have you ever thought of moving to the city?"

"Denver? Why would I?"

"Well for one, we could see more of each other, especially in the winter months."

"I would like to spend more time together. However, I'm just getting my business going, and I would need other work."

"You're talking about the Good Hour."

"Yes, I have to be able to make a living. You know as well as I do, these are extremely hard times." I'm waiting for him to say what's really on his mind, but he seems apprehensive. I wait. The silence makes me uneasy, so I mention that Becky and I are planning a trip to Savannah in the spring.

"You haven't forgotten our trip to Ouray?"

"No, I'm looking forward to it. I have my ticket. Just don't you forget."

"Me forget? Never," he answers.

The server brings our lunch to the table. The soup smells and tastes delicious.

"It is great having all the family here."

"It was the first time we were together in years. We had a nice dinner and opened gifts. It was wild with the girls. They're so spoiled."

"It sounds lovely. I'm glad you were together … Oh my gosh!"

"What is it?"

"I forgot to give you my gift. It's in the closet at the hotel. I'm so sorry. I can't believe I did that."

"It's okay. Now, I have something else to look forward to."

"Yes, you do, and I hope you like it."

"Are you going to tell me what it is?"

"Absolutely not. You're going to have to wait just a while longer."

"You're tough."

"I'm not. I just want to see your face when you open it."

"This afternoon *was* my gift."

"That's very sweet, but I do have something I think you'll like."

"But I liked what I got."

"Stop now! I'm blushing pink."

"Sorry, dove. You surely are beautiful."

"Now I'm really blushing. I love my gifts, thank you."

"I'm glad you like your paints and brushes. Now, you can start that painting you were talking about."

"I can't wait. So tell me what you got for Christmas."

"We'll, you know J.W. He goes all out. He surprised me with a really great saddle. The craftsman used three different colors of leather, just like the colors on Arapaho. It's a fine saddle. It should last me a lifetime."

"What did you give him?"

"It's hard to buy for J.W. He's got everything, but I came across a man in Abilene. He had made a pair of ivory-gripped pistols. When I saw them, I said, 'This is J.W.'. We set a day next week to shoot. J.W. is a good shot. I wouldn't want to go up against him. We used to practice when we were young. I was fast, but J.W. is accurate ninety-nine percent of the time."

"Is your mother enjoying her stay?"

She's enjoying herself. Every time I turn around she has tears. She says its tears of joy. She and Uncle J.P. stayed up past midnight night talking about the past holidays. They love each other's company. They've spent a lot of time together, more than my father and mother have over the years. Father worked hard all these years making sure Mother had whatever she wanted. I think he's given her everything, but what she really needs … him. Two people can be together and still be lonely."

"Your mother's a beautiful woman. I bet Peggy enjoys her being here."

"Yes, she loves to entertain. Mother does too. She has done nothing but make sure were taken care of, and feeds us four meals a day."

"I had a short conversation with Philip when we visited on Christmas Eve. He seems to be a kind man."

"Yes. He's a good man to my sister. I played billiards with J.W. and Philip until two in the morning. We got talking about business."

"Do you do business with J.W. and Philip?"

"No, not exactly. They were talking about a mutual business partner of theirs, Daniel Caruthers."

"Daniel Caruthers … I've heard that name before."

"Exactly what have you heard about Caruthers?"

"Well, I know he spends a lot of time at The Pineapple Delight. The talk is he has money, but he's always looking for something for nothing. It was girl talk at the hot springs."

"Well, I hope you never run into him. J.W and Philip just agreed not to do any more business with him, and they hired a new auditor to go over the company's books. They believe they may have evidence that he's been embezzling. I don't trust him. I think he lives really well off of other people's money. I have a bad feeling about Caruthers, but J.W., he's no fool."

We finish our lunch and walk back to the hotel. The weather has turned fowl and bitter cold.

In the room, Mac unwraps his the Waltham pocket watch I gave him.

"This is beautiful Alex." He opens the watch.

"I'm glad you like it."

"It really nice, thank you. There's just one thing wrong."

"What is it?"

"There's no picture of you in it."

"Mac, you made me think something was really wrong."

"I'd like it better if it had a picture of you."

"I was hoping you would say that. Next time you're passing through Durango I'll give you one."

"It's a beauty. I'll carry it always." He gives me a kiss. "I love the gold and silver combination. You really shouldn't have Alex."

"I wanted to. It looked as if it should be yours."

"Thank you."

"I have one more gift … for Arapaho."

"Arapaho? He gets a present too?"

"Last time I saw Arapaho; he needed a new blanket."

"I agree it's seen better days, but Arapaho's never complains." Mac unwraps the gift.

"What made you think of Arapaho?"

"When I think of you, you're always riding. One day, in the mercantile, they had a new shipment of blankets in the window. I immediately thought of Arapaho and Indy."

"We'll, I'll thank you for him. He's a good horse, and this will keep his backside warm."

"I sewed your initials on the blanket."

"Yes, I see that. Thank you."

We meet everyone downstairs in the dining room for dinner. I introduce Mac to the family. Aunt Jenny smiles approvingly. Uncle Scotty likes him too. I can see uncle isn't sure what's going on. I heard uncle say to Aunt Jenny, "Is she bringing a new man to every meal?" Aunt Jenny frowns at his humor. It is a relaxing evening. George excuses himself early to go see Abigail Reynolds. He is very taken with her.

John makes an announcement. They may have a change in plans, and they may not be moving to Europe. Everyone is delighted. One of Teresa's relatives knows of two schools looking for art teachers. John says he is going to see what they have to offer. We're happy to hear their news. The newlyweds excuse themselves from the table. It has been a long day. We say goodnight to them. William is exhausted, and he asks to be excused as well. He's ready to call it a night.

Surprisingly, J.W. shows up at the Brown Palace. I had no idea he was coming. Uncle had invited him. The men gather for their cigars and brandy in the smoking room, while Aunt Jenny, Becky, and I reconvene in a small little area in the lobby, which is comfortable next to the fireplace. The bustling lobby has now become very quiet at the end of the day.

"So what do you think about Mac, Aunt Jenny?"

"He's as handsome as you said and then some," Aunt Jenny answers.

"What about you Becky? What do you think? It's been over a year since you saw him."

"I think he's very nice Alex, but I like J.W. too."

"So do I. That has been the problem. I love J.W., but it's not the same as love I have for Mac. I waited until now to tell you, Aunt Jenny, J.W. had proposed to me."

"What?"

"Yes, after we returned from Savannah."

"Oh my gosh, tell us all about it. He seems to be such a wonderful, caring man," Aunt Jenny says.

"Well, J.W. is wonderful, no doubt; but I had to say no. I am still in love with Mac."

"I know J.W. loves you child," says Aunt Jenny. "It's plain to see."

"Mac loves me too."

"You know best dear. You're very fortunate Alex. They're both handsome, intelligent and caring men," Aunt Jenny says.

"Both men come from good families, and you will be very well-taken care of. That is, if you plan to marry one of them," Becky adds.

"There's such a resemblance between the two men and J.P. Reynolds," Aunt Jenny says.

"I told you they look alike."

"Yes, but I never dreamed ... Oh my, and when they smile ... I can see why you are drawn to J.W. He has to be the most handsome man I've ever seen, besides my William of course," Becky says blushing.

"They are handsome." I agree.

"Mac has a larger physique, but they could be brothers," Becky says.

"Well I'm glad they're not brothers, for my sake."

"Wouldn't that have been something," Aunt Jenny interjects.

"It was bad enough that they are cousins. The night I found out, it was a nightmare," I say.

"Yes, but for whom," Auntie chuckles and then we all laugh.

"If you marry J.W. Alex, you will never have to go back to the Good Hour. He's rich. He'll take care of you. You'll never have to work again," Becky says with passion.

"Becky, I'm eighteen years old, and you don't know me at all. I'm not going to marry for security. I can't believe you said that."

"I'm concerned is all, and I know you have strong feelings for the man."

"Yes, and that's even more of a reason not to marry him. I care for him deeply, but I'm not going to take advantage of his love. I'm not that kind of person. Please tell me you didn't marry William Stanton for that reason."

"No; of course not."

"So please have a little faith in me. I've proved I can take care of myself. Maybe not the way I'd like, but I will not take what is not mine. When I marry, it will be for love and not any other reason, I promise."

"You don't have to promise me anything."

"Girls please, let's all take a breath and calm ourselves. Becky is concerned. I'm concerned … we all are. If you were in our shoes you would understand why we are a little worried," Aunt Jenny says.

There is silence for a few minutes.

"Okay, I understand you are concerned; but I'm a strong woman, and you have to accept that and respect my integrity."

"I'm sorry Alex. You are right. Please, I don't know what's wrong with me. I don't want you to sell yourself short. You are strong, much more than I'll ever be. I know you can support yourself, and I honor your choices sister. I admit I was being selfish and shallow."

"I know you worry, and I love you both for it; but I have to do what's right for me."

"I understand. That's all we can really ask Alex," Aunt Jenny says.

"Yes," Becky agrees.

"So please dear, tell us your plans," Auntie asks.

"J.W. and I are friends. We parted yesterday after the wedding, and I'm seeing Mac now."

"How is he Alex," Becky asks.

"Disappointed, but he's a true gentleman."

"I believe that. He's been raised well. I know he loves you," Aunt Jenny says.

"He does, but he was man enough to let me go."

"I admire him. It's plain to see he's a good man. You're lucky to have such a friend," Becky says softly. "I just want to say, I'm sorry for how things turned out, with you going to the Good Hour. It breaks my heart."

"It's okay, I'm alright. I'll get this turned around you'll see. I've helped the girls there, and they have helped me too. They're like family. We watch each other's backs."

"I'm scared you'll be hurt … or worse."

"Mother said you have to use all of your abilities, did she not? So I used one." Becky let her head hang low. "Look at me Becky, I'm the same person, and I'm still your sister." We both have tears.

"I love you Alex."

"Don't cry."

"I'm crying because I should have been there to take care of you. I'm the oldest. I feel horrible that you did this for me."

"It's ok Becky. Like I said, I would do it again if I had too. I love you."

Chapter Forty-One: THE TREASURE MAP

Aunt Jenny and Becky are tired and go up to bed. I go downstairs and find the men talking in the smoking room. I enter and pour myself a glass of wine from the crystal decanter that's sitting on the server. Mac and J.W. are both here. Uncle Scotty, the Captain of the Spice Queen, interrupts the individual conversations between them and the ones between Terrance, Christopher and George. He asks the men to step into a private room down the hall. He smiles and motions for me to follow and says, "Since you were there at Tall Trees when this adventure started, I'd like you to join us Alex."

"Thank you Uncle," I answer and hurry to catch up.

The men gather around the large, smoothly polished mahogany table. I wait for everyone to be seated, and I shut the door and take a seat in a high leather wingback next to the fireplace. The captain announces he will start at the beginning when we were at Tall Tree's in Bimini in October. While Uncle Scotty is talking, he and J.W. place the two parts of the map onto the center table, fitting them together like interlacing fingers.

"Thank you for coming tonight, Uncle Scotty says. "As some know, my good mate, Gillson Estavan was murdered recently in St. Lucia. He was found bloodied under the docks, not long after he had confided and given me half the treasure map that most presume to be responsible for his death.

"He came to the America's with his uncle and worked for the English Trading Company, but he was a Spaniard at heart. He was a good sailor, and I chose him as my first mate aboard the Spice Queen. He was with me for five years before getting a commission as a ship's captain and awarded the Horizon.

"Together, we had sailed these waters for forty years. Gill and I depended on each other; we were good mates through thick and thin. Last year, we docked in St. Lucia and met at The Hold Fast Tavern.

We were laying whiskey down, and that's when he confided in me that he had a map that his uncle had given him on his deathbed.

"He said the map was dated 1733. It read *Nuestra España Fleet*. The Nuestra España Fleet was one of the last real treasure fleets. It left Havana, Cuba on Friday the thirteenth in 1733. The fleet consisted of three armed galleons and eighteen merchant ships full of tanned hides, precious jewels, gold, silver and rare spices.

"A hurricane scattered the fleet along the Florida Keys and sank with the treasure. One of the ships, the San Pedro, sank in shallow waters, so the Spanish burned it to the waterline to prevent pirates from finding it. It was a rich fleet, rich beyond measure. It's rumored that most of the treasure still lies beneath the water. This map shows the location of a number of ships that went down in the storm. Gill believed the map to be authentic."

"How do you know whether any of the treasures remain," Mac asks.

"Because of this," Uncle Scotty says and lays down a copy of the Spanish manifest. "The Spanish are known for their accurate recording keeping. I also checked to see whether any of the treasures from this particular fleet was recovered." The men pass the several pages among them. "Now that you have seen all the evidence I have, is there anyone here up for the challenge and the adventure of recovering this treasure? But, before we go on, I'm asking that if we do, and we make a find, that the Estavan family receives a double share. This is their family map."

"I agree to that, but I can't speak for these other gentlemen. This is like a horse race. You view the field; you get all the information on the horses and the jockey and place your bet. I have a good feeling about this. I'm in," J.W. says.

Everyone at the table agrees.

"How much do you think we need to go ahead," George asks.

Everyone just looks at each other.

"Let's make up a general list and see what is needed," Terrance suggests.

An hour goes by, and the men are still smoking cigars, drinking bourbon and speculating about their venture capital investment. They come to an accord that J. W. will be the principal investor.

Everyone will have to pay a portion of the initial layout. When and if there is a treasure discovered, or a claim, they agree to divide the shares. If the project goes bust, J.W. will retain all equipment and vessels. He will sell them to recoup his investment. Toward the end of the second hour, they start to put the plan together, discussing what each man may bring to the table.

Christopher says, "Being that George and I are teachers of geology and archeology at the university, we can come up with a story to cover any curiosities about the research."

"Good. The less attention we have, the better," Uncle Scotty says.

"Plus, we are experienced divers. I predict that most of the diving will be in the summer months while the seas are calmer. Classes finish up by the end of May," George adds.

"When can we get started," Uncle Scotty asks.

"It's the holidays. However, the day after New Year's I will contact my attorneys and have them set up a corporation," J.W. says.

"What shall we call it," Uncle Scotty asks.

"Something simple like, J.W. and Associates, everyone here will be on the board of directors for an equal share except the Estavan family; they will receive a double," J.W. says. "What size vessel are we looking for?"

"Nothing too large, maybe sixty to eighty feet. We need something built like a skipjack, something with a shallow draw and a wide beam that can hold a cargo," Uncle Scotty explains.

"There are plenty of vessels like that in the Baltimore area," Terrance suggests.

"Then can we leave that up to you," George asks.

"I'll start looking."

"Terrance and I can start a list of materials and supplies we'll need," Uncle Scotty says.

"Don't forget, Father, to make sure you add replacement parts. We can't afford down time," Christopher reminds him.

"I know a man in Boston that handles diving equipment," Mac says, "and he won't ask questions. I'll make sure you get the information."

"So, we have agreed. As I see it, we need to verify the map," Christopher says, "When we get back to the east coast, I'll get on it."

"Keep in mind that this map might have been drawn over a hundred years ago. Everything might have been changed by nature. For me, this is a personal matter. Someone killed my best friend. I don't want his murder to be put in the background over a treasure."

Mac speaks up, "Do you have any suspects?"

"I do not," Uncle Scotty says.

"Well, this is what I do. I hunt people. There's always a common thread. It may be someone that worked for the English Trading Company, maybe another captain. Give it some thought along these lines and let me know what you come up with. You may know more than what you realize."

Uncle Scotty and Terrance look at each other and acknowledge the information.

"How did you find out about the murder," Mac asks.

"Terrance heard men talking at a grog house in St Lucia."

"Good, Terrance, that's where you start. Write down everything you remember about that night. Go back as far as when you first docked. Do you remember what ships were in the harbor? Scotty, you do the same for the night you were with Gillson. More than likely the killer was in earshot distance. He might have seen Gillson give you half of the map, or at least overheard part of your conversation."

"I made a stop in St. Augustine to talk to his wife after learning about his murder," Uncle Scotty says. "She had Gill's half of the map buried in the courtyard."

"Then, someone in St. Augustine could have seen or overheard something. You know they didn't see him bury it, or it would have disappeared. Someone was intrigued, intrigued enough to kill to get their hands on the map, but to their surprise, Gill didn't have it on his person. It may go back as far as when his uncle had the map. You don't know until you start digging," Mac says.

"We will find out," Terrace replies.

"I'll concentrate on finding Gill's killer while the rest of you concentrate on finding the treasure. If that's agreeable, then I have my work cut out for me, as do you," Mac says.

"Here's to bringing the killer to justice," Terrance says.

"To Estavan's treasure," J.W. toasts.

"To a good friend," Uncle Scotty says.

The men raise their glasses and drink.

"I think we better call it a night mates," Uncle Scotty suggests.

"I propose we meet tomorrow night, since we have so little time," J.W. says.

"Tomorrow, we'll work on the equipment list and cost. Don't forget, a man's life has already been lost just over the possibility of a treasure. Don't share this with your wives, sweethearts, nobody. We don't want anyone to be in danger here. Tomorrow night at nine, we'll meet here in this room. J.W., Mac, boys, Alex, thank you. I appreciate your expertise and your willingness to take part in this adventure."

"J.W. wait up," Mac says. J.W. stops at the door. "We've hardly got to talk," Mac says.

"Well, I figured you were busy," J.W. says.

"No not too busy for us to play a game of billiards or something."

"Well, I can't tonight. I've got a game at the Navarre House. Hey, maybe you want to sit in? Lorenzo's going to be there."

"Heck, I wouldn't have a chance between the two of you."

"Then sit at another table and we'll get together for a big steak and drinks afterwards."

"No thanks. What about tomorrow night?"

"We can get together before the meeting," J.W. suggests.

"You're on. I'll meet you in the tavern at seven," Mac says.

"You got it."

"Hey, good luck tonight."

"I'm going to need it, especially if Parrish is at the table. That man can see through cards," J.W. says as he goes out the door.

Chapter Forty-Two: BACK IN THE ROOM

"Are you ready to go up," Mac asks.

"Yes, but don't let me hold you back."

"No, J.W. and I will have time together. I'll walk with you." We get back to the room.

"Then, you'll stay awhile?"

He looks into my eyes and says, "It's late. Don't you want to be rested for tomorrow?"

He kisses me tenderly. I hand him the key, and he unlocks the door.

"I had the most wonderful day with you."

"I enjoyed our time too."

"Do you care if I run water for a quick bath?"

"Go ahead. I'm going to pour myself a drink. Would you like one?"

"No thank you. I think the wine I had earlier went to my head." In the bedroom, I strip from my clothes and start running water for a bath. I smile thinking it is so good having Mac here.

I get into the tub, lean my head back and close my eyes. I didn't realize how tired I am until now. The lights go out. Even with my eyes closed, the room seems darker. I sit up, opening them. Mac is standing in the doorway holding a candle. He glows in the amber light, moving the candle to the side I see he's nude, wearing only his black beaver cowboy hat, which brings a smile to my face.

"My, my, Marshal, what is this? I see you've got your hat on, but where's your badge?"

"First you ask for a hat and now you want my badge. You're pretty demanding, dove, don't you think? Won't my hat get me what I what?"

"What do you want? Come show me."

Mac sets the candle on the vanity and walks over to the tub.

"Are you willing to share your water?"

I scoot up to one end. "I believe so, stranger."

He sits down, and the water splashes over the side. "Damn, this tub must be from Europe. European tubs are long and deep."

"How do you know about European tubs? Have you been to Europe?"

He puts his head back and pushes his hat over his brow, in total relaxation, and says, "Yes, I'm a tub connoisseur." The steam rolls up around his neck.

"Really, have you been to Europe?"

"Yes. I was born in Ireland. We still have family and a home in the Emerald Isle."

"Is that right? What kind of hat did you wear in the tub in Ireland?"

"No hat, same suit." We chuckle.

"Now, what have I done to get a handsome cowboy into my tub?"

I slide to him, feeling my nipples touch his chest. They become taut, sending a rush of desire throughout my body. I encircle my arms around his neck, teasing and kissing him with my moist lips. His hands explore and rove over my wet, soft, soapy skin and firm buttocks. Feeling him, I push away and submerge, taking him into my mouth. Immediately, I taste his sweetness. I feel his body become tense. He pulls me to his chest. Wet and dripping, I straddle his hips, taking him. Connecting, I experience pleasurable warmth, and our fury grows. I hear bathwater hitting the floor as we rise and fall in a syncopated passion.

"You're in so deep," I say softly.

"And you're so tight," he says with a husky voice. "God, you make me feel good," he takes my lips. His tongue explores my mouth, and I hungrily return the kiss.

"I love taking you Mac McClellan."

"I love it when you do."

"When you're gone, I dream of having you in my bed."

"You've bewitched me. I can't think of anyone but you."

"I'm glad, because you've done the same to me." I grip the side of the tub, and we look deeply into each other's eyes. My heart is racing as our passion crests. Hearing him moan only heightens the sizzling ecstasy, and I feel his release deep within. Afterward, I wither, resting on his chest. I hear the strong beating of his heart.

"You sweet thing, you surely know how to make me weak," Mac humbly says.

"And you, cowboy, know how to take me for a ride in the saddle." He chuckles and kisses me hard on the lips, flashing his perfect smile.

"Your hat, what happened to your hat?" We look over the edge of the tub and see it sitting in a puddle of water. "Oh Mac, it will be ruined."

"No, dove, it's beaver. Beavers live in water." I lean over and retrieve it, putting it back on his head. "There, handsome. That is some beaver you've got there."

"I could say the same myself."

"Mac! You're terrible."

"You brought it up."

"Shame on you. Shush now. Just kiss me."

Chapter Forty-Three: LAST FULL DAY IN DENVER

Waking with Mac beside me is the best gift. I stoke his hair with my fingertips and trace his strong jawline. I stare at him, remembering the first time we met and how he took my hand without waiting for my answer so that I would dance with him. He led me around the dance floor in smooth, perfect motion. We danced the night away in one another's arms, as if there were no one else in the room. He was new in town and had all the women's attention. It was like something out of a fairytale.

He stirs and opens one eye.

"Good morning, dove; what's the smile for? Did I already please you?"

"Not yet partner, but do I need a reason, Marshal? Can't I just be happy you're here?"

"Absolutely, I'm happy you're here."

"Good," I say as I crawl on top of him.

"You're wasting no time."

"No, I'm not. Especially since you're under the impression I had already used you."

"I don't mind, but I don't want to miss out," he laughs.

"I'm hungry for you."

"Didn't get enough of me last night."

"No. If I live until the end of time, I'll never have enough of you." He flashes a wide smile and pulls me closer.

"That's the nicest thing anyone has ever said to me."

"Really? I know you've had your share of women. Don't forget, I live half the time with the girls at the Good Hour."

"They talk too much."

"Maybe they do, but I know what I feel when I'm with you."

"Well, I hope it lasts forever then pretty woman. Come here, I haven't told you I love you today."

"No, you haven't," I say softly and bring my lips to him. We kiss long and tenderly, and it makes my tummy flutter as if I have butterflies inside. The sensation awakens a sensual tingling in my loins. He cups by breasts, bringing them to his warm lips and nibbles on my rosy nipples. It takes my breath away looking at him in the soft morning winter light. My lord, he is attractive. I can't seem to get enough of him. Being inside his strong muscular arms is the upmost feeling. I'm safe from the outside world and loved beyond measure. It is a good feeling, a very good feeling.

"Do you have something on your mind little lady?"

I give him a light kiss and say, "Yes I do. I was just thinking of the day we met. Do you remember?"

"I do. You were the prettiest girl in the room. I remember how you smelled of lilacs. I love lilacs, and your pretty blonde hair hung practically to your waist, and your eyes looked like huge sapphires, and your lips were the color of a pretty, pink rose. I said to myself, *she's lovely, I want to dance with her*. And, once you were in my arms, the evening just got better. You were beautiful, Alex, and even more so now."

"Mac McClellan, you do have a way with words."

"It's not just words. I speak from my heart."

I whisper, "Make love to me." He gently rolls me on to my back and uses his knee to open my thighs before I have a chance to say anything more. I feel his length penetrate deeply into my warm moist valley. Slowly, he grinds his hips against my pelvis. He lifts his head, closes his eyes as my name rolls off his tongue. I raise my hips to meet him fiercely, seeking his every inch, wanting and needing more and more. Our lovemaking is hot, steamy, with animal instincts taking us higher and higher to a point of no return. What a beautiful way to start the day, in the arms of my love.

Later in the morning, Mac receives a message from Peggy inviting us to lunch. I check with Aunt Jenny and Becky to see whether they have plans. Together, they were having lunch and going back to a few of the stores we went to before Christmas. Therefore, it works out to be a perfect time. I'm a little nervous about seeing them and J.W., but decide to go. It is good that I decided to go, for almost everyone made me feel at home. Peggy still seems to have an issue with me, and I never know what is up her sleeve. Although J.W. is there, he is always polite and genuine. After a lovely meal, everyone gathers in the parlor. Peggy, Maggie and I have a seat. Mac's mother, Shannon, says she has an announcement. She goes to J.P.'s side. I see the surprise on everyone's faces. J.P. rises and sets his brandy on the mantel. Shannon takes his hand. She states that what she has to say is family business, but that I may stay. I'm relieved, just how awkward would it be if I were asked to leave? She nods to me, and I make a half smile, hoping she will go on with whatever she has to say.

"I want to make an announcement," Shannon repeats. The whole room is quiet; the only sound is the crackling fire. "I will be returning to the plantation after the holidays with J.P. I have made a decision not to return to Ireland. I am leaving your father, Peggy and Mac."

The girls start to chatter. J.P. says, "Please girls, I have something to say to the family. Shannon and I are in love, and we have been for almost thirty years. It's time I take her home. I apologize, Mac and Peggy, for what this may do to you and your father. Your Mother has been faithful all her years of marriage. We have chosen to live the rest of our lives together. Life is too short, and we're growing older as we speak. I spoke with your father face to face on my last visit to Ireland. He is willing not to stand in Shannon's way. He loves her, as he loves all of you. We ask for your blessing, and we realize this may take some time for all of us to adjust. We couldn't be happier, and we hope you find it in your hearts to be happy for us. Your Mother was bound by honor to the McClellan clan at the age of twelve. And, of course, they married much later, but we are too old to deny our true feelings for one another. J.W., it was your dear mother's dying wish for me to marry your Aunt Shannon."

Everyone is quiet. Mac and J.W. come forward. Both the men embrace Shannon and then shake J.P.'s hand. Peggy tries to dry her eyes. I know she is hurt by their news. Who wouldn't be? She goes to them, and they have an emotional moment. Shannon tells Peggy and Mac that she was sorry that she could not continue with their father. They both say they understand, and that the situation will not change the love they had for both of them. Philip takes Peggy upstairs. I believe Maggie is pleased with their announcement. Maggie loves them both dearly. I take her hand and she says softly, "You know Alexandra, the truth is always the best for everyone involved."

The young girls go to their room. Mac asks me if I would like to go back to the hotel. I thought I should say good night. I go up to J.W.

"J.W. I know how much you love your Aunt Shannon."

"Thank you. I take it Mac is going to see you back to the hotel?"

"Yes, thank you."

J.W. give me a kiss on my cheek. I squeeze his hand as we leave. It is an emotional evening for them all.

Chapter Forty-Four: TEA FOR THREE

We women gather for the English high tea in the lobby of the Brown Palace. The harpist is playing beautiful Christmas music. The Palace is known for their four o'clock teatime. We fit the part, dressed in our fancy hats and holiday dresses with our very finest gloves and breeze into room. It's so much fun dressing up and having somewhere fancy to go. I tell Becky and Aunt Jenny of what little I know about Henry Brown, all J.W.'s doing of course. The server gives us two options. One includes tea with a variety of wonderful small bites; the other includes a glass of champagne. Of course, we choose tea *and* champagne.

The tea list is two pages long and includes everything from classics such as Earl Grey and English breakfast to more surprising options such as Vanilla Rooibos and Black Currant. The tea is served in fine China, perfect for sipping, and the champagne is in crystal flutes. We sit at a small table near the Christmas tree and gaze at the atrium eight floors above, to which all floors open. The gilded ironwork is spectacular, and the huge area rugs burst with color. The walls are made of Mexican onyx and marble and fixtures that look like the sun that seems to give it an Aztec flavor. The hotel is amazingly beautiful.

Aunt Jenny and Becky are filling me in on yesterday's shopping adventure. The server brings a tray of wonderful scones with Devonshire cream, and tea sandwiches with ingredients such as cheese and cucumber, and a variety of desserts such as chocolate cake, truffles and cookies. We enjoy the experience of the luxury hotel, especially on the holiday, indulging in such marvelous foods. We take our time and enjoy every bit of it.

"I hate that our time is coming to an end," I say.

"I wanted to plead with William to stay a few more days, and I wanted to see whether you think you could stay longer Alex," Becky says.

"You ask William. As for me, I will stay for a few extra days."

"What about you, Aunt Jenny," Becky asks.

"I can't possibly stay longer girls. I must get back. It's such a busy time, and I've already been gone too long from the dress shop."

"I should be sewing too," I say taking a sip of the flavorful hot tea and notice Becky seems to be ready to burst. "What is it Becky?"

"I have something to announce," Becky says in a soft voice, and then starts to bubble as she continues.

"I have two wonderful things I want to sure."

"Well go ahead, we want to hear," Aunt Jenny says.

"We are moving to Durango, and I'm going to have a baby."

"Rebecca Jennifer Highland Stanton, I'm thrilled for you," Aunt Jenny replies sincerely.

"Thank you. I'm so excited. I wanted to tell you, but I thought with the wedding and Christmas…"

"You should have. There's no holding back in this family. We are happy for you."

"Well, I could hardly contain myself this morning, and William said, 'what are you waiting for darling? Share your news. It's wonderful news.' He's such a dear man."

"Yes he is," Aunt Jenny says. "When is all this happening?"

"Mid-June William says. I mean the baby is due, and we are having a house built. In fact, it is to be started in a few months."

"Tell me where and how?"

"William contacted the hospital there. They want him to come immediately. It will be so different in the small town, but it will give him the opportunity to develop a medical practice in a place that is in such need."

"This is a cause of celebration," I say joyfully. "I make a toast of good health, to my sister the mother-to-be, and to my new niece or nephew!"

"I'll be a great Auntie, this is wonderful. I'll start on the layette right away," Aunt Jenny says.

We pat Becky's hand, and both Auntie and I say, "This is good news."

Chapter Forty-Five: THE MEETING OF MEN

At nine p.m. sharp, the men meet in the conference room.

"Uncle," I ask, "Do you mind if I sit in?"

"Not at all, little one. On this venture, we need lady luck."

"Then, I'm happy to be her." I just left Auntie and Becky in the lobby; they're playing a game of cards. I opted to be with the men.

"You're a lot like your mother, Alex. She would have been right into this. She had a heart for adventure. Did you know she sailed with your Grandfather Lawrence every chance she could get? She loved to be in her sailing britches as much as she loved planning a Cotillion. Your Momma she was something. She had more backbone than most men."

"Really Uncle?"

"Why yes. She saved your Aunt Jenny's life. They were stranded in the ocean, and she swam with Jenny on her back and crawled through the marshes, encountering the bloodsucking leeches and poisonous snakes when she herself was injured. She had been in the water all night before coming upon your grandma and Jenny. Your Auntie was in a bad way … shock, they say. That's the night that your grandparents were killed in the Savannah River. She cared for Jenny; she saved her and I'm grateful. Your Momma was a truly courageous woman … many times … many times."

"Thank you for telling me."

"Didn't she ever talk about it?"

"Not like that. She said she did what anyone would do in that situation."

"She was like that, never one to give herself credit when credit was due. I liked your Momma. She was a good person. I want you to know that."

"Thank you for telling me. I loved her lots."

"You're welcome, little one."

"Uncle, I'm not so little."

"Oh, but you'll always be little to me Alexandra. Come, we better get started. The men are waiting on us."

The men take their seats. I close the door and say hello to J.W. who comes in last. He says hello and initiates a conversation with Terrance. I take a comfortable seat in a high wingback chair by the fire while the men gather around the table, lighting pipes and smoking cigars. I don't like the smoke. Nevertheless, I'd much rather sit with the men than play cards. It will be much more interesting. Just the thought of treasure gives me a twinge of excitement. Treasure has a romantic flavor, and immediately I think of huge ships, tall masts and high seas. Who hasn't dreamed of treasure and exploring deserted islands and finding chests of gold and jewels? Flashes of the Caribbean turquoise waters and long sandy beaches come to mind.

"Men, shall we get started," Uncle Scotty asks as he pours a brandy with the rest. "Who would like to go first?"

"I'll start Captain," Mac says. "Gentlemen, I've been thinking about how to catch Estavan's killers. The areas that we need to cover, and the number of suspects, are too numerous to plot. Therefore, the most practical idea is to bait the killers and get them to come to me.

"How will you do that," Uncle Scotty asks.

"With a story of disinformation, the plan will evolve when I leak information for treasure driving expedition in the Caribbean ports. I'll need your help with a list for personnel. I'll make up a contact name and hire someone to do the interviewing. I'll set this up in three different locations to do so. I'll work out all the details. This is just the rough overlay of the plan.

"It does sound easier than searching the entire Caribbean," Uncle Scotty says.

"It's a start, a process of elimination. Men's ears perk when they hear the words 'treasure map'. Let's hope the plan produces the killers. One more thing, I wrote down the man's name I mentioned out of Baltimore for dive equipment. Give him my name; he will be glad to help. He's a long-time family friend. Captain and Terrance, maybe before you leave we can review exactly what you remember about Estavan, and then I'll get started?

"Thank you," Uncle Scotty says.

"The Captain and I have a partial list of materials. It's progressing, but I believe we have enough information to put some numbers together."

"Good; May I take a look at it," J.W. asks and Terrance passes it to him.

"And, I have made a research outline and will take it further once back in Georgia," Christopher adds.

J.W. picks up the paper, "This is enough information to get started. I can make the business plan. I will contact my banker and attorneys, and then we will decide on the earnest amount that everyone will put in, if that's agreeable." The men agree.

"Mates, let's bring our hands together. I want to thank J.W. and Mac for joining us. J. W., we're very aware that this is a lot of money for you to invest. We want you to know we will hold up our part."

J.W. chuckles, "Your men will be doing heavy lifting. I'm just supplying the gloves." The men laugh. This is why J.W. is respected. He makes the men feel of equal value.

"Mac, I thank you for your concern in bringing justice to my friend," Uncle Scotty says.

"I'll do what I can, Captain."

"Good luck to us all. J.W., Mac, I hope to hear from you soon."

"Captain, when I've received the contract from the attorneys, I'll make the trip to Savannah so we can get started. Gentlemen, I'm going to call it a day. I hear cards shuffling somewhere," J.W. chuckles. "Everyone is welcome to join me. I'm going over the Navarre House. The boys give a whistle. "Lorenzo is just few hands away of winning the good old sporting house. He has been playing cards for twenty-four hours. I want to see how this game turns out. Denver could have a new proprietor in town. That would surely shake things up around here. Join me if you will."

"I couldn't help but overhear you and J.W. Tell me Mac; why did J.W. take the elevator to the basement?"

"He's going to the Navarre House, next door."

"Through the basement?"

"Yes, there's a tunnel to the sporting house."

"How do you know all these things?"

"It's part of the shadow culture. Passageways like the tunnels in Durango. You can walk from here to there without being seen or going out in the weather; but they're not meant for everyone."

Later, back in our bedroom, I hear Mac come in. It must be close to two o'clock in the morning. He gets into bed, moves my hair from my shoulder and kisses my neck. Feeling his caress, he awakens my desires. I feel his hardness against my leg. Under the covers, I feel his rough cheek on my belly as his hot lips sear my skin. Lower, he tastes my nectar with his velvety tongue, giving me great pleasure. I push back begging him to stop, but he continues to suckle, spinning me in a world of rapture. For moments, I'm lost in layers of bliss. Floating like a feather falling to the earth, I come back into the warm reality. I desire to please him, as he did me, and take over. Beside him, with my warm lips teasing him, I bring him to an intensifying climax. I snuggle into his arms; he takes a fist of my hair in his hand.

Sleepily he breathes, "Your hair is as soft as silk, and I love the scent of lilacs."

"I love you, Mac McClellan."

With my cheek upon his chest, I hear the strong pounding of his heart. We sleep.

Chapter Forty-Six: FAMILY GOODBYES

It is December 29, and the sun was up and the morning was upon us. I like waking with him in my bed. I will be leaving today and taking my memories of this short time we have had together. We haven't talked about the future. I guess for now, this is all it can be. I will be back in Durango, and Mac will be riding on a snowy trail to wherever the next business takes him.

Cuddling in bed, I give him a morning kiss. "I wish we had more time," I say.

"Isn't that always what we always say, dove?"

"Let me lie in your arms for just a few more minutes."

"I'll hold you forever if you like." He strokes my face and hair.

"How long will you be staying at Peggy's?"

"Just a few more days. I plan to talk to Mother and J.P. today. Father is alone, and evidently, he has known about this for quite some time. I want to find out what plans they have made and what happens to the family now."

"I don't know what to say."

"I know Mother has been miserable for years. It's not that she couldn't do things, because she did, but she didn't want to do them alone, and Father, he can't help himself; he has to be busy with his work constantly."

I start to pack my things. My train leaves at noon. I want to spend every minute with the family I can, before they leave at eleven. I hurry about with my bath and dress.

"Have you got your things together," he asks.

"I'm packed. When do you think I'll see you again?"

"Maybe in month or so. I'll write every week."

"I look forward to getting your letters." Mac opens the door to the hall.

"Come, everyone will be waiting, and I'm hungry."

"You're always hungry."

"I'm a growing boy."

We meet Becky and William in the hall and the rest of the family in the dining room. We have a hearty winter breakfast of sausages, griddlecakes, potatoes, eggs and ham steaks. We struggle with our conversation. Our hearts are already saying goodbye, and holding back the tears is difficult.

We take carriages to the depot. Everyone would have like to have the good times to go on, but we all have our own agenda's. Tears flow; we make a family vow to have Mother's memorial in the spring, if possible. I watch them board the train going east. My heart sinks. Thank God, John and Teresa have made the decision to stay in the states. For now, they will be in Boston while John is interviewing for a teaching position.

I'm waiting for last call to board. "I hate to say goodbye Mac."

"It won't be for long love. We are going to see each other in June."

"That's five months. Is there any chance you may come to Durango before then?"

"I'd like to say yes, but I really don't know."

"We had a nice few days, didn't we?"

"Yes, dove, we did. I'm looking forward to spring. I will write when I can. If you do the same, we'll always be opening a letter."

We hear someone shout "Victoria." Our heads turn. "It's Philip," I say.

"Hey, what are you doing here," Mac asks.

"I'm on the train to Durango. I have business. I was hoping I would catch you. I thought maybe you'd like some company Vicky."

"This is a surprise. I'd love to have your company."

"Good, I'll let the two of you say your goodbyes and I'll go on ahead."

The whistle blows; it's time to board. We embrace. I don't want to let him go.

"Don't forget our plan is Ouray, in the spring," he says flashing a smile. "And let me know when you're leaving for Savannah. I'll try to get to Durango before then."

The whistle blows again.

"Is there any possibility you can go with me," I ask hurriedly.

"I'm afraid not. Not if I take time off for Ouray."

"I suppose you're right."

"I'm counting on you taking care of yourself."

"And you too."

"I plan to keep Arapaho and me alive."

"You better Mac McClellan." I swallow hard, once again, I'm saying goodbye. He hugs me one last time.

I hear the conductor yell, "Last call!"

I take the bottom step and look down at him. "Take care Marshal. I'll be waiting." The train starts to roll.

He takes a few steps to stay with me. My eyes filled with tears.

"The time will go fast, you'll see," he says looking up at me. The train whistles blows. I can barely hear his last words.

"I love you Mac McClellan!"

"I love you too. I'll see you soon; you can bet on it."

"I'm going to hold you to it Marshal" I shout, as the train picks up speed. He smiles, lifts his hat and waves. My heart aches. I can't take my eyes from him. Soon, he's just a speck in the distance. The wind is blowing, and the snow stings my face.

"Ma'am, you need to come inside," the porter says.

When will I see him again?

Chapter Forty-Seven: THE JOURNEY HOME

I dread leaving Mac in Denver. Time went too fast. It seems as if I had just arrived, and now we've said goodbye. We did express our love for one another, but the issue of taking our relationship to the next step was not discussed. When we are together, it seems as if we are both afraid to talk. Neither wants to pressure the other. Maybe because we know it will be too painful, too honest, and one or both of us will get hurt. Possibly, my employment at the brothel is the underlying problem. We have strong feelings, but to make that solid commitment really isn't in the cards, as I see at this time. Our relationship is comfortable and still feels somewhat a fantasy. I love that part, but the reality is that he'd never be home. I don't want his job to be a wedge that would build contempt or resentment. I would want him to look forward to coming home. A family needs the head of house there on a regular basis. That's what makes it a family.

The trip from Denver to Durango takes at least twenty-four hours. With Philip riding with me, it helps pass the time. Our conversation flows, and we take our meals together. It's nice; he's nice. I've liked him since the first time we met, at the gala they held at their home on Capitol Hill last July. We have much in common, a love for art, music and traveling.

I write as Philip dozes off. The sun shines on the mountaintops. They sparkle with snow. If only the window would stay clear, I could see. By the time we arrive in Durango it's close to five o'clock. It took us a few more hours than expected. We were delayed when workers cleared snow from the track. The longest part of the journey is coming through the valley, and finally, we arrive in town. I can hardly wait for my feet to hit the depot platform.

For the last fifty miles, thoughts of Father, Inspector Southerland and that rat bastard, Mr. Brody, come to mind. I'm tired of the whole thing hanging over my head. My patience is wearing thin. I pray the inspector has some news. My fear has turned to anger. I must keep it in check. Anger doesn't solve anything, and it can get in the way when something needs to be done.

At the station, I see to my luggage. Philip hires a carriage and insists he is taking me home. He's a big man, and carries my bag and trunk as if were as light as a feather, up the flight of stairs and inside. I'm grateful for his help and thank him. I'm sure it's all in my head, but I feel a little eerie after being gone. It was nice having a man see me home. Philip and I talked on many topics, but I didn't say a word about my family's horrible secret.

"Will you have dinner with me Thursday, Alex? It will be New Year's Eve."

"I don't know Philip; is it alright?"

"Of course, if you are referring to my wife," he chuckles.

"Yes, Peggy. She doesn't like me very much."

"Peggy is just being Peggy. Come to the Strater Hotel, or I'll be glad to pick you up. We'll have ourselves an innocent dinner. Please; we enjoy each other's company, true?"

"Yes, yes I do. I don't have plans, and if you're sure it's okay, I would love to have dinner with a friend. It will be lovely."

"Good, then you accept. Shall I pick you up?"

"How about I meet you at the Strater dining room at nine?"

"Okay, but I insist on a carriage to pick you up. We'll have a great meal, good conversation, and ring in the New Year."

I stop and look for Sam … no welcoming committee here. Of course, Sam is with Mrs. Brody. The moonlight casts an eerie light through frosted windows making it feel colder than it actually is. It's not welcoming. It portrays a lonely, desperate and isolated life. In an instant, I'm depressed. I put the makings of a fire in the potbelly stove. Striking a match, I smell the sulfur; the flash catches the kindling aglow. The growing flame mesmerizes me, and I can't quite bring myself to this reality. My mind is dancing with a plethora of conversations and incidents of the journey. It's all rolled into one ball of good, bad and beautiful.

Suddenly I'm in the moment and add another piece of wood to the fire before closing the potbelly door. Turning to the table, I strike another match and lift the chimney to light the lamp. I turn the wick up, and the glow illuminates the room like the sun rising from the east. I hang my coat and place a shawl around my shoulders. I look out the partially frosted window to the town bellow and watch a lone rider come into town. A cold chill runs up my spine. For a moment, I'm frightened. I close the drapes. Opening my carpetbag, I take out my pistol and sit in a high-back chair at the kitchen table stiffly, with the pistol held by both hands. This thing with Mr. Brody and Father makes me anxious. Tomorrow, I will contact the inspector.

After an hour sitting, my imagination has got the best of me. Moving to the window, I peak through the drapes. It's quiet; the town is settled for the night. There is nothing to fear. I heat up water and wash the light soot from my face and hands. I bring my bedding to a chair by the fire. When warm, I take it and jump into bed, pulling the covers over my head. I feel foolish and giggle, tucked into the darkness … just my pistol and me, missing Sam. Soon, I fall fast asleep.

Chapter Forty-Eight: DAYBREAK

At daybreak, I wake; my heart is pounding from a horrible dream that Father was chasing me. I'm gasping for air and feeling exhausted, instead of refreshed from a good night's sleep. Plopping back down in my bed, I stare at the ceiling. *It is only a dream Alex, calm down, and take a deep breath.*

I'm missing room service. Isn't there someone to make my tea? Maybe I can teach Sam. I love my little place, but it's not the Palace. Swinging my feet over the side of the bed, I search for my warm sheepskin slippers. I put a chunk of coal on the fire and start a list of things I must do, in the order of their importance, while I wait for water to heat. I've spent most of my money from my savings on gifts and travel. So now I need to come up with a plan to save money for the trip to Savannah in the spring. That means I'll be taking time off work again, and time off means less money. I'll be gone at least two weeks in March and two weeks in June. Can I be gone this long? I don't know how, but Mother always said, "If there's a will, there's a way."

Opening the nightstand drawer, I take out my train ticket. It's for June, six months away. I'm looking forward to this trip with Mac. I look at the time; I must go downstairs and pick up Sam. In the mercantile, Mrs. Brody is busy taking an inventory of clothing.

"Hello, Mrs. Brody."

"Alex, you're back child. Happy holidays, and it's mighty good to have you home. And actually, you couldn't have come in at a better time."

"Really, what can I help you with?"

"I'm fretting about not having enough winter clothing to last through the season. I need to place an order."

"Let me get pencil and paper." Sorting through the inventory, she gives me an order for men's trousers, long-sleeved wool shirts and three blanket coats. It's exciting and makes me feel good about getting back to my sewing. I've been waiting for orders. The more money I make sewing, the less time I need to put in at the Good Hour. I give Mrs. Brody a delivery date of February third for half the order, and the rest I will deliver on March third. That suits her fine. It's not uncommon to have snow up until July because of the higher elevation.

I asked whether Mr. Brody was back from his trip. She says he's due home any day.

"Alex, I hate to ask, but do you think you could give me a hand for a couple of days until Mr. Brody gets home?"

I hesitate, and then say, "Yes; of course." She is so good to me. I will have to let Grace know that I need a few more days. Sam lies in his basket on the counter, looking fat and lazy. He barely gets up to greet me. He licks his chops, savoring every smidgen of his fresh cream and fatty canned salmon. After I finish with Mrs. Brody, I take Sam upstairs.

Outside, the air is so cold it freezes your nostrils together. I think about Savannah and how mild of a winter Aunt Jenny and Uncle Scotty have. Mother had told me before she and Father moved to Chicago, she had only seen snow twice. After experiencing the tropics, I hate to put on heavy clothes. I'll be in my boots until June or July. Bundled, I walk briskly through town and turn down Ninth Avenue heading to the brothel.

It's early, but Grace may be up. I promised that as soon as I got back to Durango, I'd go back to work. The back door is unlocked. I go inside; there is no sign of anyone stirring. I add a chunk wood to the hot coals in the stove and fireplace, and put on a pot of coffee. I gather what I need to make a double batch of cornbread. Mrs. Kane will not be here for another hour. Soon, Grace smells the coffee and the bread baking and strolls into the kitchen.

"Holy cow, look who's back." She gives me a hug. "It's good to see ya girl. It's about time you came back. I thought maybe you'd be staying in the city. Are ya ready to go to work? We've been busy, and we're one girl short. Bevie left with some John and headed for Salt Lake. I think we're better off without her as she was caught givin' it away. I need ya girl."

"Well, I'm here for two reasons."

"Let me guess, they're both about money," she says laughing. "I need you to go to work."

"I need a couple of days."

"You got it, but don't take too long, or I'll have to hire somebody. You said you'd give me three nights a week after New Year's, and I'm gonna hold you to it. Now, how was your trip? How is the handsome tycoon?"

"J.W.?"

"Yes, did he pay ya well? I'm jealous because you got him. I hope you didn't spoil it for us."

"He'll be back. We're very good friends."

"Is that all? I thought you might fall for him. We all have."

"It's a long story Grace."

She shouts up the stairs to wake the girls. They appear like mice storming the cookie jar to see me. I brought the girls a handful of fashion magazines, chocolate mints from the Brown Palace and a can of French talcum. They couldn't wait to look at the magazines and sample the chocolates, all under the canopy of a fine, white, violet smelling powder. They give me hugs and thank me for the velvet handbags I gave them for Christmas. They have a package for me.

"Go ahead Vicky; we want to see you open it. We all chipped in."

I open the box. Inside, I find a blue china teacup and saucer. The cup has little gold legs, painted with gold leaf and a painted daisy. "Girls, it's beautiful. Thank you."

We have coffee, and Grace gives me the rundown of the brothel since I've been gone. We have plenty of interesting affairs to discuss. After two hours of catching up, I leave the brothel. Inspector Southerland crosses my mind, but I think I'll wait until tomorrow to see him. I'll give my emotions a rest. Walking briskly, bundled from the cold wind, I walk back home. I try to think what life would be like living in the city. It would be nice to have all the modern conveniences, but it would really change everything. At least here, I have work and a clean and safe place to live.

Mrs. Brody comes to the door with a small kettle of soup.

"Mrs. Brody, please come in."

"Thank you child; it's too cold for my old aching bones. I thought you'd be hungry. You should have woke me last night and slept in the guest room. You must have frozen up here."

"Oh Mrs. Brody, that's so nice. I have something for you. I really appreciate your taking care of Sam." I hand her a gift.

"Oh, you shouldn't have."

"Go ahead, open it."

She opens the pretty package.

"A cardigan with pearl buttons! Why, you shouldn't have. It must have cost you a fortune."

"You take care of Sam and me, and I can't thank you enough for all you do." I give her a hug. Sam hears his name, runs to Mrs. Brody and rubs up on her legs.

"See? He loves you."

"Yes, I believe we've grown very fond of each other."

I scoop him up in my arms, and tell Sam that he will have to be satisfied staying with me tonight.

"Well, I'd better be getting back. Thank you for the lovely gift. It's too nice to wear in the store; but Sunday, I'll wear it to church. Enjoy the soup."

"I'm going to have it right now. I'll see you in the morning."

"I appreciate your giving me a hand dear. I'll bake you a nice meat pie!"

I close the door and get out of my clothes. I pour Sam a little broth with a few pieces of chicken in his bowl and bring my bowl in to eat by the fire. I can't seem to get warm. I taste the hearty chicken noodle soup. The broth is rich and delicious. I pull the side table closer and set my bowl aside while I catch up on my journaling.

I help Mrs. Brody for three days and really enjoy working at the mercantile. After closing the store, I walk to the brothel. Gracie is under the weather and has had a little relapse. I tell her it is wise to hire Mrs. Kane and Jessie on a permanent basis. Having them to rely on will take some of the pressure off her.

The girls are gearing up for the New Year's Eve celebration. Grace always has a large party with the same group of men every year; and on New Year's Day everyone rests.

Chapter Forty-Nine: IN THE SHADOWS

Thunder rumbles from one end of the valley to the other, and lightning lights up the sky. The town of Durango looks as if God has turned on the lights. A huge storm is festering. Inside, I remember I left rugs to air on the balcony railing. I dash to bring them in as lightning flashes, exposing a man standing at the corner of the drug store across the street. He looks up. When it flashes again, he has disappeared. It gives me the chills. Why was he standing there looking up at me? Maybe it's just a cowboy trying to get out of the storm. *Come on Alex. Get a grip on yourself. Are you going to start seeing danger at every corner?* I grab the rugs from the rail, and put my back against the wall, waiting for the next flash. Will he be there or not? The sky goes bright, then dark; I see nothing, but still I'm apprehensive. I go inside and turn down the lamps. My heart is racing. I stand at the door again, and the sky provides the light to see the corner of the drug store. He's there, watching. With another flash of light, there is a hard, loud, knock on the door, sending me out of my skin. My feet seem glued to the floor, and I shout, "Who's there?"

"It's Mr. Brody. The Mrs. sent me up with a slice of her apple cake."

"One minute!" I reply. I take another look at the drug store corner … nothing. I go to the door and open it. "Mr. Brody."

"It's kind of dark in here, isn't it? Are you out of lamp oil? I can get you some. You really need to get used to using the alternating current. It's so much easier."

"Thank you, but no. I have a headache. Please thank Mrs. Brody," I say as I take the plate from his hand. "This is very nice. I'll have it with my tea later … I don't want to be rude, but I need to tend my headache."

"No problem," Mr. Brody says. "I hope you get to feelin' better. It looks like we're going to get one hell of a storm."

"Thank you," I say as I close the door. I wait to hear the sound of his boots retreat down the stairs. I have myself worked up, and it may be all in my head. Mr. Brody gives me the creeps. Is this his way of checking up on me? Does this have anything to do with the man in the shadows? The hair rises on the back of my neck.

Just then, the rain starts pounding the roof. Back at the balcony door, I see the sky as it lights, and the watcher steps off the boardwalk and moves toward the mercantile. I hear the front door of the store open. My God, is the bastard signaling I'm home? I hear the door close. I'm right above, and they can hear my every move. My pistol is in the nightstand drawer. I retrieve it and check the chamber to see whether it's loaded. I feel my anxiety ease. I remember Mac telling me, "Hold the gun with both hands, firm. Pull the hammer all the way back and squeeze."

Chapter Fifty: THE INSPECTOR AND THE RED-HAIRED WIG

Costumed in my dark clothing and red wig, I enter the Rochester House where Inspector Southerland is staying. At the front desk I ask, "I understand you have is a Mr. Southerland staying here. May I have his room number please?"

"We don't allow female companionship here. This is a respectable house."

"I'm glad to hear that because I'm a respectable woman. I'm his sister."

"I'm sorry, I meant no disrespect."

"I've just arrived from Denver."

"Mr. Southerland is out. If you like, you can wait in the lobby."

"Thank you, I shall."

Within a few minutes, I see Inspector Southerland appear. I rush to the vestibule.

"Hugo, I've come all the way from Denver to see you. Aren't you happy to see your sister?"

Inspector Southerland has never seen me in my wig, but he's a quick study. "Sister dear, what a pleasant surprise! You must be hungry. Allow me to take you to dinner; but first I need to change. Please come up and fill me in on all the latest news." He turns his head and thanks Mr. Rochester.

Satisfied, Rochester goes back to his duties, and I follow Southerland up the stairs. Once inside the room, he closes the door.

"What's the news with Father and Mr. Brody," I whisper.

"I like the disguise, but it's still dangerous for you. Have you forgotten what kind of monster he is? He's killed his own child, and he'll kill again."

I show him the pistol in my handbag. "I'm prepared."

He shakes his head and says, "You're prepared? Let me tell you, just because you have a weapon in your hand doesn't mean you're prepared. If you don't handle it properly, the killer will use it on you. I do this for a living, and no matter how many times I run scenarios in my head; I don't have all the answers. Killers are unpredictable."

"Thank you," I respond, "for taking away my only solace."

"I want you to know how serious the situation is."

"What have you found out," I ask as I place the pistols back into my bag.

"What's so important for you to risk coming here?"

"I'm being watched."

"What makes you think so?"

"Last night, I saw man standing in the shadows at the corner drug store. I watched him for thirty minutes. Just as I saw him step off the boardwalk and cross the street, I heard Mr. Brody open the front door downstairs. I couldn't get a good look at him. Do you think it could have been Father?"

"I don't think so."

"Why?"

"Frances Highland doesn't need to spy. He and Mr. Brody know exactly where you. They don't need anyone watching you."

"So, it's not them."

"So, what other interests do you have?"

"I work and come home."

"Work where?"

"I work part time at the Good Hour."

"In what capacity?"

"I'm a lady of the evening."

"Did you ever think it could be an admirer?"

"Possibly ... so, what do I do?"

"Stick to your routine. I'll check him out. I don't need him botching things up. We don't need to draw any unnecessary attention."

I smile and ask, "So, are you taking me to dinner?"

"No, I'm not taking you to dinner, not till this is over; but I will escort you back to Main Avenue."

Chapter Fifty-One: NEW YEAR'S EVE

It is now the end of the year, and I choose to recall nothing but good memories. I've done and seen more than I've ever expected. I look forward to new and wonderful horizons. I'm blessed to have so many new and wonderful friends, and I'm grateful for my travel adventures reaching as far as Savannah and Bimini. Two trips I will never forget. My life has bloomed, and I have hopes and dreams of making a life with the man I love.

Heating water for my bath, I go through my wardrobe trying to choose an outfit for the evening. I wish I were dressing for Mac, but that can't be. Therefore, I will enjoy Philip's company. I'm glad he has invited me. He's fun, sensible, has a great sense of humor and I loved listening to his childhood stories about growing up in New Orleans. He is so different from Peggy, but they say opposites attract. She would have a tizzy if she knew we were having dinner together. Rest assured, I would not be the one to tell her. I doubt she would ever understand we enjoy one another's company. She'd automatically read something into our friendship. Anyway, I plan to have a good time.

Now, what shall I wear? I dance to the wardrobe to pick out my clothes. The first two dresses are nice, but not a good choice to wear for dinner with a friend. I put them aside and continue looking and finally take out a scarlet gown with a black beaded bodice, silk cap sleeves and skirt and an overlay of black chiffon. I have a simple headpiece I bought in Denver. This will do nicely. It's festive, not suggestive. I hold it against me as I dance in the mirror. I'm looking forward to this New Year.

I wonder what Mac is doing tonight. A flash of Elizabeth VanBuren comes to mind. She may be hanging off the arms of both my men. Am I jealous? Maybe, but if they were interested in her, J.W. wouldn't have asked for my hand, and Mac would have not come for Thanksgiving. *Forget the jealously, Alex. It does not look good on you.* I, for one, have always been resentful of any woman that has that trait.

    I make a sandwich, but only take a bite. I put a chunk of coal on the fire before getting dressed. Philip is sending a carriage to pick me up at a quarter to nine. I want to be ready. I hear a band playing in the park. I step out onto the balcony and into the cold night air. Children are running up and down the street with sparklers, and fireworks burst against the black night sky. I'm excited to be going out. My other alternative, working at the brothel, wouldn't be pleasurable. I finish putting my hair into a twist and add a hint of my favorite perfume. I slip into my gown and look into the mirror. I look respectable and festive, and I'm ready for a nice evening out with Philip.

    Sam has had his dinner, and I know he will be warm. He'll stay under the covers with all the outside noise tonight. I pick him up. He's gained weight staying at Mrs. Brody's. Kissing his big orange head, he pushes off my chest to leaps down. I guess in his old age he figures he doesn't have to put up with me anymore. I giggle, thinking back to the days when I would dress him in my doll clothes. He was tolerable of me then. "I love you, Sam." I hear the carriage roll up. I put on my wrap and grab my bag.

    It's cold, but there is no wind. The town is lit up, and everyone is celebrating. I know Grace, and the girls are busy. I'm fortunate to be out having dinner instead of the alternative. The carriage pulls up near the Strater. We wait our turn in line. The driver helps me down from the carriage. I try to give him a tip, but the man says, "No thank you, I've been taken care of, Miss Highland." I smile and thank him. He's an honest man. He could have received payment on both ends. However, this is one of William Bearup's drivers. Bearup is reputable, and I guess he hires good men. The entrance is crowded, and couples are waiting for tables. Dinner music plays, but from where I stand I can also hear piano music coming from the saloon. There is access to the Diamond Bell from lobby. I see Smokey Bearup bartending. As I enter, men tip their hats. I smile in acknowledgement of their politeness. An elegant and elaborate bill of fare is posted at the dining room entrance.

Strater New Year's Eve Celebration
Pimiento Cheese and Liver Paté with Crackers
Fresh Oysters and Cocktail Sauce
Spicy Lamb Kabobs
Bacon and Onion Quiche Squares
Onion Dill Bread and Cheddar Olive Scones
Butternut Squash Soup
Spicy Pumpkin Soup with Green Chili Swirl
Orange Wild Rice
Baked Sweet Potatoes with Butter and Brown Sugar
Whipped Russet Potatoes with Butter and Sour Cream
Beef Tenderloins in Wild Mushroom Sauce
Apricot Glazed Holiday Ham
Baked Rosemary Chicken Quarters
Fresh German Brown & Rainbow Trout
Veal Loin Stuffed with Roasted Red Peppers with Goat Cheese and Basil
Tomato and Pepper Stuffed Leg of Lamb with Garlic Chèvre Sauce
Fiesta Pork Roast Served with Roasted Sweet Onions
Creamy Holiday Vegetable Bake
Cream Corn Casserole with Onion and Red Peppers
Cold Cherry Mousse with Vanilla Sauce
Spiced Apple and Cranberry Compote
Chocolate Raspberry Avalanche Cake

Even in Denver, I never saw a menu with so many wonderfully delicious choices. My mouth is watering. Within minutes, I'm shown to Mr. Bouvier's table and surprised he is not there. Glancing around the room, I see that the women are dressed in dramatic fashionable dresses, celebrating sending out the old and embracing the New Year. Several of the men approach and offer to buy me drinks. I politely inform them that someone is joining me. They wish me a happy New Year and walk away.

I like watching people. It's always interesting. I recall when Becky and I stayed at the Strater the first few weeks we arrived in Durango. How exciting it was to stay in this grand hotel. We met the bachelors, two single men living at the Strater on the fourth floor; and I met Lila. We made friends, and she's one of the entertainers here. I'm sure she is working in the Bell tonight, God bless her. I'll never forget her taking me up to the Monkey Room; boy did I get an education in a few short hours. I smile. Mr. Barker comes in with a beautiful woman on his arm. Mr. Barker comes in with a beautiful woman on his arm. Mr. Barker is one of my first acquaintances in Durango. He works in the assay office. We've had dinner a few times and he gave me a diamond in the rough from Brazil.

"Alexandra, how have you been? This is Miss Rose D'Abroscio."

"It's good to see you Rob and very nice to meet you Miss D'Abroscio."

"Miss D'Abroscio is visiting from Italy. Rosa, I would like you to meet Miss Highland."

"Very pleased to meet you."

"How do you like the West, Rose?"

"It is very different from home," she answers in broken English.

"I hope you enjoy your stay. I don't want to keep you but, have you heard from Henry lately?" Henry Strater built and owned the Strater House at one time. We became best of friends and would meet a few times a week to ride together. Soon after I came to Durango, Henry left to go to Cuba on another business adventure. Oh, how I miss him.

"I'm afraid not lately. The last letter I received was in September. He was excited about his new business … cigars."

"I hope he does well," I say smiling. "Good to see you."

"Happy New Year, Alex."

"Happy New Year. It's so nice to see you."

They make a handsome couple; however, I don't know whether it's serious or just an evening out. Anyway, how very nice it was to see him. Now, he is a man that can tell stories. I remember the evening he gave me a rough diamond from Brazil. I smile warmly at the memory. Then, there is Henry Strater. *Wherever you are Henry, I wish you a happy New Year.* Cuba, it's a long way away, but really no farther than Bimini. Funny, it's the first time I have thought about how close the two islands must be. How could I have been there and not thought about him? I wonder, does he love Cuba as I love Bimini? I start to feel awkward sitting alone. It has been over an hour since I arrived, and no Philip.

I order a bottle from the J.W. cache; He said he had put me on his guest list. I wonder what fortunate woman he has on his arm tonight, or is he sitting with a group of men drinking fine bourbon and smoking cigars at a high stakes poker game? The wine arrives, and the wine steward pours a tasting glass for my approval. I nod. He departs after pouring me a glass and leaves the bottle. I have plenty of time to sip the Burgundy merlot and think. I drink a couple glasses, watching the clock strike ten. Twice, the waiter has asked whether I would like to order. I say no both times. I don't know what to think. Did Philip fall asleep? Did he get held up on business? I finally ask the waiter to have Mr. Bearup from the Bell come to my table. A quarter of an hour passes. Smokey comes into the dining room.

"Hey Alex, what may I do for ya?"

"I'm supposed to have dinner with Mr. Bouvier at nine. It's after ten o'clock, and I'm getting a little concerned. Have you seen him?"

"I saw him come into the hotel around eight this evening. In fact, I served him a drink before he went upstairs. However, I haven't seen him since."

"Thank you. I hated to bother you, but I'm concerned."

"Can I get you anything?"

"No, I'm fine. I'll wait a little longer. Thank you for your time."

"I'll keep an eye out for him."

"Thank you. Happy New Year Smokey."

"You too."

The server feels bad for me and brings a plate of paté and crackers. I nibble, but decide not to have any more wine. The fermented juice is making the tip of my nose numb. The clock strikes eleven. He's two hours late; something is wrong. Philip is a gentleman and wouldn't strand a lady unless there is good reason. I ask myself, *should I go back home? What should I do?* My stomach is queasy. I leave the dining room and walk into the saloon. The men hoot and holler. Smokey sees me coming and says, "Make way men, there's a lady coming through."

"I'm sorry for interrupting, but I'm worried about Mr. Bouvier. Is there any possible way you could take me to his room?" Smokey calls someone to take his place. "I'm truly sorry."

"No need to be, it's time for me to take a break." I follow him to the lobby. He stops at the front desk and asks the manager what room is Mr. Bouvier's. We proceed up the stairs and knock on his door. There is no answer. I ask Smokey if he will ask for a key so we may check the room. He dashes back downstairs, returning with a room key. He knocks again. There is still no answer, but I thought I heard a noise. He slips the key in, but the door is unlocked and opens. The room is dark, and the shades are closed. Smokey lights the lamp next to the door. The amber glow lights the room. Shockingly, Philip is lying face down in a pool of blood. We rush to his side.

"Philip!" Bearup turns him over. Philip moans, "Oh, my God," I gasp.

"It's Mr. Bouvier. He's been shot," Smokey yells. He quickly lights another lamp on the dresser. Philip's coat, vest and shirt are soaking with blood.

"Oh my God Philip," I say, loosening his tie. "Philip, its Alex. I'm going to get you help." I pull his tie through his collar. It snaps with force, and I toss it aside. Unbuttoning his shirt, I see that his eyes are dilated; he's pale and barely breathing.

Smokey says fervently, "I'll get the doc."

I'm horrified. "Who did this," I ask. I'm freighted. There is so much blood.

Feathers are all over the room, and there is part of a pillow on the floor. Obviously, it was used to muffle a gunshot. Philip tries to talk, but blood is bubbling from his lips, and he's incoherent. Smokey runs into the hall and bellows downstairs, "Get the doctor! Philip Bouvier's been shot!" He darts back to say, "I'm going for supplies and whiskey."

"Hurry, please."

Grabbing a pillow, I put it under his head. He tries to talk, but blood streams from his mouth. I take my hankie to wipe his lips.

He's fading in and out. I unbutton the first button on his vest, decide it is too tedious and rip his vest and shirt open. I see a gaping wound below his rib cage. The bullet went through, but I don't know whether that's good or bad. Grabbing clean towels from the stand; I apply pressure on the wound from the front and back. *Oh my God, there's so much blood.* Distraught, I call for my late mother to help. "Tell me what to do Mother." Immediately, I hear her say, "Keep your head. Keep the pressure on the wound, and his air passage clear. Do not panic."

"Philip, help is coming." I put another pillow behind his head. Dear God, please help him. "Hold on, Philip. Stay with me. Open your eyes. Look at me." He is trying to speak. He mumbles, but I can't understand. "Are you trying to tell me who did this? Is it someone you know?" He blinks. "Is that a yes?" He blinks again. "Good; stay with me." People have crowded into the room.

I yell, "Get out! Please, all of you, get out." Smokey makes his way through the door with Doc Garrison.

"Let the doctor through" Smokey snarls, disgustedly, clearing the way.

I start to move aside to give the doctor room, but Philip reaches for my hand. "I'm here Philip." He mumbles something that sounds like udders. I put my ear to his mouth. He struggles to speak again.

"Udders? Are you saying Udders?"

Philip fashions the letter C using his finger and thumb. "Caruthers? Daniel Caruthers?" Philip's eyes opened wide, and he blinks. "He said Caruthers. Caruthers shot him."

Smokey replies, "Son of a bitch! I'll send for the sheriff."

The Doc tries to stop the bleeding.

"He's got a belly wound, in the worst way. He's bad miss. It's real bad. He has lost a lot of blood. He won't be with us long," the doctor says softly.

"Don't say that," I say frantically. Philip squeezes my hand. He turns his head and looks at me with desperate eyes, trying to speak. "Its okay, Philip," I whisper. "I'll tell her, Philip. I promise." He squeezes my hand, blinks his eyes and is gone. "Philip, Philip!"

I'm stunned and tears roll. Philip Bouvier has left this world. I don't want to let go.

The Sheriff appears. I stare at Philip's blank eyes before closing them. Bringing his hand to my lips, I kiss his knuckles. "I'm so sorry, dear friend."

The sheriff questions me about the night's events. I tell him that Bouvier named his attacker, as witnessed by Mr. Bearup and Doc Garrison.

"Bearup, is this true. Did you hear this?"

"I did, Sheriff."

"Garrison, what about you?"

"I saw him blink when Miss Highland said Caruthers."

"Miss Highland, aren't you the woman I met at the Good Hour a few weeks ago?"

"Yes, I can explain."

"I thought so. Let me get on with this. We'll talk later." The sheriff already seemed agitated, as if I were trying to confuse him.

"So, there is no question that the three of you know, for a fact that, Caruthers is the murderer."

Simultaneously, we answer yes to the sheriff's question.

"Did anyone hear the gunshot?"

We answer no. I explain that I was to have dinner with him, and became concerned when he didn't show.

"Sheriff, I think the shooter stayed with him for a while. Mr. Bouvier has some bruises. He's a big man, so I think the shooter inflicted them after he shot him, leaving Mr. Bouvier helpless and hurting."

Smokey picks up a bloodied cane sticking out from under the bed. "Sheriff," Smokey says, holding the cane up to view. "I believe the killer used this to inflect pain to the wound."

"Why, why would he do something like that," I ask.

"Maybe Philip Bouvier had something that he wanted, money, information, I don't know, but he kept him down so he couldn't get to the door or until he was too weak to call out. Then again, he may just have enjoyed torturing him." The sheriff looks over the room. "You said you were to meet him Miss Highland."

"Yes, at nine for dinner."

"Do you know if anything is missing from his room?"

"I have no idea. This is the first time I've been in this room." There is a moment of silence.

"I'll put word out that Caruthers's is wanted for murder. Miss Highland, do you know whether Mr. Bouvier had anyone traveling with him?"

"No, Philip was in Durango, alone on business. If it's alright by you, I'll take care of things from here. Just so you know; I'm having the body shipped to Denver. Marshall McClellan is Mr. Bouvier's brother-in-law. I'm sending him a wire."

The sheriff gives his okay and says, "I'll be sending a wire also." After he inspects the body, he adds, "I'll send a Deputy to pack his things."

"That won't be necessary. I'll pack his things and bring them to you."

"Very well," he steps outside the door. I hear him question the onlookers, asking whether anyone knew Caruthers or had seen him. Smokey asks me what he can do.

"I need lots of water, clean linens and towels."

"I'll have Lori, the room maid, tend to him."

I sit in the dimly lit room with Philip until she arrives. Standing at the side of the bed, I catch my reflection in the mirror scaring myself. My face, hands and dress are covered with blood.

Lori asks how she may help. I see it is all she can do to hold herself together.

"Thank you Lori, but I want to be alone with Mr. Bouvier please." I can't let this young girl do this. Besides, Philip is my friend.

"Ok, Ma'am. I will wait outside in case you need something."

"Thank you."

I pour the tepid water into a basin next to the bed and dip the face cloth into the bowl, wringing it out; I apply soap. It is as if I'm watching myself. One part of me feels as if I'm invading his privacy. Another feels as if I'm his sister. I am determined to do this alone. I take off his bloody clothes, folding them piece-by-piece, and placing them in a stack on the floor. In the dresser, I find clean clothes to dress him. I gently clean the blood from Philip's body and place clean linens under him.

In my head, I hear our laughter when we were on the train. He had his young life in front of him, and now he's gone. His eyes will never see light of day again. His wedding ring is caked with blood. I work diligently. I didn't want to take the ring off. I take special care. I didn't know Philip that well, but I knew him better than anyone here. I wouldn't want anyone to see me like this. Everything I know about out Philip Bouvier is good. When he gave the Christmas Eve blessing, he talked of how we need to remember people's needs all year long, not just on the holidays. His generosity fed hundreds at the soup kitchen.

The noise from the other side of the door makes me angry. It must be midnight with all the hooting and hollering. I want to turn the noise off. My hands are shaking, squeezing the blood out of cloth into the Basin. The bright red water turns my stomach. I must remain stoic. Mother's belief was that the soul remains to absorb their passing since it is a shock. If this is true, I don't want Philip to see his care as a burden, but one of respect and sorrow.

Once I have dressed him, I open the door and Lori is waiting.

"Yes, Miss Highland?"

"Please Lori, I need more water and towels," I say, as I hand her the soiled ones. Closing the door, I walk to the desk, pour a heavy drink, raise my glass, and resolve that Caruthers will be caught and punished. Putting it to my lips, I drink it down. For a second, the burn is so great I can't breathe. I take another drink and welcomed it. I whisper, Happy New Year and hear the crowd downstairs singing *Auld Lang Syne*. Sitting down next to Philip I brush his hair.

"Philip, I'm taking you home to Peggy. I pat his hand and rise. I look for his suitcase and start packing his things. The last thing I put in it is his toiletries and soiled clothing. Tomorrow, I will ask the doctor for his report.

I find Smokey standing outside the door. I ask him whether he will assist me with Philip's suit, coat and shoes. I can't stop weeping. Smokey says he's called for the undertaker. I could expect him anytime. I stare at Philip. Peggy's husband is dead, and she doesn't know. I have nothing but sorrow for the family. All I can think about is Peggy. I have to wire her now.

There is a rap on the door. It's the undertaker.

"I'm Mr. Bartell, the undertaker, of Bartell's Furniture and Funeral home. I'm here to claim the deceased."

"I'm Victoria Highland; I'm in charge of the deceased. I've already taken care of the cleansing and dressing of Mr. Bouvier. Please put him in a suitable coffin for travel. Mr. Bouvier will be going to Denver on the morning train. He is wearing his gold wedding ring. I expect it to be on his hand when you deliver him to the train."

"Are you insinuating that I would steal?"

"I'm not insinuating anything. I just want to make sure it doesn't get lost in travel. Are we clear, Mr. Bartell? This man is Marshal McClellan's brother-in-law."

"Nothing to worry about, Miss Highland, I'll keep Mr...."

"Bouvier, his name is Philip DuBois Bouvier."

"Very good, Miss Highland. I will meet you at the morning train."

I stand stiffly with fists clenched as Philip is removed from the room. I close the door and sit down at the desk, exhausted. Pulling pen and paper from the drawer, I write:

Dear Peggy,

With much regret, I am writing to inform you of Philip's death, murder by Daniel Caruthers. I am bringing Philip on the first morning train from Durango. Please meet us at the rail station.

Condolences,

Victoria Alexandra Highland

Setting the letter aside, I take another sheet of paper.

Dear Mac,

I need you help! Philip has been murdered by Daniel Caruthers. I am bringing him on the morning train. If possible, please meet me.

Heart sick,

Alex

Smokey sees me to the post. I send the wires. We drop Philip's belongs at the sheriff's office. The sheriff says we may pick his things up in the morning. Smokey sees me home.

"Are you going to be alright, Alex?"

"Yes, thank you."

"Do you need anything?"

"Yes, I'm going to Denver on the morning train. Can you deliver me to the depot?"

"Sure, I'll be here at eight."

I pour water from the stove into the tub and strip from my bloodstained clothes. They lay in mute testimony of the heinous act. Wadding the dress into a tight ball, I put it into the hot stove and burst into tears. In a fog, I forget to test the water and I burn myself getting into the tub. There is blood under my nails. I recall the night's events while scrubbing my fingers raw.

Sam jumps onto the chair and meows to get my attention. Poor Sam; he's hungry He needs a little attention. I sit next to the fire after my bath and count money from my handbag for a train ticket. I'm down to my last few dollars. This is exactly why Mother said to put something aside for a rainy day. I put a few things together, packing a suitcase and setting it by the door. In the morning, I'll I have to do is get dressed and take Sam down to Mrs. Brody. I doubt I will be staying in Denver too long.

Looking into the mirror; I see my eyes are swollen. I take a cold cloth, soaked in lavender water, to put on my face and get into bed. Flashes of Philip come to mind. Each time, if it's bad, I change it to something good.

Chapter Fifty-Two: THE DARK DAY TO DENVER

At six o'clock in the morning, a messenger delivers two envelopes to me. One is from Peggy and one from Mac. I read Mac's first.

Alex,
I'll meet your train in Denver.
Mac.

Typical Mac, short and to the point. I open the envelope from Peggy. The wire reads:

Miss Highland,
Thank you for the notification. I appreciate your bringing Philip home. Please plan to stay with us. Enclosed is train ticket and travel expense money.
Regards,
Peggy Bouvier

Typical Peggy.

I dress and take Sam to his second home, the mercantile. Smokey arrives with a Surrey. Mr. Bartell is waiting at the depot with the coffin. I don't like undertakers. I know it's not fair to Mr. Bartell, but they're like vultures, always in the wings waiting. Approaching Bartell, he says "Good morning, Miss Highland. I will need your signature on these documents." After I sign, he hands me a small envelope and says, "This is the deceased wedding ring. I had it removed for safekeeping. Please give my condolences to Mrs. Bouvier. Have a safe trip." He turns to two men standing by the wagon and motions for them to load the coffin in the baggage car. It is like déjà vu. Philip and I had been on this train just three days ago. How life takes its twists and turns. I'm glad Mac will be waiting on the other end. I dread telling Peggy what has happened. I thank Smokey and board the train. *This isn't how I planned to start the new year*, I think as I take a seat by the window. I hope Peggy's mother is still in Denver to give her support. At Christmas Eve dinner, I remember someone saying the family would be staying until New Years.

The train pulls into the Denver station. From the window, I see Mac waiting on the platform. Before anyone is out of his or her seat, Mac boards the train. He commands everyone to stay seated and calls out my name. I make my way to the front of the car. Mac takes me by the arm.

"Mac, thank you for meeting me."

"Thank you for coming."

"The last twenty-four hours have been a blur."

"I can imagine. I'm glad to see you are okay."

We hustle into a small office inside the station. He pulls out a chair sitting around a table.

"I'm not okay. I met a nice man, and now he's dead." He closes the door and sits down beside me.

"The only redeeming feature is he told me who killed him. I'm so relieved to be here with you. Do you mind if we slow down?"

"Of course, I'm sorry." He takes a deep breath and sits back in his chair and says, "The sheriff says he was murdered at the Strater and that Daniel Caruthers's is responsible."

"That's true. He named his killer."

"I want you to tell me everything; but I want J.W. to hear. He should be here any minute."

J.W. enters the room just as Mac finished his sentence.

J.W. comes to me. I stand, and we embrace. "Vicky, are you alright?"

"It's so good to see you JW."

"I'm glad to see you too. I'm sorry it's under these circumstances."

"I'm okay, just a little withered."

"I can only imagine. Sit down please. Can I get you something?"

"No, thank you." We sit down.

"Why don't you tell us what happened," J.W. suggests.

"Try to remember everything," Mac says.

My emotions are getting the best of me. I swallow back my tears.

"Take your time," J.W. says, as he pats my hand.

"Philip invited me to have dinner with him at the Strater on New Year's Eve." Both men are looking at each other. "What," I ask. "It wasn't like that; Philip and I developed a friendship on the train. Neither of us had plans. We were to meet in the dining room at nine. He didn't show…" I give them all the details of the dreadful event.

"I know you're tired," Mac says.

"Yes, it's been thirty hours since I left Durango. I really want to get out of my clothes and have a bath. I need something in my stomach before I have to talk to Peggy."

"Let's get you out of here."

"I packed Philip's belongings. It should be with my things."

"If you two will excuse me, I'll see to the luggage and Philip," J.W. says.

"I'm exhausted and weak. I can't remember when I ate."

Mac had arranged for Philip's body to be taken to the funeral home. J.W. has the luggage loaded in the carriage. We three stop to have a bite at a restaurant.

"I want to thank you for coming to Denver with Philip. It means a lot to all of us," J.W. says.

"Yes, we're glad you're here," Mac says.

"How is Peggy?"

"She's taking this really hard," Mac says. "It was a terrible shock for all of us."

I have something light to eat. Immediately, I feel better. We arrive at the Bouvier's, and a servant greets us at the door. We are told that Peggy and Mac's mother, Shannon, is waiting for us in the lobby.

"Alexandra dear, please come in," Shannon says.

"Mrs. McClellan, I'm sorry for your loss."

"We took Philip to the funeral home," Mac says. "Is Peggy resting?"

"She is. I finally got her to eat something."

Mac pours J.W. and he a drink.

"You must be tired, have you eaten," Shannon asks.

"Yes, I am tired. We just had a little something to eat."

"Mac, the black suitcase is Philip's; you may want to remove the clothing. I brought everything."

"I'll take care of it."

"Is it possible to see Peggy, Mrs. McClellan?"

"Yes, of course. She is waiting."

Upstairs, Shannon takes me to a small sitting room that adjoins her bedroom. "Please have a seat, Alex. I'll tell my daughter you are here."

Peggy comes into the room and sits down. She whispers, "Thank you for coming."

"I'm sorry, Peggy." I can barely talk without sobbing. I kneel down in front of her.

She takes my hands and looks me in the eyes, "Tell me everything."

"Of course." Mac and J.W. come quietly into the room.

"Were you with Philip when he passed?"

"I was."

"Where did he die?"

"He was shot in his room at the Strater."

"What were you doing at the Strater?"

"Philip had invited me for a casual dinner at the hotel. I was to meet him in the dining room at nine. He didn't show, and I became worried. I asked for someone to check his room."

"I'm confused. I'm not sure why he would ask you to dinner. Were you acting as his escort?"

"I was not. We were just two friends have an innocent dinner?"

"Tell me everything Victoria. I'll find out sooner or later."

"Please, Peggy. I've come a long way out of respect for your husband. I made him a promise, and I plan to keep it."

She breaks down. "I'm sorry, go ahead. I'm trying to understand what happened."

"Alright," I say softly. "I will tell you everything." I relay the tragic event and tell her Philip's last words, and I wanted her to know I took very good care of him, just as if he were my brother.

"I'm sorry for my rudeness. Thank you for taking care of my Philip. Now, if everyone would please excuse me, I would like to be alone."

Shannon takes Peggy back to her bedroom. The three of us leave. The men walk me to my room.

"If you need anything Alex, we'll be downstairs," J.W. says.

"I'll have Alma, the housemaid, bring you some hot tea. She'll see to your needs," Mac says.

I thank them and retreat into the room and have my own little private cry. I lie on the bed and fall asleep.

Early evening, I dress and go downstairs. Mac is sleeping in the chair and awakens to the sound of the doorbell. The funeral caretakers have arrived with Philip's body. They place the coffin in the parlor. I join the rest of the family, Maggie, J.P. and the girls. It is a very sad, sad day. Mac takes my hand.

"Did you get some rest?"

"Yes, a few hours."

"Good." He squeezes my hand gently.

"Mac, what's going to happen. Will you go after Caruthers?"

"You can bet your bottom dollar. I won't rest until I catch the son of a bitch. J.W. and I will be leaving right after the funeral."

I sit down with the family. Everyone is heartsick. Maggie asks whether I plan to come to the plantation this springtime. I say I would love too, but I'm not sure at this time. She says she is hoping Peggy will come after things are settled. We have a small meal in the breakfast room.

Mac announces the funeral plans and tells the family Peggy wants to sleep in the parlor with Philip tonight. The news brings everyone to tears. We retreat to our rooms early, giving her private grieving time. Shannon plans to sleep within hearing distance. I say goodnight to J.W., giving him a hug. "I'll see you in the morning J.W."

"I'll be here. You get some rest."

Mac takes me to my room. I melt in his arms. He carries me to the bed and lovingly helps me undress.

"I've missed you, dove."

"I hated saying goodbye," I say.

"I feel terrible for Peggy. I know she loved Philip," says Mac.

"Come lay with me."

Mac sits on the edge of the bed and undresses.

He lies down, and I come to his side. Our lips meet, and we kiss long and tenderly. We are hoping to ease our sorrows within the arms of each other. Our bodies mold into one as we make love.

The day after the funeral, J.W. receives the auditor's report. Philip and he were right; Caruthers had embezzled over one hundred thousand dollars. J.W. and Mac are eager to get on the trail. Mac says it's his job to find Caruthers, but he also has a personal axe to grind.

Chapter Fifty-Three: THE TIDE TURNS

I go to the post office to check to see whether I have any mail. Unexpectedly, I have two letters, one from John and one from Becky. They must have written the day they got home for me to receive word already. I'm excited and hurry home to read them. I open John's first. It reads:

Dear Sister,

We had a safe trip home and a wonderful holiday. We want to thank you for being there on our most important day. I pray you are safe and well. I wanted to be the first to tell you, I've taken a position at the Savannah Arts College. Aunt Jenny and Uncle Scotty have offered us the Mathieson house. We have accepted and plan to move in three weeks. Mother always loved Savannah. I hope we do too. It will be nice being close to family, and they are delighted. I will teach and head a new project for the college. This is a dream come true, and I'm glad to be staying in the states. Please keep me abreast of Southerland's findings. I hate that you are in Durango alone. We love you!

Your brother,
John

John is moving to Savannah. That is marvelous news. I'm so proud of him. I must write.

I quickly open Becky's letter:

Dear Alex,

I couldn't wait to write, so I started this letter on the train. William has secured property on Second Street in Durango! With it still the winter, they won't be able to start construction until spring, but I am so excited. I know it will be a huge change for William. He's never lived anywhere but Baltimore. His family disapproves, of course. They are unhappy that their only grandchild will be living several thousand miles away. William heard from the hospital, and the doctors are thrilled to have him. I'm so glad we will be together again. We had a wonderful Christmas. I'm eagerly awaiting meeting you in Savannah in March. Stay warm, take care, and write when you can.

Love,
Becky

I'm glad to hear they are home and well. Becky will have a busy spring, traveling to Aunt Jenny's for Mother's memorial, packing their things and moving to Durango all with a new baby on the way. I must write and tell them of Philip Bouvier.

I go downstairs for groceries. The sight of what's on the counter stops me in my steps. Low and behold, it is the mysterious brass box sitting in plain sight. I gasp in amazement. Mrs. Brody coming out in a rush and sets a box of old newspapers right beside it.

"Good morning, dearie. Is everything alright? You look as if you've seen a ghost."

I quickly close my gapping mouth and force a smile to change my expression of disbelief. "I like this box," I say in a low voice.

"What, this old thing?"

"Yes."

"Mr. Brody had it sitting on the top shelf in his office. He told me it was useless and didn't know why he was hanging on to it. It's rusted shut. I don't think it even has a key. He's always collecting junk. Since he's gone, I'm cleaning the place up and getting rid of things."

"Would you sell me the box?"

"Yes, I guess so," she chuckles. "It can't be worth much."

"I'll give you a dollar."

She pauses and says, "I accept. It can't be worth more than that! I hate to take you money."

"I like boxes. It's rusty and old, but I'll find a use for it."

"I guess it would look nice as a decorative piece, if you put a little elbow grease on it, it might shine up like a pretty penny."

My heart is pounding. We have been planning on how to steel this box, and here it is, right here under my nose. I feel a little bead of perspiration forming on my forehead.

"Where is Mr. Brody?" My stomach flips and a shutter as a rush of energy goes through me.

"Oh, he is making a delivery at the Silver Pick Mine. He'll be back tomorrow after lunch. Did you need him for something?"

"No, no ... nothing."

"I'm almost done cleaning. Won't he be surprised?"

"Let me run upstairs and get you a dollar, Mrs. Brody."

"No hurry. Don't you want to take this up with you?"

"No, I have some errands to run, and I'd like to drop this off at the locksmith."

"Okay, if I find a key. I'll let ya know."

"No need. If there's anything of value inside, I'll be sure to return it."

I run upstairs with my heart in my throat. I can't believe my good fortune. I need that box. If it's not Father's, I'll bring it back and saying I've changed my mind. However, if it proves to be some kind of evidence, Mrs. Brody will be in danger when her husband finds out it's gone.

When I reach the locksmith, I'm winded. The locksmith isn't there, but the jeweler says he'll be in later this afternoon.

"Can't you open it," I ask him.

"No, I'm sorry. I'm a jeweler. I work on watches and clocks. Mr. Roberts works on the locks and safes. If you have some errands to run, stop in later. He should be in by then."

"Will you tell him please, that I will be back before five? It's very important."

"It's always important," he mumbles.

"Excuse me," I ask.

"I'll give him the message."

"Thank you, I'll be back."

Walking, I head to the Rochester House. I have to tell the inspector. This time, I pass the registration desk, march up the stairs and knock wildly on his door.

"Excuse me miss," the clerk says from the bottom of the stairs. "If you're looking Inspector Southerland, he's not in."

"Can you tell me where I can find him?"

"No, I can't."

"It's very important that I speak with him."

"I'm sorry, I can't help you. I don't know where he is."

"May I wait in the lobby?"

"Certainly."

I wait all afternoon, hungry and thirsty, with no sign of Southerland. I ask the desk clerk if I may leave a message. He points to the pen and paper on a small writing desk in the corner. I scribble, *I have the box, Victoria*. Stuffing it into an envelope, I go to the reception desk. The clerk takes the envelope.

I dash off to tell Gracie I can't possibly work tonight. I'm worried she will tell me I'm through. I don't blame her it does. First, I take off for the holidays. Second, I need a few days to help Mrs. Brody. Third, I went to Denver to deliver Philip's body, and now I'm running from Brody. It will be just my luck to have Brody come back early. Oh God, if he does, we will be in grave danger.

I enter the back door of the Good Hour. The girls are in the kitchen, sitting at the table ready to have lunch.

"Hey, look who's here early. You're just in time for dinner. Have a seat," Grace says.

"I can't stay."

"Sure you can, help yourself to some stew." Frannie picks up a bowl and ladle.

"Thank you Fran, but I really can't."

"What's up with you, you look as if you've seen a ghost?"

I try to smile.

"Something has come up Grace. I can't work tonight. I'm sorry it's short notice, but it's really important."

"Sweet Jesus, you are becoming so undependable. I don't think I can keep you on."

"I know I've let you down; but this is a matter of life and death."

"We need to talk girl."

"Yes, we do. I guarantee I have good reason."

"Okay, if you say so; but we need to get this straightened out. I'm lettin' it slide this time because it's the crazy season, but don't make me be sorry now. I don't want the other girls to get any ideas. I'm not soft on them Vicky."

"I'm sorry, Grace. I'd appreciate a second chance."

"You go take care of your business, but this is the last time."

"Thank Grace. I'll see you girls soon."

My feet are quick, and I look in every store window where I think Inspector Southerland might be. By the time I reach home, my stomach is in knots. I pour some hot water over peppermint leaves and drink it down to try to settle my stomach. My hands are shaking. I'm a mess. All this over a stupid box, and I don't even know what's in it, for goodness sake. Mr. Brody could have been telling the truth, that he has a box just like Father's. Now I'm second-guessing myself. I wait for Southerland to come to me, but he doesn't come. It's a quarter to five when I head back to the locksmith's. He never showed. I take the box with me. I thank the jeweler and say I'll be back tomorrow.

"It must be something really important lady, if you don't want to leave here. It's as safe here as anywhere."

I say nothing and wait for him to open the door for me. Out on the street, I struggle with the box. William comes by in a wagon and stops.

"Hey, Alex. What do you have there?"

"William, I'm so glad to see you. Will you give me a hand?"

"Sure, where are you headed?"

"Will you take me to the livery?"

"Of course. Let me help." He gets down and takes the box from me and puts it in the back of the wagon, and helps me into the wagon.

"Thank you, I'm so glad you stopped."

"No problem. Where we're you headed?"

"Home I guess, but I need to ask a favor."

"Shoot," he says with a smile.

"May I leave this box with you? I don't want anyone to know I have it."

"Then why are you dragging it around Main Street," he chuckles.

"It's a long story. Could you keep it for a little while?"

"I guess I can do that." We pull in front of the livery, and William gets down and comes around to my side.

"So, you want me to take the box in?"

"Yes, please."

"I suppose you need a ride home?"

"If you don't mind, I would really appreciate it."

"I'll take ya. Give me a minute, and let me take this inside. Where do you think I should put it?"

"How about it in your office out of sight."

"You got it." He comes back, gets in the wagon and takes me down to the mercantile.

"Thank you, William. You're a life saver."

"I'm glad to help. Is everything alright?"

"I'll know shortly. Look, if something should happen to me, see that the box gets to the Sheriff."

"It's that important, huh?"

"Very, but I can't risk explaining it to you now. Thank you for helping me."

"My pleasure." He snaps the reins, the wagon wheels turn and down the road he goes.

I hold Sam while pacing the room and checking the windows and door to see whether they are locked. I don't know why. If Mr. Brody wants to get in, he will. It's going to be a long night, and where in the hell is Inspector Southerland? Damn it! I hope nothing happened to him. I decide to write a letter telling the sheriff what I know, in case I should go missing … or worse. I get a pen and paper and sit down at the kitchen table to write.

March 15, 1895

Law of the State of Colorado:

I, Victoria Alexandra Highland, write this information as I know it to be. Inspector Hugo Southerland is investigating the death of Sarah Margaret Mathieson, from Creede, Colorado as well as other related deaths in Philadelphia, Baltimore and Savannah. He has evidence that Dr. Frances Highland is connected with these deaths and may be a killer.

I fold the letter, place it in an envelope and put it in my Bible on the bookshelf. I wait on pins and needles, later falling asleep in my clothes.

Chapter Fifty-Four: THE ONE-ARMED MAN

Sam wakes me as he walks across my pillow. It's barely light, but as soon as my eyes open, my heart is racing. Dashing to the back door, out on the stoop, I look to see whether Brody had returned early. I take a deep breath ... no wagon.

I rush back inside to brush my hair, splashing a little water on my face, pulling on my clothes and wig. I've got to get the Rochester House to find Southerland. Why didn't he come last night? Oh my God, is he alright? Something must have happened, or he would have been here by now. Is he dead? Dear Jesus, please I pray he is safe. If I ever needed a Mac, the time is now. Mac McClellan where are you?

I dash out the back door and down the steps, running as quickly as my legs will carry me. It is a steep run uphill to Second Avenue, and the Rochester House is just two blocks away. I hope my hunch is right, and the box is the key to everything. For, what are the chances that Mr. Brody and Father have the same box? It would be more than a coincidence.

Mr. Brody has to be lying. I know it's Father's, but what's in it ... money? Maybe the fifteen thousand dollars the banker said Father withdrew from his account two weeks before the accident. If it's not money, then what is it? If it is Father's and important, why would he leave it behind? Why would he take it with him, unless Mr. Brody is his partner in crime?

I arrive at the Rochester House out of breath. I feel as if someone is watching me and stop for a minute, glancing back the way I came. Beads of perspiration run down my back. The wig is hot. I look toward town, wiping my brow with the back of my hand, when all of a sudden, I see Mr. Brody rounding the corner in his wagon. He's coming this way. My hearts sinks. He must know! I'm dead. Climbing the porch steps, I accidentally step on the hem of my dress and hear it rip as I go flying into the door. The door opens with a bang. I pull myself off the floor, and I run for the stairs, yelling for Inspector Southerland at the top of my lungs. I get to the middle landing and collapse. Others open their doors to see what's amiss.

Southerland flies out of his room; he takes two steps into the hall. His braces are hanging at his side, his face is covered with soap, and he holds a razor in one hand.

"Victoria what the…?"

"Help," I gasp. "Mr. Brody's coming." Running down the stairs, he gathers me from the floor.

"What have you done?"

"I have the box," I gasp, "he knows."

"Dear God!"

We take the last step. Mr. Brody's inside the house, in a psychotic rage. He's up the stairs before we enter the inspector's room. He roars, "I'll kill ya copper, you son of a bitch! You couldn't leave things alone!" He's a monster, frothing at the mouth, and wielding a knife, slashing wildly at the two of us. Inspector Southerland tosses me into a corner, out of Mr. Brody's striking distance. Inspector Southerland goes for his pistol. His holster is hanging on the bedpost; but he's not quick enough. Mr. Brody slices his forearm and makes another swipe across chest. He makes contact, blood instantly soaks through his shirt, and Inspector Southerland goes sliding to the floor. I lunge for the pistol. Mr. Brody backhands me, and I go flying through the air.

"Give me the box, bitch. I'm gonna kill you," he growls, grabbing my throat and lifting me off the floor. "I'm gonna kill you, God damn it!" Struggling to pull Mr. Brody's hand from my throat, there is no escaping. He squeezes my neck. I feel the life leaving me as my arms drop to my sides.

I hear a shot. Mr. Brody loosens his grip. His eyes are bulging, and his nose flares. He makes a grunt sound. "Ugh!" His face freezes. Bang! Another shot is fired; I hear a dull thud as the bullet hits his flesh. I'm sprayed with blood. Mr. Brody plunges forward, his arms out like a spread eagle. His eyes go wide, and we go crashing to the floor, our faces inches apart. The beast shakes and quivers. Blood is coming from his mouth, spreading a garnet pool onto the pine board floor.

Inspector Southerland's head is hanging. He's badly injured. I tell myself to move. Grabbing the knife, I go to the inspector's side. Cutting one of his braces, I use it as a tourniquet for his arm. Sensing a man in the doorway, I grab the knife, spinning around in self-defense. A strange man is standing in the room.

"Easy Victoria. I'm not here to do you harm," he says. The one-armed man lowers his pistol and comes forward.

The man knows me.

"You killed Mr. Brody"

"So, that's his name."

"Who are you?"

"Edwin Morgan."

The clerk peaks around the doorjamb into the room.

Morgan looks over his shoulder and says, "Go get the doc and the sheriff. Be quick about it!"

"Give me a hand, will you? I need to get Inspector Southerland onto the bed."

We move the inspector to the bed. I can't take my eyes off the one-armed man. I've seen his face before. Sheriff Brookstone and Doctor Garrison come bolting through the door. There's a crowd gathering.

"Give us some space," the sheriff shouts. The doctor pushes past him. The sheriff kneels to look at the dead man and says, "What the hell? That's Mr. Brody! What happened here?"

The doctor rushes to Inspector Southerland. "This man's lost a bit of blood. He tears open his shirt, "Christ, he's gonna need a hundred stitches. The sheriff comes over and gets in his way. "Sheriff, you've got to let me do my job."

"I need to take a look."

"Who's the doc here?"

"Little edgy, aren't ya Doc?"

"I'm working! If you want to look at something, look at the dead man, and get out of the way."

"That's it, everybody out of the room," the sheriff shouts.

The deputy pushes through the crowd, "Doctor where do you want Mr. Brody's body?"

"Take him to the morgue, but don't let them fools do anything until I get there. They're quick to strip 'em and throw 'em in a box. Tell 'em this is no potter's field. Mr. Brody's an upstanding citizen."

"The Mrs. has to be told," the sheriff says.

"Upstanding citizen, my ass. The son of a bitch tried to kill us. If it hadn't been for this man," I point to Morgan, "you'd be looking at my corps."

"You, lady" the sheriff points, "I just saw you at the Strater. You were with Philip Bouvier the night he was killed." The sheriff studies me as if I'm a suspect. "I've seen you before. You were involved in another killin' just a few weeks ago, at the Good Hour. You put a knife in a man's back. You may be going away for a while. You're a dangerous young woman. Isn't your name Vicky Highmount?"

"Close enough," I say.

"What did you say?"

"My name is Victoria Highland."

"You lied to a lawman? I know you said Highmount the first time I questioned you at Gracie's."

"I thought it was close enough."

"Oh, did ya now Victoria Highland? Well, I'm watchin' you. I don't take it lightly when someone lies to me, and now you're involved in this killin'?"

Before I can answer, Morgan says, "We're all involved."

"Who are you? What's your name," The sheriff asks.

"Edwin Morgan from Savannah, Georgia," There's a short pause, and then Morgan points to me and says, "She's my daughter."

"What!" I shout. "I don't know you. I don't know him Sheriff."

"Oh, the tide has turned. Now you're askin' me to believe you don't know him. I see."

"I don't know him!"

Morgan says, "I've come to claim you."

"No one is claiming me! I'm an adult, if you haven't noticed."

"I see you're all grown up, but it doesn't change the facts. I knew your momma, but we'll talk about this later."

"Wait, I'm confused. You, lady, said your name is Highmount," the sheriff says.

"Highland … Highland." I say sharply.

"Highland, Highmount … Morgan, which is it?" the sheriff is very irritated. "Never mind. It doesn't matter. I'll find out at the jail. But you, mister; you're Morgan, and you say she's your daughter."

"Yes, that's right," Morgan says.

"What's your part in this, Morgan?"

"I'm the shooter."

"Okay, give me your gun. You, Morgan and Miss Highland, follow me. I was gonna handcuff ya, but you only got one arm. Are you going run on me?"

"No," Morgan says.

"Did she do that to ya?"

"No sir."

"Do ya know her very well?"

"No sir."

"Well I got's some advice for you, Morgan. Before y'all go claiming her as your daughter, you might want to do a little background check. I've seen this woman three times, all in situations callin' for the law, mind ya, and all of them involving a dead man … Henderson, Bouvier and Brody." The sheriff looks at me with squinting eyes and says, "I'm watchin' you. You better hope you've got an alibi young lady for the night that Bouvier was killed, 'cause I've got questions rollin' around in my head now." He looks over his shoulder. "Doc, you let me know when I can talk to the man you're stitching up."

"Well, he won't be going anywhere for a while."

"His name is Inspector Southerland, and he deserves respectful treatment," I snap.

The sheriff points to me and says, "I don't want to hear from you."

"I'm not going anywhere Sheriff," Inspector Southerland says. "Victoria?"

"I'm here, Inspector Southerland."

"I'm glad you're okay. Morgan, thank you for saving my life."

Morgan tips his hat to Inspector Southerland, and we follow the sheriff downstairs.

"I don't think I like the way you talk to people Sheriff," I say.

"I don't care what you like. Damn, this is the sixth death in town, in four weeks and you've been at the scene half the time. Would you call is coincidence? What's this town comin' to anyway? We're supposed to be cosmopolitan. Instead, I get cuttings, stabbings, shootings and now, a one arm thug."

"I'm not a thug," Morgan says.

"Shut up; you fucks are making work for me."

"I need to talk to William Bearup, Sheriff," I say urgently.

Sheriff Brookstone stops quickly. I step on the back of his heel and bump into him like a post. He turn and says, "Why, you gonna stab him too? You're not gonna talk to anybody until I have my lunch. Let's go."

"Do we get to eat too," Morgan asks with a grin.

"Shut the hell up. It's people like you who give our town a bad name."

The deputy runs up to the sheriff and asks, "Sheriff, should I go tell Mrs. Brody? Do I bring the body to the morgue?"

"First, break up the crowd up and then see to Mr. Brody. Then, get the Mrs."

"Sheriff, she may be injured." I say.

"Why, little missy? You know something I don't?"

"Mr. Brody could have taken his anger out on her first, before he came to the Rochester House."

"Is she involved?"

"No, not exactly; but I got the box from her."

"What fuckin' box?"

"The one William Bearup has."

"What the hell has he got to do with this? Never mind, just keep movin'." The sheriff points his finger at a young boy. "Son, you know Mr. Bearup at the livery? Tell him to come to my office now."

"Yes sir." The boy takes off.

"William has nothing to do with this. I hid it so Mr. Brody couldn't find it."

"I can see you are the root of all this mayhem. Not another word."

"I don't like you, and I don't like the way you're treating me. You're rude and foul mouthed," I snap.

The sheriff stops dead in his tracks, turns around and says, "I don't care what you think. You two are under arrest. You're criminals. Which is why we're going to jail."

Weaving through the town, people are pushing and shoving trying to see what all the commotion is. Inside the jail, I think of Mac.

"You two, in there," the sheriff says.

"In the cell," I ask "… with him?"

"Yes, in a cell with him. This isn't a boardinghouse. Have a seat. You're going to be here a while."

"Well, I'm going to tell Marshal McClellan."

"How in hell do you know Marshal McClellan? Great, another killer."

"I'm going to tell him you said that."

"Shut the fuck up!"

Morgan and I take a seat in the small cell. I sit on one side, and he sits on the other. There is a long silence between us.

"I am your father, Edwin Morgan."

"I wish you'd quit saying that. Not that the father I have is good because he's not. This mess is all about him."

"Okay, I won't say it again. I know it's a surprise."

"Please, just stop talking like a crazy man."

"I've come along ways to see you."

"You've got the wrong person, I don't know who you have been talking to, but I'm not your girl."

"I've been watching you for days just trying to get my courage up."

"You've what?"

"I admit I've been watching you for days, to get my courage up."

"What kind of man are you?"

"I'm…"

"Wait, it was you hiding in the shadows? You scared me half to death."

"I've waited a long time to meet you, but I never thought we'd meet like this," Morgan says.

"Don't talk to me. I don't know who you are."

"Sorry."

There's a long pause between us. "How long have you been in town," I ask him.

"More than a few days."

Here I am, sitting inside a jail cell on a hard, rough bench used by dirty butts. The place smells like a livery stall. I don't want to look at anything. What I may see will only make it worse. William comes in with the deputy.

"William," I say.

"Now, little lady, you be quiet, and let me do the talking," Sheriff Brookstone says.

"Mr. Bearup, do you know this woman?"

William looks over, surprised. "Alex, what in the devil is going on?"

"So, you do know her."

"I do."

"What does she want with you? Are ya family or something'?"

"Something; can I speak with her?"

"Go ahead, but make it quick. She said something about a box."

"Thanks, Sheriff."

William comes over and says, "Who's the one-armed man? Is it his box I'm hiding?"

"No," I say looking back over my shoulder. "That's Morgan."

Morgan leans forward and says, "I'm her father."

William extends his hand. Morgan gets up to shake it.

"Don't listen to him. He's from Savannah and just happened to get himself involved in my business."

"You sound just like your Momma," Morgan says.

"William, I need you to bring the brass box to me."

"Sure, I can do that. Do I need to wire Mac?"

"I wish, but he's out on the trail hunting down Caruthers."

"I'll send a wire if you like."

"No, thank you. I plan on getting out of here soon."

"Don't count on it missy," the sheriff says.

"I'll get the box for ya." William spins on his heels and is out the door.

I sit down. Morgan smiles.

"What are you smiling about?"

"I'm not a bad guy. I don't know why you're mad at me. I guess I have some explaining to do."

I leap from the bench and into his face and say, "You don't know my Momma. And if you mention her again, I'm going to be all over you like an avalanche mister!"

"Easy woman," the sheriff says. "Sit down!"

"That silver bracelet you're wearing was your Momma's. There's an engraving inside, the initials E.A.M." My mouth flies open, I'm holding my breath. "Elizabeth Alexandra Morgan, my grandmother, your great grandmother."

I back up to the bench and plop down, dumb founded. "Okay, if that's true, where did I get this bracelet?"

"You would have gotten it from your Momma, Sarah Margaret Mathieson."

"You knew my mother," I question confused.

"I did, since she was ten. She was my best friend. We were to be married, and then the war came to Savannah." There's a silence.

"Why didn't my mother tell me about you?"

"It's a long, long story, and she married another man, a Dr. Highland."

"I don't believe you."

He pulls a letter from inside his jacket pocket and hands it to me. "This might explain things."

I recognize the stationery. It was my mothers. I open the well-creased letter; it looks as if it he has read it a hundred times. I read the introduction ... *Dearest Edwin* ... I recognize it as mother's handwriting. My hand goes to my mouth to stifle a cry.

"Please don't cry Victoria."

"I'm sorry, I'm so confused," I say wiping my eyes. "You must excuse me; it's been a pretty tough morning."

"Take your time."

Dearest Edwin,

After all these years, I've decided to write. It has been sixteen years since my last visit to Savannah. I've always hoped I would have the opportunity to come home again. However, it never seems to materialize. Although you sent me away, you have always remained my true love.

I have three children, John and Rebecca - who are twenty-seven this year - and Victoria Alexandra who is sixteen years old.

I don't know how to tell you this news, so I will just get on with it.

I believe Victoria Alexandra is our daughter, yours and mine, Edwin. The timing is right. We were together on December ninth and tenth of that year, and Victoria was born September ninth the following year. For years, I was not sure, although I did think about it. The older she grows; the more obvious it is that she is yours. She has blonde hair, unlike either of us, but has your blue eyes, smile, teeth, sense of humor and heart.

Victoria is a sweet, sweet, young woman. Not long ago, I received photos from Jenny taken on the last Fourth of July. Some of them were of you. It was then I could no longer tell myself she was not yours. I'm relieved to get these words on paper, but I don't know what your feelings will be on this news. I felt that it was important to let you know. I have not shared this with anyone, and I would appreciate your letting me know if you want to be a part of Victoria's life before I say anything to her or Frances.

I can't say I'm sorry, for she is a very loving, joyous soul. I always wanted to have your child, and God has blessed me with a part of you, which I will always be grateful. I don't want you to feel pressured in any way. If you would like to be known as her father, I will make things right.

Yours truly,
Sarah

"You were born September 9, 1875."

I nod yes. "Did you write Mother?"

"I had planned to. Two days after I received this letter your Aunt Jenny came to my door and told me the terrible news that you're Momma was died." He looks down and rubs his eyes with a finger and thumb. "For days, I couldn't move. Although we weren't together, I never gave it a thought that she may go before me. I've loved her all these years."

"It says here that you sent her away."

"Like I said, I'd like to tell you about it. That's why I made the trip, to tell you about the love we had for one another."

"So, it's true. You are my father."

"Yes, I fathered you. It was because I loved her so much I sent her away. We were young sweethearts when I joined the Confederacy. I went missing. Two years your Momma waited and waited. Finally, it was time for her to move on and she took another's hand, France Highland. He promised to take her north, away from all the death and destruction. After the terrible incident of losing her parent's she had to take on the responsibility as head of household at the age of sixteen.

"For the next two years, she worked herself to a frazzle taking care for everyone. Your Momma assisted in surgeries, cutting men's damaged limbs from their bodies. She needed an escape. Your mother moved to Chicago and had a good life; I was told. Later, I was found, a distant family member recognized me and brought me home. I had memory loss. Eleven years passed, and she came to visit your Aunt Jenny. She told her I was alive and well. During your Momma's visit, she looked me up."

There's a moment of silence.

"When we laid eyes on one another, it was like time had stood still. We were in love, just as we were at sixteen. We spent two days and two nights together, and you were conceived. It was the best two days of my entire life," He says, choking on his words. "Your Momma wanted to stay, but I had to say no. I had nothing to offer. I was just a one-armed man. Our families had lost everything in the war. I could hardly support myself, let alone her and two children. It wouldn't have been fair to anyone. I loved her enough to give her up. She begged me to let her stay."

Tears stream down my cheeks and my chest aches so badly I think I'm going to die.

"I wanted to come and get her a thousand times," he continues. "I fought with myself continually. I thought I knew what was best for her, but now I know I was wrong. We were meant to be together. I let her down. I thought I was doing the right thing. I learned the hard way; you never let you're head do the thinking. If you want to make the right decision, go with your heart. I never married. There has only been one woman in my heart, until the day I received this letter. Sarah had given me the most precious gift, a daughter. That day; I fell in love with you."

I lift my head, and tears roll down my cheeks. I remember Mother on the front porch the day she received a letter from Aunt Jenny. Aunt Jenny had sent photos of a Fourth of July picnic. This man, my father, was in the pictures. I remember Mother crying. She didn't want me to see her upset, but I was sixteen and knew something was wrong. She was in love with him. He was her Savannah. She wanted to go back home, to my father, and Frances Highland made sure that was never going to happen. He wanted to keep her from those she loved so deeply. He didn't want her happy. He dragged her thousands of miles away, to keep her to himself, and for what? He didn't love her. He just wanted to own her.

I see by this man's eyes that Edwin Morgan's love for Mother was real. He's traveled all the way here to tell me so. I can't describe what's going on in my head and heart, but I'm so relieved Highland is not my blood.

Chapter Fifty-Five: THE DEVIL'S SOUL

The deputy stumbles through the door. "Everything is under control. The crowd is dispersing."

"Good." Sheriff Brookstone says. "Now, go see whether Southerland can be moved. Get him down here right away. I want to get to the bottom of this."

"Yes sir."

"Did you see to Mrs. Brody?"

"Not yet."

"Well, get Southerland, and I'll see to Mrs. Brody." He takes his hat, and they leave.

William comes through the door minutes later, carrying the brass box. He sets it on the sheriff's desk. "Where's the sheriff?"

"He'll be back in a little bit."

"Is there anything else I can do?"

"You can hand me the keys or get me Mac McClellan."

"You need Mac. I don't know if I trust the sheriff." William looks around. "The keys are gone, probably with him."

"I'm kidding about the keys," I say.

"I'm not. Is Mac in Denver? What about J.W.; he may be in town."

"They're together last I heard, out for Caruthers. After he hears the inspector's report; hopefully, we can get to the bottom of this. You want me to stay?"

"No, thank you. You're a good friend William."

"I'll check back later." William leaves. I stare at the box sitting on the desk.

"That your box," Morgan asks.

"I believe it's Frances Highland's box, left in the hands of Mr. Brody. I'm hoping it will answer a lot of questions. I'd tell you; but you might as well wait and hear the whole story."

"I'm sorry you had to find out I'm your father this way," Morgan says.

"Me too. And I'm sorry you haven't seen the real me," I answer.

"There's more," he laughs.

"You'll have to forgive me. Right now I'm not myself."

"You don't have to apologize. It's not my average day either. I killed a man, met a young woman who is my daughter and am sitting in jail for a murder I didn't commit." He reaches into his pocket for the makings of a cigarette.

"I can do that for you if you like."

He looks at me and grins, "I've been doing this a long time, and I'm probably better at it than most men with two hands; but thank you." In less than a minute, he has the finished product in his mouth. He strikes a match and pulls a long draw.

"Mr. Brody was a very bad man. You shouldn't feel bad about it."

"I had seen enough of his handwork, and I wasn't going to stand there and let him kill you."

"I'm sorry, I haven't thanked you for saving my life."

"No need to. It's a blood oath."

Inspector Southerland, with the assistance of the deputy, comes through the door.

"Are you okay," I ask, concerned.

"I'm like a newly stitched saddle bag," he tries to joke as he winces in pain. He sits down slowly in the chair next to the desk. "So, that's the box. How did you come by it?"

"I bought it from Mrs. Brody for a dollar."

Inspector Southerland looks puzzled, but smiles. "Honestly?"

The Sheriff comes through the door and acknowledges the deputy and Inspector Southerland. He takes off his hat and hands the keys to the deputy. "Let them out."

"Sheriff, is Mrs. Brody okay," I ask.

"She's with the doctor now," he answers. "She's pretty scuffed up, but she'll recover."

"This is my fault," I begin.

The sheriff puts up a hand to stop me. "First, I want to hear from Southerland."

The inspector takes out his badge and lays it on the sheriff's desk. "My name is Hugo Southerland. I'm and inspector from the Philadelphia Police Department, and I've been tracking the suspect, Dr. Frances Highland, in connection with multiple murders, which I believe has committed since the Civil War. The trail of bodies, which includes men, women and children, has led me from Philadelphia to Baltimore, Savannah, Chicago, Creede and Durango."

"What does this have to do with Brody," the sheriff asks.

"I'm getting to that."

The sheriff pauses to reflect on the information given and then says, "Continue."

"I believe Brody to be Highland's accomplice. The trail led me to Creede, where I hoped to find Frances Highland, but when arrived, I was informed there had been an incident, which took the lives of Sarah and Frances Highland. During my investigation, I noted that neither one of the bodies was found. The Highland girls had moved to Durango because Brody, a friend of their father, had offered them shelter and a place to set up shop. I believe the contents of this box will prove Highland is a multiple killer and that Brody assisted him. Up until yesterday, this box was in Mr. Brody's possession."

"How did you get it?" The sheriff asks.

"I got the box when Mrs. Brody was cleaning out the back room and offered it to me for a dollar since the box has no key," I answer. "I'm sure this is my ... I'm sure this is Dr. Frances Highland's box."

The sheriff turns to Morgan. "Where do you fit in all this?"

"I'm her blood father, and I came to Durango to tell her so."

"You're not from around here?"

"I'm from Savannah."

"How long have you been in town?"

"Several weeks."

"And you hadn't contacted your daughter yet?"

"I was waiting for the opportune time."

"That was today?"

"I followed her to the Rochester House, hoping to have a word with her when I heard
a woman screaming, and so I ran into the hotel and followed the sound. I saw the man you call Brody pull a knife on this man here and Alexandra."

"I thought your name was Victoria," Sheriff Brookstone asks.

"Sometimes it's Alex…"

"Don't talk to me. You're too confusing."

"Brody was after them with a knife. His intent was to kill. I shot him. Then, you and the doc showed up, and here we are."

"So, you don't know anything about Highland or this investigation, or the box; you're just the shooter?"

"That's right. I stopped the man from killing these two people."

"I don't need anything more from you now." The sheriff instructs the deputy to give Edwin Morgan back his pistol and says there are no charges. "Everything seems to stem around this fuckin' box. Let's open it."

"I don't have the key," I say

"But we do," the sheriff says. "I stopped at the funeral home, and this key was around Brody's neck. So, if this key opens this box, then Brody's connected to it."

"This became the lynch pin of my investigation. I became suspicious and believed Highland wasn't working alone, but I could never confirm it," the inspector says.

"Since this is the center of your investigation, I'll need you to verify its contents."

By this time, we are all looking at the brass box. It is approximately twenty-four inches long, twelve inches wide and a foot high, with handle on both ends. The sheriff slips the key in, the lock turns, the mechanism springs open, and slowly the sheriff raises the lid revealing a flat piece of stiff leather covering the contents. Inside the lid, there is a small, leather-bound journal. Inspector Southerland removes and opens it. All is quiet while he scans the first few pages. The inspector closes the book and pauses.

"This book belongs to Dr. Frances Highland. His initials are on the front. Inside, he has listed his victims as if he were taking inventory."

I waiver, and grab for the desk.

"Why don't you sit over here Victoria," Morgan takes me by the arm to the chair.

"I don't think Miss Highland should be present," the inspector says.

"I'm okay," I manage to say.

"Go ahead, an inventory of what," the sheriff asks.

"Victims. He's listed his victim's names, dates and locations. It's dated as far back as far back as 1851."

I can't believe what I'm hearing. The blood rushes to my head. The inspector puts the journal onto the desk and removes the stiff leather cover to reveal the contents. The box has many compartments, like a jeweler's case. The sheriff lays out newsprint. I feel as if I should be here, but I have no idea of what is coming. The inspector starts taking items from the box placing them on the table.

He says, "These look like trophies from each of the victims. I will match each piece of evidence to each if the victims later."

It is a compulsion to see what Southerland sets on the table. I stand, and the men step back. The first item he places on the paper is a ring that appears to be on a short stick. I gasp in horror realizing the stick is a petrified finger. My feet are glued to the floor. I want to look away, but I can't move. Without a sound the Inspector places more items on table, spectacles, earrings, opera glasses, money clips, hat pins, broaches, gold teeth, cameo's, necklaces, pocket watches, braids of hair, a rabbit's foot ... *When will it end?*

A buzz gets louder in my ears, and bile rises in my throat. My head spins. Memories come bolting back. We lived with this beast; he slept beside Mother. I sat on his knee, held his hand ... I can't breathe. It's the same feeling as when Brody was choking the life out of me. Everything is a blur, and I hear Southerland say in hoarse whisper, "We are looking into the devils soul."

I grab for the chair, it goes out from under me and slides across the floor. I feel myself falling into oblivion, tumbling further and further into the deep. My heavy breathing is the only sound. Cold as ice, curled in a ball, I lay in the darkness. Incoherent voices echoes in my head. I try to open my eyes, but my lids are too heavy, and I can't. I try to scream, but I don't make a sound. Deeply unconscious, I'm in a dark room. I see Mother and reach out to her; but she stands aside as another woman comes forward.

I recognize her as Harriett Southerland Highland, and she is holding the hand of her little boy, Christopher. They are Southerland's sister and nephew. It was he and his mother I saw earlier in a vision where they were buried behind a wall in their basement. The men and women keep coming; there's a crowd. They are solemn but clap their hands as if they are in appreciation.

A cold compresses wakes me. For a second, I don't know where I am. Morgan and the deputy lift me from the floor and set me into a chair.

"Are you alright Alexandra," Morgan asks. I nod yes.

"Do you want to be excused Miss Highland? I can speak with you later," the sheriff offers.

"No, I had a little dizzy spell is all."

The deputy hands me a glass of water. I take a sip.

The sheriff says to the deputy, "Go down to the paper, and don't let them print about Brody's death."

"Wait. Let's play this out. This is the perfect opportunity to lay a trap for Highland," says the inspector.

"Well go and tell them not print anything just *yet*. We've got to work this out. Are you well enough for us to continue miss?" I nod my head.

Southerland discovers a pouch of gold coins, and underneath, a letter of credit from the Chicago Merchants Bank for up to twenty thousand dollars. "This is a link, evidently. Highland has been contacting Brody for money. I need to go through Brody's possessions to see whether there are any other leads. I know Brody has been in contact with him, but right now, we have the edge. He doesn't know Brody's dead, and we have the box."

"As soon as he finds out Brody is dead and the box has been compromised, what do you think his next move will be," the sheriff asks.

"He'll run. He's lost his edge. He'll somewhere to recoup, but where ever that is, you'll find death. Sickness drives this man."

"My God, he is not a man. Is this the Highland you've been tracking for over twenty years?"

"It is. This is the monster I've been hunting."

I'm numb and sit in the chair as if I'm comatose, drained of all energy. The sheriff digs further into the box.

"Here Southerland, there's an envelope. I'll let you do the honors." The sheriff hands the letter to Southerland and asks him to it read aloud. Inspector Southerland opens the envelope.

My dearest Sarah, you're lying deceiving bitch.

I drop my chin on my chest and swallow hard.

Under the circumstances, I was unable to collect a personal trophy, and I apologize your life didn't end as elegantly as I would have planned; but I must say seeing you pierced, hanging like a piece of meat on hook, was definitely to my satisfaction. I will have you know I plan to take my trophy from your living testimony of your adultery, Victoria Alexandra Morgan. You thought you were so clever, so I let you play your game, all along knowing I would have the last dance.

Eternally yours, Frances

"This man is one sick fuck," the sheriff says.

Inspector Southerland says in a solemn voice, "I'm puzzled once again." He looks at me. "If you are the target, then why hasn't he come forth? You've been in plain sight, so why?" He picks up two Chicago Police Department shields from the evidence and says, "It must be his game."

Chapter Fifty-Six: SILVER LINING

The sheriff has called it quits for today. The inspector needs to rest. Mr. Morgan escorts me home. Arriving at the mercantile, I see the closed sign on the mercantile door, and my stomach turns.

"If you would like me to come up, I will. I'd prefer you not be alone right now."

"I'd like to stop in to see Mrs. Brody." I go to the side entrance.

"I'll wait here. I'm the last person she wants to see."

"I live upstairs."

He smiles and says, "I know."

"It's open, make yourself comfortable. I need to see Mrs. Brody, and I don't know how long I'll be."

"Please take your time. Don't worry about me."

I knock on the door. Mrs. Gerkin, a close friend of Mrs. Brody's, answers.

"Mrs. Gerkin, I've come to see Mrs. Brody."

"She's not so well I'm afraid."

"Of course, do you think I might talk to her for just a moment?"

"I'll check with her. Wait one minute please." She returns. "Mrs. Brody says she will see you."

"Thank you." Mrs. Brody is on the sofa covered with a blanket. Her face is bruised, and one hand is bandaged. "Mrs. Brody, thank you for seeing me."

"I'm glad you're safe Alex. I'm so sorry this has happened. I don't understand."

"Are you okay?"

"Yes, Doctor Garrison says I'll be fine in a few days. My heart aches more than anything. I've never seen James so upset. He was totally out of control. There was no talking with him when he found the box missing. I tried to tell him I could get it back, but he wouldn't listen. Over the years, he's been possessive with certain things. I've always made excuses for him. He was an orphan you know. He had no one to care for him. I thought that was the reason he was a little on the rough side. I'm sorry he came after you. You're not hurt are you?"

"No, no I'm okay. Like you, my heart aches too."

"What's this all about, Alex?"

"Today, I found out that my father, Frances Highland was a very bad man. It's so hard for me to talk about it." I wipe tears with shaking hands. Mrs. Brody hands me a hankie from a stack on the table next to her. "You see Mrs. Brody, today, in that box, was evidence that my father is a monster."

"Don't you mean *was* a monster?"

"No, they think my father is still alive."

"Really, without your knowing it?"

"Yes, but that's not the bad part. There's proof that my father has killed many people." I sob.

"Dear God in heaven, what are you saying? Are you sure?"

"Oh yes, there is no doubt. The brass box was given to Mr. Brody for safekeeping. He and my father were somewhat partners in crime. I don't know the whole story."

"My James?"

"I'm afraid so."

"So, that's why James was so violent. The box was more than something he was keeping for a friend."

"Yes, the box contained, money and evidence against my father. The sheriff is investigating."

"Lord have mercy; it's so hard to believe. I don't want to believe."

"I understand. If I hadn't seen for myself, I would never believe it; but today, I saw it with my own eyes, evidence of something beyond evil by my Father's hand. It's all so horrible."

"You poor child."

"I will be alright. If you want me to move out, I understand."

"No, why would I want that? You are not responsible for your father's doings any more than I'm responsible for James. We have a lot in common, don't we? Please, you must get some rest. You and I just need to get through one day at a time. Do you want to stay here with me?"

"Thank you, but I have someone to stay with me for now."

"Alright. You know Mrs. Gerkin is staying with me the next few days. If you need anything, just let me know."

"You're too kind Mrs. Brody."

"I consider you the daughter I never had."

"What a beautiful thing to say, thank you."

"If you need groceries or anything, help yourself. You know where the books are."

"Yes, thank you."

"Thank you for telling me the truth. The sheriff didn't want to tell me anything, but then again, he didn't know the story at the time. I won't be opening the store for a while, unless I can get someone to take over, and I just can't think about that now. As I said, help yourself."

"I hope you can get some rest. I'm sorry for your loss. Thank you for letting me stay."

"I wouldn't have it any other way. You're a good girl Alex. I do have one question before you leave. Do you really think your father is still alive?"

"Yes, I do."

"Well, you should have nothing to fear. He wouldn't hurt his own kin."

With a face of stone I answer, "I'm afraid it's not that simple Mrs. Brody. Inside the box was a letter he had written. My mother was in an accident. Father left her to die, alone, in the cold abyss on Aspen Ridge. He looked on and did nothing. He left her hanging on a branch until she bled to death out in the wild. I pray that God took her quickly. He said my Mother was unfaithful, and now he is coming for me. What he doesn't know is that he gave me a gift today, surely unexpected. The fear I was carrying is gone. When I found out the truth, it gave me courage. And now, if I ever see his face again, I hope I'm the one to meet his match. It will be me killing him, and I will be the one watching him bleed to death." I leave and go upstairs to my flat. Drained, relieved, sad and worn, I open the door to another page of life. I have a new father to get to know.

Chapter Fifty-Seven: MOTHER'S JOURNALS

Behind the privacy screen, I clean my wounds and put on a robe. At that moment, my mind is on the enemy. It's recalling one ghastly incident after another. I'm reliving the whole frightful day. I will make a tea to help settle my stomach and calm my nerves.

Mrs. Brody has lost her husband. Inspector Southerland has been damaged, but he will survive. Nevertheless, he has spent his whole life tracking one man across the continent and his quest is not finished. I feel bad for him. Frances Highland robbed him of his life, a normal life with family and friends, while striving to bring him to justice. Dr. Highland has destroyed many lives and families. Me, I'm healthy, whole but not unscathed. My life is upside down, and facts can't be changed, no matter how much I wish too. It's beyond my mental capability to fathom that we lived with this beast, not for a day, a week, a month, but years.

He used us to do exactly what he wanted, making what we had a lie. Others saw him as normal, respectable professional, but the monster lived within. He played one character to hide the other. He used his skills to mutilate people for his enjoyment, his pleasure, his need to feed his nefarious soul. He never loved us. A man such as he is incapable of love. He is the devil. It makes my skin crawl. Dear God in heaven, he must be dealt with. My Mother is dead, but her death wasn't grotesque enough for him. John and Rebecca are my half sister and brother, and though I'm glad of not being of Highland blood, my heart aches to have our family be torn apart.

Leaning my head against the screen, through thin fabric, I see Mr. Morgan standing at the balcony doors looking at the town. I find it hard to believe, but he's my real father. My mother loved this man. I must give him a chance. He's came two thousand miles to meet me and tell me the truth. From that action, I know he is honorable and loyal. Behind the screen I ask, "Would you like some coffee?"

"That would be nice."

"I must warn you. I don't make the best."

"How about you let me make it for us?"

I set the coffee on the table and fill the pot with water. Edwin Morgan takes a tablespoon and measures the coffee.

"I don't think you should be alone tonight. I'll stay if you like."

"I have Sam."

"Yes, you do and he's a good boy, but I don't think Sam can protect you."

"Do you think it's necessary?"

"You've opened a snake pit today, and Highland's made his intentions clear. If you don't feel right about having me here, then we could go to the General Palmer Hotel or the Strater, or where ever you want. We'll get a couple of rooms until we figure this out."

"I'd rather stay here."

"I can sleep in the chair, if you don't mind, with my clothes on."

"The spare bed is made up. You may sleep there."

"Thank you for appeasing an old man. You have a real nice place here. I recognize a few of your furnishings; they must have come across the country with your mother. This rug used to be in the foyer of the Mathieson house, and this rocking chair was your great grandfather's favorite. Your Grandfather, as I remember, was a real connoisseur of furnishings."

"Yes, Mother brought a few things with her. I have Grandfather's journals and Mother's too."

"Your mother wrote journals?"

"Yes, many of them."

"I wonder if she wrote about me?"

"After her death, I didn't want to open them. I felt as if I were invading her privacy. I've just started to read them."

"I understand … you must be hungry, I know I am."

"I can make us some eggs and bacon."

"That's nice, but I'm going to skip down to the Strater, get some of my things and pick up dinner from the kitchen. This way you don't have to cook. You can just relax for the evening."

"I can't argue with that, thank you." There's silence as he puts on his hat and coat until I say, "I have an idea."

"What is that?"

"Well, we don't know each other,"

"True."

"So, after we have dinner, would you like to read one of Mother's journals, together, back when you both were young? It could be our common denominator. I haven't read it, and I'd love to read it with you."

"That would be nice; I'd like that.

"Good, me too. The coffee will be ready when you get back, and I saw a blueberry pie downstairs. Mrs. Brody makes good pie. The store is closed, and she said I could help myself. Mother said pie helps fix everything." We both chuckle.

"If you say so, then we'll have pie … daughter," he says with a warm smile. He's unbuckling his holster and says, "I'll leave my gun with you for protection."

"That's not necessary. I have one of my own."

She goes over and pulls the pistol from the nightstand. "I'll be okay. This gun was Mother's and it's killed before."

"That sounds like another story. Save it for when I get back."

"Deal." He turns and is out the door. I hear the clicking of his heel until he reaches the boardwalk below. I lock the door.

This time is as good as any to get to know each other. Reading, it will just be the three of us. I'm eager to know and understand their relationship, and the journals just may help.

I set the table and go downstairs. The store seems a little eerie. I turn on the current and put a few items in my basket: eggs, bacon, bread, butter, a small ham, and a wedge of cheese and blueberry pie. I list my purchase in the book, and tally up my total of $2.60 and return upstairs.

Mr. Morgan is back within the hour. I take his basket as he hangs his coat. Sam smells dinner too.

"The kitchen was busy," he says, "but they were willing to accommodate my order. I brought us mashed potatoes, brown gravy, meatloaf with creamed peas. I need to return the tins tomorrow. They seem to be good people."

"You can put your things anywhere you like. I've set out some soap and towels for you if you want to wash up, and hot water is on the stove."

"Thank you. I'll just be a minute."

Sitting across the table, I see I have my father's sapphire eyes. He's handsome for an older man. His hair is jet black and shiny with light graying around his temples. His teeth are nice, straight and look like mine. I enjoy our light conversation. We exchange a few stories. I tell him of Indy and me riding in the mountains and down the Rio Grande, and he tells me stories. Once, he and his brothers made a raft and floated down the Savannah River at the age of six. He said they were lucky they didn't drown. The tide was going out and carried them fast and furious toward the ocean, and my grandfather rescued them by taking them aboard his ship just before they entered the sea.

We have our coffee and pie, and after, I pull Mother's first journal from the shelf. Sitting around the fire, I take the first turn reading.

"What shall I call you?"

"I go by Alex."

"We don't know what we'll hear, so we need to keep an open mind. Even through your mother and I were serious; this is unknown territory."

"I completely agree. So, let the adventure begin."

We pull our chairs closer to the fire, and I open to page one and read:

April 8, 1862

I live in a beautiful port city that opens to the Atlantic. Ships enter her harbor from around the world. The architecture is a blend of Greek, Gothic and Italia, among other gracious styles. Fancy ironwork fences that are covered with a variety of flowering plants, whose fragrance perfumes the air, surround stately homes and parks. The live oaks that shade you from the afternoon sun are festooned with Spanish moss. The land is graced with an abundance of resources. Pines grow endlessly toward the sky, and cotton covers the land like snow covers Maine in the winter. The tidal salt marshes line her hundred-mile coast and changes color each season. You can sail to her barrier islands where the green waters are fertile with blue crab, shrimp and fish. Washingtonia palms sway, and pelicans soar on the ocean breeze.

Savannah is beautiful. I, Sarah Margaret Mathieson, call this home. Springing from bed, my feet hit the cool plank floor as the morning sun shines through the Priscilla curtains hanging over the east bedroom window. Stretching, I reach to the sky. I've never felt more energized and full of life at sixteen, bubbling with excitement to start my adult life as the wife of Edwin Morgan. My soon-to-be fiancé is just waiting for the opportune time to speak with Father. We have been best friends since the age of twelve, and over time, our friendship has turned into one of true love.

I love the way Mother describes Savannah. I can practically feel the warmth of the sun and smell the flowers.

"Your Momma and I had a favorite place in the city we would go."

"Where?"

"Forsyth Park, we would meet there for picnic lunches under the big live oaks. In fact, the very last time we were together, we went there. I can still see her sitting on the blanket with the warm sunshine on her face smiling. We were happy, very happy," he says warmly as he looks down and takes a sip of coffee. I see his eyes wet with tears.

We discuss the circumstances of the war and the concerns of city at that time. He describes my mother and her family in comparison with his own. We continue:

April 9, 1862

My plan this morning is to rush through my chores, do my studies, practice the piano for one hour and take a nap after lunch. I'll be fresh as a daisy when Edwin stops by. I haven't seen him in a couple of days, which is very unusual. I wonder what he is up to. Anyway, I will not dwell on that now. Mother says too much energy spent on negativity is not favorable. I believe she is right. Momma always has something constructive to say. She has so much wisdom, and one day I hope to be just like her, educated and wise.

I know Momma approves of Edwin, and after he asks Father for my hand, which will be no surprise, Mother and I will set a date. I would love to have a June wedding.

We'll be married in church, of course. However, our reception will take place right here in our own gardens. I can see it all, Momma's silver punch bowl sitting on her finest linens, trays of peach tarts, with a huge wedding cake surrounded by flowers. Roast pig on the spit with iron kettles full of low seafood boil, and there will be plenty of music and dancing. Oh, it will be a marvelous day, a lovely celebration! I do love my dear Edwin. I truly do. I've waited too long this year to become Mrs. Edwin Morgan.

Hours fly bye as I read, and he reminisces, adding small quips about Mother. Mother's journal is a terrific bridge and allows both of us to fill in the blanks. Maybe this is her way of introducing us. We agree to read the next entry:

Straightening my room, I pick up my secretary's notebook for Savannah's Young Women's Society, and place it in my top dresser drawer. I took the position as secretary two months ago. Fifteen of us women take turns being the hostess for luncheons and short excursions around the city, and right now I'm busy making last-minute preparations for our spring cotillion. It's in two weeks. I pray I'll have my engagement ring by then. I plan to wear a lovely rose silk and taffeta dress, Edwin loves me in pink.

Opening my wardrobe, I pull out the dress and hold it to me as I stand in front of the dressing mirror. Savannah is an elegant city, and the spring cotillion is the most elaborate celebration. Everyone who is anyone will be there, and I'll be on the arm of Mr. Edwin Morgan. He'll be in his white tails looking as handsome as a peacock. He's one of five brothers and comes from a prominent Savannah family. My father and his father have known one another for years. Edwin is educated, and studying to take over his father's freight business. He's gorgeous and all mine, and I'm the envy of all the available young women in our society!

"I believe I have that exact dress. Mother saved it!" I say excitedly, rushing to the wardrobe, seeking out the garment. In a flurry, retrieving the dress, I bring it to my neck and spin.

His face lights up and broadens with a grin. He says, "You are your Mother, beautiful."

Laying dress across the bed, I hurry back to pick up the journal.

We continue reading the next entry:

TIMES ARE A CHANGING

Father must have been up early and laid the Savannah Morning News *on the front porch swing. The headlines read, "President Abraham Lincoln Favors Northern Interests." Dear God, what is this all going to lead too? It's been less than a year, and eleven southern states have seceded from the Union. Our social and economic differences have caused our country to divide.*

The paper says Lincoln is tightening the blockade on all southern ports in hopes to strangle and starve the South. Chills run up my spine. Oh my Lord, what will Father do? He's on the river every day. I'm afraid for him! Momma's from the North and Father's from the South. I've overheard some pretty heated discussions between them. He told Momma that it's his duty to see that Savannah's resources are sold and delivered. Momma reminded him that his duty as a husband and father is to stay alive and take care of his family. She also said, "If push comes to shove, there is no reason that we couldn't become just as prosperous in the North as we have in the South."

Father said, "We may leave Savannah, but we'll never leave the South. This is where my roots are, and as long as you're a part of my family, this is where we will stay." And that was his last word!

"This is the time when the war had really heated up. My brother's and I were talking of enlisting. Your grandfather knew exactly what was going on. He was on the river. The river was the lifeline of Savannah."

We read:

Father said this morning, "I've been running the blockade at night. It's been pretty quiet although we know the Union is making plans. We've been fortunate and have had only a few minor incidents. However, yesterday someone reported seeing a Union ship anchored out at sea on the Atlantic side of the island. We surmise the ship brought supplies and more armed forces. That can only mean one thing; the Union is gaining in strength. They could be ready to strike the city or at least try to take Fort Pulaski. Father said that Savannah would become a dangerous place. On that note, Father stops and took a deep breath and said, "I'm thinking of moving you out of the city." The news hits me hard. He then went on to say, "Your lives have been sheltered thus far, but things have changed. From this day forward there will not be any more socializing at cotillions, carriage rides in the parks or picnicking in the squares. And do not even think of asking Mathis or Jeffrey to take us town. You'll go nowhere and do nothing until I have given permission." Exasperated, he slams his hand down on the table making us jump, and then in a calmer voice he said, "I'm sorry, but the war has invaded our space, ladies, and the good times have ended."

"It was this very day I enlisted. I hadn't told your mother. I was pretty much a romantic as she, but it had come time that we had to face reality. The war was here, and everyone and their brothers had to protect their land and beliefs. It was a crucial time."

My mind is racing and full of questions, what about Edwin? What about our marriage? Leaving will change everything. I won't go. I just won't. What will I do if something happened to Father, or Mother or anyone, in fact? If Edwin gets word, he'll join the Confederacy. He has talked about it before. Lord, this is bad, very bad. Father will never give my hand in marriage with all this happening. I hate the war, damn them all!

When Edwin turned seventeen, he secretly asked me to marry him. We have already decided where we will live and how many children we will have, but he has been waiting for the right opportunity to ask Father. Oh, why did he wait so long? I must talk with Edwin today. This is terrible. It will ruin everything!

"This must have been torture for my mother. This was a very scary time."

"It was. This action was unknown to us. It was an idealist dream, quickly evaporating as the first bullet takes the life from the man beside you as another loses his head. All those romantic notions are quickly dissipated. Then, it comes down to survival and when the smoke clears, if those standing outnumber the enemy, you have won. Then, you face the wounded. You hear their screams, moans and the cries of their suffering. Next, you are off to a prison camp, to be left at the mercy of your captors and treated no better than animals. This is war, and both sides pay the price.

"I can't fully imagine how the horror of it all, but I had a small taste of violence today. Did Mother and you have a chance to say your goodbyes?"

"We did. Your grandfather had decided he was taking the family out of the city. She and Jenny had been sent to their room to rest; for they were sailing on the high tide, around midnight, down the river and out to the sea, south to Darien, Georgia. Your mother snuck out and came to me. I was getting ready to leave. I was to report to Fort Pulaski at midnight. Keep in mind, I had not told her I had enlisted. I was just getting ready to go to her. My brothers and I had made the decision at the last minute. When she got to the house, I had to tell her. She was heartbroken, angry and scared. I'll never forget what she said to me."

"What did she say?"

She said, "Something tells me that after tonight our lives will never be the same." I told her she would always be in my heart. We made love that night for the first time. We were together less than an hour. I told her I would come for her as soon as I was relieved from duty. If she were not in Savannah, I'd find her. I told her to be strong, and everything would be alright. She wanted to run, but I said no. She told me she hated the war and made me promise to come back and not let anything happen to me. I promised. I could only keep half my promise, I did return and you know the rest from there.

"I feel for both of you. Your world was coming undone."

"I loved your mother dearly, but I had to do my part. If the North won, life as we knew it, our business, land, currency, our workers, everything would be destroyed. They had burnt Atlanta, and Georgians were starving. Sherman was raping the state, and he planned to do the same in Savannah. Damn right, we were scared. We had to take up arms. There was only us to defend our city. I'll never forget the look on your Momma's face that night. She had a way of seein' things. When I look back, she knew what was comin'. It was just as she said. After that night things were never the same."

It is after midnight when we said goodnight. Edwin and I aren't strangers anymore. I am discovering there is more than a common thread between us. As we open our innermost thoughts, the thread turns to spool. I feel Edwin's pain and his love for Mother. I remember Mother said that most only have one true love in a lifetime. Edwin was Mothers, and she was his.

I get into bed with my back toward Becky's bed, where Edwin lies down with his clothes on. I don't how to say goodnight, so I just start somewhere.

"I'm glad you're here. Not just because if you weren't, I probably wouldn't be here now. I'm truly glad you loved my mother, and that I know you as my father."

"That makes me feel good. Sometimes things don't work out between people, but then it doesn't mean you forget that person, for your heart can hold onto that love forever. I missed your momma, but I gave thanks each morning I woke, for she was my first thought of my each day."

"Weren't you ever lonely?"

"There were times, but there was no reason for me to try to fill that void. No one could fill her shoes, and it wouldn't have been fair for me to try to give my whole heart to another."

I think to myself, *I've said these exact words.*

Chapter Fifty-Eight: THE VISION

I've started my prayer over and over, drifting in and out of sleep. The angels are probably tired of listening. I talk to Mother. "Mother, I know you are looking down on us tonight. Today, I met Father. You probably overheard our reading your journals. I know you don't mind because if you did, you would have never kept them. They're helping Father and I bond. It is so strange to say that word on both accounts. One, I want to forget, and the other, I want to get to know. For as bad as the day was, I feel a little relief and excitement. I have something to look forward to. I love that he loves you, for now and eternity. It is such a blessing. I wish you would have had more time together, but as Edwin explained, and I've heard you say it before, true love remains in your heart forever, and forever is a very long time."

I feel her taking my hand, and I'm comforted. Snuggling down into the covers, I drift off to sleep. In this sleep state, I'm back in Creede, in Mother's classroom. She's sitting at her desk, and I'm at mine. We're alone, and she smiles and motions for me to come. Standing beside her, she shows me an open book. At first, the page is out of focus, but slowly it comes into view. It's a map of the United States. She points to the west coast. She turns the pages and, each time, I see something else. I know she is trying to tell me something. I feel almost frantic that I may not remember.

The Durango Silverton Train whistle blows and disrupts my apparition. I sit up in my bed. Images are flashing in my mind. I need to hang on to them. It's a necessity to talk with Inspector Southerland. I throw off the covers, springing from the bed, and I begin dressing hurriedly and between breaths I say, "Thank you, Mother! Thank you! Mr. Morgan, wake up!" I say startling him. He throws back the covers, clicking the hammer back on his pistol.

"Woe, it's okay, we're alone! But, I've got to see the inspector." Morgan swings his legs to the edge of the bed, rubbing his face as he tries to shake off sleep.

"Here, I've poured you some hot water, but I'm afraid there is no time for coffee."

Morgan gets ready, and we leave immediately, out into the dark, blistery cold, for the Rochester House. Knocking on Inspector Southerland's door, the inspector is slow moving to answer.

"Miss Highland, Mr. Morgan, what's wrong?" We step into his room. The information bursts from me. "I have clues where Dr. Highland is. Mother showed me in a vision."

The two men look at each other. Morgan shrugs his shoulders, and the men stand waiting for the next piece of the puzzle.

"I couldn't wait for daylight. I was afraid I would forget. Mother came to me in the night. I saw some things, similar to the time when I saw your sister and nephew. Do you remember?"

"I do. I'd like to know how that works," the inspector says, inquisitively motioning for us to take a chair.

"I don't think I can be of help with that, but if you have pencil and paper, maybe you can write down the information as I try to recall."

"Very well." The inspector sits at the desk. I know he is in pain from his facial expression. He pulls paper and quill and is ready to write.

Mr. Morgan and I take a seat by the window. For a moment, I'm distracted by the bloodstained floor and turn my head to stare out into the darkness. It takes me a moment to recall the vision. "I remember being in a classroom. Mother was showing me a book. Inside was a map of the United States. She pointed to the west coast."

"Everything and anything may be a clue Alex," Inspector Southerland says, "Tell me the details, if you can.

"Yes, yes," I say anxiously.

"Mother turns the page. I see something that looks like a newspaper; it says something about a new frontier."

"What else? Do you see the name of the paper?"

"No, but there is an advertisement. They're looking for men and women to fill positions."

"What positions? Can you read it?"

"Cooks, teachers, dentists, lawmen, tailors and physicians!"

"Physicians, yes! Good."

"There is a street scene, with many people; it's crowed, wet, cold, dreary. I see water and tall ships in the background. A man's face comes to mind."

"Who is he?"

"A Russian man we knew in Creede."

"Are you sure?"

"Yes, he's wearing a long green wool coat, tattered with a fur trapper hat. Dr. Highland used to sew him up all the time. He was a scrapper."

"Does that mean anything to you?"

"No ... maybe."

"Tell me the first thing that comes to mind."

"He was always telling Father that he'd like to show him his home."

"Where was that?"

"Sitka ... That's all I recall."

Inspector Southerland reviews the information and says, "West coast, tall ships, Russian man, personnel, Klondike."

"Start of a new life," Morgan says, "The New Frontier."

"You're right. He's headed to Alaska, God Damn. You did real good Miss Highland. Thank you!"

"Thank Mother."

"Yes, I should have had you with me years ago. I have to make sure that every newspaper between here and there has his description and photograph. He'll have to hide underground, and that takes money. Mr. Brody held his bank. Highland has Brody wire money to accounts that he set up, using fictitious names."

"It would be wise to notify the Chicago Bank to freeze his account," Morgan says.

"I agree. I'll do that immediately."

"He won't have money to fall back on, not that it will stop him, but it surely slow him down. As soon as I'm healed, I'm headed to San Francisco," the inspector says.

"I'm coming with you."

"Father?"

"This man has destroyed too many lives. It's time for his to end. How long will it take you to heal, Mr. Southerland?"

"Give me ten days, two weeks at most."

"You've got a partner," Morgan says.

Chapter Fifty-Nine: GOOD BYE FOR NOW

"Here we are the station. I can't believe two weeks have gone by so fast," Morgan says.

"Goodbye Victoria. We'll be sure to keep in touch." The inspector promises.

"Inspector, you take it easy and keep safe."

"I will. I just want to say you are a brave young woman. I have the box because of your efforts."

"Thank you, inspector."

"I'm going on ahead. It will take me a while to get on the train."

"I can't tell you how grateful I am that you came. You've changed my life," I say to Morgan.

"I hope for the better."

"Of course, it's for the better. I hate to see you go."

"I must. I will not have anyone threatening you. I don't want you to worry. I'll be alright. The inspector and I will watch each other's back."

"Promise me you'll come back, alive and well."

"I promise. I'm looking forward to grandkids someday. You're gonna help rebuild the Morgan family. I won't be alone." He pats his left upper jacket pocket.

"What's that?"

He pulls out a worn photo of Mother. "Your Aunt Jenny gave me this a few years ago; it was taken the last time Sarah was home. She's a beauty."

"Yes, she is."

"And so are you. I'm real proud that you're my daughter."

"I'm far from perfect."

"You're perfect to me."

"I love you." There is a pause. I see his eyes well.

"You just gave me the best gift in the world."

"I'm sorry I didn't say it sooner."

"It's perfect timing. I'll be back before spring, for Sarah's memorial. That's a promise."

"Really?" I say smiling, trying not to choke on my words. "I'm going to hold you to it."

"You bet."

A release of steam sprays into the air from the massive engine. The train bell rings, and the conductor shouts, "Last call! All aboard!" We embrace. I don't want to let go. What if this is the last I see him? All we've had is just a few days together, under unfortunate circumstances. *Dear God, please keep him safe.*

"Now, what's the tears for," he asks lifting my chin.

"I'm worried. I don't have a good feeling about this."

"Worried, not for me, I hope. You know I'm a good shot," he chuckles.

"We're just getting to know each other, and I want you in my life."

"There now, dry your tears. I have every plan on coming back alive. I don't want your thinking anything different. I'm just going to make things right. I've got a lot of people on the other side rooting for me. Justice must prevail."

"Just be careful. Don't let your guard down, please. Keep me informed will you, and write when you can."

"I will, and you listen to the man I hired, he's a professional and don't be bull-headed about this."

"I wish you would have talked to me about him first."

"I would have, but I can't leave you alone, not now. Highland may be in San Francisco, but he may have another Brody somewhere. I couldn't forgive myself if something happened to you. I left you a letter on the table. You don't have to read it now, just hang on to it. When I get home, you can give it back. Enough said."

The train whistle blows. "I know you have to board."

"Yes, I do. I'll be in touch. Take care Victoria." He takes my hands and squeezes them lightly. Our watery eyes connect. "I love you, daughter."

His words are genuine. I feel it. My heart aches. I swallow hard and say, "I love you too Father."

I watch him board and wave goodbye.

THE END

**Read on for a preview of Book V in the series
Let The Wildflowers Bloom**

Ride Like The Wind

Chapter One: END OF SUMMER, 1895

The sound of my heart is almost as loud as our horses' hooves pounding the earth. In the dead of night, I'm riding Indy full bore to put as much distance as possible between the Pinkertons, the law, and me. In the last hour, my life with those at the Good Hour has changed. I've left Durango and my fiancé', Mac McClellan, with nothing more than the clothes on my back. J.W. Reynolds, cousin to Mac, and close friend, was drafted into helping me escape. In single file, three of us ride. J.W. leads, followed by Grace Talbot, the madam, and me riding like the wind.

Indy has labored breathing and sounds like a blacksmith's bellows with steaming breath that vanishes like a ghostly figure against the black of night. The cold night air is chilling to the bone. With reins in one hand, I snap the collar of my jacket up around my neck. I pray our horses are sure footed. A couple miles south of Durango, we dismount, and climb to the high mesa. From there, we see an orange glow emanating from town.

"There goes everything," Grace says remorsefully.

"I'm sorry Grace, maybe I should go back and give myself up."

"There's no going back," J.W. says, nodding towards Durango. "Mac has already stuck his neck out."

Warm tears run down my cheeks for a plethora of reasons. I expected my life to change today, but not like this. Troubled, I can barely think. I look at J.W. and ask, "Where are we headed?"

"Mexico."

"Mexico, that's over a thousand miles from here."

"Yes and we're not getting any closer standing here, we've got a few more hours of night ride before daybreak and we need the distance." He gives us a silent command by mounting up. We do the same, turning south.

I can't stop thinking of Tilly, sweet Tilly, beaten to death, and that son-of-a-bitch who did it. I know what happened is my fault but if the situation presented itself again, I'd react the same.

My heart is racing as hard as Indy's but he's doing all the work. Ahead, I see Jim Cantor's farm, the road splits there. J.W. slows and signals for us to do the same. On the fence post in the moonlight, I read a sign, Aztec, New Mexico. Passing the farm, J.W. takes the track south and picks up the pace. We're fortunate to have an easy ride on the hard packed dirt road. My head is full with thoughts of Mac. I recall him saying goodbye. We were just getting our life together and now this. What will Becky think? She just moved to Durango, and I'm running away in the night. Dear God, what's next? We come to the sleepy little the town of Aztec, a few dogs are roaming the streets, but none bark. J.W. stops at the fountain in the center of town, we fill our canteens and let horses drink from the trough.

Quietly J.W. says, "Bloomfield is the next outpost town. We'll be taking the in-country trails once we leave the road. It will be extremely dangerous."

"Why is that, because of bandits?" Gracie asks.

"No, because the desert hides its pitfalls at night. A horse and rider can disappear off the trail right before your eyes. So stay behind me, we can't afford an accident or to lose a horse, move slowly and carefully. We'll walk the horses for a while, giving them and us a chance to stretch our legs."

I see Grace limping, I know she's sore. I ride every day and I hurt. J.W. mounts up and we do the same. The sun will be up soon. Scrub oaks and thorn bushes tear at our clothing, piercing the flesh. Nasty branches sting when they hit us. Finally, the sun rises in the east, I see what J.W. means by dangerous terrain. The landscape has changed drastically from Colorado. The parched land is high mesas, bluffs and canyons, ranging in colors of cinnamon, sage, grey, beige and yellow, all shaped by the harsh elements exposed to the open sky. Previous flash flooding cut gorges into the earth and from the high mesa the riverbed curves around, looking like a monster snake. After noon, the panorama view of the hot desert shimmers like a mirage. With a bandanna over my face, my tongue feels swollen and my mouth is gritty. I take a deep breath and try to swallow, but my throat practically sticks together. Hours pass, the sweat is running in my eyes. Wiping my brow with the back of my wet, dusty glove, I blink repeatedly to remove the burning salt. Tumbleweeds sail across the prairies and strange gusts of wind send sand whirling into small cyclones. We ride hard, my eyes dart right and left scouring for danger. I've seen a few rattlesnakes cross our path. Indy jumps over deep crevasses in the baron, cracked soil. My hat flies off, I'm thankful for the stampede strap or it would have been gone. I used to classify myself as a rider but I've never ridden like this and it's hard to fathom riding a thousand miles to our destination. Right now, I'm just concentrating on making the next mile, the heat is getting to me. Indy's neck is in a lather but he shows no sign of weakness, Paints are known for their endurance, but the question is will I have the grit to make this journey? By now, all hell has broken loose in Durango, and I'm an outlaw, all I know is running from the law scares me. I close my eyes for just a second and the hot tears actually feel good. I'm physically and mentally exhausted, my body aches and my ass is chafed and sore.

We're a good sixty miles south of Bloomfield, New Mexico. Parts of the Rio Grande are dry at this time of year, but around the next bend the shallow river has created a small pool, shaded by a few scruffy oak trees, thank God, it is an oasis. We stop, I push my hat off my head and pull my stiff bandana from my face, as I struggle to get down from the saddle. My body feels as if I've been beaten. I collapse at the water's edge, there's a reflection staring back at me that I don't recognize. A quick attempt as my hand cramps, I try to remove my sweat stained gloves. I say in a whisper, "Fuck the gloves." I splash the water on my face, expecting it to be cool but it's tepid, another surprise. I rinse my bandana and use it as a face cloth. I feel the heat in my face, my skin stings from the wind, dirt, and salt. Indy shares my space, by sticking his lips to the water for a drink. To him, it's water, he doesn't mind if it's warm or cold. I sit back on my butt and see J.W. and Gracie doing the same. I look across the way, the land is harsh, unforgiving, and yet I see a lonely, deep yellow, cactus flower sprouting from the parched earth, reminding me God is here.

Luann and Patrick Reynolds and Family

About the Author: Luann Reynolds, "The Intuitive Novelist", derives her inspiration from the various places around the country she has called home, as well as her intuition. She has learned to listen to her inner voice and trust it to guide her. This book was born from an experience in Colorado while driving home from work. She glanced over at the side of the road and sighted a woman in 1800's attire. Looking back again, the figure had disappeared but what was left in her stead was a flow of information that Luann was driven to write, and after ideas for at least seven novels, she is still writing. This is book two in the series.

Luann is passionate about art, swimming with sea turtles and walking on the beach. Currently residing in Gulf Breeze, Florida, she is a mother and grandmother. She is married to artist Patrick Reynolds. Please visit www.LuannReynolds.com

About the Artist: Patrick Reynolds is an artist and illustrator with a varied and extensive background. As a young man, he earned tuition money drawing caricatures on the boardwalk in Atlantic City. As a Vietnam combat veteran, he used his talents to draw portraits of his teammates. This he says, helped keep his sanity intact. Since that time, he has been a sign painter, portrait artist, muralist, book illustrator and art instructor. In recent years, he has turned his talents towards miniature oil paintings. He describes the process as very complex, where mistakes are difficult to correct but the results are extraordinary.

Milton Keynes UK
Ingram Content Group UK Ltd.
UKHW050214250324
439991UK00013B/1724